SO-BDP-805

ALL HELL SUDDENLY BROKE LOOSE!

"Contact, contact!" came Allen's cry over the ta-comm. "Tee-dad infantry units with small arms—co-ordinates seven-one-six by delta-one-eight-zero."

"Commence firing," Capt. Curt Carson ordered, and then to his own ACV: "Sensors out! Drop the ramp! Warbots! Power up! Deploy as skirmishers on west edge of road. Fire at any and all targets."

His two General Purpose Mark 33 warbots had been in pre-combat standby. Now they replied verbally in sequence that they were ready and trundled out the hatch door down the ramp.

But Curt never got the chance to dismount the ramp himself, because the scream of enemy heavy seeker projectiles tearing overhead in search of targets suddenly filled the universe!

ACTION ADVENTURE

SILENT WARRIORS   (1675, $3.95)
by Richard P. Henrick

The Red Star, Russia's newest, most technologically advanced submarine, outclasses anything in the U.S. fleet. But when the captain opens his sealed orders 24 hours early, he's staggered to read that he's to spearhead a massive nuclear first strike against the Americans!

THE PHOENIX ODYSSEY   (1789, $3.95)
by Richard P. Henrick

All communications to the USS *Phoenix* suddenly and mysteriously vanish. Even the urgent message from the president cancelling the War Alert is not received. In six short hours the *Phoenix* will unleash its nuclear arsenal against the Russian mainland.

COUNTERFORCE   (2013, $3.95)
Richard P. Henrick

In the silent deep, the chase is on to save a world from destruction. A single Russian Sub moves on a silent and sinister course for American shores. The men aboard the U.S.S. *Triton* must search for and destroy the Soviet killer Sub as an unsuspecting world races for the apocalypse.

EAGLE DOWN   (1644, $3.75)
by William Mason

To western eyes, the Russian Bear appears to be in hibernation — but half a world away, a plot is unfolding that will unleash its awesome, deadly power. When the Russian Bear rises up, God help the Eagle.

DAGGER   (1399, $3.50)
by William Mason

The President needs his help, but the CIA wants him dead. And for Dagger — war hero, survival expert, ladies man and mercenary extraordinaire — it will be a game played for keeps.

Available wherever paperbacks are sold, or order direct from the Publisher. Send cover price plus 50¢ per copy for mailing and handling to Zebra Books, Dept. 061, 475 Park Avenue South, New York, N.Y. 10016. Residents of New York, New Jersey and Pennsylvania must include sales tax. DO NOT SEND CASH.

#2

OPERATION STEEL BAND
G. HARRY STINE

WARBOTS

PINNACLE BOOKS
WINDSOR PUBLISHING CORP.

PINNACLE BOOKS

are published by

Windsor Publishing Corp.
475 Park Avenue South
New York, NY 10016

Copyright © 1988 by G. Harry Stine

All rights reserved. No part of this book may be reproduced in any form or by any means without the prior written consent of the Publisher, excepting brief quotes used in reviews.

First printing: July, 1988

Printed in the United States of America

TO:
REGINALD BRETNOR

"Wars may be fought with weapons, but they are won by men. It is the spirit of the men who follow and of the man who leads that gains the victory. In biblical times this spirit was ascribed, and probably with some justice, to the Lord. It was the spirit of the Lord, *courage*, that came mightily upon Sampson at Lehi which gained the victory—not the jawbone of an ass."

—Lt. Gen. George Smith Patton, Jr.

CHAPTER ONE

"Captain, carry out the sentence of the High Court of Justice!"

"By your command, General!" The officer wearing the striking and colorful uniform of the Presidential Guard, First Regiment, Trinidad Defense Forces, barked his acknowledgement of the order and snapped a crisp salute to the bemedalled General who wore six stars on his collar tabs. The young captain performed a sharp about-face, letting his gaze sweep over the horde of people crowded along both sides of the Independence Square thoroughfare at Frederick Street.

Few of the thousands of spectators were there of their own will. The execution by firing squad of former President Clarke Chamberlin was planned as a media event by the new president, Gen. Austin Drake, and media events require lots of people. The Trinidad Defense Force had seen to it that a suitable crowd of thousands had been trucked to the execution site from the city and its environs. As a result, the people weren't very happy, but they had an incentive to be there and maintain good behavior.

Soldiers kitted-out in the gaudy uniform worn by the captain stood along the wide center median of the street called Independence Square in the heart of Port of Spain; each carried the futuristic and impressive Brazilian Mekanika Uru 9mm submachinegun, strictly an anti-personnel weapon. At each intersection, a war robot waited impassively, its sensors swinging back and forth across the crowd of people while it held its massive Argentine AE.77 riot gun at the ready. Self-propelled artillery from the First Artillery Battalion stationed at nearby Fort George watched over the throng as it normally monitored the harbor of Port of Spain. This was not a military force equipped and trained to defend the island nation; it was an instrument of police power over the people.

Although flags were flying, it was not a festive occasion. An island nation which for generations had celebrated Carnival and given the world calypso and the steel band was now a military camp. Freedom had disappeared under the heel of Gen. Austin Drake and a military establishment supported and supplied by the ABC Allianza—Argentina, Brazil, and Chile— in its effort to clamp a stranglehold on the economy of South America and the Caribbean.

Two soldiers and four verbally-commanded war robots surrounded a tall, lean, haggard man as they marched him from a nearby armored car to a wall facing the bright sun. The two soldiers held the man on each arm, an unnecessary precaution as his wrists were shackled behind him. The four warbots formed the corners of a square around him as their oil-drum bodies rolled on squat treads across the pavement, their 15mm high-velocity Argentine Bersa automatic robot rifles held at the ready in their multi-jointed arms.

The man was unsteady on his feet. He stumbled at the curb. But he tried valiantly to march proudly, head held high. Although the crowd wouldn't get closer to him than 50 meters, nonetheless considerable effort had been expended to cosmetically hide most of the welts and bruises on the man's face and arms. Video cameras with their long lenses could and would bring Clarke Chamberlin's image close to viewers. The telltale signs of physical torture would not make good press for the new military regime of the island nation of Trinidad.

It wasn't necessary to hide the mental damage of the torture. It was not expected that Chamberlin would be permitted to speak. General Drake had no intention of giving the man any last words to the people and the world.

But as the robots and soldiers marched Chamberlin past the bemedalled Gen. Austin Drake, the condemned man managed to shout in a voice loud enough to be picked up by the shotgun mikes of the news media, "Damn you, Drake! You've betrayed the people of Trinidad!"

One of the accompanying soldiers hit him across the Adam's apple with the barrel of his Astra pistol.

A murmur arose from the crowd as they heard Chamberlin's words. He still had followers out there, the people of Trinidad who'd swept him into the presidency in the last free election. Basically, Chamberlin had done nothing new; he'd followed in the footsteps of others who'd sensed the yearning for more change that overpowered the boredom of a successful, emerged nation. Worldwide, people had faced different problems in learning how to be rich in a post-industrial world. The people of Trinidad had been told they should not only take a bigger piece of the commercial and economic pie, the materials and technology of which had come from elsewhere, but also the crust and filling they'd baked with their own efforts. They were told to take the whole pie and the bakery to boot. Chamberlin had promised basically bread and circuses. But others like Drake felt he hadn't gone far enough in concentrating economic power in the hands of a few "men on horseback" who preferred to take it rather than make it, holdovers from a world of the past in which everyone had a little bit of something but no one had very much of anything.

The two soldiers stood Chamberlin against a brick wall facing south so that the sunlight was directly in his eyes. His manacled wrists were shackled to a ring on the wall. The two soldiers stepped away. No one made the offer of a blindfold or hood.

The eight soldiers of the firing squad stood stiffly at attention facing the condemned man at a distance of only ten paces—point-blank range for their Mekanika Uru submachineguns. "Ready!" barked the captain.

Eight guns snapped up. Eight bolts were drawn back to chamber rounds.

No one had told the Captain or the eight men of the firing squad that they'd been issued special 9mm ammunition for this occasion. Each had a clip of ten rounds of this special ammo. Contrary to custom, but unknown to the firing squad, *all* rounds in *all* clips were live; there were no blank rounds.

"Aim!"

The eight submachineguns came up to eight shoulders.

Suddenly, Chamberlin began to sing. His voice was cracked and hoarse from being hit sharply on his Adam's apple:

"God save our beauteous land,

"God save our bounteous land . . ."

It was the tune of the national anthem of Great Britain, of course, with new words put to it when Trinidad ceased to be a Crown Colony and became an independent republic.

Chamberlin's choked words were suddenly drowned by the cry, "Fire!" and the roar of eight submachineguns firing eighty rounds into the man.

He ceased to exist. The special ammunition had soft, hollow-point expander bullets, the sort used by hunters who stalked game with pistol-caliber guns to bring down their quarry with the first shot rather than wound it and possibly leave it to suffer.

When these bullets hit Chamberlin, he literally exploded.

This was deliberately intended by General Austin Drake. He wanted this execution not only to be public but to be shocking. He cared little for the ineffectual "voice of world opinion." This was an internal matter. Only by means of the initiation of terror could he maintain his rule with a minimum of military might.

The crowd gasped but was then silent.

Only a few thousand people were close enough to have seen the details. But nearly everyone within sight of the wall now saw a huge splash of blood on the white stucco and a heap of red meat on the sidewalk below.

"General, do you think that was perhaps a bit overdone?" asked one of his staff colonels.

Austin Drake shook his helmeted head, his jaw set and a grim expression on his rugged face. "Not at all. Everyone now knows we mean business. And that we will act decisively without mercy against anyone who opposes us." He noted that he had several spots of blood on his uniform, even standing more than ten meters from where Chamberlin had ceased to exist. He didn't dare reveal the fact that the execution had been far more grisly than even he, a veteran of twenty years' service in the United States Army in places such as Tunis and Aden, had ever expected. His lunch was not sitting well in his gut right then, and he couldn't reveal that fact, either. "Disperse the crowd and dismiss the troops!" he snapped to a colonel at his right. Turning on his heel, he strode to his awaiting armored car, trailed by his aide and bodyguard.

"Keep a guard stationed on the place of execution. Announce that those who stop and tarry there for whatever reason will be shot. I don't want it turned into a shrine to Chamberlin," he told his aide as he clambered into the armored car for the drive back to the Red House, now remodeled into a heavily-guarded palace and headquarters. Parliament had not met there since Drake had staged his *coup* and dismissed the body. He'd taken it over as his private residence and bastion of power.

A cloud slipped between the bright sun and the semi-tropical city. The weather was hot and humid. The rainy season was upon the Caribbean. It would begin to rain soon again on Trinidad and Port of Spain. Perhaps the rain might wash some of the blood off the wall, but Drake hoped enough of it would remain to be a constant reminder to the people of Trinidad that the new regime would brook no dissent.

CHAPTER TWO

It was raining also on St. Croix in the Virgin Islands 970 kilometers northwest. It was the usual brief morning downpour, but it was enough to get Capt. Curt Carson quite wet as he crawled through the underbrush on his belly. His portable tactical radio had already quit, and he was forced to communicate with Bravo Platoon of Carson's Companions by visual signals and, when feasible, voice.

He had no war robots he could count on—no assault bots, no recon bots, no fire support bots. He and 1st Company, Carson's Companions, of the 3rd Robot Infantry Regiment, the Washington Greys,* had been given the task of relearning what it was like to be real soldiers again. The other three companies of the Greys still maintained their human troops who operated war robots through remote sensor and command links. The warbot brainies, as these warbot operators were known, were supposed to study what Carson's Companions learned and eventually phase over to become the other special combat companies, the Sierra Charlies, capable of fighting with a mix of humans and voice commanded warbots. In the meantime, Carson's Companions were making all the mistakes.

*See Order of Battle, p. 425.

The rushing sound of raindrops hitting the leaves of the rain forest masked the sounds of movement around him, so he turned his head to where Lt. Alexis Morgan was crawling five meters to his right. "Anything?" he asked laconically.

"Nothing," she replied, her fair face caked with mud and grime.

"They're out there somewhere," Curt muttered.

"I know. Jerry and that old fox, Henry."

"Both know more about this than anyone in the outfit . . ." Curt observed, then stopped to listen again, trying to discriminate unusual sounds amid the noise of falling rain.

"Don't be so sure," Alexis whispered back. "Don't short-change our new squad leaders."

Alpha Platoon led by Lt. Jerry Allen and accompanied today by M. Sgt. Henry Kester was out there somewhere in the rain forest. Curt and Lt. Alexis Morgan along with Platoon Sgt. Nick Gerard and his two corporals, Tracy Dillon and Tom Cole were trying to find them without getting ambushed and shot by them. It was rough going. The short rainstorm had turned the ground to mud, and water was dripping from the lush vegetation of the semi-tropical rainforest.

Once it had been a sugar plantation. Now it was overgrown with a lush secondary growth of palms, vines, and ferns. Visibility was a few meters at best. The only way to win this war game was to surprise the other team and shoot first. There wasn't enough skirmish room to engage in a fire fight with movement. Warbots would have been useful here only in a brute force way, provided they were amply supported with recon bots and air support. Warbots were great, Curt knew, for fighting in places like Europe, the steppes of Asia, and the open spaces of the Middle East. But there had been no national requirement to station Army robot infantry forces in the tropics.

The paint pellet pistol in Curt's hand felt strange; he disliked pistols and preferred rifles and carbines as personal weapons. He recalled the lack of stopping power exhibited several months ago by Sgt. Edwina Sampson's 9mm Beretta in Zahedan during the first hand-to-hand personal combat experienced by the United States Army in nearly a generation.

And Zahedan was the reason why Curt and his company were out in the rain forest of St. Croix crawling through the mud like the doughboys, GIs, and grunts of yore. The rescue of more than a hundred hostages in the eastern Iranian city of Zahedan had taught them a new verity of warfare: war robots can't do it all and can't shield their human operators from all the hazards of combat. The human soldier, using war robots as support, was suddenly perceived by the Army as a new tactical element. Somebody had to work out the doctrine and tactics. Carson's Companions were the "somebodies."

But they weren't supposed to be out in the rain forest of St. Croix playing survivalist war games. If Col. Belinda Hettrick of the Washington Greys found out that Curt and his company were doing this, Curt knew he was going get his ass chewed for not following orders. But he believed that the simulators were no more realistic when it came to personal combat than a pornographic video was a substitute for real sex.

But orders were orders, and they said that the new tactical doctrines of combined human-warbot operations were to be worked out in the computerized simulators and war gamers at the War College Annex in Charlotte Amalie. Twenty years of robot warfare still had a legacy which said, "Don't risk human beings!"

Curt didn't think that crawling on his belly through

the mud and decayed vegetation was risky. It was just plain, downright uncomfortable.

But *someone* had to go out and learn how to fight infantry tactics again!

So the Companions had decided to do it, and Curt was placing heavy reliance on Lt. Jerry Allen who'd graduated from West Point last year. In an era of warbots, personal combat was still taught at the U.S. Military Academy in its continuing process of turning children into adults.

The fact that Jerry was in command of the adversary force, Alpha Platoon, accompanied by the experienced veteran soldier, M. Sgt. Henry Kester, made Curt very wary indeed.

"Well, maybe we can count on the fact that experience and deceit can overcome youth and zeal," Curt remarked.

"Got news for you," Alexis reminded him. "They've got both."

"Nick, see anything?" Curt asked Bravo's platoon sergeant on his left.

"Not a damned thing, Captain," the platoon sergeant replied quietly.

"How about Dillon and Cole?" Curt wasn't too worried about his two new squad leaders, Tracy Dillon and Tom Cole, teen-aged recruits from Montana and Tennesee respectively. Both of them had grown up in rural areas and had hunted since the time they could pick up a gun. Curt had carefully chosen them and the other two troopers, Jim Elliott and Charlie Koslowski, because of their backgrounds, regardless of their lack of military experience. If he had to integrate four soldiers into his tight-knit group to handle the new voice-command warbots of the Sierra Charlies, he wanted people who hadn't fought with standard warbots.

"No report," Nick Gerard shot back.

18

"Okay, they're out here somewhere. On your feet. As skirmishers, forward," Curt finally decided.

However, as he got to his feet, he heard the crack of breaking wood. He didn't drop to his belly again.

Curt wasn't wearing a helmet; he had on a soft green beret that didn't cover his ears. The shape of the human ear hadn't evolved by accident or without useful purpose. While having an ear on both sides of the head permits a person to locate sound left or right, the shape of the ear allows location of a sound in the vertical direction. Had Curt been wearing a helmet or even a cap pulled down over his ears, he wouldn't have heard the snap of wood as Platoon Sgt. Edwina Sampson's foot slipped while she was high in a palm tree, waiting in ambush.

He looked up, saw his target, raised the pellet pistol, and fired. "Bang, you're dead!" Curt told her and immediately began to look around.

"Arrgghh!" she snarled, the left leg and hip of her cammies splattered with washable red paint. "Blew my ass off!"

Curt heard the *whish* as a paint pellet sped past his ear. Then he heard Alexis Morgan fire.

"Damn! Missed!" Alexis hissed.

Nick Gerard's pellet gun went off, and the front of his cammies suddenly became bright red. "Shit!" he growled.

"No, it's paint!" came the voice of Lt. Jerry Allen from the underbrush.

Suddenly, the humid air was full of the sound of pellet guns being fired. Then a slow Tennesee drawl called out, "Okay, we gotcha! Drop 'em! War's over for you all!"

Another two reports came from pellet guns, then another voice with a Western twang to it, "Told ya to drop 'em, folks. Now let's march right on out there and formally surrender to the captain. Or do you wanna get painted some more?''

The bushes parted and Lt. Jerry Allen walked out, hands in the air but still holding his pellet pistol. He was followed by M. Sgt. Henry Kester who didn't bother continuing the sham and had his pistol in his belt and his hands stuffed into the pockets of his soaking wet cammys. Jim Elliott and Charlie Koskowski followed, both of them showing bright red paint stains on their camouflage jackets.

Curt stuffed his pellet pistol in his belt, too. ''Okay, troops, the war's over. Let's figure out what happened.''

''Can we go somewhere and get dry?'' Alexis asked. She was soaking wet, and her corn-colored hair hung wetly around her head.

''Edie, can you get down out of that tree without help?'' Curt called up to his Alpha platoon sergeant.

''I got up here by myself, Captain, and I'll damned well get down by myself . . . in spite of this goddamed paint,'' came the hoarse reply from the little sergeant in the tree.

''Don't bust yourself up,'' Curt warned her. ''Bad enough we're out here with non-reg weapons playing non-reg war games on company time. Hettrick would have a tizzy fit if any of us got hurt doing something we're not supposed to be doing in the first place.''

''She's gonna have a tizzy anyway,'' Henry Kester growled. Sampson dropped the last two meters to the ground, breaking the drop by rolling which got her covered with mud and other things. But it tended to cover up the bright red stain on her cammy pants. A string of curses quite uncharacteristic of a petite woman, albeit a redhead, issued from among the fronds and ferns where she landed.

"Edie's been taking lessons from Henry again," Jerry Allen ventured.

"Not a chance, Lieutenant," came the gruff, no-nonsense reply from the old master sergeant. "She's been watching old war movies in the post theater."

"You okay?" Allen called to his sergeant.

"Yeah . . . Yes, Lieutenant. The mud broke my fall. Whup! Wasn't mud. Goddammit, when did they start running cows in here?" came the reply. Then Edwina Sampson emerged from the underbrush.

"Well, you sure as hell win the prize for camouflage," Nick Gerard told her.

"Shut your mouth, Nick, or I'll stand upwind of you!" Edwina Sampson told him, trying to wipe her face with the sleeve of her jacket. "Captain, can we go somewhere and get dry and clean again?"

"Quoting the field manuals," Jerry Allen quipped, " 'an experienced field sojer will figger out a way t' keep clean an' dry.' "

Sampson looked at him as he stood there, wet and bedraggled. "Yes, sir," she replied with just the proper amount of respectful sarcasm in her voice. "Lemme know when you do . . . sir."

Curt turned to look at his two new Bravo platoon troopers. They were both grinning ear to ear. "Okay, where the hell did you two go and how did you do it?" he wanted to know.

"Shucks, Captain," Corp. Tom Cole replied easily in the Good Ol' Boy down-home drawl that was a natural part of him, "you all gave the command, 'As skirmishers, forward.' So I went forward with Tracy here. I could hear Lieutenant Allen rustlin' around in the puckerbrush, so Tracy and me decided to bushwhack 'em. So much rain comin' down that the sound covered our slitherin' through the grime until we outflanked 'em."

"Was real simple," Tracy Dillon went on. "Hell, Captain, it was like playing cowboys and Indians back home in the scrub oak . . . 'cept it's a tad wetter here."

"You've had personal combat training somewhere? National Guard?" Lt. Jerry Allen asked incredulously, having difficulty believing that these two recruits could have gotten the better of a West Point graduate.

"Shucks, no, Lieutenant," Cole replied with a smile. "I just had Basic at Fort Benning, that's all."

"Never been deer hunting, have you, Lieutenant?" Dillon asked.

"I didn't think hunting wild game was allowed any longer," Jerry Allen offered.

"Oh, we got plenty room out west. Lot more space than people," Tracy Dillon explained. "Drive a hunnert miles to borrow a pair of pliers from a neighbor if we have to. And gotta hunt the deer and elk to keep them from over-breeding; damned few natural predators out in the Rockies these days."

"Okay, looks like Bravo won this time," Curt adjudicated. "While it's fresh in our minds, what did we learn?"

"I wish I'd had some good recon," Jerry Allen observed.

"You've been spoiled by being able to see what you wanted to see through recon warbots," Henry Kester told him. "Even reconbots would have trouble detecting and tagging an enemy in this cover."

"I learned something in Zahedan," Sgt. Edie Sampson put in, brandishing her pain pellet pistol. "These pop guns may be great stuff for non-lethal engagements like this, but I want stopping power in my personal weapons now."

"Yeah," Nick Gerard added, "this thing has too much drop in its trajectory and the underbrush can deflect the projectile. I don't need range in conditions like these, but I do want the damned bullet to go where I aim it and not get deflected by a leaf . . .''

"I'd like infra red, laser, and chemical detector sights," Alexis put in. "Sometimes in this cover, you can't get a visual for aiming."

"You think a chem pointer would work with all the musty smells around here?" Curt wanted to know.

"Eventually, yes, especially in Edie's case," Nick remarked.

"I should stuff this paint gun down your throat for that remark, Gerard," Edie Sampson snapped, "but I'll just remind you that a chem pointer wouldn't be able to descriminate me from hundreds of piles of the stuff laying around out here . . .''

"How about tactics?" Curt changed the subject. "As for myself, I felt I'd lost control of my unit because my tacomm* unit failed," he added, referring to his plastic waist unit.

"Captain," M. Sgt. Henry Kester advised him, "anyone who goes into personal combat believing that radios and other such high-tech gear are going to work in the normal battle environment is counting on nothing. The Russkies learned it. We learned it."

"How come the warbot sensor and command links always seem to work?" Alexis Morgan asked rhetorically. "We've *never* had them jammed!"

"They're multiple-redundant," Curt pointed out. "Ordnance and Signal won't tell us how it works, so we've just got to assume its cosmical magic stuff and count on it. Never failed us yet."

"Why can't they come up with personal tacomm units that operate on the same principles?" Jerry Allen asked.

"Because there's been no stated and justified mili-

*See Glossary of Robot Infantry Terms, p. 422.

23

tary requirement for these personal tacomms working in a personal combat enviroment, and nothing ever gets done in this Army without a J-M-R," Curt said with finality. "However, these rear echelon units seem to crap out under field conditions. I'll report it and maybe Signal will eventually give us one that will work in the mud and slime."

"Things *are* kind of wet out here," Alexis Morgan pointed out, her soaked camouflage uniform shedding water it could no longer absorb. "Captain, can we continue this critique somewhere that's dry?"

"Agreed," Curt acquiesced as he looked around at his bedraggled unit. These survivalist war games weren't very comfortable, but as far as he was concerned they were a lot better training that playing computer war games and running simulator battle scenarios in the comfortable surroundings of the War College Annex. "We'll continue this critique this afternoon after we get some chow. Let's get the hell out of here and back to Charlotte Amalie. Where's the vehicle?"

"Over to the west, toward that hill," Henry Kester indicated. "I got a line of sight on it. If we spread out as skirmishers, we'll find it."

Ten minutes later, the call came down the line to Curt as they thrashed their way through the thick foliage, "Captain, Sergeant Kester says the aerodyne isn't there!"

"What the hell?" Curt exploded. "Can't be!"

"Someone steal it?" Alexis Morgan wondered.

"Not unless they knew the start code," Curt reminded her. "Everyone, assemble toward Sergeant Kester. Henry, give us a locating call."

As Curt walked into the clearing where they'd landed the saucer-shaped aerodyne which had brought them from Charlotte Amalie, he could see that it was indeed gone. The three landing pad impressions still remained in the soft ground. "Sonofabitch, we're stranded!" he growled with frustration.

"That's just what you think, Carson!" the familiar voice of Capt. Marty Kelly boomed through the air. "You forgot to cover your ass!"

Four tactical aerodynes suddenly lifted into the air above the treetops, their armament ranged directly on Curt and his troops. Around the clearing, a dozen war-bots suddenly broke cover. "Hettrick sent me to find you and bring you back. We found you, but we're gonna have a little fun with you first . . ."

With that, the warbots and the aerodynes opened fire on Carson's Companions.

CHAPTER THREE

It was damned near for real. And the warbots under Capt. Marty Kelly of Kelly's Killers, the most bloodthirsty outfit in the Washington Greys, were firing live rounds from their assault warbots and tactical aerodynes.

The rounds went over the heads of Carson's Companions, but just barely over their heads.

Curt thought, *That goddamned sonofabitch Kelly is playing his usual bloodthirsty games again!* The Killers wouldn't deliberately attempt to kill any of the Companions; Colonel Hettrick would view that with less than enthusiasm and probably convene a general court martial as a result. Curt believed that Kelly wouldn't let this little game go too far, although Curt found himself wishing that his old nemesis would make some kind of a mistake which would lead to some sort of a reprimand or disciplinary action. He'd had enough of Kelly over the years, starting in his West Point "Beast Barracks" plebe days. This little gambit was only the latest in Kelly's string of harassing stunts.

He looked around. He couldn't see the rest of the Companions. Some of them had barely entered the jungle clearing when Kelly's loudspeaker voice had boomed forth. Now, they'd melted back into the rain forest. Kelly had been overanxious and premature in revealing himself, but Marty Kelly had never been known for his patience.

"His aerodynes can't lower their fire without hitting his own warbots," Alexis Morgan observed.

"Right! Stay on your feet and rush the nearest warbot! Use your paint gun! Aim for the sensors!" Curt told her.

But Curt's troops had already figured out how they could incapacitate Kelly's warbots with their paint pellet pistols. From the underbrush came the muffled sounds of pellet gun discharges. Four warbots were suddenly covered with bright red paint. Before the ambushed warbots could stop firing their heavy weapons—much heavier, larger, and more powerful than a human being could possibly fire without physical injury—they were blinded and their projectile weapons began to slew uncontrolled. Three robots on the other side of the clearing suddenly stopped firing; they'd been hit by another warbot's gun in the wild crossfire.

"Sierra Hotel!" Alexis shouted. "Now Kelly's got himself into deep yogurt! His warbots have shot each other!"

Curt steadied his paint pellet pistol and took aim at one of the remaining untouched warbots. He fired and his paint pellet found the target a fraction of a second before two more pellets from Companions in the underbrush also hit the warbot, blinding it completely.

"You sons of bitches!" Kelly's amplified voice roared.

"And a few real bitches, too!" Sgt. Edie Sampson's voice yelled back.

The four aerodynes began moving in for what appeared to be a tacair strike.

Suddenly everything stopped. The two remaining warbots quit firing. The aerodynes stopped their forward flight and went into automatic hover.

There was relative silence for a moment before Henry Kester's amplified voice boomed forth from one of the aerodynes, "Okay, Captain, me and Nick and Tracy just took the Killers' command post. Caught Kelly and his people in linkage with the warbots and unable to personally resist. They've parked our aerodyne over here. Can you locate magnetic north?"

Good old Henry Kester! The man knew more about personal combat than anyone in the whole regiment! "Got my trusty Boy Scout compass," Curt called back.

"Okay, take up a heading of zero-five-zero magnetic, about three hundred meters through the Tarzan stuff," Henry's voice came back. "We'll hold 'em until you get here. They ain't very spunky now. We threatened to pull them out of deep linkage with their warbots, and they haven't got their biotechs along with them. So no rush. Captain Kelly and his troops aren't going anywhere or doin' anything . . ."

Kester and two of the Companions had found and captured the command post for Kelly's Killers. It was an armored air-mobile vehicle from which the warbots and aerodynes were being controlled by the Killers themselves. Normally, the physical capture of a warbot command post wasn't considered a realistic threat because warbots fought other warbots as much as ten kilometers away while defense warbots protected the command post. Rarely was a command post endangered by surprise capture in actual warbot combat. But Capt. Marty Kelly, unused to dealing with real human soldiers as adversaries, had let down his guard. Not only had Curt and his company blinded most of the warbots with simple paint pellets, but the Companions had over-run the command post itself.

Standard war robots were, of course, commanded by human beings carefully and securely protected in a remote command post. The individual nervous systems

28

of the human operators were connected by nonintrusive skin electrodes to artificial intelligence electronics and intelligence amplifier computers that fed the visual, auditory, laser, and radar sensor outputs from the warbots directly to their nervous systems and brains in such a way that the humans perceived exactly what the warbots perceived. In turn, the human warbot operators relayed commands by similar data links back to their remote robots directly from their minds, merely thinking the commands as if they were the warbots themselves. Even though robot operators might be miles away from the dangers of battle, they could fight their warbots as if they were there in person . . . without the risk of being killed.

There was little that Marty Kelly and his people could do about Kester's capture of their CP. Although the electronic linkage with their computers and warbots was nonintrusive—only a series of external electrodes on their head, shoulders, and backs—if they were unplugged suddenly from these electronic harnesses, the mental jolt of coming quickly out of the unreal electronic world of remote linkage was a very traumatic experience. When a warbot brainy soldier was suddenly disconnected from his warbots during action, the result was known as "being killed in action" or KIA. Sometimes the mental jolt required months of hospitalization and convalescence in order for the warbot soldier to separate the two realities—the real world versus the neurally-linked warbot world. Without trained biotechnologist support troops present to monitor each warbot soldier's physical and mental condition during an "un-link" operation, Kelly and his troops could be KIA, and even Curt wouldn't wish that on his worst enemy.

Curt grinned at the thought of having caught Marty Kelly and his warbot brainies in that condition. "You know, Alexis, maybe there's something redeeming about this personal combat after all . . ."

"You tell me," the attractive but dirty young woman officer replied. "I haven't been this wet and scared in a long time. Thank God it's just a game. All I really want to do right now is to get clean and dry again . . ."

"Oh, I'm sure you'll have time to do both before we have dinner at Bluebeard's Tower tonight . . ."

She looked back at him and a smile spread across her face. "I guess I'll manage somehow. These days, a woman can't afford to turn down an attractive offer like that . . ."

Carson's Companions converged on the Killers' command post, but Curt didn't enter. The Companion's transport aerodyne squatted on its landing gear a few meters away. As Kester, Gerard, and Dillon came out of the command post vehicle, Curt remarked, "I wish I could have left Kelly a calling card."

"I did, Captain," Nick Gerard said with a grin. "No latrine aboard, so it seems a panel marked 'olfactory sensor modulator' got used for a urinal . . ."

"Serves the bastards right," Edie Sampson muttered. "Trying to bushwack us like that . . ."

"Done under my orders!" The voice of Col. Belinda Hettrick suddenly blurted forth from an aerodyne quietly hovering about 20 meters away. There were four of the saucer-shaped aerodynes hovering up there, and only then did Curt notice that one of them didn't carry the markings of Kelly's Killers, but those of the Third Robot Infantry Regiment, the Washington Greys, "Captain Carson. embark your company at once, return to the War College Annex, and report to me in person immediately after landing!"

"Oh, shit!" Curt said under his breath. "It's hit the

impeller now!" Then he straightened up and snapped, "Carsons Companions, load up! We've moving out!"

Neither Lieutenants Alexis Morgan nor Jerry Allen said anything to Curt during the 20 kilometer flight between St. Croix and St. Thomas. M. Sgt. Henry Kester was impassive; he'd been in the Army long enough to have caught hell from hundreds of officers for dozens of different offenses, some serious, some minor, and some trivial. The old soldier considered this to be a trivial occasion. Besides, Hettrick wasn't likely to bust him; he was far too valuable as a combat infantry soldier who'd transitioned from personal combat to warbot combat and was now transitioning back. Kester knew too much about personal combat tactics. He also knew a lot about other people in the Washington Greys but he was extremely discreet. It was pretty hard to dress down a man with a sleeve full of chevrons, rockers, and hash marks plus a chest displaying five rows of ribbons, the legendary Combat Infantryman's Badge, several Presidential Unit Citations, and so many oak leaf clusters that no one bothered to count them any longer. Kester's most recent oak leaf clusters were on his Purple Heart and Silver Star from the Zahedan hostage extraction mission.

If rank has its privileges in the Army, so does longevity.

CHAPTER FOUR

On the ramp before the War College Annex, Curt told his company to shower down, get cleaned up, hit the chow hall, and he'd see them at 1400 hours in the Orderly Room for a final debrief. Still in his wet cammys with mud streaked and splattered all over them and over his face and arms, he looked more like a classic infantry grunt as he slogged down the hallway to Colonel Hettrick's office . . . being careful, of course, to wipe the mud from his combat boots before he set foot on the shining polished floors of the War College Annex.

It was 1135 when he rapped on the door, went in, stood at attention, removed his soaking beret, and saluted.

"Captain Curt Carson reporting as ordered, Colonel." Col. Belinda Hettrick was looking down at the terminal screen in her desk top and didn't bother to acknowledge him for a few seconds. When she did so, she returned his salute with a scowl. "I hope you had fun crawling on your belly through the mud over on St. Croix," she finally said.

"Colonel," Curt tried to explain, "we've had it with all this academic bullshit in the simulators and war gamers. It just doesn't match the real thing worth a damn. So we—"

"I know what you were doing," Hettrick interrupted him gruffly. "I don't like the academic war gaming environment any more than you do. But the General Staff says to do it in the sims and gamers so no one gets hurt. They've grown a big set of chicken feathers in the last twenty years. They can't conceive of putting a human solider at risk. But, they make the rules and they issue the orders. I'm just an old soldier and I've been trained to follow orders. But you, you young warhorse, I'm having a hell of a time with you. Always have."

Curt said nothing.

Hettrick leaned back in her chair and ran her hand over her shaved scalp. She wasn't wearing a wig today. Like all warbot brainies, she shaved her head daily so that the sensor and command electrodes in a linkage helmet would make better contact. She envied Curt and his company; in the months they'd been developing the new multi-phase, human-warbot special combat tactics, doctrine, and operational procedures at the War College Annex in Charlotte Amalie in conjunction with the McCarthy Proving Ground's tropical annex, Carson's Companions had allowed their hair to grow again. They were thus unique among the Washington Greys, all of whom proudly sported the shaved heads of warbot soldiers.

"Sergeant Henry Kester put you up to these survivalist war games, didn't he?" Hetterick suddenly asked.

"Colonel, I'm responsible for my company engaging in that activity."

"That isn't what I asked."

"It was my decision to do it, orders to the contrary notwithstanding," Curt told her, still standing stiffly at attention. "If I'm going to ask Carson's Companions to go out and put their physical bodies in the line of

33

fire, regardless of how many voice-commanded, artificially-intelligent warbots we've got under our command and supporting us when we do so, I want them to have experience and training on how to survive in battle on their own if the warbots go toes-up like some of them did in Zahedan."

"Captain," Colonel Hettrick said slowly, "I've got to give you a reprimand for disobeying orders and putting your officers and NCOs in a hazardous situation."

Curt sighed inwardly. An official reprimand in his 101 File was the first signal of the beginning of the end of a professional Army career and a ticket to the bottom of the promotion list . . . which was short enough in these days of non-war robot combat in which the human strength of the Army had dropped to its lowest level in over a century. With warbots capable of handling so many combat tasks, huge manpower rosters were no longer necessary. The Third Robot Infantry Regiment, the Washington Greys, of the 17th Iron Fist Division now boasted less than a hundred people, even though it was the first of the new Special Combat or Sierra Charlie regiments with more people and one-tenth the number of warbots.

"But it's going to be a personal reprimand and won't go in your One-Oh-One, Curt," Hettrick went on in softer tones. "You're too damned good an officer; you don't deserve an official reprimand in your One-Oh-One. But you do derserve an ass-chewing, which this is. Curt, you and your company are among the few people in this Army who've been shot at and fought back in personal combat. We're all down here on TDY so the War College staff stooges can pick our brains and use us as guinea pigs to test new doctrine. It's an honor for the Washington Greys to be chosen to do this. But, dammit, man, why do you have to make it so difficult for me?"

34

"I told you why, Colonel," Curt replied levelly.

Hettrick sighed. "Consider that you've been personally reprimanded, as I've been ordered to do. Now, at ease and sit down. What did you learn over on St. Croix playing games in the mud today?"

Curt carefuly took a seat alongside the desk. "That it's a dirty job but someone's got to do it."

"I can see that. Dirt, that is. Got rained on, too, didn't you?"

"That's a minor discomfort, although my ladies didn't think so," Curt admitted, thinking of Lt. Alexis Morgan and Sgt. Edwina Sampson. "They don't really dislike personal combat; both of them are somewhat more bloodthirsty and sneaky that the male members of the company. But they feel a bit insecure."

"Insecure? Why? In what way?"

"When the General Staff decided that the experimental TO of a Sierra Fox company should include four squad leaders in order to handle the voice-commanded support warbots we're supposed to use, four young men were assigned to Carson's Companions," Curt pointed out.

"So?"

"So Lieutenant Morgan and Sergeant Sampson have the sneaky feeling that the Army's swing back to personal combat is going to be accompanied by a return to the old Army policy of prohibiting women from serving in combat units. Morgan and Sampson are part of our team. They don't want to find themselves reassigned to another company or even back to a noncombatant job where they're exposed to danger but aren't permitted to defend themselves," Curt tried to explain.

"Well, withdrawing women from combat units certainly isn't contemplated at this time . . . I hope," Hettrick replied, thinking that she wouldn't relish being in command of a divisional logistics support regiment herself. She was an experienced warbot brainy herself and had come close to personal combat at Zahedan. "What does the assignment of the four troopers to the Companions have to do with it?"

"No women were assigned. Only four young men."

"Oh."

"Pretty good men, too."

"I thought they might fill the bill, judging from their backgrounds."

"They did and they're going to. We're learning a lot from them. Two country boys in Morgan's platoon, and two city types from the asphalt jungle in Allen's platoon. I asked you originally for two men and two women."

"I couldn't find two women who filled the bill," Hettrick explained. "I told you that."

"I believe you. But I'm reporting on the consequences of posting four young male recruits to my company."

"I'll see what I can do about it."

Curt knew she would. Hettrick was an excellent regimental commander, a leader who knew when and where to cut through the red tape, forms, bureacracy and bullshit to get what was needed.

"What else? Certainly you didn't go out there and get wet and dirty without learning something." Hettrick went on.

"Well, I thought you probably knew since you were observing."

"I didn't start observing until I learned you'd gone. Never mind; no one ratted on you. I've known you and the Companions were sneaking off on these survivalist games for weeks now. This time, I followed in a stealth mode." She smiled and added, "I also called in Kelly's Killers on you."

Curt nodded, but he didn't smile. "Yes, Colonel, I know you did."

"Don't you want to know why?" she asked after about fifteen seconds of silence.

"No, Colonel, I've got that figured out already."

"Oh?"

"A little game of surprise-surprise makes the cheese a bit more binding. After all, if you knew we'd been over on St. Croix from time to time for several weeks, the best way to find out whether or not we were learning something or just screwing around was to pop Kelly's Killers on us with a full warbot compliment and see what happened." At this point, Curt did grin. "Paint pellet guns aren't bad as an anti-warbot weapon, but they're inaccurate. They have a lousy low velocity trajectory so they don't hurt a person when they get hit. Leaves, branches, and other underbrush deflect the pellet too easily. Okay for disabling warbots in war games, but I think we want something in the way of a personal small arm that will kill an armored warbot and do a reasonably good job of messing up an enemy soldier as well."

"How about a small arm that will kill both robots and humans?"

"Because I'd rather wound a soldier," Curt explained. "Been reading some of the books by Patton, Bradley, Ridgeway, Westmoreland, and the other generals who led troops in the days of personal combat. Kill a soldier and it takes only two men with shovels to bury him plus one or two guys from Graves Registration. Wound a soldier, and you've created a logistical and personnel problem for the enemy because that wounded soldier needs medical evacuation, medical care, and rehabilitation. Ties up a lot of the enemy's capabilities."

"I read you," Hettrick admitted. "Okay, what *do* you want in the way of a personal small arm?"

Curt thought a moment. "Seven-point-six-two caseless ammo. Five hundred meters effective range against body armor. Selectable full auto, semi-auto, or three-round burst. Ten centimeter dispersion at five hundred meters. Weight about two to three kilos, length about seven-fifty centimeters."

Hettrick snorted and remained silent for a moment while she thought about Curt's requirements. "Won't kill an armored warbot."

"Don't want to kill them. I'll let my voice-commanded artificially intelligent support warbots carrying the fifteen-millimeter, high velocity stuff that would bust my shoulder but penetrate most warbot armor. If I come up against a warbot, I'll aim for its sensors, which is why I want the low dispersion. My dream weapon will stop a human, and we found out we can run up against a lot of non-robot human troops out there in parts of the world that can't afford warbots."

"What's the matter with the standard issue Hornet submachine carbine?"

"No range. No accuracy. Worse than the old M1 Carbine. It'll scare someone who sneaks up on you in the rear echelon, but we learned in Zahedan that it can be out-ranged and out-shot by any of the fifty million old Soviet Kalashnikovs still out there in the real world."

"Elephant guns," Hettrick muttered, using the soldier's vernacular for those old, large caliber assault rifles.

"No, real old elephant guns were smaller than the current warbot rifles," Curt pointed out.

Hettrick sighed. "Well, the requirements you've just set forth for the new Sierra Charlie personal weapon eliminates every small arm in the Army's inventory. If we could ever get an Operational Requirement Statement approved and get Congress to cough up some funds for development, we might get a few experimental rifles in about twelve years or so . . . Well beyond even your effective combat career, Captain.''

"Oh, we've found a personal small arm, Colonel," Curt admitted with some hesitation.

"What?"

"The Mexicans make a perfectly excellent version of the Heckler and Koch G-22 called the FABARMA M3A4 'Novia.' The Mexicans are right; it's a sweetheart.''

"That's a foreign weapon; the Army couldn't possibly think of buying it without a lot of Congressional lobbying . . .'' Hettrick advised him. "Besides, the Novia isn't an automatic weapon.''

"Henry Kester makes a few minor modifications to it, something the designers at Fabrica de Armas Mexico or the people from the Bureau of Alcohol, Tobacco, and Firearms didn't think could be done.'' Curt admitted.

"You mean Kester has one?"

"We all do."

Hettrick started to say something, decided not to, then settled back in her chair and brought her fingertips together in a steeple before her lips. Then she said incredulously, pausing momentarily between words, "You mean, you all purchased personal small arms for use in Army activities?''

Curt nodded. "Cheap. Couple of hundred bucks each. We've been out practicing on weekends. Nice weapon. Beats the hell out of the Hornet.''

Hettrick clasped her hands together and shook her head in dismay. Although the Hornet was the standard personal weapon of the U.S. Army Robot Infantry soldier and intended for individual protection in rear areas or unusual combat situations, Army policy had reverted to that of the Indian Wars when support troops were permitted a choice in small arms because they were so seldom used. Technically, a warbot brainy in the Robot Infantry wasn't supposed to engage in personal combat at all but was expected to do all his/her fighting through warbots; therefore, the matter of standardization of personal weapons became nearly a moot point. Warbot brainies either carried their choice of personal weapons or relied upon the Hornet standard-issue weapon. Hettrick had no real grounds for complaint about the Companions chosing a nonstandard personal weapon.

Except that now the doctrine was changing again. The complete reliance upon warbots was suddenly seen to be inappropriate for some combat situations. The human being was being integrated back into actual combat. They would be out there on the foward edge of the battle area or FEBA like infantry of old, but supported by armored personnel/warbot carriers and commanding newly developed warbots that responded to verbal commands and contained a very high level of artificial intelligence computer circuitry.

Personal weapons had again become important in combat. But the Army policy concerning them hadn't yet caught up with what Curt Carson and his company were learning about integrated human-warbot combat.

So Col. Belinda Hettrick couldn't chew out Capt. Curt Carson for selecting a Mexican sporting rifle and converting it into an automatic combat weapon. It was their job on St. Thomas to learn and develop the Army's new special combat or Sierra Charlie doctrines and operational procedures. This obviously had to include testing different sorts of weapons in the new combat environment.

Or so Hettrick rationalized to herself.

"All right," she snapped to Curt, "I'll not stand in your way of selecting and testing the best personal weapons for Sierra Charlies. But playing survivalist war games with paint pellet pistols could get someone hurt. Then my eagles are on the line."

"Colonel," Curt replied, trying to convince his regimental commander that what he was trying to do was right and that what the staff stooges wanted to do was nothing more than playing games, "we're leaning too heavily on the voice-commanded AI warbots in the doctrine and tactics the War College people were trying to stuff down our throats. It's going to get us killed in real combat."

"What makes you believe that?"

"Because, except for a few people like Jerry Allen who are just out of West Point, we've all forgotten how to fight like infantry soldiers. Even me. Ten years ago, I'd just graduated from the Academy; I'd had personal combat training, which was considered to be quaintly old-fashioned but was supposed to turn children into adults. It did. But then we were thrown into the RI environment and sat on our duffs in nice air-conditioned vehicles fighting through warbots. We forgot things. The NCOs—with the notable exception of Henry Kester, of course—never learned personal combat at all."

"What are you getting at?" Hettrick asked him. It was patently obvious that Curt Carson was rather passionately defending his non-reg company training procedures. The Colonel was under pressure from higher brass to do it the Army way, and from her fighting troops, to react to the real world of combat. In her particular position as a regimental commander, she was caught between staff and warriors. In fact, it had been the particular and unwelcome position of most field officers for centuries. Hettrick tended to fend off the brass and listen to her combat commanders.

"Simply this: We're going to have to learn how to fight all by ourselves first. *Then* we should learn how to use the AI warbots to help us. Not the other way around. If the warbots catch it in the pan—as most of them did in Zahedan—we've got to fight without them. *We cannot count on machines to do our fighting for us!* And that's what we're learning down here in the Virgin Islands, Colonel."

"The military academicians around here aren't going to believe you."

"And those staff stooges aren't going to get shot at, either."

"Got any suggestions I might try to sell them and they might buy?"

"Yes," Curt Carson said firmly. "Real, honest-to-God war games. Not in a computer. Not in a simulator. Out in the rain and mud and the heat. Over on St. Croix. The sort of thing you tried to pull off with Kelly's Killers today, but a little bigger and more realistic. Look, split the Greys, two battalions like the TO shows but we never follow. Match my Companions as Sierra Charlies with Walker's Warriors as the Blue Force. Our opponents: Manny's Marauders and Kelly's Killers as the Red Force. Put us in the field, give both Red and Blue an objective as well as a position to defend. Let us go at one another with the War College people and your staff as umpires."

Hettrick shook her head. "They won't buy it. Too dangerous."

"Dangerous? Hell, Colonel, kids play that game all the time and never get hurt!" Curt pointed out. "I can't believe you've forgotten how you used to play when you were a kid—"

"What do you mean?"

42

"For chrissake, we aren't going to get hurt and we're going to learn a hell of a lot by playing a super-sophisticated warbot version of 'Capture The Flag!'"

Hettrick smiled. "Why, of course! But, Curt, they won't buy an exercise if we tell them it's a grown-up version of Capture The Flag."

"Who's going to tell them that? This is a 'field exercise' to realistically test what we've supposedly learned in the simulators."

"Now *that* I can sell!" She stood up and looked at him. "You're a mess. Now I've got to get the room-policing robot in here. Go get cleaned up. Dismissed! And, uh, Curt, if I'm going to go over to St. Croix and supervise this field exercise, what do you recommend for keeping clean and dry?"

Curt grinned. "One each, coat: rain, Army, and a green field coat with hood."

CHAPTER FIVE

"Mr. Priest," the tall, handsome woman with snow-white hair said diplomatically, "are you officially requesting the assistance and participation of the United States' government in an overt *invasion* of Trinidad?"

"I am, Madam Secretary. And I do so with the full agreement and support of the people I asked to join us here today in Arecibo." The lilting accent of a native of Trinidad was on the lips of the dapper British-looking man who waved his arm around the circle of people gathered on the sun-drenched patio which commanded a spectaular view of the ocean to the north.

The Secretary of State of the United States of America let her hazel eyes follow the sweep of the man's arm, then dropped to her lap to scan the sheet of notes that had been prepared by an aide. It was indeed both an august and unusual group of people—high representatives from the governments of Venezuela, Panama, Colombia, Jamaica, and Curacao in addition to the man speaking, the former President of Trinidad, Morris Priest, who had been forced out of office and the island itself by the questionable election of the late socialist, Clarke Chamberlin.

Seated in the circle as well was a round-raced, bearded man wearing a kaftan and burnoose who was cited on the crib sheet as the official representative of the Oil Ministry of Saudi Arabia and the Petroleum Federation or PetroFed. The Saudi had a more than usual dour expression; that was understandable to the Secretary who knew full well from her former profession as a petroleum geologist that Trinidad was the third largest crude producer in the Western Hemisphere and second only to the United States in refinery capacity, most of which was owned in convoluted corporate arrangements by the PetroFed and the other multi-nationals whose vice presidents also sat in the room to look after the interests of Shelexxo and Texarco.

"The United States government," she intoned roundly, "would find it extremely difficult to justify participating in an armed conflict to protect purely commercial interests of other countries and multi-national corporations." She knew she had to say that, even though more than ample historical examples could be cited to the contrary. She also knew from briefings on the flight down from Washington that more than commercial interests were involved in the Trinidad matter. One of the men in the U.S. delegation who was ostensibly a Deputy Secretary and had been introduced as such was indeed a Deputy Secretary, but of the Department of Defense, not the Department of State. Another quiet woman behind the Secretary was an Assistant Secretary of Commerce. The representative from the Central Intelligence Agency had remained in the aircraft at the airport.

The Secretary of State knew exactly what the situation was and why the President had sent her to this unannounced, unheralded, and quite unofficial meeting in Puerto Rico. The various White House and en route briefings had only served to fill in what she already knew from the last meeting of the even more quiet Council of World Economies, about which the

45

less said the better because very little was known of this multi-national power group . . . and that was exactly the way they wanted it.

"I believe this is far more complex than that," intoned the Saudi representative from the PetroFed, the successor to OPEC. "We have a sizeable investment in the refining and processing capability on Trinidad because of some of the protectionist laws of the United States which limit the amount of imported crude but ignore the matter of importing processed crude products. Our information sources report that General Drake's government, such as it is, will shortly nationalize these refineries which in turn will put their products exclusively at the disposal of the Allianza. The PetroFed may be forced to shut off shipments of crude and refined petroleum products to North America as a result—"

"Now, Sheik, we believe some sort of accomodation can be worked out if such a thing happens," was the quickly inserted input of one of the petro conglomerate executives. "It may be costly, but we can certainly recover the capital expense through a modest increase in retail prices . . ."

The PetroFed representative merely scowled in reply. "We do not intend to sit back and allow our investments to be seized by military adventurers."

Morris Priest, who was trying to orchestrate this meeting so that the conclusions actually matched the anticipations, quickly put in, "This is not a purely commercial matter, Madam Secretary. The security of the Caribbean nations is at stake. Trinidad is not only economically powerful because of its petroleum industry but also because cheap energy permits other industries to flourish there."

"We do not object to free competition among nations," the Jamaican representative attempted to explain. "But we cannot survive a situation in which Trinidad forces us to the economic wall because of massive inputs of capital and materials from the ABC Allianza."

"Argentina, Brazil, and Chile have grown constantly and slowly as a power base in South America ever since they had the temerity to mediate the Pancho Villa border dispute between the United States and Mexico in 1914," the Panamanian prime minister recalled. "Now, there is no question that the Allianza has grown in economic and military power to the point where it can openly utilize Trinidad as a satellite nation to gain physical control over the air and sea lanes of the Caribbean. I would like to present evidence concerning this."

The Panamanian withdrew a sheaf of photos from his briefcase and began to pass them around the table. "We have purchased high quality, earth resources satellite photos from Japan within the last week; you may wish to look at them to confirm what I tell you. We can see that a new military airfield has been put into operation at Napirima, south of San Fernando. It is the base for twenty-four Embraer Piranha-B strike aircraft and an anti-shipping squadron consisting of twelve Argentine IA-88 Delfin maritime patrol/attack aircraft. These have a radius of action of a thousand kilometers. In addition, the Trinidad Defense Forces have eighteen Aero Boero *Diamante* interceptors and twenty-six IAR Model 20 transport aerodynes based in a new military compound at the Piarco International Airport. The Trinidad naval forces have taken delivery of two new Viagens Class corvettes and four new Argentine hydrofoil gunboats based at Port of Spain and San Fernando. Some of the aircraft and naval ships may be manned by Allianza military advisors. We also know from our own resources that the Trinidad Defense

Forces' army now numbers more than ten thousand troops and an unknown number of war robots.''

The American Deputy Secretary of Defense had to supress a grunt of total amazement at the clarity, resolution, and detail shown in the Japanese commercial landsat photos. He'd recently seen similar images from super-secret, high-tech Air Force KH-44 spy satellites whose image resolution pushed the limits of optical technology. The Panamanian photos from the Japanese satellite were good. Very good. But he said nothing. The photos merely confirmed what he already knew. Damned civilian space equipment was getting almost as good as the CIA and DIA stuff . . . and at a lot lower cost.

''We are forced to ask ourselves the question,'' said the prime minister of Curacao, ''why the people of Trinidad need such a strong military and naval presence on their island. General Drake claims it is necessary for the defense of the island. But we have a very equitable series of multi-lateral trade agreements among the Caribbean nations, and none of us maintains large standing armies capable of attacking one another. It's not as if we wanted to remove Trinidad as a competitor by using military force. So why is Trinidad building a massive military and naval establishment on the pretext of 'defense'?''

''It is our conclusion,'' the foreign minister of Venezuela put in, ''that the activity on Trinidad is backed by the Allianza for the specific purpose of controlling a choke point of both sea and air trade.''

''At the moment, should they chose to exercise their existing air and naval power, Trinidad would be able to control the air travel node between North and South America through Piarco International Airport and extend the threat of aerial interdiction over the eastern Caribbean sea lanes. The 'coastal defense' naval forces

48

would easily be able to interdict the major maritime trade routes,'' the Colombian prime minister added. ''Madam Secretary, the transatlantic and South American trade of all the nations represented in this room passes through Trinidad's choke point at the southeastern end of the Caribbean. That includes the maritime trade of the United States of America from your Gulf ports and Mississippi Basin to South America, Africa, and the Far East around the Cape of Good Hope.''

The prime minister of Jamaica added, ''We also know of plans and initial work on the establishment of a new spaceport on the eastern coast of Trinidad; this will give the Allianza a space launch capability far closer to the equator than Gran Bahia. They will be able to use the local petroleum industry as a source of both energy and rocket fuels. With a Trinidad spaceport, Brazil's strong space activity will be bolstered by the participation of both the Argentines and the Chileans. This should have significant impact on space commerce because of the fact that Trinidad has never signed the various United Nations' agreements, treaties, and protocols relating to space commerce; they will be able to do whatever they wish if they complete a spaceport in the Nariva swamps . . .''

The Secretary of State knew what she had to do and say first. If she were later to be subpoenaed before a congressional investigating committee in the event that the inevitable military action didn't succeed, she had to be able to testify that she'd been properly reluctant to participate and had asked all the right questions. She already knew what the answers were going to be and what her ''report'' to the President was going to say; that had been decided days ago in the Cabinet Room of the White House. But the United States of America had to touch second base and play by the rules. ''Why

49

are you so concerned about the Allianza? Isn't the economic union of Argentina, Brazil, and Chile seen as comparable to the formation of the European Common Market, a concentration of economic power for internal as well as international trade benefit of this part of the world?''

The answer surprised her. She didn't expect such candor. Everyone looked at Morris Priest, a man educated in history and political science at Oxford, who quietly stated, ''Before World War Two, Sir Winston Churchill commented about the attitude of many Britishers who felt that it was unfair for England to help preserve French military superiority over Germany. He pointed out that it wasn't an issue of competition between two similar nations. If the French were superior, peace would result; if Germany became superior, war or disasterous appeasement would probably ensue. Thus, Churchill believed that for Great Britain to take a netural stance between France and Germany was both foolish and dangerous. I submit to you, Madam Secretary, that the United States now faces a similar situation. We represent concerned Caribbean nations that have lived for over a century in the shadow of the enormous economic power of the United States. We have learned to live with you and to work within your system. We would rather continue to live and trade peacefully with the United States. We do not relish the consequences of being subservient to an economic conglomerate whose history is rife with military juntas, socialist revolutions, and leaders who loot and run.'' What he didn't say was that, in asking for United States' military support in eliminating the threat to the Caribbean posed by a strong Allianza presence in Trinidad, they were choosing the lesser of two evils.

''Is the threat to the security of the Caribbean by Trinidad sufficiently documented?'' she asked. The

50

CIA had told her it was. But she raised the issue anyway.

"We can make strong a case for it. Far less justification was used when the United States Marines were sent to Central America, when Cuba was blockaded, or when Grenada was invaded . . ." Morris Priest pointed out.

"Precisely what do you want the United States government to do?" the Secretary asked.

Priest replied quickly, "We want to displace the present military government of Trinidad with an interim government of occupation pending free elections to be held within three months. We desire that the military operation be carried out with the minimum loss of life and destruction of property. Venezuela, Curacao, Panama, Colombia, and Jamaica have committed a total of fourteen hundred troops. We request United States naval action, naval transportation of troops, air strikes, air lift, and sufficient army units to quickly carry out the overthrow of the present government of General Austin Drake. Speed is essential because a protracted conflict would kill people and destroy facilities. Therefore, it must be a large operation with overwhelming strength and military superiority. Because of the size and complexity of such an operation, we request that the United States be in charge of the combined command. You have the knowledge to carry out this sort of operation; we do not. So we will follow your tactical orders based upon a jointly agreed-upon strategic plan."

Silence fell over the room. The sea breeze whispered through the open doors and windows.

"There are precedents, Madam Secretary," the president of Panama pointed out.

"Yes," the Secretary of State admitted, "but some

of them are old and from a world that no longer exists—"

"The world has not really changed, Madam Secretary," Morris Priest observed. "Only the individuals and their ideologies have changed. Basic human instincts, motivations, and interests have not. We are not rational beings; we are *rationalizing* beings. We can work out the necessary rationalizations . . ."

The Secretary was a realist; she knew that. But she had to report back to the Oval Office. "When?" was the simple question she asked.

"We are ready now," Morris Priest replied, equally as brief.

But the Americans in the room knew that the United States of America was not. It never had been. But that fact had not deterred it before.

"Your military staffs are with you?" she asked.

Affirmative nods came from the leaders of the Caribbean nations seated around the room.

"Can they accompany us on our aircraft back to Washington?"

They could.

The Assistant Secretary of Defense was already running through his mind the current world disposition of the Army's forces. It was a lean picture. Actually, the general staff had already briefed him on what might be accomplished. The 50th "Big L" Division (Robot Infantry) was due to be withdrawn from the Sub-Saharan Theater because the region was now under the control of local organizations; the 50th could easily be moved to the Mid-East. The 22nd "Double Deuces" Division (Robot Infantry), was in the process of shipping out to the Mid-East from Fort Carson and the Cheyenne Mountain reboubt; it could be diverted without drawing attention to the diversion. Elements of the 17th "Iron Fist" Division (Robot Infantry) were being rotated out of the Persian Gulf Theater to the home base at Diamond Point, and the First Regiment, the Washington Greys, was already in the Virgin Islands on TDY. With the diversion of of the 22nd and the movement of the 50th to cover the withdrawal of the three regiments of the 17th, two of the four most advanced and powerful of the US Army's robot infantry divisions could be brought into action on Trinidad.

In addition, this would be an excellent opportunity to try out the new robot warfare doctrine being honed to perfection by the 17th Iron Fist Division.

But his civilian communications channels didn't go much below the level of the Army Chief of Staff. He didn't know that this new doctrine was far from being perfect, much less operational.

CHAPTER SIX

The Washington Greys were learning it the hard way on St. Croix.

They weren't helped by the fact that the umpires for the Grey Flag war games were more than slightly biased because they were old warbot brainies. Even though only one company, Carson's Companions, had been training in the new doctrine of Sierra Charlie operations involving mixed human and robot warriors, the whole Sierra Charlie concept was a severe threat to the hallowed turf of field grade staff officers who'd made their reputations on the basis of their performance in the Robot Infantry. The mere fact that human soldiers were going to be placed at physical risk in combat was also slightly repugnant to them; they liked nice, clean warfare: machine against machine, and may the best systems manager win.

Besides, the Sierra Charlie doctrine was something new, and the United States Army in peacetime had always been resistant to major changes. It always took an "armed conflict" ("war" had been outlawed by the United Nations charter in 1945) to get the Army to move.

Colonel Hettrick had divided her regiment into its two tactical battalions of two companies each. Her staff of five officers and five NCOs from the headquarters company was to serve as umpires.

The Blue Force consisted of Carson's Companions and Walker's Warriors with Capt. Curt Carson as field commander and Capt. Samantha Walker as second-in-command. The Companions were a Sierra Charlie company—three officers, three NCOs, six squad leaders, and thirty-two highly modified war robots.

Unlike the other warbots in the regiment, the Sierra Charlie warbots were highly experimental units as yet unqualified for combat. They were stuffed with new artificial intelligence computers and circuitry so that they were capable of responding and reporting by both verbal means and radio. They were about the nearest thing to an artificial replacement for a human soldier yet developed by the Army because they would accept orders from a human soldier, ask for clarification if the orders were not understood, carry out the orders, and report back to the human. They had no remote linkage capability, but they were far more self-sufficient and self-programming.

Walker's Warriors, on the other hand, was a regulation robot infantry company—three officers, three NCOs, and 144 standard warbots run by remote linkage with the six humans esconced in a command vehicle. The standard warbots served as extensions of the minds of their human commanders, although these warbots had a limited amount of artificial intelligence which permitted them to carry out orders and operate without constant human direction.

The Red Force was made up of the remaining two regular warbot companies: Manny's Marauders and Kelly's Killers. With malice aforethought because she knew of the animousity and competition between Curt

Carson and Marty Kelly, Hettrick had given command of the Red Force to Capt. Martin Kelly.

Both forces had a redoubt they had to defend while attempting to capture the redoubt of the opposing force.

But both sides had some restrictive rules of engagement laid on them.

First of all, no air support in the form of tac strikes or recon would be available, although Red Force and Walker's Warriors of Blue Force could use airborne recon warbots.

Secondly, no artillery support would be available, even at the company level; the warbot companies could use whatever large caliber smart projectile or rocket capability their warbots happened to have.

This last rule of engagement threatened to cause some difficulties for the Sierra Charlies of Carson's Companions because their new AI self-sufficient warbots didn't carry anything bigger than 25mm or 50mm weapons. But Carson's four Light Armored Maneuvering Vehicles each carried the new 75mm universal projectile—shell or rocket—gun which had been developed by *Atelier de Construction de Tarbes* in France and was thus immediately tagged the "French 75" in remembrance of that ancient cannon of World War I. And, like its namesake, its French nomenclature, *soixante-quinze* (seventy-five) was perverted immediately to "Madamoiselle Saucy Cans," which is the way Henry Kester pronounced it.

Thus, Grey Flag was to be strictly an infantry operation conducted with the philosophy that RI and Sierra Charlie troops would have to work out their operational problems among themselves before getting involved in combined arms operations with air, armor, artillery, and such.

In retrospect, that turned out to be a mistake. Marty Kelly was his usual ebullient, obnoxious self as the units were moving out on St. Croix. His last jibe at Curt Carson was, "You'd better stay on the defensive, Carson, because we're going to pin you mud-slogging swamp rats down with fire so you won't have time to think about assault! Just don't forget to check minus-x because I'll be on your ass the whole time!"

Curt didn't reply. He knew two things that Kelly didn't.

First, he'd found out that, although Hettrick was basically pulling for him and the new Sierra Charlie concept, the regimental staff had been briefed by some of the War College people who really didn't see anything to be gained by putting human beings directly back into combat; they believed it was a step backward in warfare. Thus, the umpires, and therefore Grey Flag, were probably already rigged against him if he tried to use anything resembling robot infantry tactics. So he'd read up on how Merrill's Marauders, the British Commandos, the Green Berets, and other Special Forces outfits had operated in the past. He'd also listened carefully to both M. Sgt. Henry Kester who had actual experience in personal combat before warbots were introduced and to Lieutenant Jerry Allen who was fresh out of West Point with recent training. Then, too, all of Carson's Companions remembered very well the personal combat of the Zahedan hostage rescue strike which had precipitated the Sierra Charlie experiment.

Secondly, he'd worked with Capt. Samantha Walker in training her regular warbot company to work in co-operation with Carson's Companions using the Sierra Charlie tactics. Their joint battle plan made use of the strengths of both human and warbot soldiers to cover the weaknesses of each. Sam was a good officer; she wouldn't let any of it slip out, even though her Warriors would be carrying the brunt of the physical action.

But they hadn't bothered to tell Hettrick or anyone else; security was important, and both Carson and Walker were counting on surprise.

Grey Flag was to last no more than three days. If neither force had prevailed by that time, Hettrick would call a truce.

Curt knew it wouldn't last that long.

As anticipated, contact between Red and Blue first came along Mahogany Road. Sam Walker's Second Platoon under Lt. Dave Coney moved off the road and secured it under fire against further Red advance. Walker's First Platoon under Lt. Joan Ward moved north of the road as if to flank the Red Force.

The word came back via frequency-hop tactical communications with two levels of security. Curt and Samantha were the only two who knew the frequency-hopping sequence, pulse rate, and rep rate programming. And they were the only two who knew the digital coding that would be used for the messages themselves—actually voice would not be used, only bursts of digitized symbols and coded phrases from the 44 standard commands, reports, and responses. The messages would appear on the displays of each person's field communicator. Special messages could be typed in using the miniature keypad. There was literally no way that Red Force could eavesdrop on the Blue Force communications or use electronic countermeasures or jamming against them.

But the same held true for Blue Force; they couldn't snoop on the Red Force communications, either.

Curt saw the encoded report, grinned, and told

Henry Kester, "Okay, this is what we wanted! Let's move out!"

"Hold them by the nose with fire, then kick them in the ass with movement," Kester observed, unconsciously repeating an earlier tactician.

"Kelly's going to have a hell of a time finding our command post, much less capturing it, isn't he?" Alexis Morgan remarked.

"Let's just hope he doesn't move his, too," Jerry Allen warned.

"He won't. Nothing was said in the rules of engagement about moving a command post. In standard warbot tactical doctrine, a commander doesn't move the CP. So Kelly won't move his. Let's hope the umpires don't call foul on us for doing it. Okay, now let's move," Curt snapped anxiously. The anxiety of combat was rising in him. He didn't get it in the sims the way he did in the field. "Sam Walker's expecting us to do the butt kicking while she holds them, but she can't hold them forever."

He began rattling off orders, although everyone in the Companions already knew what they had to do. He wanted the Sierra Charlie warbots to hear the orders, too. Curt believed in redundancy—*Tell 'em what you're going to tell them to do, tell 'em what to do, then tell 'em what you just told 'em to do.* "Allen, get Alpha Platoon out on point. If you happen to make contact, hold it long enough to allow Bravo to engage, then disengage and move!"

"Check! I'll put the Mobile Assault Warbots out in front; they look like regular warbots and may confuse the Red Force," Jerry Allen observed.

Curt turned to his other lieutenant. "Morgan, follow up and watch the flanks. If contact is made by Allen, be ready to establish the fire base."

59

"Gotcha! I'll pin 'em down with my Saucy Cans plus the Heavy Fire Warbots to make like we're regular RI troops using regular RI tactics," the attractive young woman officer acknowledged.

"Remember," Curt admonished them, "that we've got mobility, shock, and surprise on our side. We can maneuver like no warbots ever could. We'll use the roads for movement and the fields for fighting. Be prepared to abandon the vehicles at any point and proceed on foot."

The umpire who'd been assigned to them, a natty little field officer named Maj. Frank Wardwell from regimental S-4, acted very antsy during this entire briefing; it was very obvious that he wanted to object to most of it on the grounds of adherance to tactical doctrine, but his role of umpire required that he merely observe and declare the casualties that resulted. Curt laughed inwardly; these staff stooges were going to get a bit of a lesson today if his plans worked out even fifty percent as well as he hoped.

The North Shore Road between Northside and Cane's Bay was winding and treacherous, threatening to slow their forward movement, but Curt pushed hard to keep up speed. They moved in communications silence, listening only to reports coming from the battle shaping up on Mahogany Road. Umpires were wiping out warbots on both sides. Neither force could withstand that sort of attrition much longer.

"Kelly's going to have to commit his reserves pretty damned quick," Kester pointed out. "I'm keeping a log here; the Manny's Marauders have lost almost half their warbots."

"How's Sam Walker doing?" Curt wanted to know.

"Not as good as she was at first," Kester reported.

60

"The Red Force tried to fight from the road and were creamed by Walker's warbots operating from the fields and woods alongside. Now Red's moved off-road into the jungle where the Warriors were fighting. It's become almost one-to-one with the warbots over there, and the Warriors are having trouble handling more than one warbot per person in the jungle. But so are the Marauders from Red Force."

A burst of digital data suddenly came in. The command vehicle's computer deciphered it and Kester whooped, "Captain Walker reports Kelly's split the Killers! He's sent his Alpha Platoon under Lieutenant Frazier into action to reinforce the Marauders!"

That meant only one Red Force platoon under Lt. Phil Messenger remained to guard Kelly's warbot command post.

"Tell her to keep it up. We're getting ready to turn the flank." Curt checked the map on the command vehicle's display. He poked his head out of the turret and saw what he wanted. "Okay, Companions, pull it off the road here in this clearing. Dismount all troops and warbots. Proceed on foot. Get under cover in the jungle alongside the road; we don't want to take the chance of being spotted by any of Red's recon warbots . . . if they've got any up in this area."

Curt had subrogated the principle of mass to the principles of movement and surprise. He knew how Kelly would be thinking. Marty Kelly would have his airborne recon warbots searching for the Companions moving to flank him within a kilometer of Mahogany Road and not along the winding North Shore Road. Standard warbot assault doctrine recommended frontal assault following a near-fight flanking attack, especially at battalion level. Warbot brainies liked to keep a tight, well controlled battle, emphasizing the principles of mass and economy of force.

In spite of his company-sized force, Curt had adopted regimental doctrine instead because of his much greater mobility. The past few months had helped the Companions shuck their preconceived notions derived from standard warbot tactical doctrine; they'd learned to think in more versatile terms.

"What are you doing?" Major Wardwell who was wearing the white brassard of an umpire asked as Curt began to dismount the command vehicle.

"If you're supposed to stay with our command post, you'd better dismount and come along," Curt replied, giving as much of an answer as he thought the occasion justified. "Isn't it true that the command post stays with the commander?"

"But you can't abandon your protective vehicles and proceed on foot!" the major objected.

"Oh? Is there an operational rule that prevents me from doing it?"

The umpire looked up at the hills to the south. "Do you expect to go through that?"

"Sure as hell do. On foot, too. If our warbots can't hack it, my soldiers can and I'll deploy my warbots through easier terrain along with my four squad leaders and an NCO. At any rate, we're only about two kilometers from the Red command post on the other side of that ridge." Curt grabbed his FABARMA rifle to which had been fitted a suitably modified laser target kill indicator. He scrambled out of the command van and tried to remain civil to the umpire who also outranked him. "Major, shag out of there and come with me, or you'll ride this vehicle back to where it came from! Command vehicle, this is Indian Scout," Curt addressed his vehicle using his code name.

"Ready, Indian Scout," the artificial intelligence computer of the vehicle replied verbally.

62

"Return with all vehicles down this road to the original command post location. Then report to Captain Samantha Walker and follow her orders. Execute!" Curt wanted the vehicles with their Saucy Cans to be available to Walker as part of her fire base. Furthermore, to Kelly, it would look like the Blue Force was putting its reserves into the fire fight.

The major scrambled off the vehicle just as it began a one-eighty spin about.

As Curt rushed for the cover of the forest alongside the road, he couldn't see the Companions or their warbots anywhere. They'd dismounted and faded into the vegetation.

But Kester was waiting for him under cover with their four General Purpose Warbots.

"What have you done to your warbots?" the umpire wanted to know as he scrambled into the underbrush behind Curt.

"Painted them while we were en route," Curt explained. "Little chameleon low-observable camouflage." He opened his kit, took out a container of camouflage cream, and began to spread it on his face and arms. "Major, I request that you spread a little cammy grease on your face and arms. If you're spotted, Red will know we're around. And I'm damned if I'm going to get this unit trashed because my umpire was seen and we weren't!"

"But—"

"The rules say that the location of a unit cannot be revealed by the actions of an umpire. Want me to call foul on you this early in the game, Major?" He tossed the can of cammy cream to Wardwell and called out, "Companions, forward!"

"Yo! Into the breach!" Jerry Allen's voice came back.

63

"Jerry, shut your face and go to tacomm!" Alexis Morgan's voice replied.

"Right on!" Curt called. "Don't break audio silence now unless you make contact or get into trouble. Move it! We've got maybe an hour to go two kilometers and take Red's command post! Haul ass!"

CHAPTER SEVEN

It wasn't as easy as it looked. The hills on the north side of St. Croix weren't very steep, but they were well covered with secondary growth. At one time, the area had been a coconut plantation before the palms got too old and the American diet shifted away from the use of coconut oil as a saturated fat food additive.

About half a kilometer into the bush, Curt got the tacomm signal from Lt. Jerry Allen indicating he wanted face-to-face communication.

Curt sent a signal for the company to hold present position and then the code for "officers assemble."

"I can't get my heavies along these primitive hillside trails," Allen explained when the three of them gathered. He was in command of Alpha Platoon, the heavy fire base of the company with the new Mark X44 Heavy Fire Robots, the "Hairy Foxes." These were essentially super-light but compact tanks about the size of a sub-compact car; they had heavy firepower, heavy armor, and chassis designed to be solid firing platforms; they were the fire base of the company in action. They needed greater power to move their greater bulks, and there was little that could be done to disguise the high-pitched whine and muffled rumble of their gas turbine engines. "The trails are too narrow in most places for these Hairy Foxes. And the slopes are a little steep for them to maneuver. I'm going to have to take them down the bottom of the valleys and gulleys where the trails may be more like this little road and where the gradients aren't so great. They'd run quieter, too, if they didn't have to use some much power . . ."

"Sounds like Ordnance is going to have a headache when they read our field reports from Grey Flag," Curt remarked, then turned to the woman who was commanding Bravo Platoon. "Alexis, how about your lighter warbots?"

"We're getting through without too much trouble," she reported simply. The warbots under Alexis Morgan's command were the rapid-moving multi-wheeled Mark X60 Mobile Assault Robots—the "Mary Anns"—with lighter armament, light armor, and enough power to enable them to achieve speed and maneuverability. Their mounted sensors had better discrimination and used faster AI computers with greater memories. They had smaller engines than the Mark X44s but ran quieter. Kester once referred to them as "wheeled horses," which was perhaps an inept description because they had no heads, only horizontal barrel-like, main-frame bodies from which sensors could be extended on telescoping stalks if it became necessary to look over or around an obstacle. Their three wheels allowed them to negotiate terrain like a sporting off-road cycle, and they were therefore more maneuverable. "Gerard, Dillon, Cole, and I are staying behind the Mary Anns and letting them blaze the trail. How much further before we top this ridge?"

Curt reached into his backpack and drew out a folded sheet of paper. It could be considered an ancient artifact; an actual printed map of St. Croix Curt had bought several weeks before from the Virgin Islands Tourism Board's office in Charlotte Amalie. "Okay, my map says this valley comes up on a pass through

66

the ridge about three hundred meters ahead, then snakes down the south side to where the Red command post is situated here, just about fifty meters north of Mahogany Road," Curt explained, tracing his finger on the map.

Major Wardwell watched in fascination; it had been years since he'd seen a printed map because, like other officers, he'd become accustomed to using maps and charts generated by computer graphics and displayed on the tactical screens and three-dimensional holographic tanks of a command post. What Curt had was strictly military Stone Age. But the major could see no reason why he could legitimately deny the use of a printed map. The war game rules said absolutely nothing about prohibiting their use because no one on staff who'd planned this operation had even considered that such a thing might be used at all!

"Alexis, when you get Bravo Platoon to the pass, split your force and send Nick Gerard down the west side of the valley with half your troopers and Mary Anns while you take the east side with the rest," Curt went on. "You'll move slightly ahead of Jerry and Alpha Platoon down along the bottom of the valley. Henry and I will stay slightly behind Alpha. There's a little clearing about twenty meters wide just north of the Red command post. Alexis, you'll get there first, but don't reveal yourself. Let Jerry deploy Alpha Platoon along the north side of the clearing as a base of fire. Find out where Kelly has his remaining warbots stationed as cee-pee defenses. Then Jerry will pin them down with fire which is your signal to move in on the cee-pee from the east and take it from behind. Got it? Questions?"

"When can we break audio silence?" Jerry wanted to know. Sometimes in close battle, verbal commands to both warbots and troops were far more efficient than taking time to send a tacomm signal; while his Hairy Foxes wouldn't lose any time receiving and complying with it, his NCOs and squad leaders would have to look at their tacomm units to get the message.

"As soon as Bravo Platoon locates Kelly's warbots," Curt explained. "After that, the more noise we make, the more confusion we'll generate. Lieutenant Allen, can you make your outfit sound like a whole damned regiment?"

Jerry Allen grinned. "Sure as hell can!" He opened a waterproof pocket on the side of his pack and drew forth a plastic bag. It was full of Chinese fireworks he'd bought in town—firecrackers, smoke bombs, whistles, and assorted aerial-type shells. "Just don't be surprised when this stuff starts going off. I was supposed to be commanding a fire base platoon, so I got enough for Sampson, Elliott, and Koslowski, too."

"Good man!" Curt clapped him on the shoulder. "Okay, every one's counting on everyone else. If there's a screw-up before we make actual contact and the fire fight starts, send the 'hold' code and I'll try to improvise."

"No problem," Lt. Alexis Morgan promised. "I'm going to take Kelly's command post without firing a shot."

"Let's not get over-confident," Curt warned.

"You know the sonofabitch better than I do," Alexis Morgan pointed out, "but I'll bet he's got his mind on the offensive and couldn't care diddly squat about his defenses. He thinks he's got us pinned down somewhere along Mahogany Road along with Sam Walker's outfit. He'll see our vehicles coming up to add to Samantha's fire base, so he'll probably decide that some of the Warriors were left to guard the Blue cee-pee and what he's facing on the road is a mixed unit of Companions and Warriors."

"That's the way I work it out," Henry Kester put in quietly. "We haven't seen any of his airborne recon warbots, so he's not looking for us here. If he's seen anything from the air, he's spotted our abandoned vehicles aeither heading westbound on the North Coast Road—and that's probably got him confused as it was supposed to—or he's seen them moving into position as fire base. Damned good thing our assault doesn't depend on those vehicles getting into position first . . ."

"Our empty vehicles were only a distraction to him. Confuse him. Draw his attention away from our dismounted assault," Curt reminded them. "Okay, resume positions and move. When we start down the valley on the other side of the ridge, we're on assault. Behave accordingly." He turned to the umpire. "Major, are you going to make it all the way to the ridge okay?"

Major Wardwell looked totally bushed; it was obvious the man had spent far too much time keying a computer terminal and not enough in heavy exercise such as this. He wiped his face with the sleeve of his sweat-stained field uniform and put his cap back on his shaved head. He was dirty, sweaty, and obviously uncomfortable. It was also obvious that he hadn't believed that a war game umpire's job could be this difficult. He didn't catch his breath, but merely nodded. This whole maneuver was beyond his control now; but he decided he'd have to do something to display his authority as an umpire other than start declaring hits and casualties once the assault began. So he pointed to the fireworks that Jerry Allen was stuffing back into the pack. "You can't use those," the Major directed. "Nonregulation. This war game has to be fought with regulation equipment so we can properly assess problems and effectiveness when we review the outcome."

Curt simply told him, "Lieutenant, you heard the umpire."

"Yessir," was Jerry's short reply. But he was thinking that it wouldn't make a whole hell of a lot of difference if the Major ruled Alpha Platoon destroyed as long as Alexis Morgan's Bravo Platoon took the Red CP in the process. Allen would gladly "sacrifice" his platoon in this war game in order that the Blue Force won. And his company commander had not given him a direct order not to use the fireworks. To Allen, this meant that Curt Carson had listened to what he and Kester had told everyone in the Companions: In the thick of a fire fight, even in a war game, it was damned-near impossible for an umpire to call "foul" in the middle of the action because of the classical "haze of battle."

Taking the Red CP by the rules was the way to legitimately win the game. However, winning Grey Flag wasn't the primary motivation of Carson's Companions. What they really wanted was to prove the viability of the tactics they'd worked out among themselves, regardless of what the staff stooges had dreamed up as the ideal tactical doctrine in the sterility of their war gaming computers, regardless of the bias in the rules and attitudes of the umpires. All of the Companions knew they were essentially renegades at this point. But the long-range task that had been given them when they'd started this TDY with the War College was to develop the new tactics the Army decided it should have in the wake of Zahedan.

When Curt reached the saddle at the top of the ridge, he stopped and exclaimed to Henry Kester, "Sonofabitch! I can see the bastard's cee-pee!"

Kester looked, then trained his field glasses on it. "I'll be gone to hell! It don't look like he even tried to hide it!"

Lt. Jerry Allen joined them. He saw it, too. "That isn't even standard RI doctrine!"

A commander hid his CP because it literally contained the brains of the whole warbot operation. Inside the CP vehicle, which was about the size of a sixteen-wheeler, semi-trailer truck, a dozen people reclined in their operational linkage couches whose sensory pickups and electrodes connected their nervous systems to the warbots out there in the field doing the fighting for them as extensions to their own brains.

"The sonofabitch is so confident that he didn't bother to hide himself," Curt breathed in disbelief.

"Well, Captain, without the threat of air interdiction strikes or recon as well as long-range artillery fire," Jerry Allen observed, "Kelly obviously built his battle plan around a strict ground operation involving overwhelming Blue along Mahogany Road followed by continued contact as Blue retreated to its own cee-pee whose location was known to him from aerial warbot recon."

"Too damned risky, Lieutenant," Kester pointed out.

"Not if he took a calculated risk that he could pin down the Blue Forces so no one would get close enough to his CP to bring it under fire," Jerry Allen countered.

"Well, I recall," the old master sergeant mused, "that when you're winning or think you're winning, or in peacetime when you don't think anyone's gonna shoot at you, you don't camouflage. Everything's painted one standard color becuz it's cheaper to buy a million gallons of one kind of paint. Or you don't paint things at all, the way they did with airplanes when the Allies finally got World War Two air superiority. You could be right, Lieutenant . . ."

"Sure, Red doesn't think it makes any difference whether or not Blue knows where he is."

"Well, you're missing the point," Curt broke in. "Kelly did the obvious. He followed standard warbot doctrine. Except he ignored the principle of security because he hasn't recognized the mobility and versatility of our Seirra Charlie force. So that's the way we clobber him . . . just the way we planned it. But I didn't think it would be this damned easy!"

"Still may not be," Kester cautioned. "He's probably got some warbots around the cee-pee."

"Damned few, according to reports. I'll bet we outnumber them," Allen ventured. "And that wins war games."

"We'll see," Curt decided. "No change in plans. Forward!"

Halfway down the valley, Nick Gerard reported on the tacomm, "Enemy air recon."

Curt saw the message and fired back, "All units, take cover."

"An RCV," Kester remarked as he located the Remotely Controlled Vehicle in the air to the south of them.

"Is it in range?" Curt asked.

"Captain, I'd advise we don't shoot it," Kester said. "If we fire on it, Red will know we're here. If we do nothing, he won't know the extent of our forces even if the RCV happens to get a visual or radio fix on us. Suggest it's time to go to verbal commands and shitcan the tacomm; the RCV has no audio sensors."

Curt tapped his tacomm unit. "Have to go verbal anyway. My tacomm just died on me."

"Maintenance check it out before Grey Flag?"

Curt nodded. "Supposed to. I'll nail somebody's hide to the wall when we get back. It's deader than a depowered warbot . . ."

"Problem with all this high-tech crap," Kester muttered, "is that it craps out when you need it. Always."

"So you think people are more reliable?"

Kester shook his head. "In battle, nothing's as reliable as it oughta be. Including people."

Curt raised his voice, "Go verbal! Don't shoot the RCV. Forward under cover."

CHAPTER EIGHT

"Roger from Bravo!" Alexis Morgan's voice came back.

"Yo from Alpha!" was Jerry Allen's call.

Curt turned to the umpire. "Going to make it, Major?" Major Wardwell was still sweating, but he'd caught his breath."Now that we're going downhill, yes."

The three of them—Curt, Kester, and the Major—caught up with Jerry Allen's Alpha Platoon before they reached the edge of the clearing. Allen motioned them down, then crawled back to Curt. "My Hairy Foxes are deployed and ready."

"How about Bravo?"

"Don't know. My tacomm quit."

"Yours too? Henry, send Lieutenant Morgan the signal that Alpha is deployed and ready," Curt told his master sergeant.

Kester keyed the code into his wrist tacomm. He waited, and then part of the reply flashed on its tiny screen before his unit also went dead. "Lieutenant Morgan's ready, Captain. I got that much of her reply before this damned thing crapped out, too. Don't know where the Red warbot guards are."

"Okay, Allen, you may fire at will," Curt told the young lieutenant.

"Roger, Captain," Allen replied and began to crawl back through the underbrush to his command at the edge of the clearing.

At this point, Major Wardwell got to his feet. Curt laid a hand on him, "Major, get down! You're revealing our position."

"I've got to do my job," the major replied curtly. "I need to contact the umpire at the cee-pee. Together, we'll assign casualties as this fire fight progresses."

Curt didn't get the chance to tell the man that he'd just compromised the surprise element in the assault. A bright red spot suddenly appeared on the Major's chest. He'd been accidentally targeted by the laser designator of one of the Red warbots guarding the CP. "Dammit, I'm an umpire!" the major called out and strode boldly into the clearing.

Jerry Allen seized the initiative. "We've opened fire!" he called out loudly.

In war games, some blanks are used to create the illusion of the sound and fury of a fire fight. But most firing is done with bore-sighted weapon laser designators and laser target responders affixed to equipment or worn by human troops. The corruscating red spots of laser weapon fire dappled the side of the Red CP and nailed one of the guarding warbots. Major Wardwell dashed forward to declare that warbot out of action, but never got there.

Real explosions began to go off all around him. In defiance of the umpire's ruling, Jerry Allen was using the fireworks he'd brought along.

Major Wardwell found himself dancing between exploding M-80s and cowering under the blasts of aimed aerial shells. Screaming whistles were going off all around the clearing, and whizzing chasers wobbled through the air.

The human soldiers in Alpha Platoon also opened up with their FABARMA rifles firing blanks. Curt never got anyone in Alpha Platoon to confess to doing it—he never really conducted a thorough inquisition—but someone aimed for and hit Major Wardwell in a very large part of his anatomy with the wax wad from a blank cartridge. The major screamed in agony and clutched with his hands where he'd been hit. Curt glanced and saw that the major probably wasn't going to be able to sit comfortably in a chair in front of a computer terminal for a couple of days.

As quickly as the firing began, Curt saw Alexis Morgan rush out of the east side of the clearing. She wasn't following even temporary doctrine; she was accompanied by Nick Gerard and her two squad leaders while they, in turn, were followed by the Mary Anns firing rapid-fire with their laser designators. The official Sierra Charlie doctrine required that the Mary Anns precede humans in the assault.

But the dash of twenty meters to the CP van was made so quickly that none of the human soldiers in Bravo Platoon were hit. And it was Lt. Alexis Morgan who pulled the CP van's door open and led the others inside.

"Cease fire!" Curt yelled over the din. He had to yell it several times. The Mary Anns stopped when they heard his first command given, but Sgt. Edie Sampson and squad leaders Jim Elliott and Charlie Koslowski kept on firing their weapons and tossing fireworks, even though all of the visible Red warbots had already been "put out of action" in the brief fire fight.

It was all over in thirty seconds. Lt. Alexis Morgan appeared in the doorway of the Red CP van and yelled, "They surrendered! We won!" Then, in sheer exhilaration, she pointed her FABARMA assault rifle to the darkening skies and fired off the remaining rounds of the 50-round clip.

"We won," Curt repeated.

"Don't be so damned sure, Captain," Henry Kester put in. "The Major looks miffed . . ." Kester was understating it.

"Alpha Platoon, all dead!" Major Wardwell was yelling. Lt. Jerry Allen stood up. "Major, no laser spot hit me . . ."

"I told you to put away those fireworks, that they'd be illegal if you used them," Wardwell replied angrily.

"What the hell, Major, we were just adding a little realism to the assault," Allen replied with a grin. "No one was hurt, and none of the fireworks came anywhere near the cee-pee or the guard warbots—"

"I rule them nonregulation weapons and I also rule your platoon out of action."

"Major, isn't that a little bit academic?" Curt Carson wanted to know, getting to his feet and walking over to the umpire. "We surprised Red Forces and took their cee-pee. You and the other umpire inside the Red cee-pee can now call a cease-fire. Grey Flag is over . . ."

"But it's been underway for only five hours," Major Wardwell noted. "It was scheduled to last for three days . . ."

"Well, Major," Curt told him easily with a smile on his face, "sometimes you can't schedule battles and have them go as planned . . ."

Another major with a white brassard stepped out of the Red CP. "Fred," he called out to Wardwell, "what the hell happened? How did the Blue forces get here?"

Curt answered for him as he walked toward the CP,

"Over the mountain, over the great divide. . . . Do you agree that Blue got 'em?"

"Well, yes, but nothing like this should have happened until day after tomorrow . . ."

"Welcome to the world of Sierra Charlie forces, Major," Curt told him. "Please call off the war because we just won and Red can't continue to fight. Lieutenant Morgan, did any of your troops disconnect any of the Red warbot brainies?"

"No, sir!" she snapped back. "Didn't want to put a whole battalion through the trauma of being KIA." She was referring to the traumatic mental and emotional shock of a Robot Infantry soldier being suddenly cut off from all the warbots that were providing sensory information. The effect was like suddenly being knocked cold but remaining conscious. Sometimes it took more than six weeks of therapy for a warbot brainy to get over the effects of being KIA. It had happened to Curt twice in actual combat; he didn't like it and was glad Alexis had followed orders by not pulling the plugs on Kelly and his battalion.

However, there were times when Curt wished he could pull the plug on Captain Marty Kelly.

"Is everyone in the cee-pee okay?" Curt continued.

"Yes, sir. I've called in the biotechs so these people can be properly de-linked."

"Captain," Major Wardwell broke in, "you're being paged by Colonel Hettrick. Is your tacomm unit working?"

"No, it crapped out before the assault," Curt admitted. "That's why we went to verbal commands. Who's got a tacomm I can use?"

"Why not use the battalion unit in the cee-pee, Captain?" Henry Kester suggested.

Curt did, entering the van to smell the distinct odor

78

of human beings sweating anxiety, fear, and lots of adrenalin, smells no environmental control system could totally remove from the atmosphere of the CP. It was the typical RI stink of battle. It struck him even more than it usually did because he realized that he and his Sierra Charlies probably also stank, but in a different and older way. They'd been out there in the jungle and coconut palms with the high humidity and the moldy ground. He stepped up to the blank terminal plate of the wall-mounted tacomm, laid his palm on it, and watched while it came to life. He touched the display label for verbal. "Colonel Hettrick, Captain Carson here."

He could have called up video as well, but was glad he didn't. His reflection in the terminal plate showed that he was dirty and sweaty. On the other hand, he didn't need video to know that Hettrick was both a bit angry as well as somewhat pleased. "Captain," her voice came through with a valiant attempt to maintain its coolness, "you've screwed up Grey Flag."

"Colonel, with all due respects, I think we won it."

"I admit you took the Red cee-pee."

"That was my assigned objective, Colonel."

"Yes, it was. But, goddamit, Carson, why did you have to do it so quickly?"

"I don't understand, Colonel." Curt did indeed understand. Grey Flag had been designed to test the new Sierra Charlie tactics under controlled conditions that would allow the regimental staff and the War College people to properly evaluate the new tactics, the use of weaponry, and the effectivenss of their preconceived beliefs about how people should fight alongside robots with the least risk.

He could hear Hettrick's sigh. "Critique will be at oh-nine-hundred hours tomorrow morning at the temporary regimental headquarters snake pit in Charlotte Analie,'' she told him. ''In the meantime, I'm cancelling what's left of Grey Flag . . . which isn't much. You're right; you won by capturing the Red cee-pee. The fight on Mahogany Road collapsed the instant your Blue forces took it. Now, cool your heels. It's going to take more than a couple of hours to reschedule the recovery airlift to get everyone back here . . .'' Hettrick cut the circuit from her end.

''You dirty sonofabitch. You sneaky bastard,'' was the growl in Curt's right ear.

Curt turned to see Capt. Marty Kelly standing there. The man still wore his linkage cap and he was unsteady on his feet; he held on to whatever he could grasp inside the van. Curt knew the man had come out of linkage on his own—a very risky thing to do from both the physical and mental standpoints because it was literally like going from one reality to another. ''Kelly, you should have waited for your biotechs to come up.''

''To hell with them!'' Kelly snarled. The man was not only suffering from unlinking with his warbots without help from the biotechnicians, but he was livid with anger. ''I heard you here in the cee-pee talking to the Colonel, and I wasn't about to let you get out of here without letting you know exactly what I think of your goddamned sneaky, grandstanding actions! You bastard, you didn't play by the fucking rules!''

Curt faced him. ''No, Kelly, you didn't understand the rules. You forgot the principles of maneuver, surprise, and security. And you didn't pay a damned bit of attention to all the discussions about Sierra Charlie tactics, or you would have clobbered my company when we debouched from our vehicles on the North Coast Road. Or caught us coming through the pass to the north of you. I was just damned lucky you had a fixation on the Mahogany Road battle, but it's typical of you to love the big fight. So I held your nose with fire power while I kicked you in the ass with maneuver . . .''

''I'm not going to hold your nose; I'm gonna bust it!'' Kelley snapped and started to swing.

Curt was in much better condition at that moment than Kelly. He simply ducked. Kelly's fist slammed into the wall of the van. He hit it hard enough to break several fingers, if not his wrist. As Kelly gave a yelp of pain, Curt decided that enough was enough and it was time to really end this little war game. Curt thrust his FABARMA rifle so its butt caught Kelly in the solar plexus. When Kelly's breath exploded from his mouth and he instinctively bent over, Curt merely swung the rifle upward and caught Kelly on the point of the chin. The agressive captain's head snapped up, then his entire body crumpled to the floor.

''Nice work, Curt.'' Lt. Alexis Morgan was standing in the external door of the van.

''Glad you saw it,'' Curt told her. ''I'll probably need you as a witness when this sonofabitch files charges.''

''You've got two witnesses, Captain,'' came a groggy voice from one of the linkage couches. It was 2d Lt. Phil Messenger, Kelly's new platoon officer. It had been hinted around in Rumor Control that Messenger wasn't getting along too well with his company commander; people said they were too much alike. ''I would have done the same thing, Captain, but I wouldn't have done it after self-delinking. But I don't think Captain Kelly will file charges. You're going to be up to your asshole in alligators when the Colonel gets through with you at the critique tomorrow . . . Where are those damned biotechs?''

Curt turned and left the CP van, motioning Alexis

to follow. The sky was darkening even more. The typical afternoon thundershower would soon commence. He raised his arm above his head and rotated his hand in a horizontal circle. "Carson's Companions! Assemble! Fall in! On the double!" he called out in the parade ground command voice taught to him by Henry Kester. It was a sound driven by his diaphragm in the manner of a company commander of old. Major Wardwell, who was conferring with the other umpire nearby, was startled by the sound.

With comparative rapidity—comparative only because some of the people and warbots were in the deep jungle at the edge of the clearing—Carson's Companions formed up. Close order drill was an anachronism from the days when troops had to be maneuvered from column to line and back again under battlefield conditions, and the Robot Infantry didn't bother with such things. But the basic assembly formation, modified to reflect the smaller number of people in the RI company and further modified by the Companions to account for the changes involved in the Sierra Charlie unit, remained basically the same.

Sgt. Henry Kester took the forming position on the right. The two companies formed on him, each rank forming on a platoon sergeant or a squad leader as a guide. Once all had fallen in, Kester walked front and center. Curt and his two lieutenants then walked to their positions. Kester saluted Curt to turn the company over to its commanding officer, then resumed his position as the right guide.

"Comp'ny . . . At ease!" Curt snapped. "Congratulations! We did it! Nice work all around. Don't worry about the critique; we did what we were supposed to do, and that was to test the new Sierra Charlie tactics—whether the regimental staff and the War College knew it or not. It may be a couple of hours before pickup and recovery; we sort of brought Grey Flag to an end a couple of days before anyone expected us to, so Transportation got caught with their bots down. Looks like the usual afternoon rain shower is about to begin, so take cover but stick around for pick-up. Don't go wandering off. Fall out!''

It began to rain within a minute. Curt found himself a dry spot under the CP van. Alexis Morgan slipped in beside him.

"Found a place to keep warm and dry, I see?" Curt observed.

"God, I want to get the hell out of these grubbies and scrape this cammy grease off and take a hot shower and shampoo," Alexis replied. "Reminds me of Zahedan . . .''

"Except for the humidity."

"And the smell."

"Same feeling of getting shot at."

She nodded. "Except nobody shot at anyone else here."

"We did everything but."

"Yeah. We did. Right. Same feeling."

"I think that's why the Army kept women out of combat . . .''

"Why? The feeling?"

"Yeah. The results of getting shot at. Or thinking you were getting shot at."

She looked at him carefully. "Well, we can certainly do something about that."

"Not while Rule Ten is still in effect," Curt reminded her unnecessarily of the Army Regulation 601-10 prohibiting physical contact of any sort between personnel of different sexes while on duty, one of the most stringently enforced of all Army regs.

"And not until I take a shower and get cleaned up," she promised. "But, yeah, it certainly is a pretty strong feeling . . . and made even stronger by these war games.''

"Remember what it was like in real combat?" Curt asked, thinking of the aftermath of Zahedan.

"Words fail me," Alexis admitted. "But, then, words weren't necessary . . ."

CHAPTER NINE

"The Blue Force won the Grey Flag exercise," Col. Belinda Hettrick, commanding officer of the 3rd Robot Infantry Regiment, the Washington Greys, announced. "But they shouldn't have."

The briefing room or "snake pit" at the Army War College Annex in Charlotte Amalie was exactly like the one in the regimental headquarters at Arizona's Diamond Point casern of the 17th Iron Fist Division (RI). The main three-dimensional, full-color holographic display was located in the center of the circular stadium-like room in which ascending rows of linkage couches were arrayed. All couches were occupied for this critique of the Grey Flag war games. Combat unit officers, NCOs, squad leaders, staff officers, and umpires lay back so that electronic sensors in the couches could detect the electrical impulses of each person's nervous system along their spine. All also wore linkage caps that placed other electrodes in critical locations to detect nerve impulses of their brains.

These electrical signals from each human nervous system were digitized and deciphered by computers which, in effect, could "read the minds" of each person. Actually, all the people in the briefing room had been thoroughly trained so that the nervous system impulses read by the electronics were commands to the system—inputs to the computers, so to speak. In turn, the computers could send signals back to each person's nervous system through the electrodes, thus creating verbal and even visual sensations in the person's brain. It took a lot of computer power to do this, and even then it would not have been possible without intelligence amplifiers, computers that acted as high-speed, large-memory extensions and supplements to human brains.

The human beings were in control, however. The programming of the computers and intelligence amplifiers contained highly sophisticated instructions which could not be overridden by any means and which made the computers the electronic slaves and mind-extension tools of the humans linked to them.

The computers and intelligence amps of the snake pit were modifications of the regulation, government-issue systems installed in robot infantry command posts which allowed the human soliders of the robot infantry to know what their remote robots sensed and to control what their robots did. For more than two decades, the United States Army had embraced robot warfare which allowed the risks of battle to be borne by robots while human beings were safe and protected in their remote command posts.

And robot warfare had worked well . . . in theory and some limited engagements against other robot adversaries and undermanned irregular forces.

Until the RI had tangled with the Jehorkhim Muslims in the backwater eastern Iranian town of Zahedan. The Jehorkhims were poorly armed but well trained religious fanatics who'd been brainwashed by a crude modification of RI technology. They'd used the Mongol tactics of mass, firepower, and maneuver against the Washington Greys . . . and would have whipped them had it not been for the hastily improvised tactics developed by Capt. Curt Carson and his Companions who'd had to revert to personal combat.

"We were looking for two things in the conduct of Grey Flag," Colonel Hettrick went on, her image being presented larger than life in the holographic display at the center of the snake pit. "We planned the field exercise carefully to get the answers we needed. We wanted to learn whether or not we'd developed the proper roles and missions of the new Sierra Charlie human-plus-robot troops. We also wanted to find out whether or not we'd been successful in developing the proper ratio or mixture between robot and Sierra Charlie forces. We'd worked all these out in the computers here at the War College Annex. In Grey Flag, we needed to confirm that our experimental tactical doctrines were correct. We failed to achieve those goals."

There was silence in the snake pit. No one present wanted to comment at this point. Curt and Carson's Companions simply listened and observed. Curt knew what was coming.

"In violation of doctrine, Captain Carson who was in charge of Blue Forces split his battalion, allowed his fire base to absorb most of the battle damage and casualties, and engaged in a flanking sweep outside the limits of battalion action. This resulted in Blue's capture of Red's command post within six hours. Grey Flag was scheduled to run for three days . . . I'd like to know why the umpires allowed Carson's Companions to deviate from tactical doctrine. Major Wardwell, you were with the Companions. Why didn't you blow the whistle on Captain Carson's maneuver?"

Much to Curt's surprise, the rather flabby staff officer replied, "Colonel, it was my responsibility as an umpire to ensure that the Grey Flag rules of engagement were not violated and to declare hits and casualties. That responsibility was carried out in spite of the fact that my tacomm unit failed and I lost all communications with War Game Central. I saw no violation of the rules of engagement. However, in the final assault on the Red cee-pee, nonregulation equipment in the form of commercial fireworks was used, and I declared the Alpha Platoon of Carson's Companions to have violated very basic Army war gaming rules and therefore destroyed. But it would have made no difference; the Bravo Platoon of the Companions would have captured the Red cee-pee in any event because of the overwhelming surprise of their maneuver.''

"Major, were you not aware that the actions of the Blue commander were violating the doctrine to be tested?" Hettrick wanted to know.

"As S-3 Operations on regimental staff," Wardwell replied quickly, "it became apparent to me and was confirmed by the results of Grey Flag that the experimental doctrine to be tested was conservative, narrow, and restrictive. It ignored the time-tested principles of maneuver and surprise, two elements which have been subordinated in robot infantry tactics in favor of the principles of mass and economy of force. The Blue Force violated unity of command, but that was justified in light of their overall strategy which stressed the principles of offensive, simplicity, maneuver, surprise, and security. These principles were neglected by Red Force. I believe we learned that regular warbot forces should be used to provide a base of fire to pin down enemy forces while the Sierra Charlie forces emphasize maneuver, shock, and surprise to break through, outflank, and strike deep into the enemy rear echelon of command. I believe we tested the experimental doctrine and found it to be wrong.''

Hettrick was apparently not satisfied with the explanation and rationale of her staff officer and umpire.

"Captain Carson," she asked Curt directly, "why did you as Blue commander deviate from tatical doctrine?"

"The principle of objective," Curt replied briefly.

"Explain."

Curt said slowly, "The principle of objective states that every military operation must be directed toward a decisive, obtainable objective."

"I don't need a lesson in the basic principles of warfare, Captain," Hettrick snapped.

Curt thought she probably needed to be reminded of them, but he said, "I knew what the strengths and weaknesses of my command were because I've been out in the field learning about them. I knew the strengths and weaknesses of my adversary because I'm also a warbot brainy and have fought with warbot tactics and equipment. I was told that the objective of Grey Flag was to capture the enemy's command post while protecting my own. I had to do that without permitting prohibitive losses on the part of Captain Samantha Walker's company who was likely to be outnumbered and outgunned. So I had to move fast before Red Force discovered what I was doing and so I could bring the operation to a conclusion before Sam took those losses. She knew what I was doing and I knew what she was doing; we had tacomm until less than an hour before my assault on the Red cee-pee, so unity of command wasn't compromised. We had a simple battle plan: She was to hold 'em by the nose with fire while I moved around and kicked 'em in the ass . . . And that's just what we did. Kelly was caught with his bots down . . . Or somewhere else."

"Goddamit, Carson, I wasn't expecting you to come over that ridge . . . and on foot, to boot! Or I would have moved to counter you!" Marty Kelly put in.

"Yeah, that's just exactly what I figured, Marty,"

89

Curt replied with a smile in his tone. "I knew you'd fight down there on Mahogany Road with good old warbot assault tactics, plus your own unique doctrine of kill 'em all, let God sort 'em out. Next time, check your flanks!"

"Hell, we damned near wiped out your units on Mahogany Road!" Kelly countered.

"I took only thirty percent warbot casualties and no warbot brainy casualties," Capt. Samantha Walker put in. "My company command post wasn't touched because you couldn't find it. If you had, I was prepared to prevent you from attacking it."

"Carson, you lost a whole platoon," Kelly pointed out.

"Not because of battle conditions," was Curt's rejoinder. "My Alpha Platoon would not have been wiped out in a real fight; Lieutenant Allen just got carried away and decided the fireworks added some needed realism. Our casualties were acceptable, not Soviet. We did the job fast and surgically . . . and guess who won?"

"But you didn't follow the rules!" Kelly objected.

"Damned poor excuse for losing your ass, Marty," Curt chided him.

It might have been out of place for a lowly captain to discourse on tactical doctrine in front of regimental staff people (and, eventually division staff and even Army staffers because this debrief was being recorded for later analysis higher up the chain of command). But Curt felt he was on solid ground in giving a little lecture about what had happened. He and his company had been the ones who'd crawled on their bellies through the rain and mud to relearn ancient infantry and cavalry tactics long-forgotten in this era of robot warfare.

He did something no officer had done for decades

during a debrief. He rose from his linkage couch, feeling the jolt of disconnecting himself from the computers and intelligence amplifiers but not the total shock of delink because he had deliberately refrained from going into deep linkage. He walked down to the center of the snake pit and stood there in the midst of Colonel Hettrick's bigger-than-life image. Hettrick dissolved her image to allow Curt to hold center stage. Curt felt that the Washington Greys had to get used to doing without their computers and warbots if the Sierra Charlie concept was going to work right. His actions in appearing personally in the snake pit were designed to drive this home. He looked small but hardly invulnerable in comparison to an enlarged holographic image. He'd deliberately worn his camouflaged field uniform in contrast to the other officers who'd switched back to garrison dress after Grey Flag.

"The big problem is that the RI hasn't fought a real war in almost fifteen years," Curt told everyone. "And the warbots used at Tibesti by both sides were primitive compared to what we've got today. Yeah, we've been in a fracas or two since then, but nothing we couldn't handle with warbots. Then Zahedan came along and blew away our cherished and ill-conceived ideas of actual robot warfare against determined human adversaries. Down here in the Vee-Eye during the last few months, we've had the chance to work out the ungarbled word on how to put humans back on the battlefield in a limited role. Grey Flag was the best possible damned test of Sierra Charlie versus warbot tactics. Colonel, may I suggest that we look on Grey Flag not as a failure but as the first field test of the Sierra Charlie concept in which we all learned a hell of a lot?"

When the heated exchange between her two war game force leaders erupted, Hettrick had let it run its course. She knew very well that Curt's unorthodoxy was historically justified even if it wasn't officially sanctioned. More than two decades ago as a green second lieutenant fresh out of West Point, she'd been involved when the Army was cautiously backing into robot warfare. She'd sat quietly in a similar critique and debrief when her first regimental commander, Col. Silvo Thayer of the Golden Dragons, had defended his use of the robot warfare tactics he'd worked out and proved in the famous Steel Claw war games. She knew now she was seeing a pattern of history repeating itself.

"And what do you think we learned, Captain?" Hettrick asked.

"That the Sierra Charlies should be considered as a special mobile assault force," Curt replied briefly. "We move fast and do things that ordinary warbots can't do. Grey Flag showed beyond a shadow of a doubt that we're capable now of making a warbot with enough artificial intelligence so it can act almost on its own like the old infantry rifleman . . . provided there's a human soldier nearby to issue orders to it correcting paradoxes and re-directing its activities. There is no longer any need to get 'inside' our warbots and run them as direct extensions to ourselves. We can and should get out there with them; we should use them as the perfectly obedient warriors that field commanders have longed for over the centuries."

"That will be difficult to sell," Hettrick advised him. "The high brass is scared of losing human soldiers."

"They asked us to develop the human-robot mixed force concept, didn't they? Did they also expect that no Sierra Charlie would get hurt in combat?"

"Sometimes what the Army asks for is not what the Army really expects to get," Hettrick admitted. "All right, I want to go over the action in detail. I want all company and platoon commanders to note what happened right on down to the individual warbot and soldier level. Forget that Captain Carson tossed the experimental doctrine down the latrine and improvised. Let's see how good the improvisation was, where it could have led to trouble, and how it could be improved. Then I'll forward a staff report up the line and we'll get on with our job of working out the new Army doctrine . . .''

But Col. Belinda Hettrick and the Washington Greys regiment wouldn't get the chance to do this in the usual leisurely peacetime way.

CHAPTER TEN

Back in the Army world of direct mind-to-mind communication made possible by the high technology of existing robot warfare, a major operational planning conference was taking place on high-speed, high-bit-rate data channels between the Pentagon, the Diamond Point casern of the 17th Iron Fist Division (RI), the Taum Sauk casern of the 22nd Double Deuces Division (RI), the Emerald Bay Fleet Headquarters of the United States Navy, the Air Force Strike Command redoubt at Tincup, and a temporary communications node set up at Willemstad on Curacao by the United States for the use of the Caribbean allies in Operation Steel Band.

Digitized data streamed out at ultraviolet wavelengths along fiber optic cables where such networks existed on land between installations. Where the information had to leap seas and oceans, it bounced off satellites as a thin, sparkling beam of laser communications. It was a totally secure communications network. No one could tap it. No one could reach down into the noise level and pick up the weak electromagnetic fields radiating from ordinary telephone systems. No one could search for and detect antenna side lobes from radio communication. The information rode on scintillating threads of light waves down glass strands or on the pencil-thin and nearly invisible indigo-purple beams of tightly focused ultraviolet lasers.

"We have excellent intelligence concerning the disposition of the various units of the Trinidad Defense Forces," came the electronically processed thought of retired Air Force four-star Albert Murray who was in charge of the covert National Intelligence Agency's military/naval division. "Incidentally, our spooks are calling them 'Tee-dads,' which is a hell of a lot easier to say. The Tee-dads don't have a sophisticated, modern military establishment; it exists primarily for internal security. The Tee-dad government has taken few steps to stealth any of its military, naval, or air units."

"If you don't mind, Al, I'll accept your 'excellent' intellgence with the proverbial grain of salt," was the comment from Maj. Gen. Jacob O. Carlisle, commander of the 17th Iron Fist Division (RI) at Diamond Point. "It left us totally unprepared for Zahedan."

"Not a fair comparison," Murray replied quickly. "That was out in the middle of the land God forgot; this is right in our own back yard. I guarantee you won't be unprepared this time, Jake. Here's the good and ungarbled word:

"Drake's supreme command is located in the Red House; his cee-cubed is maintained by land-line telephone, some fiber optic lines from Port of Spain to San Fernando and Sangre Grande, a co-ax cable TV net between those same two places which can be commandeered if necessary, and the usual spread of electromagnetic radio frequencies which can easily be jammed or spoofed because none of the Tee-dad comm gear uses frequency hopping."

As the NIA official's electronic "voice" was heard in the minds of those linked to the net, a computer-generated visual image of a three-dimensional Trinidad topographical map was projected into their minds as well so that it appeared to be projected on a nearby wall in front of everyone. Symbols appeared and disappeared on the mental image map as the "conversation" proceeded.

"The Tee-dad army is the most powerful element. It contains almost fourteen thousand men organized into five regiments. Only the Presidential Guard battalion of the First TDF Regiment is roboticized, and it's based in Port of Spain. The rest of that regiment consists of a special forces battalion at Arima, an engineer battalion at Pointe a Pierre, and an artillery battalion at Fort George. The other regiments are basically human infantry based at Sangre Grande, Chaguanas, San Fernando, and Rio Claro. Their basic arm is the five-point-five-six millimeter SAR 80 assault rifle and the CETME light machine gun, same caliber; the support troops carry the Astra Model A-80 automatic pistol and the Mekanika Uru submachinegun, both using nine millimeter parabellum ammo. They're fairly mobile with EE-9 Cascavel recon LAVs and EE-118 Urutu armored personnel carriers. The artillery ballation uses the Brazilian X2A106 self-propelled one-oh-six-millimeter gun, and they have some one-oh-six-millimeter recoiless launchers along with eighty-one-millimeter mortars at the company level."

"What about their warbots?" asked Maj. Gen. Daniel Miles of the 22nd Double Deuces RI division.

"Four companies equipped with the Argentine AutoMech Mark Four, a rip-off of the Swiss Model Two assault warbot," Murray replied offhandedly. "They carry the fifteen-millimeter MEC-10 machine gun. Light armor. Can maintain ten klicks speed on level ground. Very primitive robotics, no linkage, simple remote control via infra red links from single warbot operator in an accompanying APC which carries six such operators. So, Danny, tell your people to concentrate on the APCs, not the warbots; take out the APCs and you've got undirected warbots running around doing nothing.''

"That's only about seventy-two Tee-dad warbots we'll have to contend with," Miles muttered. "No problem. Doesn't bother me as much as the potential resistance from manned vehicles and artillery.''

"We'll discuss the operational plan when Al finishes his intel report," said the Army's Chief of Staff, Gen. Otis R. Brooke, from the Pentagon. "Go ahead, Al.''

"Tac air," General Murray went on. "They've got some. Twenty-four Embraer Piranha B strike aerodynes operating out of that new air base they built near Napirima. That's also where their twelve Delfin maritime patrol and ASW aircraft are based. Eighteen AeroBoero Diamante interceptors are based at the Piarco International Airport over at the new military compound they've built on the field. Also twenty-six IAR-Coanda Model Twenty air transport aerodynes mostly used for VIPs and to move generals around. Can be used for transportation of their special forces battalion. Finally: naval force situation . . .''

"Wondered when you'd get around to us," came a remark from Vice Admiral Arthur Hamlen. "Whatever they've got, we'll take care of it. We'll deliver firepower to sink ships or soldiers to hit beaches . . .''

"Afraid it's mostly going to be the latter for the Navy, Art," Murray came back. "Tee-dad has minimal naval forces at the moment, but indications are they're buying fast from the ABC Allianza. The eight patrol gunboats can make eighty knots on powered hydrofoils, but their two ASW corvettes are ABC handme-downs. Same goes for the two coastal mine layers.''

"Where are they?" Hamlen wanted to know.

"Evenly split between Flotilla One at Port of Spain and Flotilla Two at San Fernando.''

"Ought to be able to sink them in the Gulf of Paria if we do it right."

"Any questions on the force situation?" Murray concluded his presentation.

"Everything seems to be concentrated on the western part of the island," General Miles observed. "Is the eastern side that rugged?"

"No. The Gulf of Paria amounts to the largest sheltered harbor on the east coast of South America," was the comment that came via satellite from Curacao where General Hans Sturtevandt, the man who would lead the Caribbean forces, was plugged into the operational briefing. "Trinidad was settled on the western side because the Gulf was such a large sheltered harbor back in the fourteenth century. Still is. Only two entrances to the Gulf: The Dragon's Mouths on the north and the Serpent's Mouth on the south. An easy sea defense situation."

"Weather?" came the one-word question from Gen. Phyllis Cochran of the Air Force.

"Touchy," was former General Murray's intelligence input. "We're in the rainy season's lull."

"It's called 'Petit Careme,' " Sturtevandt explained. "Sort of an Indian Summer lull in six months of the rainy season. It could break at any time."

"So the sooner we can get Operation Steel Band moving, the better," Cochran put in. "It's tough enough to conduct tac air operations in good weather, even with robotic smart weaponry and electro-optic image enhancers. I take it you'll want Air Force to sanitize those airports . . ."

"You're getting ahead of us, Phyl," the Army Chief of Staff told her curtly but diplomatically. "No further questions on the situation as it stands?"

"I may wish to get some additional information as

98

the operational plan is revealed," said the 17th Iron Fist Division's commander, Jacob Carlisle.

"There will be opportunity for that, Jake," General Brooke told him.

A new map image was presented. Brooke went on, "Here's the operational plan. Code name: Operation Steel Band. It consists of five missions tagged Operation Lightning, Operation Rainbarrel, Operation Tenor Pan, Operation Bass Boom, and Operation Baritone Pan."

"Sounds too complex," Admiral Hamlen remarked.

"Not with modern telecommunications," Brooke told him. "Phyl, Operation Lightning is yours. You'll launch from Grenada, Barbados, and Venezuela. At oh-three-hundred hours, your birds will hit Piarco Airport in a low-level air strike to knock out the *Diamante* interceptors on the ground. Over the top of this goes the second wave to hit Napirima Airport and take out the Piranha tac strike aircraft and naval air contingent. The Piarco strike is to be surgical: Take out *only* the military side of the field, not the commercial terminals or aircraft because they belong to Pan Am and Carib and other air carriers. But at Napirima you have no such restrictions. Napirima is a military base; neutralize it."

"We'll be in the dark," General Cochran pointed out. "Our infra red and millimeter radar are both pretty good, but I can give you more positive results at dawn."

"Oh-three-hundred hours, Phyl, has been approved by JCS," Brooke added.

" 'The difficult we do immediately; the impossible takes a little longer,' " General Cochran quoted.

"Stick around. The impossible comes later," Brooke told her. "Art, at oh-three-thirty, a naval surface feint will emerge in the Dragon's Mouths. Purpose: Draw

Flotillas One and Two out of Port of Spain and San Fernando."

"Do you want Navy just to draw them out?" Henlen asked.

"No. Sink 'em. Your primary task is to secure the Gulf of Paria."

"Will do. If we don't catch the whole TDF navy, we'll hunt 'em down and send them to the bottom."

"No, your naval feint has an additional purpose," Brooke warned. "By this time, the Tee-dads will be alerted by Phyl's air strikes. We want them to think that an assault is either coming through the Dragon's Mouths or on the north coast of the island. Actually, we're going to jerk them around a little bit. At oh-five-thirty, Operation Tenor Pan will commence. That's yours, Jake. You'll take the Iron Fist ashore on the south side of the island near Port Fortin, Siparia, Sadhoowa, and Basse Terre. Objective: Capture Napirima Air Base and San Fernando. Purpose: Draw the Tee-dad land forces south to meet the threat."

"Going to be tough to put four regiments ashore spread out like that, General," Carlisle told him. "I'd like to use the Washington Greys and their new Sierra Charlies to hit the west flank at Point Fortin. They may be able to move fast enough . . ."

"That's an experimental outfit, Jake, but if you think you can pull it off, let me have your detailed operational plan as soon as you can get it worked out," Brooke told him. The Chief of Staff had been assigned the job of commander-in-chief of the Trinidad invasion by JCS, and he felt that the operation was already bordering on the limits of simplicity. Thus, he was openly reluctant to introduce any new and untried elements into an already complex equation. But inwardly he realized that Operational Steel Band could be the critical test of the next and somewhat disturbing doctrine that

100

would put human soldiers again at risk on the battle-field.

Brooke had been in the Army for nearly thirty years, and he remembered the dirty and dangerous early times of personal combat before warbots assumed those risks; he liked robot warfare. However, he had no choice but to accept Carlisle's suggestion; the battle plan depended on overwhelming superiority in numbers, and he couldn't expect Gen. Jacob Carlisle to carry out his mission with a division operating with only three regiments; the Washington Greys had to be involved. Brooke had studied what had happened at Zahedan. To him, the near disaster had been brought about *not* because the warbot soldiers had come up against a zealous, fanatical foe using ancient tactics, but because Brig. Gen. Victor Knox had used inadequate forces; to Brooke, it had been a shoestring operation with a preciatable outcome, if Knox had only been able to admit to it.

"Phyl, as soon as you can get your aircraft refurbished—or if you can draw in additional tac strike capability," Brooke went on, "I want you to sanitize that artillery battalion stationed at Fort George on the hill overlooking Port of Spain. I don't want our ground forces to have to contend with those one-oh-sixes and tac rockets. I want them out of the equation early. Can you take out Fort George with a tac strike by oh-eight-hundred?"

"Is timing critical?" the Air Force commander wanted to know.

"Yes. We don't know how long it will take them to begin deploying south, and we must knock them out before they get into Port of Spain and into the industrial complex between Port of Spain and San Fernando. You need to take out that battalion in its casern at Fort George.''

"Wait one—" General Cochran withdrew momentarily to consult her staff and computers, then came back with, "If JCS will authorize me another A-Twenty wing, can do."

"You have one handy?''

"Closest one will have to deploy today from Sakhalin."

"Authorized. Do it.''

"Roger.''

"The main strike comes at eighteen-hundred hours when the 22nd Double Deuces go ashore on the western shore between Waterloo and Ponte a Pierre,'' Brooke went on as military symbols appeared and danced across the map. "Art, that's why the Navy must secure the Gulf of Paria by twelve hundred hours. Dan, your division will hit the unprotected right flanks of whatever Tee-dad troops are moving down the Solomon Hochoy Highway between Port of Spain and San Fernando. You'll also be able to take the Second Tee-dad Regiment at San Fernando from the rear while Jake's troops are keeping them busy to the south. All this is intended to draw as many Tee-dad units as possible south of Port of Spain and engage them. Because on Day Two at oh-five-hundred, Sturtevandt will hit the north coast with Operation Baritone Pan at La Vache, Maracas, Chupara, and Blanchissuse. He'll have fourteen hundred non-robot troops from the Caribbean allies and will cross the Northern Range to catch the entire Tee-dad force in the rear. Sturtevandt should be able to take Port of Spain by sundown . . . and that should lop the head off the Tee-dad forces.''

There was a slight pause, then General Brooke asked, "Any questions?''

Maj. Gen. Jacob Carlisle ventured a critique. "Otis,

This is a damned complex operational plan. Any way we can simplify it?"

"We ran a couple hundred battle scenarios in the Old Hickory computer under the Pentagon," Brooke told him. "This was the simplest one to fall out of that exercise, given the rules of engagement."

"All right, Otis, what are those rules of engagement you're going to saddle us with?" asked General Dan Miles of the 22nd Double Deuces.

"Except for taking out the military side of Piarco Airport and sanitizing Fort George and Napirima Air Base," Brooke told them slowly, "you are *not*—repeat, *not*—to engage in any activity that would destroy or damage non-military equipment or installations, civilian homes or businesses, the industrial complexes along the west coast, and especially the petroleum producing and refining facilities."

Silence fell over the teleconference. It was Carlisle who finally spoke up, "Otis, we may have to bust that R-O-E if the Tee-dad forces learn about it and take up positions that would cause us to violate it."

"Surround them and starve them out," Brooke told him. "That's what warbots are good for."

"Otis, I can see a situation where the Tee-dad units initiate a scorched earth policy. Can we keep them from doing that by assault, regardless of possible damage?" General Miles wanted to know.

"Dan, this primary rule of engagement is intended to spare the island's industrial base. It will be violated only upon specific case-by-case considerations and approvals by me," General Brooke advised him, then added by way of explanation, "We can't turn Trinidad into an economic basket case just because our Caribbean allies called on us to help them oust a military dictatorship which is already doing just that. That R-O-E was laid on me from higher up. We're professionals who are used to operating under such restrictions. Let's carry out our orders. Put your staff people to work on your individual assignments for Operation Steel Band, and we'll link up for another go at this in eight hours.''

CHAPTER ELEVEN

"General Carlisle, did I understand you correctly, sir? We're *invading* Trinidad?" Col. Belinda Hettrick was having trouble believing what the commanding general of the 17th Iron First Division (Robot Infantry) had just told his officers.

The snake pit serving as a temporary briefing and communications node for the Washington Greys in Charlotte Amalie was silent. Other officers linked to the Division's supercomputer and intelligence amplifier—familiarly called "Georgie"—located back at the Diamond Point casern were sitting in their linkage couches in disbelieving silence.

The three-dimensional, full-color image of General Carlisle filled the holographic display tank in the center of the briefing room. Although he was thousands of kilometers away at Diamond Point, it was as though he were right in the room. "Colonel, this is not an 'invasion.' A consortium of Caribbean nations requested the assistance of the United States in an effort to head off a potentially disruptive economic and military situation in Trinidad. I'm sure you must have been following the news reports of Austin Drake's activities in ousting the left-wing government of Clarke Chamberlin and his recent execution of the former president." General Carlisle carefully avoided the use of Austin Drake's retired rank of Lieutenant Colonel and the assumed rank of "General" that the mercenary now used in Trinidad. Carlisle had known Drake as an ambitious, hard, and vicious field officer who'd essentially been given the option of resigning or being cashiered for insubordination. Carlisle had never liked the man. "If not, please retrieve it from the current events data base. In any event, we're soldiers and we don't question the reasons why our national leaders give us specific orders."

He held up his hand as if anticipating a response and silencing it. "Yes, I know the Nuremberg Precedents and all the international treaties concerning aggression to which the United States is party. However, adequate precedent also exists to support Operation Steel Band—Czechoslovakia and Grenada being only two incidents in the last hundred years. Be that as it may, the 17th Iron Fist Division has its orders. We will carry them out."

Capt. Curt Carson wished he'd shaved before this briefing. Because Carson's Companions had not recently been controlling warbots in direct linkage but were using voice and other commands to control artificially intellgent robots as the first Sierra Charlie company, none of the company had shaved their heads for the past two months. There was no need to wear linkage caps in order to ensure that electrodes made good contact with the skin of the scalp, and the Companions had discovered that having hair on their heads was more comfortable in the semi-tropics of the Virgin Islands. As a result, the electric fields of the sensors and electrodes of the snake pit couch's linkage cap and spinal network didn't make intimate contact with Curt's nervous system through his skin, and General Carlisle's image occasionally wavered, dimmed, and lost color as a result of the poor contact. Curt had gotten used to this but, because of the importance of getting all the information in this briefing, he was now kicking himself for not running the razor over his scalp before coming.

General Carlisle launched into a presentation of the Iron Fist's specific activities, operations, objectives, and responsibilities in Operation Steel Band, noting first that the operations of the other units were classified and of no interest to the 17th Division (RI) at the moment.

"Operation Tenor Pan belongs to the Iron Fist," the General explained. "The Cottonbalers will depart Basrah at sixteen hundred Zulu time tomorrow; that's the earliest Air Transport Command can provide airlift for a regiment. The Wolfhounds will be relieved by the Panthers from the Big L Division today and depart ASAP; Air Force can get to you quicker. The Can Do will leave Diamond Point in seven hours. All three regiments will rendezvous with the Washington Greys in Charlotte Amalie. This is being disguised as a normal regimental rotational exercise.

"On Saturday, ten September, the Iron Fist will depart the Vee-Eye and proceed to Trinidad. The Navy will provide sealift in submersible landing craft to put the various regiments ashore on Trinidad here." As General Carlisle spoke, a three-dimensional map was projected behind his image in the holo tank; computer-generated symbols and indicators appeared on the map and moved as he spoke.

"We're scheduled to hit the beaches at oh-six-hundred hours on Sunday, eleven September. Here's the breakout for the various regimental commands.

"The Washington Greys will go through the Serpent's Mouth strait at the southwest corner of the island to land at Point Fortin; objective of the Greys will be the Oropuche River mouth at noon."

"The Can Do will land at Quinam Bay; initial objective by twelve hundred hours is the town of Siparia moving to eventual link-up with the Washington Greys at the Oropuche River line for the assault on Naprima Air Base.

"The Wolfhounds will land between Roja Point and Negra Point, moving north along the Morne Diablo Quarry Road to take Sadhoowa and Pinal by noon.

"The Cottonbalers will come ashore at Moruga to move north along Moruga Road to Basse Terre and Preau.

"Here are the probable movements of the Tee-dad units during the first six hours of the operation.

"Our objective: Engage the Tee-dad units and render them unable to offer further resistance. Capture is preferable to killing. The ultimate objective of Operation Steel Band is to secure the island militarily so that a temporary government headed by former President Morris Priest may be set up and free elections of a new parliament can take place within six weeks. Therefore, this is an extremely surgical operation with definitely limited objectives.

"We expect Operation Steel Band to be completed within four days. You will deploy in the field with rations and ammunition for one fighting day; subsequent supplies will be brought up to the forward line of troops each evening at eighteen hundred hours.

"We could achieve our overall objectives in less time if it were not for the following rules of engagement which are in force for Operation Steel Band:

"One: You will *not* open fire on any target without opositive identification that it is a military target; you will not fire upon people unless you have a positive visual identification of the individual as a member of the Trinidad Defense Forces. This does not restrict you from opening fire upon any individual or group which

108

fires on you; the act of opening fire is presumed to be a hostile act of an opposing military force.

"Two: You will *not* attack and/or destroy non-military equipment or installations such as the oil fields at La Brea, Siparia, and Penal. You may bring Tee-dad units under fire if they occupy non-military facilities, but the utmost effort must be made to limit the damage and destruction that ensues.

"Three: You will *not* attack or molest civilians or their homes and working places."

The map vanished into mid-air and General Carlisle turned to look around. "Any questions?"

Every regimental and company commander had an individual set of orders and battle plans available from Georgie and could study them at length and refer back to them when needed. These orders had been developed by the division staff and were effective down to the company level and out to T + 24 hours. A more general set of orders were issued out to T + 48 hours. The possible movements out to the full, anticipated 120-hour duration of Operation Steel Band were also available, but limited data on the movements of other regiments and divisions were given so that this information could not become available to the Tee-dad intellgence officers in the event that an officer or NCO were captured and interrogated.

Curt gave only a cursory inspection to the operational package for the Companions. He knew from recent experience that everything would change drastically during the first six hours of the fight. From then on, he'd have to play it by ear, taking advantage of opportunities in the field and following any orders that might come down from Hettrick.

Col. Emmett J. Calhoun of the Cottonbalers spoke up electronically through the communications channel from the Persian Gulf. "Will we have any local guides available to us?"

"The intelligence people tell me that individual units may be contacted by agents-in-place who will serve as guides," Carlisle replied. "Naturally, the intelligence people are reluctant to divulge names and locations in advance. Assume you'll be contacted, but plan your activities as if you will not be."

"How about other locals?" Calhoun repeated that part of his question.

"If a local volunteers asistance, take it," Carlisle told him. "The people of Trinidad are friendly. I understand they don't especially like the rigid restrictions of the present military junta. Use your best judgement but, yes, you can accept the help of volunteer locals, including water and rations."

A question passed quickly through Curt's mind, something he'd read from military history, something that seemed to be missing here. But it came and went so fast that Curt told himself it couldn't have been that important. He was already thinking of all the new problems that presented themselves as a result of having to run the first Sierra Charlie company in combat far sooner then anticipated. He knew the bugs hadn't been worked out of his company operations much less the combined arms operations involved with coordinating activities with the rest of the regiment. Curt was thinking about support details—ammunition for more humans and warbots than a company usually required in ordinary warbot combat, more rations, the need for clean and dry uniforms, especially socks, and contingency plans for transportation in case one of their armored personnel vehicles broke down or was hit. What if the Air Force didn't sanitize the Tee-dad tacair; could they defend against strike aircraft, and, if so, with what and to what extent?

And Curt didn't like the meteorology analysis; the rainy season could bring the Petit Careme to a sudden and soggy end at any time. Not only was it tougher to move and fight on the muddy roads of the Caribbean islands when they were wet, but human efficiency went to hell and warbots often did screwy things when the hot weather turned very humid.

The United States Army hadn't fought with robots around the Caribbean rim. Their last fracas in the region had been with human soldiers and remotely piloted recon aircraft during the Panama Relief Expedition more than twenty years before. The Washington Greys had been involved; the streamer of the Panamanian Presidential Unit Citation bearing the words "Gatun Locks" flew from the regimental colors. But none of the people currently assigned to the Washington Greys had been with the regiment than . . . except the venerable M. Sgt. Henry Kester.

Curt was also sweating a bit mentally; he had one hell of an act to put together in a very short time. If he'd had his druthers, he would have spent another six months in Grey Flag exercises working all the wrinkles out of the Sierra Charlie concept. But he didn't have six months; he didn't even have six days. Going into combat with incomplete and largely untested operational doctrines and procedures was a super way to buy lots of trouble. Since nothing was yet set in concrete or in the book, he was going to have to improvise . . . and that could be dangerous because sometimes there was no way out of a tight corner in combat.

He was planning to use the inputs from the people in his company. They were the only ones in the Army who'd lived and breathed Sierra Charlie operations for the past several months. Lt. Jerry Allen's recent training in personal combat at West Point would be invaluable. So would the field experience of M. Sgt. Henry

Kester who knew enough not to re-invent the square wheel in the typical Army fashion. And he would rely on Lt. Alexis Morgan and Platoon Sgt. Edwina Sampson to pick up little details that men would miss. Platoon Sgt. Nick Gerard was street savvy because of his background, and that would come in handy in the little towns and villages they'd pass through, especially if any Tee-dad troops laid ordnance on them there. The fresh outlooks of his four "country boy" squad leaders would be helpful, provided they didn't freeze up too badly in actual combat before they got dry behind the ears.

Learning how to perform while getting shot at—actually getting shot at rather than having your warbots take the incoming—was something new to the Army. Curt knew from experience that it was like sex; until you'd done it for the first time, you didn't know anything about it, and there was no way to anticipate everything that could happen.

CHAPTER TWELVE

No one in the snake pit had further questions. To the other company commanders in the regiment, this was just another mission. They'd be sequestered safely in their armored command vehicles with their warbots out in the fracas. The worse thing they might anticipate was being suddenly delinked from the sensors of the warbot they were controlling at that instant, thus becoming vulnerable to the severe psychological shock of suddenly and unexpectedly losing all sensory input from the outside world known as being "killed in action" or "KIA." It could be traumatic if a biotech wasn't there to help . . . and sometimes there was too much action and too many warbot brainies being KIA for the biotechs to handle them all.

Curt was far more concerned with the possibility of actually being physically wounded or even killed. Soft body armor would help, but it was heavy and would be very hot. The biotech battalion attached to divisional headquarters wasn't prepared to handle actual battlefield casualties beyond minor wounds; medevac and MASH capabilities were practically nonexistent. On the other hand, it was quick and easy to get a damaged warbot repaired. . . .

M. Sgt. Henry Kester had advised the Companions concerning the basics of personal combat, "Just don't get yourself into a situation where you get your ass shot off. In short, don't get heroic; shoot the other bastard instead of letting him shoot you. . . . Better yet, wound him because that usually takes his buddy out of the fight to help him. The high brass will tell you to take prisoners; do that only if the enemy surrenders because taking care of prisoners ties up a lot of our people and uses up our rations. Make the enemy run. That blows away the confidence of rear echelon troops and reserves, and will make them run, too.''

The divisional briefing was dismissed but Colonel Hettrick held the regiment in the snake pit for her briefing. She advised the Washington Greys, ''We've been given the dirty end of the stick again as usual. Don't bitch about it; the Washington Greys are good enough to handle the impossible missions other regiments can't hack. So we've got to figure the Navy will get us through the Serpent's Mouth and onto the beach at Port Fortin. That may put us right under the guns of the Napirima tacair strike squadron if the Air Force doesn't rip their shorts properly. The Tee-dads haven't installed any defenses along Irois Bay or Guapo Bay; manpower-wise, they're too thin to defend every beach on Trinidad. So we'll put two companies in on both beaches and thus surround Point Fortin and its petroleum facilities. If a constabulary unit of Tee-dads happens to be garrisoned in Point Fortin, our landings will surround them and cut them off; that's why I'm assigning landing points as follows:

''Kelly's Killers will go ashore on the right flank and proceed inland on Erin Road to the Southern Main Road.

''Manny's Marauders will hit land on the southern edge of Point Fortin. Their initial objective is to secure Point Fortin itself and, if no Tee-dad troops are garrisoned there, to join the Killers on the Southern Main

Road moving to the northeast and the noon objective. If there is a Tee-dad garrison in Point Fortin, the Marauders and the Killers will move into the town to overhwelm them. Standard urban warbot tactics.

"The Warriors and the Companions will go ashore together in Guapo Bay and move inland on Vance River Road to the Southern Main Road. The Companions will be on point because of their greater mobility. The Warriors will move with them if possible and will have weaponry configured to serve as a fire base for the Sierra Charlies in the combined anti-air and regimental artillery roles.

"The regiment will be strung out along the Southern Main Road and thus is a prime tacair target, which is why the Warriors will cover the anti-air mission. The Companions have fourteen kilometers to cover in order to reach the Oropuche River line, and they'll get there first. The Killers, on the other hand, will have to cover twenty-three kilometers.

"Staff doesn't anticipate you'll meet any Tee-dad military resistance before reaching the Oropuche River objective. Therefore, stick to the road for speed. We're counting on speed, shock, and surprise. Move fast and, if you have to, hit hard. Move into the countryside only to maneuver.

"If the Companions reach the river line and find no opposition, they are to continue to move toward San Fernando; the Can Do regiment will link with us at St. Mary's where the Southern Main Road and the Siparia Road join. We'll then move eastward to take the Napirima Air Base in a flanking movement while the Wolfhounds move up Erin Road from Penal to hit the southern side of the Air Base. The Can Do will continue up the Southern Main Road to San Fernando where divisional staff expects considerable resistance from the Fourth TDF Regiment.

"We should have the Napirima Air Base in hand by sunset. That's a Number One objective because Air Force intends to use Napirima for logistical support. In other words, if we look forward to eating the following day, we'd better have Napirima Air Base in our hands the first night.

"Any questions?"

"Colonel, how's the footing?" Curt asked.

"The Southern Main Road is a two-lane paved highway. Off road, tropical vegetation will probably make tough going for the heavier warbots."

"Do we know anything about those swampy areas indicated alongside the Oropuche River?"

"They're probably soft. I don't know whether or not we can maneuver warbots there or not," Hettrick admitted. "Captain Carson, your company will be the first on site there; I want a recon report from you as soon as you reach that area and see what it's like."

"Roger. Will do. If we can't get our warbots in there, our people may be able to investigate it. Human footprint pressure is certainly a lot less than a warbot's," Curt told her. He was beginning to realize more and more that his Sierra Charlies were not only very maneuverable but could serve as excellent scouts, moving through territory where warbots would be unable to function. Curt Carson knew he was reinventing the cavalry. . . .

"Colonel?" It was Capt. Samantha Walker of Walker's Warriors. "Did it occur to the divisional staff that robot infantry may be at a serious disadvantage fighting non-warbot troops in this sort of environment? We're optimized for combat in Europe, northeast Asia, and the sparsely covered rolling terrain of northern Africa and the Middle East. Not jungle, not even the sort of semi-tropical environment here in the Vee-Eye."

"I don't know," Colonel Hettrick replied candidly.

116

"I do know—and you should, too—that the main combat arms of the United States Army are the Robot Infantry and Heavy Armor. The grunt infantry went the way of the horse cavalry. So the Robot Infantry has got to get in there and fight anyway, regardless of whether or not we're optimized for it. It may turn out we end up being a support element for our Caribbean allies' contingents which are personal combat units of the old type because those little countries can't afford warbots—Well, we'll just have to be flexible about that and deal with it if it happens . . ."

"Doesn't look like any battle streamers or awards coming out of this fracas," was the growl that came from Capt. Marty Kelly.

"Battle citations are awarded, Captain, on the basis of valorous action in the field," Hettrick reminded him. "They are not awarded for the best computer forecasts of the battle. We'll never manage to fully computerize warfare; it's too illogical. In fact, it's alogical."

The operational briefing broke down again to the company level, and the Companions took off their linkage caps and got up from the couches. They didn't need or want direct linkage at the moment, although they intended to use Georgie's computer capabilities through key pads and verbal address terminals if necessary. They gathered in the orderly room that Curt had requested and gotten for the Companion's use.

"Well, we damned well epitomize the regiment's motto: *Primus in acien,* first in action," Lt. Alexis Morgan remarked as they sat down around the table.

"Al, that's the place to be when you've got the heavy stuff behind you," Lt. Jerry Allen reminded her.

"Russian tactics," Henry Kester muttered.

"You want us to ride our warbots like the old Soviet tank riders, Sergeant?" Allen asked.

"Hell no. Too vulnerable. Soviets developed the

117

tank-riding infantry because they had lots of soldiers,'' Henry Kester reminded him. "We don't."

"Those Soviet tactics were once used in modified form in the Army's Battle Twenty-One doctrine," Curt said, recalling the old personal combat doctrine that he'd been studying for several months now. "That was a half-assed wedding with the old Air Land Battle doctrine. Infantry rode inside armored personnel carriers and dismounted in the assault. Then the APCs followed them to provide heavy fire cover."

"That's what we've been trying," Jerry Allen recalled.

"Yeah, now we're going to see if it really works," Curt reminded him. "Ride if we can. Walk if we have to. And don't button-up unless the chemical sensors pick up soldier stink."

"Uh, Captain, how do the chem sensors know how a Tee-dad grunt smells? We've never fought 'em," Sgt. Nick Gerard pointed out.

"The first time a chemical sensor picks up a scent and the computer verifies with a visual that it's coming from a Tee-dad grunt, the signature will be tagged and communicated to every other unit in the division," Curt said. "At least, that's what I've been told. The chem sensors are new. We'll use them only if they're needed." The new sensors were capable of detecting the odors of human bodies—the aldehydes and other complex organic chemicals that are continually exhuded by human beings everywhere and had been widely known for years as "locker room" odor, "sweat sock stink" and other such sobriquets. Because of differences in the food they ate, most people had a distinctive chemical or odor signature. It was the recent development of high resolution chemical sensors far better than the human nose which had made such "chemical radar" possible and useful to combat troops.

Like the Sierra Charlies, the chem sensors were experimental and hadn't been used in combat before.

"Okay," Curt went on, "bullshit session is hereby delayed until after we get our ducks set up for Operation Tenor Pan. Nonregulation as they are, the battle kits we've been using will be standard for this. Light cotton cammies over soft body armor . . ."

Sgt. Edwina Sampson groaned. "Aw, Captain, body armor in tropical heat? How much water are we going to carry to replace what we lose by sweating under that stuff?"

"You'd rather take incoming than have it scrunch your body armor?" Curt asked rhetorically.

But Edie Sampson felt that her commander's rhetorical question deserved a decidedly nonrhetorical answer. "What the hell do we ride around inside ACVs for? Not just so's we don't have to walk, Captain. If we dismount, then let's don body armor."

"We may not have time to put it on," Curt told her.

"Captain," Henry Kester advised him, "our direct command warbots can take the initial heat of an engagement before we have to dismount the ACVs. I really think you ought to let the troops be as comfortable as possible until they have to get uncomfortable in order to survive. This damned humid heat will wear the troops out faster that you can imagine. It did in Panama."

When Henry Kester spoke, Curt Carson listened. "Okay, we'll try it that way. Body armor in standby. First out of the ACVs are the warbots. They'll establish a fire base and give us time to don armor."

"Thank you, Captain," Edie Sampson told him.

Curt looked around and went on, "Luckily, we can pretty much call the shots regarding equipment because we're the new Sierra Charlie troops. But what we've got and how we use it must have a reasonable chance of achieving the objectives we've been assigned. It's too late to change from what we've been training with. So we'll have the usual twelve Mark X60 Mobile Assault Robots under Lieutenant Allen in Alpha Platoon, twelve Hairy Fox Mark X44 Heavy Fire Robots Mary Ann under Lieutenant Morgan in Bravo Platoon, and four Mark 33 jeep General Purpose Robots assigned to company command under Sergeant Kester. I'm going to keep the Light Artillery Maneuvering Vehicles with their Saucy Cans attached to the company command; later I can move 'em where we need their firepower. Each platoon will have the usual Armored Command Vehicle for the troops and an Armored Robot Transport Vehicle for the command warbots. When we hit the beach and on the road, I want Alpha to take point with Bravo bringing up the rear and providing fire cover if necessary. Usual tactics upon making contact: Alpha goes flankers while Bravo moves into the slot to pin the enemy down with fire.

"Personal equipment: Your FABARMA rifles and as many M100 Triple-A-T pocket rockets as you can carry; we may need personal artillery in that tropical underbrush. And the usual dozen or so M20 grenades for close-in work. Make sure your vehicles and robots have enough ammo; as a Sierra Charlie force, we'll shoot up far more ammo than a regular warbot company, especially since the Colonel put us up in front of the Regiment along the Southern Main Road.

"Officers, check to make sure everyone has one set of spare clothing along with rain gear; find room to stuff it into the ACVs somewhere. The staff says four days for Operation Steel Band, but it could last longer."

"Or be over quickly," Henry Kester muttered. "We haven't been told how well the Tee-dads will fight.

120

Captain, they may be just an internal military garrison force designed for show and not for blow . . .''

"I hope you're right, Sergeant, but we can't count on it. Regardless of the weasel-wording topside, we're actually invading their country. Defending troops fight like hell under those condition.'' Curt looked around and finally asked his Companions, "Anything else we should cover here?''

No one said anything.

"All right, we're on alert. No external communications. Don't leave the post. No talk to anyone, period. When we hit that beach, we want it to be a real surprise to the Tee-dads. God knows we don't want them waiting for us.''

"What about Rule Ten?'' It was Edie Sampson who wanted to know.

"In effect from now until this fracas is over. Sorry about that, troops. But we're going into combat, and we've either got to be sharp or we'll be dead. This is the first time we've gone into action knowing full well that each of us would be in a position to be shot at. And the rounds are real, not paint pellets. Keep that in mind. Okay, we've got about twenty-four hours before the bloody Navy stacks us aboard one of their SLVs. And we can't come back for anything we've forgotten. So don't forget anything.''

CHAPTER THIRTEEN

The U.S.S. *Tallapoosa Country* SLV-20 was a smelly, damp, and crowded naval vessel. Two days were about all Captain Curt Carson wanted to spend in her. She didn't have many amenities, but she wasn't supposed to since she was used only and rarely for transporting Marine warbot troops underwater to their landing point, and then to crawl up on the beach to disgorge them. She was intended to transport a whole company, but the twelve members of Carson's Companions, being the first Sierra Charlie outfit with more people and warbots, crowded her old and already limited facilities.

The *Tallapoosa* County had been one of the first of the class of submersible landing ship/vehicle. She hadn't been refitted with a modern environmental control system that not only recycled the air but cleansed it of smells as well. The old system was now overstressed by the additional four squad leaders.

The run from St. Thomas down the Lesser Antilles to her present position in the Columbus Channel southeast of Trinidad had been made submerged except for brief surfacings when the top deck hatches were opened and fresh air brought in by the blowers. But the last eighteen hours had been spent submerged while the Navy crew talked laconically and often endlessly with the other SLVs carrying the other three companies of the Washington Greys.

The rest of the initial invasion armada for Operation Tenor Pan had converged on the Channel. The flotilla bringing in the 17th Iron Fist Division (RI) was now on station.

Curt used his perrogative as the commanding officer of the Army troops aboard to visit the control room where he could keep track of the action. The young two-striper in command, Lt. Jack Barber, seemed to be competent if not somewhat surly, even though he did follow the naval custom of referring to Curt as "Major Carson," bucking him automatcially up a rank because there can be only one captain aboard a naval vessel. But Barber seemed merely to be serving out a duty station assignment. In fact, he confided to Curt, "One doesn't gripe about one's first sea command. The *Tally Puss* is old bucket of bolts that's seen its last overhaul; she's due for the scrapyard any time. But, what the hell, it's a command. Someday, I'll be in line to command a new Submersible Landing Ship/Dock. Those SLDs could have hauled the whole 17th Division and put them ashore in new auxiliary SLVs."

"Except," Curt pointed out, "I've heard that they can't keep the new aux SLVs from leaking."

"Well, yeah, a couple of them have gone to the bottom," Barber admitted reluctantly, aware that he was talking to an Army man and the honor of his service was at stake. "But it was in less than eight fathoms. The troops aboard got out okay. We even salvaged the hulls and rebuilt them."

"I'll put up with the *Tally Puss*, thank you," Curt observed.

"Yeah, well, you'll have to, Major. Sorry about the air system. The Chief does his best, but we can't requisition charcoal filters for this ship any longer; no one makes them," the young lieutenant remarked. "So we use the old Navy way: Force to fit, file to hide, and paint to cover."

Curt chuckled. "In the Army, if it moves, we salute it. If it doesn't move, we pick it up. If we can't pick it up, we paint it . . ."

"Nothing's changed since my grandfather sailed in the old Trident boats. But this beats the hell out of conning commercial tankers," Barber admitted. "By the way, Major, no offense intended, but why did they send you Army types on an amphibious mission? Sounds to me like a job for the Marines . . ."

"I don't know why they picked the bloody infantry," Curt admitted. "We always get the shit details. And I'm not paid to guess strategy; I just follow orders . . ." He shrugged. "Taking over a whole island the size of Trinidad is probably a bigger operation than the Marines could handle."

"Marines did a pretty good job with a couple of islands, as I recall."

"That was back in double-u-double-u-two, Captain," Curt reminded him.

"I don't know about that. They send the Marines in where you Army types are sure to get clobbered . . ."

A signal came in on underwater comm from the flotilla commander to begin moving westward toward the Serpent's Mouth. "Right on schedule, Major," Barber observed proudly. "We'll have you on that beach at oh-six-hundred tomorrow morning without fail. But first I've got to thread the needle through the Serpent's Mouth."

124

Curt moved to look over Barber's shoulder at the tactical sonar display. He could see the blips representing the four other SLVs moving with them away from the rest of the flotilla. "Any evidence of ASW on the part of the Tee-dads?"

Lieutenant Barber shook his head. He punched up another display which added the above-surface situation to the screen. "Nothing."

"What are those targets?" Curt pointed to two bright spots on the tactical surface display.

"Probably a couple of cruise liners on their way out of Port of Spain to Rio." He turned to speak to the audio terminal of the ship's computer, "Tally Puss, can you identify those targets in coming out of the Serpent's Mouth? Are their propulsion noise signatures familiar?"

The female voice of the ship's computer, familarly called "Tally Puss" in accordance with the ship's nickname, replied in friendly tones, "Aye, Captain. The nearest one is the *Viagens do Brasil* cruise liner *Rio Amazon* and the far one is the Cunard *Duchess.*"

"Tally Puss, what is their closest approach if all ships hold present course?"

"Approximately nine-point-three nautical miles, Captain."

"Tally Puss, set up an air sweep using integrated and synthesized data from flotilla command," the Lieutenant instructed the computer. "Show me current air situation over the Columbus Channel."

Two fast-moving spots of light appeared with alpha-numeric designators alongside each.

The *Tallapoosa's* captain pointed. "That's a *Panair do Brasil* subsonic airbus out of Piarco for Belen. The other is showing the code for Pan Am Flight Three Twenty One into Piarcho, a supersonic flight from

125

Buenos Aires. No sweat. On schedule according to the master flotilla computer which gets its data from Pentagon Central.''

''No military aircraft?'' Curt asked.

''None showing.''

''How about stealthed?''

''According to Naval Intelligence, none of the ASW aircraft based at Napirima are stealthed. They're simple, straightforward coastal patrol aircraft.'' Barber reported confidently.

''You trust your spooks to that extent?'' Curt wanted to know.

''Well,'' the young naval officer replied with a touch of sarcasm, ''I don't know how good the Army intellgence people are, but when the spook community wants the ungarbled word, they always rely on Naval Intelligence . . .''

It was downright boring, this underwater travel. God knows it wasn't a comfortable ride. Because of the overload, the *Tallapoosa's* environmental control system was on the utter verge of complete catastrophic collapse, making the air in the sub a little too warm and far too humid for comfort. The outside water temperature was about 20 degrees Celsius, but it made the hull cooler than the humid air inside it, causing condensation to be deposited on everything in the ship. The walls were wet, and Curt was wet with sweat himself. If the *Tallapoosa* had sported the composite plastic hull of one of the newer SLVs instead of its welded aluminum hull that conducted heat so well, it would have made things easier. As it was, everything had a film of condensation on it.

At least the Navy chow was good, the coffee hot (always, day or night), the bunks clean, and cold showers available. Things could be worse, Curt decided. And they probably would be before Operation Steel Band was over.

He'd told his company to take the opportunity of the two-day sail-in to relax and touch up equipment. Once they went ashore, it was highly probably that no one would have time to do much more than sneeze and shoot.

Curt had fretted over every detail he could think of. If he'd forgotten something, it was too late now. They were slowly moving through the Columbus Channel to pass through the Serpent's Mouth and thence to the beach north of Point Fortin.

To keep himself from becoming bored and battle anxious, he tried to maintain interest in the outside situation.

As he watched the projected charts, position displays, and situation screens in the little control room, Curt thought to himself that the Tee-dads would be have to be downright stupid not to keep a close watch on the strait known as the Serpent's Mouth. It was the southern entrance to the Gulf of Paria and one of the two choke points for the island's maritime trade.

And he really couldn't understand the strategy the Army staff stooges must have had in mind when they decided to send the Washington Greys in through the Serpent's Mouth to land on the western beaches. As he studied the projected map of the southern part of the island of Trinidad, he found himself asking the question, "Why the complexity of this operation? Why not put the whole Iron Fist ashore on the southern beaches and drive north?" Some of the strategy was readable, however. The concept of putting the 17th Iron Fist ashore on the south and southwest was logical if for no other reasons than to capture most of the oil fields and petroleum refineries. This made some sense because it didn't seem prudent to land on the beaches of the highly industrialized west coast, not with the prohibitive rules of engagement concerning non-military facilities. It also made some sense from the viewpoint of the principle of surprise; the Tee-dads certainly wouldn't anticipate the landings of the 17th Iron Fist on the south coast, which appeared to be largely undefended. It was a good place to get ashore with minimum resistance.

But it still seemed incomplete to Curt, and that was probably because he hadn't been told the whole operational plan because of security. He would have wanted to use the modern version of the multiple pincer tactics of the Red Army during World War II. Certainly, Operation Steel Band showed none of the simplicity and audacity of the breakout of Patton's Third Army from Normandy to the Seine during the same war. Instead, it reeked of the sort of complexity that had been behind the "saw tooth" tactics of the immediate pre-warbot Army where one unit would break through and hit the enemy on its flanks, then hold them down while the neighboring unit hit them with a frontal assault and in turn broke through to pincers of its own. Didn't work, of course, Curt knew, because of its inherent complexity and the requirement for outstanding C-curbed-I . . . which went to hell in a handbasket because of enemy electronic countermeasures and jamming.

Well, Curt wasn't in charge of strategy for this operation and he knew he wasn't totally informed. He didn't have to be. He was responsible for fighting his Sierra Charlie company in a new and unproven way while still following orders from above which might not reflect the strengths of the new mixed human-warbot outfit. He was certain he'd have to bend the rules and even make a few minor breaks in orders to keep Carson's Companions from getting into a combat situation where the orders had neglected to take into account their weaknesses.

And the prime weakness of the Sierra Charlie concept was that human soldiers were again present on the battlefield where the hazards were great and the chances of being killed or wounded were enormously increased. With that sort of weakness, Curt had figured out that their only salvation was to remain on the offensive and exploit the inherent mobility of the Sierra Charlies.

The regular warbot troops should be used for their excellent firepower and general immunity to fire whereas the new Sierra Charlies should be exploited for their flexibility and mobility. That's what Curt hoped Hettrick understood as a result of the Grey Flag war game.

But on the other hand there hadn't been enough time to completely evaluate that overwhelming Sierra Charlie success in Grey Flag and the reasons for the rapid and surprising defeat of regulation warbot forces. That's why Curt hoped that Belinda Hettrick had gotten the message. He knew that there hadn't been enough time for General Carlisle and the 17th Iron Fist staff to get it.

His black study was interrupted by Lt. Alexis Morgan who eased into the control room and stood alongside him. Nearly all hints of her female attractiveness were now gone, hidden under her combat gear or deliberately sublimated by her.

Her arrival triggered another of Curt's concerns: Should women be placed in a Sierra Charlie combat situation where they could be killed? It was different in ordinary warbot operations where both men and women were protected by their remote command post; now they were going to be out on the firing line, commanding the new, experimental warbots that responded to verbal orders and served as very stupid infantry troops.

"Miserable," she remarked, sweat running down her face in spite of the headband around her forehead.

"Agreed," Curt replied, wiping the sweat from his own eyes. "How are the troops holding up?"

"Uncomfortably. And some restlessness."

"Combat jitters," he told her, then asked, "You have any problems going into real combat?"

"Yes," she replied honestly and without hesitation. Lt. Alexis Morgan was an open person to Curt; he knew his second-in-command very well. "This is different than warbot command where I can relax and let technology put me into a warbot's head. And the warbot takes the fire instead of me. Yeah, I'm . . . I'm, uh, a little scared."

"I'd be worried if you weren't. And if I weren't, too. The old books say it's an ordinary reaction to the anticipation of combat," Curt tried to explain in an effort to relieve some of her anxiety. It didn't relieve any of his. "Frankly and honestly, do you think you should be permitted to fight?"

"You mean, should female officers and NCOs be restricted to straight warbot combat?" she asked in reply. Then she thought a moment before she replied, "On previous occasions where we've had to go into personal combat, there wasn't time to think about it. Now on the eve of going knowingly into combat for the first time, I don't know."

"You feel all right? You up to it?" Curt wanted to know.

"As much as you are, and hell yes! My implant injectors are working just fine, thank you. They're keeping my hormones under reasonably constant control. I'm on an even keel. So you can't keep me out of combat with the old excuse that I have 'bad days' because you don't either. You've got your own implant injectors. So I can fight just as well as you," Alexis said as she watched the slow movement of bright target spots on the tactical displays.

"Besides," she added almost as an afterthought, "I'm an officer and a soldier. This is my job. I'm here because I want to be. It's what I want to do. So—"

" 'So why don't I get off your back, huh?'"

"Yes, why don't you?" she told him curtly, then went on in more gentle tones, "Sorry, I know you've got the jitters, too And you're worried about your troops." She changed the subject. "You've been up here for hours. How does the situation look?"

Curt grunted. He didn't realize that much time had gone by. "Everything copasetic. Nominal. As planned."

"Calm before the storm?"

"Maybe. The Tee-dads apparently haven't suspected or spotted all the Navy submersibles back there in the Columbus Channel. They haven't put a single one of their coastal patrol planes out here this afternoon."

"Maybe they do it only in the morning before it gets hot. That's when the aviator types like to fly," Alexis observed.

"You're right," Lieutenant Barber commented over his shoulder. "They make one coastal sweep at dawn and another at sunset. We're trying to go through the Serpent's Mouth after the sunset patrol checks these waters."

Curt looked at the clock on the bulkhead. "They ought to be out here pretty quick, then. Isn't it about sunset?"

"Close. When we see him take off from Napirima, we'll come dead in the water, activate various stealth measures, and wait until he goes home to put it to bed for the night,'' Barber explained. ''Naval Intellgence reports that the sunset sweep is quicker and probably only a cursory look around. Seems the pigs-on-patrol types like to get back as soon as possible for the Happy Hour at the Club.''

''That makes a hell of a lot of sense. Wish we could do the same,'' Curt muttered, wiping the sweat off his forehead and from around his neck.

''Check with Henry Kester,'' Alexis said cryptically.

''Huh? Why? Something wrong?''

''I think he managed to stuff a liter in his kit.''

''Lieutenant, I can't hear you,'' Curt told her. Damn that old soldier! Sometimes he carried the perks of his age, rank, and experience too far! The regs were unambiguous when it came to packing any intoxicants or other chemical substances into combat. This had been strictly enforced during the long aftermath of Southeast Asia and the critical times in the recent experience of the warbot Army in the Middle East where hashish was readily available. Regular warbot combat was intolerant of the use of mind-altering chemicals by warbot brainies because of the problems of interefacing them with the computers when they were high.

Personal combat was no different in that respect. Even from the incomplete experience of survivalist games and Grey Flag, Curt realized that the alert mental state of a soldier in personal combat was a far more important factor than it was in warbot combat where the computers and intelligence amplifiers might factor out some of the consequences of mind-altering drugs. Curt also realized he couldn't prevent his troops from stashing something as relatively harmless as alcholic beverages in their kits. But if he caught them at it, he was bound by the regs to take disciplinary action whether or not he wanted to and regardless of the circumstances.

At the moment, he didn't want to know about it; he couldn't afford to lose the expertise of M. Sgt. Henry Kester.

CHAPTER FOURTEEN

Alexis suddenly realized her slip of the lip was a real *faux pas*. So she tried to recover by remarking offhandedly, "Kester wants you to check with him about the warbot ammo status sometime before we go ashore. Nothing critical, he says."

Curt nodded. "Will do. Come here. Look at this." He indicated the holographic topo map of southern Trinidad in the tactical plot tank. "I want to know if you see what I see. The Greys are going ashore here on the west side of the peninsula. The rest of the Iron Fist goes ashore on the south. We converge around Napirima Air Base here. What do you think?"

"Now that I look at it real carefully," Morgan admitted, "we're gonna get squeezed against the west coast, forced to fight on a limited front, and restricted in our movement by the swampland along the river. What does staff say the Tee-dads are going to do?"

"Georgie forecasts that the Tee-dads will attempt to defend San Fernando. But suppose they don't?"

"Yeah, suppose they don't. . . . The whole right flank of the Iron Fist is wide open to Tee-dad Regiment Five moving eastward from Rio Claro. They could catch the Cottonbalers from the rear if they time their movement just right."

"And Tee-dad Regiment Two could sweep down

the Cunapo Southern Road to reinforce. They could roll us up like a ball in the San Fernando area . . ."

Alexis looked at the map quietly for a moment. "It's so obvious that I'm *sure* staff must have considered it. They must know something we don't."

"Maybe they do and maybe they don't," Curt growled.

"There's Sunset Sammy," Lieutenant Barber said, calling attention to a target that appeared on the screen near the position of Napirima Air Base. "No stealth. No countermeasures. No jamming. Obviously a routine flight."

The display panel of the flotilla command net suddenly had the words "Condition Black" flashing in its center, the command from the flotilla admiral in charge of the naval portion of Operation Tenor Pan.

Lieutenant Barber responded immediately. He keyed the mike of his headset. "All hands, this is the Captain. Come at once to Condition Black. I say again: Come at once to Condition Black. All engines stop. All fans and blowers stop. Kill all electromagnetic communication, detection, sensing, and ranging. Go to low-level lighting. Coversational verbal silence. Tally Puss, play dead."

The ship's computer replied in its female voice, "Aye aye, Captain," and went silent.

The bright white lights in the control room suddenly shifted to wan sodium yellow illumination run by batteries. The yellow color matched the peak sensitivity of the human eye, allowing less power to be used. The air blowers quit. Suddenly, the air inside the *Tallapoosa County* became heavy and damp. "How long are we going to have to put up with this?" Alexis asked.

"Until Sunset Sammy goes home to the car barn for the night," Lieutenant Barber told her.

135

"Captain, suppose I need to communicate with my regimental commander or vice-versa?" Curt asked.

"Not in Condition Black, Major. And we've got to go to that condition immediately. Would you please pass the word to your troops to power down and stay quiet. Even the obsolete surplus gear carried by that aircraft can pick out a conversation in one of these boats if the ASW operator gets suspicious and dips a sensor in the water."

"Well, crap! Okay, quiet we'll be. The less we give Sunset Sammy to be suspicious about, the quicker he'll go home to Happy Hour and we'll be out of this sweat box and on the beach. Come on, Lieutenant Morgan, we've got a quick and dirty job to do," Curt remarked as he got up and began to move forward to the troop bay in the forecastle and bow of the submarine.

He found sweaty men and women accompanied by equipment covered with a film of condensed water. The yellow lights did nothing to improve their appearance. "Sack time," Curt announced. "Make it in your bunk and make it quiet. Real quiet. Sergeant Gerard, are you all right?"

Platoon Sgt. Nick Gerard looked both very uneasy and extremely upset. "Uh, I'll be okay, Captain."

"You don't look it."

"Uh, how much longer we gonna be trapped in here?"

"Claustrophobic?" Curt asked.

"Just as soon be the hell out of here," Gerard admitted.

The platoon sergeant's behavior puzzled Curt who'd known the man ever since Carson's Companions had been formed as a company. Nick Gerard was a non-nonsense NCO, a good warbot operator, and a street fighter by nature. He'd never exhibited such phobic reaction inside a warbot command post, which often was crowded. He'd never been claustrophobic in submersible transports before, but Curt had to admit that they'd usually travelled in the huge carrier subs which were little different inside than the underground casern of the 17th Iron Fist at Diamond Point.

But the *Tallapoosa County* was small, austere, crowded, uncomfortable, hot, humid, and generally oppressive. The combination of those factors had probably triggered the deeply rooted fears of the man.

"Sergeant, take a mepro," Curt told him, ordering him to take a mild tranquilizer.

"Sir, I don't want to be screwed up when we hit the beach. I'd rather be a little scared now than be happy and dead on that beach," Gerard replied.

They were due to hit the beach in about ten hours. That was well beyond the half-life of the mild trank that the biotech people had provided Curt's people in their kits. "That's an order, Sergeant. Do it and shut up. Same goes for the rest of you. We're in Condition Black. That means no talking or moving around. Climb in the sack. All of you. Now. Sunset Sammy is up there looking for anything suspicious; if he dips sensors, he could hear us talking or even moving around. So shut it down . . . now!"

So saying, Curt climbed into a net-sprung bunk.

He didn't notice that Platoon Sgt. Nick Gerard had deliberately disobeyed the order and not taken the tranquilizer.

Curt had to admit that it was an uneasy situation, enclosed as they were inside an aluminum pressure hull fifteen meters down in the muddy waters of the mouths of the Orinoco River. It was deadly quiet; he could hear the breathing of Lt. Jerry Allen in the bunk above him and that of M. Sgt. Henry Kester on one side of him. The air was close, hot, humid, and still as death.

What made it even worse was that he didn't know

what was happening outside. Where was the Tee-dad coastal patrol aircraft? Was it making its standard sweep of the Columbus Channel? Had its airborne sensors detected anything unusual? The aluminum hulls of the submerged invasion fleet wouldn't trigger the plane's magnetic anomaly detector, but what if some Navy skipper made a mistake and went up-periscope to have a look around? What if the streams of muddy water pouring out of the Orinoco delta cleared a little bit, allowing the Tee-dad observers in the plane to see an SLV? What if . . . ?

There were too many "what ifs" for Curt's liking. But he was a trained soldier who could handle the waiting. That didn't mean he liked it. Or that he liked not being in control of what was happening to him. But that had been the soldier's lot—especially the infantry soldier's—since the dawn of time.

He checked his watch. Condition Black had been in effect for 22 minutes. How much longer? He began to run the figures in his mind. The Tee-dad IAF-88 "Delfin" maritime patrol aircraft had a maximum mission duration of—what were those numbers?—about six hours at a speed of 200 knots. But the Tee-dads wouldn't fly their Delfins to the full duration of their mission capability. They didn't need to. They'd fly them only long enough to have a look at their offshore waters. The south coast of Trinidad from the Serpent's Mouth on the west to Galeota Point on the east was about 110 kilometers. A Delfin at slow mission cruise could sweep the entire south coast and back again to Napirima in about 35 minutes. Unless the standard coastal sweep included the eastern side of the island as well; if so, perhaps the Delfin would return to base overland rather than recheck the Columbus Channel. This whole Condition Black exercise could be over in another ten minutes. . . .

If Sunset Sammy didn't detect something suspicious and proceed to circle and dip sensors.

Curt told himself that the Navy was run by pros who knew what they were doing. They wouldn't break cover. He was counting on the fact that the Tee-dad flight crew would want to return to base as soon as possible, preferably before it got too dark.

There was a sudden commotion forward. Curt heard heavy footsteps on the deck and heavy, labored breathing. This was quickly followed by three sharp blows against the aluminum hull.

Curt rolled out of his bunk to see Platoon Sgt. Nick Gerard, ashen faced, eyes large, flattened up against the forward bulkhead. He'd given three blows with his fists to the hull.

Without a sound, Platoon Sgt. Edie Sampson rolled over in her bunk and quietly hit Gerard over the head with the butt of her FABARMA assault rifle. Gerard crumpled to the deck. Lt. Alexis Morgan immediately got out of her bunk and went over to the unconscious sergeant.

Curt also didn't say a word; Alexis and Edie Sampson had the situation under control. Gerard was Alexis' platoon sergeant. But Curt nevertheless rolled quietly out of his bunk to his feet and moved as quickly and silently as possible out the aft hatch toward the bridge. He didn't know what effect the three blows against the hull had had to the *Tallapoosa's* Condition Black.

Lieutenant Barber glanced at Curt. In a low voice, he said, "What the hell was that?"

"Under control," Curt replied in an equally low voice. "Did Sunset Sammy detect it?"

Barber shook his head and grinned. "Nope! My passive infra red shows he's heading home to Napirima. The admiral will lift Condition Black in a minute or so. He's got to. Otherwise, we'll get behind schedule.

We've got to make knots now in order to get you through the Serpent's Mouth and onto that beach on time . . . But Condition Black is almost over. It wasn't so bad, was it?''

"Pain in the ass," Curt retorted, then added, "And a real headache for one of my troops." He'd never known Platoon Sgt. Nick Gerard to lose his cool before, but deep-seated phobias that don't often surface can make anyone lose their cool. Curt left the bridge and went forward; he didn't think Gerard had been hurt badly by a mere blow to the head. But they were about to hit a beach and nothing was certain thereafter.

By the time Curt arrived in the forward compartment, the ship's computer announced over the bullhorn, "Hear this! Hear this! Condition Black is lifted! Resume normal under way operations." The blower fans immediately came to life, and Curt could feel the screws begin to turn in the water outside, driving them again forward to the Serpent's Mouth.

Sgt. Nick Gerard was seated against the forward bulkhead with a damp towel held to his forehead. Anticipating her captain's question, Lieutenant Morgan turned to Curt and reported, "Gerard's okay. Headache."

"Must have hit his head on one of these low overhead beams, poor man," Sgt. Edie Sampson added.

Gerard shook his head sadly. "Captain, I'm sorry. I don't know what happened to me."

"I do," Curt told him, "and someday I'll explain it to you. How's that bump on the head?"

"Feels like someone smacked me with a rifle butt."

Edie Sampson said nothing. Neither did Alexis. So Curt told the sergeant, "Your damned head's plenty hard, Gerard. A knock on the noggin won't put you out of action for long. Think you'll be ready to go ashore in a few hours?"

Gerard grinned. "Yessir! Anything to get out of the black hole of *Tally Puss* . . ."

Curt snorted and looked around at his troops. "Maybe you all ought to enjoy what you can of it while you can. The beach is going to be a different matter. So are the next five days. We'll wish we were back in the *Tally Puss*."

M. Sgt. Henry Kester shook his head slowly, "Not me, Captain. If our equipment wasn't rust-proofed, we'd be in real trouble after all the time we've spent in this high humidity enviroment."

"You expecting problems, Sergeant?" Curt wanted to know.

"Yessir. Any time you put high-tech equipment in extreme environments, you can expect troubles. But I can't tell you what they'll be. Don't forget, sir, the Army hasn't fought in the tropics since Panama more than twenty years ago. I sorta suspect we're gonna re-invent the square wheel on Trinidad . . ."

CHAPTER FIFTEEN

As the first rays of a tropical sunrise broke over the island of Trinidad and stretched out across the smooth, calm waters of Guapo Bay, Stanley Smith stuck his head out of the little green tent.

What a beautiful, unspoiled place to camp! he said to himself.

Their vacation on Trinidad had almost come to grief because of the imposition of military law in Port of Spain and the constant and rude demands of the soldiers to see passports, visas, and other documents. If that sort of thing kept up, Stanley thought, it would certainly ruin this beautiful island's lucative tourist trade. It had been Joyce's suggestion that they rent a car and some camping gear in order to spend the remaining days of their vacation roughing it and seeing what the island was really like. He agreed; anything to get away from the oppressive military presence in Port of Spain.

He pulled his head back into the tent, awakened his wife (who wasn't really asleep), and told her, "Come, watch the sunrise. It's so beautiful and unspoiled . . ."

But when the two of them crawled out of the tent and looked across the bay, something suddenly disturbed the calm water surface about thirty meters from the shoreline.

"My God, it's a whale!" Stanley breathed in disbelief.

"Can't be, Stan. Whales don't inhabit these waters. Must be a big dolphin . . ." his wife guessed.

Whatever it was broke the surface in an almost explosive eruption of water and air as it continued toward the beach. It had no head and its sides were wetly smooth and glistening blue-black as water drained from it.

In mute surprise and amazement, the two of them watched as a fifty-meter submarine hull slowly crawled out of the water.

A vertical line appeared in its bow which slowly began to open sideways in two huge doors.

A metallic ramp fell down from inside the monster and hit the unmarked and smooth white sands of the beach.

With whining rumbles, the monster from the depths of Guapo Bay vomited smoothly lined, camouflaged tracked and wheeled vehicles which crunched up onto the dry land of the beach. These vehicles, their cannon swinging left and right, didn't pause but immediately began to rumble across the sand into the immediate cover of the lush tropical foliage.

"We can't get away from them!" Stan yelled. "Goddamned military is everywhere on this island! It's a bloody armed camp! I'm going to raise hell with that travel agency for guiding us right into one of the local war games!"

His wife Joyce tugged at his arm. "Stan, look! More of them to the south of of us!"

"Wow! Uh, Joyce," the man suddenly said as he saw the nearest armored vehicles more closely, "those aren't Trinidad military vehicles. They've got the markings of the United States Army. We've got a ringside seat at an invasion!"

"Stan, forget the tent. Forget the stove. Forget our clothes. Let's get out of here . . ."

He pulled her down to the sand. "No, there's no shooting . . . yet. Let's just get down and stay down. Maybe they won't notice us. I'm sure as hell going to kick a little ass for steering us into the middle of a war. . . ."

"But we picked this spot . . ." his wife tried to tell him. "And how would American Express know there was going to be an invasion?"

What the young couple had witnessed, of course, was the landing of Carson's Companions and Walker's Warriors of the Washington Greys regiment as they disembarked eagerly but with some trepidation from the bowels of the hot, humid SLVs.

And the camping couple didn't go unnoticed. "Captain," Lt. Jerry Allen said, "I have human targets in our ten o'clock position on the beach. They're near a tent from which they emerged, and they do not appear to be armed."

"Investigate," Curt snapped over the tacomm between their two armored command vehicles.

"I'll send Sergeant Sampson covered by a Mary Ann," Allen replied, referring to a Mobile Assault command robot. This was not only a statement of intention on his part, but Allen wanted to be sure there was no objection from Curt to sending Sampson to have a personal look. There was a reason for Allen's decision, and Curt caught it right away. If these two people were indeed camper tourists, Edie Sampson would be able to put them at ease and get them to move out of possible harm's way.

"Roger," was Curt's laconic reply. He scanned his passive air display; no sign of any tactical strike aircraft from Napirima Air Base. Maybe things were working right after all. He hoped maybe the Air Force had clobbered the tactical strike squadron there. But he hadn't gotten any news of it. As a matter of fact, he hadn't gotten any news at all. Nothing had come through the tacomm net to inform him of the progress or lack of it in other aspects of operation Tenor Pan. This could be due to nothing more than the need for security at this early stage of the operation. Curt had confidence in Hettrick; if there was something he should know, he knew she'd tell him.

Furthermore, he didn't suspect that the two campers on the beach were anything more than just that. Edie Sampson would handle the matter.

And she did. Debouching from Alpha Platoon's armored command vehicle with her FABARMA rifle slung in the crook of her left arm, she followed the treaded Mark X60 Mobile Assault Robot across the sand. "Mary Ann Eight,' she told the warbot, "load and lock, but keep your weapon in the standby attitude. Do not point your weapon at the two people unless I tell you to do so. Acknowledge."

"Load and lock. Weapon on standby. Do not point weapon at people unless you order it," the synthezied voice of the warbot replied.

"Mary Ann Eight, do your chemical sensors detect the odor of human aggression from the two people?"

"Negative. My sensors detect only the distinctive odor of fear."

As they approached the two, Sampson stepped up alongside the warbot and saw two very frightened young people in their early twenties, obviously either man and wife or close companions; she didn't care which. She quickly evaluated the situation and waved her right hand. "Hi! I'm Sgt. Edwina Sampson, United States Army. Please don't be afraid of me. Sorry to spoil your camping trip, but you happen to

145

be in the path of a military operation. You're Americans, aren't you? May I ask your names?"

"Joyce and Stanley Smith, and we're American tourists," the man replied. "What's going on here?"

"Can't tell you," Sampson said. "There could be shooting. I'd suggest you strike that tent right now and retreat to the foliage line at the top of the beach. Might be a good idea to take cover so you can't be seen. We know who you are and where you are, but if the Trinidad Air Force makes an air strike on this beach, they'll shoot at anything that looks human and moves If you lay low for a couple of hours, we should be well inland by that time and you can go back to camping . . . although I'd suggest moving south for three or four days because there may be fighting in this neighborhood . . ."

"But we've got a flight back to Chicago day after tomorrow . . ." Joyce complained.

"The flight is probably going to be cancelled," Edie Sampson guessed.

"But—"

"Folks," Edie said easily, "I don't really have a lot of time to talk with you. We've got to get off this beach where we're prime targets. Suggest you do the same. Have you seen any Trinidad soldiers around here?"

"No, not since we left San Fernando," Stanley reported. "What the hell is the United States doing *invading* an independent country? Has the State Department gone absolutely insane?"

"I don't know anything about that. I'm just a soldier, and I go where I'm told and do what I'm ordered. And all of us could damned well get shot in the next second or two out here in the open. So kindly get the hell off this beach, or I'll have my robot pick up your stuff and take if off." Edie Sampson was a redhead with the legendary temper that often accompanies

146

the genotype, and she was quickly running out of patience.

"Sergeant, I don't have to take orders," Stanley Smith told her defiantly.

"Hell no, you don't. But I'm telling you that if you stay here, you might get your ass shot off. And so will I. So I'm moving." She turned to the robot. "Mary Ann Eight, pick up that tent and transport it over to the line of trees."

"Don't bother," the man's wife suddenly said, obviously vexed at her husband's attitude. "We'll do it ourselves. Stanley, don't be stupid. We got ourselves accidentally into a war for some reason we can figure out later. In the meantime, let's get our heads down . . ."

It turned out that the noise of the SLVs nosing onto the beach and the whining rumble of the vehicle turbines caught the attention of others in the vicinity. The landing force of Carson's Companions and Walker's Warriors had been right on target, landing within a hundred meters of where Le Retraite Road leading inland dead-ended on the beach itself. Other unarmed people suddenly showed themselves as Alexis began to move her platoon off the beach and onto the road. They'd apparently come from homes and houses tucked off in the foliage alongside the road.

It must have been a terrifying thing, Curt thought, to suddenly wake up on this beautiful September morning to find that your tropical paradise had been overrun by huge armored military vehicles and your pristine white beach violated by hulking blue-black hulls of submersible landing craft.

"Clear the road!" came the voice of Alexis Morgan over the audio projectors of her vehicle. She was perched with her head and shoulders outside the top turret of her ACV. She was vulnerable to sniper fire,

147

but she was also counting on the fact that the Companions and Warriors hadn't received any incoming yet. Therefore, there were no Tee-dad soldiers in this vicinity. So she felt confident no one would shoot at her with anything that would penetrate her helmet or soft upper body armor. "We're Americans. We intend no harm to those who do not resist us. Clear the road and let us through."

"Americans!" one man shouted. "We hear you bomb Napirima Air Base a few hours ago! We see the smoke in the sky!"

"Air Force came through," Jerry Allen remarked over the tacomm net.

"Sam, I hope you don't relax your anti-air capability on the basis of Rumor Control," Curt messaged on the tacomm net to Capt. Samantha Walker whose company of warbots and warbot brainies were following his outfit onto Le Retraite Road.

"Negative, Curt! Best we watch our flanks, too. Point Fortin is only a kilometer on our right."

"Can you get up a birdbot or other aerial recon? What's going on there?

Col. Belinda Hettrick's voice cut over from regimental command post. "Companions report. Warriors report. What's your situation? Give me a sitrep."

"Do it, Curt. I'm involved in linkage with birdbots," Samantha Walker remarked.

"Grey Head, this is Companion. All ashore sucessfully. No opposing fire. No opposing troops. Just locals acting surprised but non-hostile. Moving inland as planned."

"Companion, do you see a telephone line along Southern Main Road?"

"We aren't there yet."

"When you get there, look for a pole-mounted telephone cable and cut it soonest. Companion, proceed as planned. Report reaching Cochrane. Warrior, detach one platoon to move south along Southern Main Road and hold it against the Tee-dad garrison possibly attempting to retreat out of Point Fortin.''

"Colonel, that will take most of our air cover," Samantha Walker's voice replied. "I'm reconnoitering that road now. Nothing on it. We can move with the rest of the batt and engage any retreating Tee-dad forces with a rear guard if necessary.''

"Killer is having a hard time on the road south of Point Fortin, and Marauder is engaged in heavy house-to-house with the Tee-dad garrison. Both may need help.''

"What's the big problem, Grey Head?" Curt asked the regimental commander.

"Those goddamned rules of engagement!''

"That's what I thought.''

"Warrior, you're right. Cancel my last order. Proceed as planned and check minus-x. Killer will move in to help Marauder. Not more than a company in Point Fortin. Constabulary duty mostly. We'll have them nullified shortly, a little behind sked, but we'll catch up. Companion, move it fast. We've still got the initative of surprise." Hettrick's commands were emotionless and flat; Curt knew she was in deep linkage with the intelligence amplifier and tactical battle computers of the regimental command post which had come ashore south of Point Fortin with Manny's Marauders. On the other hand, he was head-out of the turret of his ACV, getting full and real visuals, audio, and olfactory inputs from the lush tropical landscape that was closing around their column as it moved inland.

This might not be as safe a way to fight as in linkage with warbots, but Curt got a better appreciation of the range and sensitivity of human sensors as opposed to those of warbots. He was now fighting in a real world, not some reality separated from him by electronics and artificial intelligence. He felt the adrenalin in his blood, hyping him and intensifying his sensitivity to his surroundings, putting him right up on the edge of the blade of battle and shortening his reaction times.

It was exhilarating! No wonder George Smith Patton, Jr. had called war the grandest of all human activities.

The warbot brainies were missing all of this. The chances of them getting killed were remote; their warbots would take the incoming. But Curt knew that if a sniper happened to be somewhere in that lush foliage alongside the road, he himself would be the target for the bullet. It made a hell of a lot of difference in the way Curt approached combat. It was even more intense than war games.

But he was almost overloaded with battle data that would normally have been selected, evaluated, and presented by the artificial intelligence of the computers. Here it was all descending upon him, being presented in bewildering array on the tactical displays just below the rim of the ACV's turret. It was almost too much to handle. He had to make the selection, and he cut out everything that didn't immediately concern him. And he delegated, assigning certain areas and functions to Kester, Morgan, and Allen.

CHAPTER SIXTEEN

The column reached the Southern Main Road. "Allen, get a warbot to cut that telephone cable," Curt ordered.

"Captain, I don't have a pole climber," came Jerry Allen's reply.

"What?"

"My Mary Anns can't get up the pole to that cable. Neither can Bravo's Hairy Foxes."

"Shoot it in two," Curt told him.

"Uh, excuse me, sir, I think I've got the answer. I just got a volunteer," Allen's voice came back.

Squad Leader Jim Elliott jumped out of the aft sortie door of Allen's ACV and, with practice evidenced from his recent youth in the country, shinnied up the rusting steel telephone pole at the edge of the road. He simply hacked at the cable with his heavy machete, cutting it in one swing of the blade. He then slipped tapping transmitters over both ends of the severed cables; the little black boxes would transmit any and all telephone messages and data bursts on either line back to regimental for the use of the S-2 intelligence types.

The Southern Main Road was a good two-lane thoroughfare thankfully paved with an abundant layer of asphalt. No one was on it that morning except the

Washington Greys' column. People peered out of houses alongside the road as the column whined past.

The column came to a wide place in the road where the tropical forest had been cut back and kept back to clear a gasoline station with a telephone call box outside it. "Grey Head, Companion here. Reporting Cochrane. We're checking minus-x but detect no bogies," Curt transmitted over the tacomm, telling Hettrick that Sam Walker's troops on rear guard were watching for the possibility of Tee-dad troops retreating out of Point Fortin but such bogies weren't in evidence. "How's the situation?"

"Keep it moving," Hettrick's command came. "Marauder has taken Point Fortin. Killer is moving up behind you."

The robot brain of Curt's Armored Command Vehicle suddenly brought the lumbering transport to a shuddering halt.

A young woman was standing squarely in the middle of the road and waving her right hand in the air. In her left arm, she cradled a shining assault carbine.

"Captain Carson?" she was calling.

"Column halt!" Curt snapped into the tacomm mike. With his hand warily on his own FABARMA rifle, still kept discreetly below the lip of the turret hatch, he peered at her.

She couldn't have been more than twenty years old, and she was beautiful. The cutoff denims belted at her narrow waist by a heavy cartridge clip belt of the old style and the white cotton shirt tied around her shoulders and torso as a halter did little to cover but instead emphasized a sensual and athletic young body with full hips and breasts. Her long, slender legs were tanned, and she wore a pair of open thong sandals on her feet. Her corn-colored blonde hair fell loosely to her shoulders while wisps and strands blew over her forehead, framing a squarish face with broadly set and intensely electric blue eyes.

But in spite of her attractiveness, there were two things about her that riveted Curt's attention.

Her beautiful face was marred by an excessive gap between her two upper front teeth. Curt didnt't know whether that detracted from her beauty or emphasized it.

And she cradled a silvery stainless steel 5.56mm Ruger Mini-14/5F rifle easily in the bend of her left arm. Its black plastic furniture was in stark contrast to the tanned skin of her arm and torso. Even its carbine size looked large when she carried it. It emphasized her small size. From the way she handled it, Curt decided she knew how to use it in spite of her apparent youth and its apparent age, because the weapon had undoubtedly gone out of production before she'd been born.

"I'm Captain Carson," he replied carefully.

"Adonica Sweet," she introduced herself.

"What can I do for you, Miss Sweet?"

"Let me come aboard." She spoke with just a hint of the lilting Caribbean English accent overlaid mostly with a slight Dixie drawl. An interesting combination, Curt decided.

"Why?" he asked.

"I'm your native guide."

"Oh?" She was a native guide? With a little orthodontic work, this girl could have a very successful and highly-paid career as a high-fashion model in New York.

"This is Operation Tenor Pan, is it not? And you are Capt. Curt Carson, Carson's Companions, Sierra Charlie force, Washington Greys, Seventeenth Iron Fist Division, are you not?" Adonica Sweet asked, her sentences taking a strange structure that was part American and part Caribbean.

"Who told you that?" Curt fired back.

"*Robert,*" she replied briefly, pronouncing it as the French do: *Row-bear.*

That was the code. "Sergeant," he called down to Kester, "open the sortie hatch. Please let Miss Sweet aboard."

"Oh, no, Captain," Adonica Sweet objected. "I'll mount the point vehicle."

"You'll ride with me for right now," Curt told her. "I have communications with my point vehicle, and I'm instructed not to place locals in jeapardy." That wasn't precisely correct, and he knew it, but he felt that he wasn't overly stretching the rules of engagement. His real motive was to check out this improbable and beautiful "native guide" who looked and acted more like an American. On the other hand, he asked himself, how did a person from Trinidad act? He didn't know. "The master sergeant has opened the aft sortie hatch. Before you come aboard, clear that weapon's chamber."

She reached down with her right hand and pulled back the slide with a positive movement, ejecting the ancient brass-cased round into the air where she deftly caught it and slipped it back into the loaded clip through the open bolt. "The weapon is clear and the action is open, Captain," she announced.

Adonica Sweet walked around the ACV with a freely swinging motion of her long legs and hips, the way of movement of one who hasn't spent her life in a teeming city but in the open, rolling countryside of a place like Trinidad. She walked like the women of St. Thomas with a smooth and liquid grace and efficiency.

When Curt heard the sortie hatch shut, he picked

up the tacomm mike while at the same time motioning forward with his arm, "Wagons ho!"

"On to La Brea!" came the reply from Jerry Allen in the point ACV. "Captain, I've got plenty of room for the native guide up here . . ."

Curt ignored the young lieutenant as he felt Adonica Sweet brush against him when she squeezed up into the turret hatch. There really wasn't room for two people in the hatch. But Curt didn't complain. Adonica had a fresh smell about her. "Captain, we must bypass La Brea," she stated at once, not waiting for any formalities. "Turn to the right down Sobo Road when we reach it. The Southern Main Road becomes plainly visible from the Gulf of Paria, and we may be brought under naval gunfire from Trinidad gunboats if we don't detour La Brea."

"Show me," Curt told her and called to Kester, "Sergeant, take over here."

Down in the ACV's command compartment, Curt called up the tactical display on the screen. The roads were plainly visible. Their present position was marked, and Curt could also see the vehicles and robots of the Washington Greys now strung out along the Southern Main Road. There was an indication that some of Manny's Marauders were still engaged in Point Fortin, but even Kelly's Killers were on the road northbound now. The location of the naval elements were not shown on the display, and neither were the location and movement of the Tee-dad forces.

"This is how we must go," Adonica Sweet pointed out to him, tracing the route on the display with her fingertip.

Curt called up the Tee-dad naval situation. He didn't get it initially until he patched the request through regimental and Hettrick, knowing that Curt wouldn't call for tactical data unless he needed it, squirted the data to him.

"There appears to be a naval threat in the Dragon's Mouths," Curt observed. "Looks like the Tee-dad navy is responding."

Adonica indicated the targets moving out from San Fernando. "Those are the ships of Flotilla Two. They may be moving into a position to bring the La Brea penninsula under fire."

Curt felt that something different was happening and that Flotilla Two was probably on its way to meet a Navy feint to the north. But he didn't say anything. "I'm reluctant to put this column on what appears to be a secondary side road around Le Brea," he told her. "What sort of surface does Sobo Road have?"

"A most excellent asphalt surface, Captain."

"On a secondary road through this jungle?"

"Of course! Do you see Pitch Lake there on the chart?" Adonica asked. "That's been a primary source of asphalt since the island was discovered back in the sitheenth century. Nearly all roads in Trinidad are asphalt paved. We have lots of asphalt . . ."

That would make sense. Curt looked carefully at her and observed, "You certainly don't look or act like a native."

"How should I act? And is there anything wrong with how look?"

"Nothing at all wrong with your looks, my dear. But this is my first trip to Trinidad. So forgive me if I seem ignorant. I'm also under just a little bit of pressure. Some Trinidad people out there may try to shoot at me before very long . . ."

Adonica Sweet laughed. It was a silvery laugh. "The General's army? That's a laugh! Mercenaries from Brazil, most of them. The only outfit you may have to worry about is the Presidential Guard, and they're up

156

in Port of Spain. The rest of the troops are stationed in the bigger towns such as San Fernando, Rio Claro, Arima, and Sangre Grande. Their main task isn't the defense of Trinidad. They control the populace."

Adonica Sweet not only knew the disposition of the Tee-dad forces, but she prounced the names of the towns with the unique rolling lilt of one who speaks Spanish.

"You seem to know a lot about Trinidad. Were you born here?" Curt asked, hoping to probe this young girl's background.

"I was born in New Orleans. I'm as American as you. My family moved to San Fernando when I was a child. My father was a refinery supervisor for Texarco . . . until General Drake's thugs put him in jail as a suspected spy yesterday."

"Was he?"

"A spy? Of course! So am I! And I'll find him before this is over. Besides, he'll be helpful when we find him; he fought with the Washington Greys in Panama before I was born, and he taught me about the Army. Captain, you're going to discover a lot of people on Trinidad who will be happy to help Operation Steel Band . . .

M. Sgt. Henry Kester couldn't help overhearing the conversation from his post in the turret not three feet away. He ducked his head into the ACV and asked, "Was his name Capt. Roger Sweet?"

"Yes! Did you know him?"

"I had the honor to serve under him as a private until he was wounded and mustered out disabled," Henry Kester remarked simply.

Adonica literally bubbled. "You knew him! Oh, wonderful! When I was given the job of guide during Operation Steel Band, I asked if I could be assigned to

157

his old outfit! I hoped I'd run into some of his old comrades . . ."

"Uh, Miss Sweet, I was only eighteen at the time," Kester pointed out gently. "I was a lowly private first class, and he was a captain. We knew one another, but I can assure you that we weren't drinking buddies. Not at that time in this Army . . ."

Capt. Samantha Walker's voice boomed in on the tacomm, "Heads up! Button down! Incoming air strike! Curt, he'll be over your point vehicle in thirty seconds and coming right down the road!"

CHAPTER SEVENTEEN

M. Sgt. Henry Kester didn't duck down out of the turret hatch and dog it shut. Instead, he reached down into the ACV and pulled out a tube containing a Mark 100B anti-tank/anti-air pocket rocket. "Stupid sonofabitch," he muttered to Curt. "It ain't very smart to attack an armed vehicle column head-on. Better to come at it from the rear. Better yet, from either flank. That poor dumb bastard is either stupid or poorly trained . . . or both. He'll take fire from the whole length of the column as he goes over it. When he breaks off the attack, he'll have to do it to either side, which means he's going to be bare-assed exposed while he's doing it."

Curt made a quick decision. "Belay the button-down order. He's swinging west but continuing to parallel the road. Let's get a positive on him before we shoot . . . unless he shoots first."

"I have a visual!" came Jerry Allen's voice on the tacomm. "Can't get a positive on him. Might be a Piranha. Low and slow. Subsonic. Radar glint signature indicates a turboprop. Okay, we've got range gate lock on him. Passing the data back on taclink."

"Let him get Fox Three . . . close enough to hit," Alexis Morgan told him.

"Guns, guns! Opening fire!"

Curt heard the *whump whump whump* of the 75mm Saucy Can on Allen's LAMV spitting out self-homing projectiles, then the *RRRIIIPPP* of a burst from the 50mm gatling on a Hairy Fox heavy-fire warbot.

"I'd better get a shot in if I'm gonna—" Kester said and aimed the Mark 100B toward the front of the column. "There's the target, baby! Go get it!" The rocket left the tube with a snort.

Curt looked up through the hatch just in time to see a civilian Cessna Caravan go over, half the left wing in tatters and the engine trailing heavy, dense smoke laced with orange flame. The large black letters on the wing identified it as Tobago-registered. As it did an uncontrolled half-roll passing overhead, Curt caught the familiar logo of International Television News on the fuselage. The huge aft cargo door was open, and Curt could see the surprised and frightened face of a TV cameraman. . . .

Even through the armored sides of the ACV, Curt and Adonica could hear and feel the explosion as the aircraft hit the ground on the west side of the road.

Kester tossed the empty tube away. "As I said, Captain, poor, dumb sonofabitch!"

"Christamighty! That wasn't a Tee-dad Piranha!" Jerry Allen's excited voice exclaimed.

"Damned right it wasn't!" Curt exploded. "We just shot down an ITN media camera plane!"

"Well, what the hell was it doing here, Captain?" Allen wanted to know.

"And why did it come in unannounced from the front?" Morgan's voice came in on top of Allen's.

"Damned if I know, and I haven't got time to worry about it," Curt fired back. He activated a switch. "Grey Head, this is Companion reporting that we accidentally torched a news media aircraft. He came at us down the road looking like a tac strike aircraft lining up to blow our lips off. My people reacted."

Hettrick's voice came back cooly, "We saw it through Warrior's recon sensors. We also have it taped for the future board of inquiry. Fortunes of war, Captain."

Damned poor excuse for killing a bunch of people! Curt thought savagely. But the news media often acted as if they were immortal and above the laws of war and civil actions. This time, it cost several people their lives. And there would probably be hell to pay.

He could hear the TV anchors intoning gravely already, "Trigger-happy Army solidiers shoot down unarmed camera plane in Trinidad invasion. Tape and details at six . . ."

Then he gathered his thoughts, attempted to quiet the adrenalin pounding through him, and asked, "Companion requests data. Can we anticipate future tac air strikes? Did the Blue Boy do the job at Napirima?"

"Post-strike recon positive," Hettrick replied, "but we won't know for sure until we take the base itself. Blue Boys are not sure they got all the Piranhas, and satellite recon has been degraded by smoke over the target area."

"Do we have air supremacy?" Curt asked openly and bluntly.

"Unknown."

"Grey Head, this is Companion. Unless I'm assured of friendly air and warned of their approach, I'll shoot at anything in the sky coming at us. I repeat: I'll shoot at any unidentified aircraft that exhibits what I decide is hostile intent. I must protect my command, the rules of engagement notwithstanding," Curt said adamantly. "Blue Boys or Navy going to continue to sanitize Napirima?"

161

"Blue Boys have hit it according to plan, but they've got to stage out of land bases a long ways away."

"Where's the bloody Navy?"

"The two carrier subs assigned to Operation Steel Band got delayed by Hurricane Nathan off Hatteras," Hettrick broadcast in the clear. That meant she was reasonably confident that their frequency-hopping ta-comm link hadn't been compromised, although there was heavy jamming on some of the other parts of the electromagnetic spectrum.

"I repeat: If it's in the air and moves toward us, and if we think it's hostile, we shoot," Curt told her again.

"I read you loud and clear the first time, Companion."

"So who gets blamed for torching the camera plane?"

"You do for right now. But don't worry about it. That's post-operation stuff. Lots can happen between now and then. In the meantime, you've got an objective, and we're right behind you. Did you pick up your native guide?"

"Affirmative."

"Any good?"

"Some native guide!"

"Say again?"

"Never mind, Grey Head. You'll meet her soon enough."

"I expect I will."

Jerry Allen's ACV turned off the Southern Main Road at Sobo Road as directed by Adonica Sweet. The side road led them around an oil field with its nodding well pumps. But Allen missed the left turn at Boodoosingh Road that would have led the column back to coast. Adonica Sweet caught the mistake as soon as Curt's company ACV reached the turn.

"Companion Alpha, one-eighty on that road, return to the junction," Curt passed the order along on tacomm. "Companion Leader will take the point for now."

It was a major switch in plans, but Curt's people were flexible enough to adjust to the strange procedure of having the company commander and his armored command vehicle with its four General Purpose "Jeep" robots inside leading the parade. At the next wide spot in the road at Rousillac, Curt had his ACV pull off to the side to let Allen's Alpha Platoon retake the point.

"Alpha Leader, when you pull alongside me, I'm transferring our native guide to you," Curt told him. "She knows where we're going. Just don't let her expose herself too much to danger. We're getting close to the point where the spooks say we might encounter Tee-dad units moving south . . ."

"Roger, Companion Leader," Allen's voice came back. "By the way, you might want to switch to the standby equipment. You're transmissions are getting weak, garbled, and unreadable . . ."

"Bravo Leader, this is Companion Leader. Radio check. How do you read?" Curt wanted to make sure it was his equipment and not Allen's. He wasn't really sure what all the humidity in the *Tally Puss* had done to the circuitry which was *supposed* to be hermetically sealed.

"Bravo Leader reads Companion Leader loud and clear. But I ought to. I'm in your minus-x."

"Alpha Leader, check your tacomm gear."

"Yeah, we got bounced around a little bit on that back road. Could have roughed it up," Allen came back. "And we'll be happy to tranfer the guide aboard at Rousillac."

"Yeah, I'm sure you will, but remember that she's a guide. Period."

163

"Yessir. I've seen the native women . . ."

Lt. Jerry Allen was going to get a surprise, Curt told himself. Especially when Adonica Sweet scowled and said, "I don't like the way he spoke about 'native women.' I guess I'll have to teach him some manners . . ."

"Companion Leader, this is Grey Head," the ta-comm barked with Colonel Hettrick's computer-processed voice. "You're opening the lead between us. We've dropped back four klicks. We can't move that fast."

Curt suspected that might happen. His Sierra Charlies and their command-activated warbots were still all in their vehicles and moving. They weren't restricted to the relatively slow, leap-frog movements of the regular warbot companies who had to maintain their direct linkage channels between the warbot brainies and the warbots out ahead of them as doctrine required. The warbot command post vehicles with their officers and NCOs lying in linkage couches and extending their senses out through the warbots could continue to move. But they had to move, stop to ensure that the linkage channels were secure and that all warbots were operational, then move again.

Regular warbot troops weren't organized for the sort of rapid movement that Curt's Sierra Charlies could maintain. On the other hand, Curt's company didn't have the massive coordinated firepower possible with hundreds of heavy warbots under multiple human control.

"Want us to slow down?"

"No, but be aware of the situation," Hettrick advised him. "If you make contact with Tee-dad forces, you may have to hold them until we move up, or make a retrograde operation until you can pick up our fire support."

164

"We'll either hold 'em or blast through them," Curt promised. "We don't like to retreat. No sense paying for the same ground twice . . ."

"Don't forget the rules of engagement, Captain. Get a visual before engaging. Don't involve non-combatants. Don't be provocative . . ."

"The ROEs are engraved on the inside of my helmet, Colonel," Curt told her sourly.

It was going to be a difficult battle when it occurred, Curt thought. The Southern Main Road was lined with houses. Many of them were quite neat and modern, undoubtedly belonging to the many petroleum industry workers in this part of the island. If the Tee-dad troops used such civilian structures for ambush or cover, Curt was going to have to ignore the rule of engagement that told him not to harm such structures. And some civilians were going to get hurt, too, but he'd do his best to prevent that if he could.

And the battle was going to occur. Hettrick sent him the latest position data on the Tee-dad forces moving out of San Fernando down the Southern Main Road to meet him. It had taken more than an hour for the Tee-dads to react and get elements of the 4th Regiment moving south. It didn't look to Curt like it was a full Tee-dad regiment moving out of San Fernando. But it wouldn't take more than another company to block their progress by ambushing them on the road.

It was just about noon when Jerry Allen's point vehicle reached the intersection with Desir Road, Curt sent the order, "Debouch your squads. Put one squad leader on either side of the road with the Mary Anns for fire support. Your should meet Tee-dad troops soon. Report contact."

"Footing doesn't seem very good off the road," Allen reported.

"Have your squad leaders check it out before you get the Mary Anns bogged down in it," Curt told him.

The road swung nearly down to the beautiful beach of Otaheite Bay. Adonica Sweet, now in Allen's ACV, advised that they were coming up on the intersection with Siparia Road.

"Alpha Leader," Curt advised, "you may detect forces moving north on Siparia Road. Get positive visual before initiating action. Repeat: Get positive visual before laying ordnance on them. They may be the point units of the Can Do, the Fifteenth Regiment."

"We don't show anything moving north on Siparia Road," Allen reported. His ACV made a sharp left turn as it passed another village center shown on the map as St. Mary's and the vehicles of Alpha Platoon passed out of sight behind foliage.

All hell suddenly broke loose.

"Contact, contact!" came Allen's excited cry over the tacomm. "Tee-dad infantry units with small arms five hundred meters range where road turns right again! Coordinates seven-one-six by delta-one-eight-zero."

"Don't be provocative, but commence firing!" Curt ordere with more than a touch of sarcasm in his voice. "Bravo, deploy to St. Mary's and lay in AP rounds from the Saucy Cans. Prepare to assume fire base. Alpha, when you get Bravo's fire cover, deploy to the right."

"It's difficult for me to disengage without getting some heavy fire cover to make them put their heads down! Bravo, give them two salvos, then I can move without getting creamed," Allen replied.

"Companion Leader, give me a sit-rep," came Col. Belinda Hettrick's voice on tacomm. "Estimate of enemy strength?"

"Looks like we've encountered company strength,

166

but there may be battalion strength up the main road behind it," Curt estimated. "Request overhead fire support from you on the road in the one-half to one hour depth. Companions can handle the narrow depth. Lay 'em on both sides of the road up to the Oropuche River to keep the rest of the Tee-dad column from moving up and deploying!"

"That your tactical estimate of best response?"

"Affirmative!"

"Roger, Companion Leader."

The tearing sound of heavy seeker projectiles tearing overhead in search of targets suddenly filled the universe.

CHAPTER EIGHTEEN

The incoming stuff was heavy . . . the heaviest they'd taken thus far.

God, I hope the Tee-dads don't have artillery around here! Curt said to himself. As a regular Robot Infantry regiment the Washington Greys had minimal artillery, mostly a few 105 recoilless projectors and a few 80mm mortar warbots. But nothing that would offer any sort of counter-fire to a Tee-dad artillery outfit with their heavier weapons. But apparently Curt's troops hadn't contacted anything larger than an infantry company with little or no artillery support behind them.

So it was a matter of maneuver right then. "Kester, where's the best place Alpha can move to flank?"

"East to the Lagoon River if the footing will stand it," the Master Sergeant replied.

"Alpha, when you disengage, move to the right flank. Bravo, move forward and pin down the enemy," was Curt's resulting order.

"Now that we've got some fire support, we can. Disengaging!" Jerry Allen replied.

"Casualties?"

"One Mary Ann mired in the goo."

"I'll pick it up," came Alexis Morgan's voice.

"Negative! Let the tech batt work on it. Fight the

168

fight. Alpha Leader, send the native guide back to Companion Leader," Curt directed.

"Uh, request to keep her up here," Jerry Allen replied. "She knows this ground. And it looks like we may get into the mire off to our right. Swampy stuff."

"Okay, but put her behind armor. She hasn't got body armor on."

"Yessir, that's obvious . . ."

"Yeah . . . And, Lieutenant, technically she's a civilian."

"Technically? More like an Indian scout, isn't she, sir?"

"Argue technicalities when this is over. In the meantime, don't send your Mary Anns into that swamp area, only your squad leaders . . ."

"Yessir. That's SOP, sir. But we're leaving the ACV and the robot transport vehicles under cover alongside the road. We can move on foot and with the armored all-terrain vehicles okay."

"Do what you have to do. Execute a standard break to the right," Curt instructed.

Thirty seconds later, Alexis Morgan reported, "Bravo is engaging enemy company strength. Apparently the point. They're withdrawing northeast along the road."

"Grey Head, can you move the fire support northeast to the river crossing?" Curt asked Hettrick.

"Roger, Companion, we're already doing that."

The sound of 105s ripping overhead continued.

"Muddy but passable," came the report from Allen. "We're maintaining contact with the withdrawing enemy."

"Bravo Leader, move up on 'em. Maintain contact."

"We're doing it."

"Bravo, Companion Leader is coming up behind
169

you to add to your fire base. Companion One, forward," Curt ordered his ACV, and it turned the corner at St. Mary's into the smoke and haze of battle.

They passed one smoking Mary Ann warbot, apparently blown off the road into the mud where it couldn't extricate itself. It didn't appear to be hit, so Curt tried the expedient of verbal commands to get it out of trouble.

"Mary Ann Fourteen," Curt snapped through the ACV's audio system, giving a direct command to the warbot, "this is Companion Leader; can you move out of that ditch?"

"Negative!" came the robotic reply. It was apparent to Curt that the warbot was attempting to carry out its function and get out of the ditch. But something had gone wrong with its artificial intelligence circuits, and it was merely burning itself out trying to extricate itself without help.

"Then I order you to power down and wait for pickup."

"Roger, Companion Leader," the warbot's synthesized voice replied.

"Companion Leader, this is Alpha Leader. I'm at the river. Don't know which one. Sensors show two rivers here, but they're pretty stagnant creeks. Indistinct, too. Swampland gets awful soft east of here. I've got about two hundred meters on the landward side of the road to work in."

"Enemy locations?"

"Don't detect them yet . . ."

Again, Curt could hear it when it started up. "Companion Leader, this is Bravo Leader! We're taking fire!"

"We're abeam you to the east, Bravo," Allen reported. "We have contact with the enemy. Major defense line at the river crossing. At least a battalion in

170

defensive positions with small arms, one-oh-six recoilless launchers, and a bunch of light machine guns."

"A bunch?" Curt asked, requesting by inference a more accurate estimate from the young lieutenant in his first heavy combat against a formidable foe. Curt knew what the young man was going through; his first combat in Chad had resulted in doing something stupid and getting his warbot shot out from under him, leaving him "killed in action." A minor oversight in estimating enemy firepower was a small mistake on Allen's part. But it shouldn't have happened; Allen had been blooded at Zahedan. All of which served to reinforce Curt's experience that strange and unusual things happened in the haze of battle and people didn't react predictably when they were being shot at.

The sound of firing was fast and furious for about a minute, then tapered off to sporadic bursts of automatic small arms firing.

"Grey Head, this is Companion Leader," Curt called to Hettrick. "We've apparently encountered a heavily-defended enemy position at the Oropuche River. I'm going forward for a personal recon."

"Roger, Companion Leader! Grey Force is moving into position in your minus-x. I have recon warbots airborne at this time squawking friendly sensor reply codes."

Curt unplugged his headset from the ACV's tacomm circuitry and picked up his transportable tacomm. He felt absolutely naked without a direct linkage to a reconaissance warbot which would allow him to go out and take a look without being there himself. Directly linking his nervous system through a computer and command channel to the eyes and ears of a warbot did indeed have some advantages, he decided. In the absence of that capability and in the present situation, he was forced to go out and have a look for himself.

171

He retrieved his FABARMA rifle from its rack on the side of the vehicle, slung the bandolier of 500 rounds of caseless ammo around his waist, and stuffed a half-dozen M20 plastex grenades in his hip pouches. Thus armed, he told his master sergeant, "Henry, I'm going on a personal recon. Mind the store while I'm gone."

Kester calmly unplugged, too, and reached over to take his own rifle off its rack. "Better to work in teams of at least two, Captain," he advised. "It's possible to get uncovered or pinned down otherwise."

"No, I want you to run the company command vehicle," Curt told him.

"Captain," Kester said with patient restraint, "this ACV will run itself while we're gone, and I'll patch in one of the jeep warbots as an overload buffer. This vehicle's too far back and too well defiladed to be hit by anything that might penetrate, much less do damage. Unless it catches a wild round from one of those one-oh-sixes Lieutenant Allen reported . . . in which case we'd be shook up a tad if we're in it, especially if the round hits at the proper angle. We'll take the other jeep with us for additional firepower and comm capability."

Curt hesitated, whereupon Kester went on, "Hell, Captain, nobody's gonna steal this ACV while we're gone! And if it has to come get us, you can holler for it."

"Let's go," Curt decided without further discussion or consideration. Only a damned fool or a stupid officer would ignore the expert advice of his chief NCO, expecially if said NCO was an honest-to-God down-and-dirty old infantry grunt.

They debouched the ACV through the rear sortie hatch, followed by a General Purpose War Robot which extended its walking stilts after it rolled off the ramp to

172

the ground. It carried only a 20mm gun with a grenade projector, but Curt knew it could serve as a potent armored firebase if necessary, capable of absorbing a 5.56mm round directly into its composite hard armor at fifty meters without damage.

They weren't exactly in a jungle, but the tropical growth was lush and thick enough to deflect 5.56mm rifle rounds at ranges greater than a hundred meters. This meant that any really significant fighting would take place in close quarters. Which, in turn, meant to Curt that the Greys would have to adapt urban fighting tactics to this environment.

Furthermore, the air was damp and opressively uncomfortable. Curt began to sweat. There was also a strange burnt smell to the air. Kester tapped him on the shoulder and pointed through the trees to the east. Barely visible were huge black clouds of billowing smoke. "Napirima Air Base," Kester said. "Smells like they got it good. That stink is burning composite plastic and jet fuel."

They worked their way down the landward side of the road toward the sound of the battle ahead, dodging from bush to bush.

Even though Curt knew that the enemy was ahead and dug in behind the river line, he was startled when he practically stumbled upon a family of five local people huddled in the dense foliage. The two youngsters, neither of them much more than five years old, looked scared to death. The mother was pallid and didn't seem to be any more confident than her children. The father tried to comfort his wife and wasn't being very successfu at it. The fifth member of the family was an older man, and Curt almost levelled his FABARMA rifle at him because an ancient American M1 Carbine was cradled in the grandfather's arms.

Curt quickly waved his open right hand at them and slithered under the brush with them. "Anyone hurt?"

The father shook his head.

The grandfather shifted the M1 in his arms and growled, "Just leave us alone!"

"Don't blame me," Curt told him. "I didn't start this, and I'm being shot at, too. Stay under cover and this will all be over in a few hours. The fighting's up by the river. Your house okay?"

"Go near it and I'll shoot you," the grandfather muttered. "You soldiers are all alike. The Trinidad army soldiers tried to loot our place; I shot two of them before you Americans showed up, and I'll shoot you, too, if you try to loot us . . ."

"Don't worry," Curt tried to assure him. "I'm probably the only American soldier you'll see, but you'll see a lot of our war robots. The warbots won't loot. And they won't shoot at you, either. Matter of fact, go back to your house; you'll be safer there. The battle's gone past you . . ."

"Why do you do this? Why do you invade our country?" the father suddenly asked.

"To help you get rid of General Drake and his soldier," Curt explained briefly. "Now please go back to your house so you won't be mistaken for soldiers and get shot at. Come on, now . . ."

They started to move out from under the brush when Curt heard Kester call, "Captain!"

Curt ducked out and toward the master sergeant's voice. Kester was leaning over a woman. "Wounded civilian," Kester explained. "Rifle round . . ."

Curt keyed his tacomm. "Grey Head from Companion Leader through Companion Cee-Pee. We've got wounded civilians up here. Send up the biotechs."

But Kester was already at work with his personal bio kit. "Pain killer, antibiotic, and coagulant," he ex-

174

plained. "That'll hold her for an hour or so until bio-techs can get to her."

"Any others?"

Kester shook his head. "I hope not. I'm not equipped to handle very many more. Ain't like it was when we used to go into personal combat with the medics. Army forgot to include medics with the Sierra Charlies . . ."

"Something else we didn't get the chance to learn about," Curt remarked. "If she's stabilized, let's get moving forward." Within 150 meters of the first river crossing —the Lagoon River—the fire fight was going on. However, it wasn't a constant fusillade, only occasional *pop-pop-pop* of individual fire punctuated from time to time by the ripping sound of an automatic weapon as a target was located. The sounds were strangely muffled by the vegetation. And there was the unusual feeling of potential death all around. It didn't look or feel like any sort of battlefield Curt had ever been on before, even in Zahedan.

The enemy was out there somewhere to the north and east, but Curt couldn't see anything except an occasional muzzle flash against which one of Morgan's Hairy Foxes immediately returned fire. Curt saw her platooon ACV hunched behind vegetation. "Companion Bravo, this is Companion Leader. Henry and I are in your minus-x and about to knock on your sortie hatch."

"Latch string's out," came the excited voice of Lt. Alexis Morgan. "Watch out you don't draw fire."

Ten meters from the ACV, Curt felt the pop of a bullet's shock wave going past him. He couldn't see where it came from so he couldn't return the fire as he wanted to. So he dropped to the ground and crawled on his belly the rest of the way.

Alexis Morgan was busy with her tactical displays

and plots. "We took a few rounds in the glacis plate," she explained, "but nothing damaging. No one-oh-sixes yet. They must be short of one-oh-six ammo; they're using it very sparingly against targets they know they can hit."

"Any response to Hettrick's supporting fire?" Curt asked, studying the display.

"No, the enemy's dug in and the one-oh-fives haven't been able to identify and home on targets. Most of the rounds have gone harmlessly into the jungle . . . but they've made the Tee-dads keep their heads down."

"Can we force this river crossing?"

Alexis shook her head. "No way without heavy warbot assault . . . and we aren't equipped for that. We don't have the firepower. We've got barely enough to hold them down and keep them from counterattacking across the river."

"Where's Allen?"

"Out on the right bogged down."

Curt looked more carefully at the tactical display. It had changed since he'd left his own ACV. "Battalion strength at least," he mused. "The whole Fourth Tee-dad Regiment was suppose to be in San Fernando. Where's the rest of it?"

"Don't know. We're not privy to that data if Hettrick has it."

"If we can't break through this choke point, can we hold it until Hettrick moves the heavy warbot stuff up here for a frontal assault?"

"The Tee-dads won't move me," she promised. "You wanted a fire base. You've got a fire base."

"Companion Leader, this is Grey Head," was the call from Hettrick over the tacomm. "Do you read?"

"Loud and clear, Grey Head. I'm in Companion Bravo command post."

176

"Consolidate your positions on a temporary basis. Grey Main Force is moving into position behind you to support. Do not attempt to force the river crossing. I repeat: Do not attempt to force the river crossing. Consolidate your positions and forces, and be prepared to withdraw by eighteen hundred hours. I'll want to see Companion Leader at Grey Head in St. Mary's at nineteen hundred hours."

"Withdraw? Retreat?" Curt wondered.

"Repositioning," Hettrick explained. "It'll be explained in the conference at nineteen hundred. Get your company together."

"Roger, Grey Head," Curt told her and remarked to Alexis as the circuit ceased, "Most reasonable order I've heard all day."

"Reasonable? To retreat?" Alexis couldn't believe him.

Curt shook his head. "Hell's great livid balls of fire! We're Sierra Charlies, not a regimental warbot assault team! We shouldn't be fighting this type of battle, pinned down and unable to move. The Colonel must know this. So we're being pulled back to maneuver, which we're good at." He keyed his personal tacomm, "Companion Alpha, this is Companion Leader." Silence.

Curt repeated his call.

Still silence.

"Let me plug into your ACV system. Maybe my personal unit's gone dead," he suggested, then did so and repeated the call to his maneuvering platoon.

Still no answer.

"Has he been hit?" Alexis suddenly asked anxiously.

"No, we'd have heard from Sampson if he had been." Curt replied. "His tacomm is out. Can you see Allen or any of his troops on radar?"

"Negative!" Alexis replied. "The foliage is too thick. No penetration."

"Damned millimeter-wave stuff!" Curt cursed the super-high-frequency radar. Longer wavelengths might not have been diffracted by trees and undergrowth. Curt hoisted his FABARMA rifle to sling it over his shoulder. "I've got to find him and get him back here. Henry, want to come?"

"Hell yes."

"Lieutenant, can I borrow Sergeant Gerard?"

"In this static situation, I can spare him. My squad leaders are doing a fine job with their warbots."

"Good! Call him in. Five minutes. When we're out there, I'll leave my tacomm in spotting mode; follow it on your tac display and give me covering fire and a directional fix if necessary. I've got to find our wandering platoon and its native guide—"

"Without getting shot in the process, please," Lt. Alexis Morgan advised. "This area's got a high pucker factor. Lots of stuff flying through the air."

"As long as it flies, I don't care. When it stops flying and hits something, I worry a lot. . ."

CHAPTER NINETEEN

It was going to be deadly out there.

"Lieutenant Allen doesn't answer on his personal tacomm unit," Curt explained when Platoon Sgt. Nick Gerard joined them in Morgan's ACV.

"Which probably means that he's been hit," Gerard surmised quickly.

"Or just that his tacomm unit went toes-up," M. Sgt. Henry Kester added from a more pragmatic viewpoint.

"Or both," Capt. Curt Carson told them. "If it's equipment probs, we'd better make damned sure our own stuff works. And if mine goes out, we'll use one of yours as backup."

"I think we'd better count on it crapping out," Kester advised him.

"But these units are supposed to meet pretty tight specs," Nick Gerard pointed out.

"Nick, mil specs are the tightest requirements you can find, but they're either grossly overdone or neglect to cover some important factor," Kester told him. "For the last twenty years, the Army hasn't operated in anything but desert climates, Europe, and eastern Asia. We haven't fought in the tropics since Panama. Sometime look at the mil specs, and you'll see this stands out all over them. Our tacomm units have been slowly

179

going belly-up ever since we got to St. Thomas. Trinidad has accelerated the deterioration."

"What the hell is doing it?" Gerard wondered.

"Molds. Fungus," Kester told him.

"Fungus? Where the hell does that come from?"

"Everywhere. That stuff us all around us all the time," Kester pointed out. "There's always spores and crap that gets in during manufacture because the parts can't be kept in clean rooms all the time. And tacomms can't be totally sealed. So put 'em in an environment like this where it's warm and wet . . . and them little beasties grow like crazy. Fungus actually causes rust and eats the equipment."

"Eats it?"

"Yeah, in Panama we used to find the stuff actually feeding on the plastic boards and enclosures. The stuff will eat right through these plastic cases. Then the humidity and more fungus gets in and *blooey,* you've lost your high-tech electronic gear . . ."

"But you said something about fungus causing rust," Nick objected. "Rust is nothing but iron oxide!"

"Nope. Otherwise it would form an oxide film on the surface the way aluminum does," Kester tried to explain. "Rust just keeps right on eating through iron, and that's because of a fungus."

"So, as our company tropical deterioriation specialist and expert on moldy stuff, got any ideas about what to do, Sergeant Science?" Curt wanted to know.

"Yessir. Take two tacomms with us. Three if we've got 'em. If one craps out, use another."

Gerard rummaged through the equipment cabinents of Bravo Platoon's ACV. "We've got two spares."

"That's better than none," Kester said.

"Set up the existing hop code and sequence," Curt told Gerard, "and we'll take them."

"Yessir." Gerard slipped each in a slot in a piece of equipment and punched the "Code Set" button. In thirty seconds, the green light flashed, indicating each of the small transceiver units had been set up with the existing secure frequency hopping code and sequence.

"Okay, final check," Curt remarked. "Personal weapons?"

"Ready," Kester said briefly, looking down at his FABARMA rifle.

"Cleaned and hot to trot," said Gerard.

"Six fifty-round clips?"

"Yo!"

"Got 'em."

"Six plastex grenades?"

"Yo!"

"Strapped on."

"Night vision sensor?"

"Ready and battery checked."

"Ready."

"Infra red laser targeting unit?"

"On the FARARMA and working."

"And bore-sighted."

"Body armor?"

"On and adjusted."

"On, adjusted, and uncomfortable."

"Helmet tactical display?"

"Checked."

"It works."

"Tacomm unit?"

"One plus a spare."

"Got it."

"And I've got the other spare. Potable water?"

"One liter."

"Likewise."

"Bug repellent?"

"Damned right!"

181

"Good thing the Tee-dads don't have chem sensors yet."

"Don't count on it," Kester warned.

"Hell, this place smells worse than the insect screen . . ."

"Robot?"

"The jeep's checked, power packs charged, ammo replenished, voice print recognition unit set to our voices," Kester reported. "It responds to the handle 'Black Jack.' "

"Pershing?"

Kester shook his head. "Nope. You were probably so busy you didn't get the chance to pay a little visit to the casinos in St. George while we were in the Vee-Eye, Captain. I named it because if any of us get stuck out there, it's going to take a push . . ."

"That's a hell of a bad pun, Sergeant."

"Sorry, sir. And it's technically not a pun. It's a simile."

"Captain, lemme take one of our Hairy Foxes for covering fire," Gerard requested.

"Have you set foot outside?" Curt asked. "It isn't soft. It squishes. And out where Lieutenant Allen and Alpha Platoon are likely to be, we'll probably be up to our necks in water standing in goo. A Hairy Fox would sink clear down to China."

"You mean we won't?"

"Not if you watch what you're stepping in," Curt advised him, then added, "By the way, there's no way for you to replenish your ammo once you're out there in a fire fight. Nick, I seem to recall that you were rather loose and free with the expenditure of ammo in some of our survivalist games and Grey Flag. This time when you get shot at, don't waste ammo by spraying the whole damned surrounding countryside."

"Yeah," Kester added sagely, "and don't play it

safe by hitting the dirt. That means you've lost forward momentum and the enemy can keep you pinned down. Shoot back from the hip in the general direction of the incoming stuff and keep moving. Keep the enemy on the scared list by continuing to fire, which makes him keep *his* head down! And if you hear one of the Tee-dad one-oh-sixes come into the trees above you, don't grab for gravel, either; you're less of a target if you're standing up.''

"Thanks for reminding me," Curt told his master sergeant. "I'd forgotten that bit of combat lore . . .''

"Hell, Captain, I'm a walking damned encyclopedia of it," Kester said lightly with a grin, betraying the fact that the grizzled old veteran was no cooler than anyone else before a combat patrol.

"Well, I figure you've got to have some redeeming virtue, Henry, or someone would have busted you years ago . . .''

"Oh, that happened from time to time when I was younger and a bit more likely to tell a stupid superior to go piss up a rope . . .''

"I hadn't noticed you'd changed . . .''

"Well, nowadays when I get a stupid order, I salute and go do it the way it shoulda been done in the first place . . .'' Kester admitted. "If I'm wrong, I just say I didn't understand the order. If I'm right, the brass takes the credit anyway. So—''

"So, okay, let's move out. We've got about two hours of daylight left, and it'll be harder than hell to find Alpha Platoon in a dark swamp," Curt said, breaking up the pre-fight humor. "Black Jack will be on point because it's got good i-rand chem sensors. I'll be five meters of less behind it. Henry, take the left flank. Nick on the right. Five meter interval. Don't lose sight of me or Black Jack." He stuck his head into the forward command compartment of the ACV and called to Lieutenant Morgan, "Alexis, monitor our ta-comms. We're going to keep open mikes."

"Be careful what you say, Captain" she shot back. "I'll be taping it."

"Still no radar contact?"

"Negative, Captain."

"Do you have a bearing on Jerry's last transmissions?"

"Try zero-eight-zero. He's out there somewhere. And, according to his last report, he shouldn't be more than about fifteen hundred meters away. The rivers sort of limit how far he can go. Those Mary Anns of his sure won't float, and I doubt that he or his troops will either, carrying all the gear they had with them when they left their ACV . . ."

It had been raining. The usual afternoon thundershower was over, but it left the foliage dripping with water and the ground under foot soggy and wet. The humidity was oppressive. Curt began to sweat under his soft body armor and with the cammy grease and insect screen on his exposed flesh. It was like stepping into a steam bath. A musty smell pervaded the air.

"Spread out!" Curt ordered. "Forward!"

"Think the Tee-dads have any patrols out, Captain?" Gerard asked.

"Maybe. Listen!"

There was the sound of sporadic firing ahead and to the left. There would be the popping of a short burst of 5.56mm rifle fire followed alomst immediately by the ripping sound of a 20mm or 50mm burst from a warbot aiming at the sound and flash of the small arms fire. Occasionally, there would be a ripping return fire from the near left where someone, probably Morgan's squad leaders themselves, were returning close-in fire.

It was typical jungle warfare in mangrove and bamboo swampland where the footing was always soft and in many places wet. The bugs were fierce; it would have been nearly impossible for Curt and his two sergeants to make any headway at all against the mosquitoes, little black gnats, and buzzing flies if it hadn't been for the insect screen they were wearing. Curt could no longer smell it on his body, but that was only because the initial volatiles that could be detected by humans had evaporated; the insects could smell what was left, and they didn't like it. In addition, the insect screen cut down the specific infra red radiations from the human body that attracted mosquitoes.

About an hour later with the sunlight beginning to fade in the west, they'd covered about 700 meters. They found nothing.

"It's getting wetter and wetter underfoot, Captain," Nick Gerard reported on the open-mike tacomm channel. "I'm having trouble staying out of water deeper than my waist."

"Yeah, Black Jack's been in up to its sensors a couple of times," Curt reported.

"Captain," M. Sgt. Henry Kester said, "Lieutenant Allen and Alpha Platoon didn't come this far."

"What brings you to that conclusion, Henry?"

"He had Mary Anns with him. Twelve of them. They ain't jeeps like Black Jack. They would have bogged down by this time," Kester explained.

"You're probably right," Curt told him. He glanced upward at the miniature tactical display on the inside of his helmet brow. In spite of the dampness, it was still working. From their present position, there wasn't much except mangrove and bamboo swamp with more water to the southeast where the Lagoon River turned southward.

"Swing to the left," Curt decided. "We'll work downstream toward the road and the center of fighting."

"You don't want to cross the river, Captain?" Gerard asked.

"Negative! Alpha couldn't have done it with Mary Anns. We haven't located any Mary Anns, so they didn't abandon their warbots and proceed across on foot. I don't want to get on the other side of this creek and find myself being shot at by our own troops. Alpha *has* to be to our left!"

"Better let me lead by twenty meters or so," Kester suggested. "The Tee-dads are on my side of this patrol, and I want to watch for zones of beaten fire."

"Do it," Curt told him. "Nick, you concentrate your search to the left. I'll concentrate forward."

They progressed through water and mud for about a hundred meters when rifle fire opened up ahead and to the left. Curt ducked behind a mangrove, but the line of fire was across their front from left to right.

"Kester? Did that hit you?" Curt asked anxiously.

"No, sir. Came close! It cut right through the underbrush. Seven millimeter stuff! Our Sierra Charlie stuff! But I'm in water up to my neck to stay below it."

"I've spotted it!" Sgt. Nick Gerard's report came in. "Tell Black Jack to look at about two-eighty magnetic!"

Curt passed the command verbally to the general purpose warbot whose turret swivelled around quickly to bring sensors into a search pattern.

"Give them another target, Henry!"

"Like hell, Captain! Not me! But give me ten second to toss my canteen up!"

In a few seconds, another burst of rifle fire cut through the mangroves.

"I have a target," Black Jack announced in flat tones. "Bearing two-seven-seven magnetic, left of line of advance, range thirty-four meters, a rifleman behind

186

a tree accompanied by two more humans. No visual contact. Infra red contact only."

"Dammit, it's probably Alpha Platoon! We've worked our way in front of them! They must think we're Tee-dads!" He raised his voice to call in a parade ground thrust of vocal energy, "Allen! Carson here! Cease fire!"

A short silence followed, then came the call, "Allen here! Stand by! We're sending scouts to check you out!"

"No tacomm?" Curt called back.

"No tacomm," Allen's voice confirmed.

"Human presence, same bearing, ten meters and closing slowly. Carrying a rifle," Black Jack reported.

There was a glint of failing sunlight on a shining piece of metal.

"Hold fire," Curt snapped, knowing that he was taking a chance, albeit a small one because he had a hunch he knew what the glint was.

He was glad he took that chance.

CHAPTER TWENTY

Adonica Sweet appeared stealthily around a mangrove, her stainless steel Mini-14 at the ready. She was soaking wet from head to toe, a fact which made her already skimpy clothing cling to her body.

"What the hell are you doing out here, and why haven't you reported back?" Curt asked her.

Adonica waved her right hand violently to silence him, then crept the rest of the way to come alongside him. "You may have put us in danger," she whispered to him. "We've been stalking a Tee-dad patrol and being stalked by them for about two hours. They're out there about where M. Sgt. Henry Kester is."

"Damn!" Curt swore and then spoke into his tacomm, "Companion Bravo Leader, do you read Companion Leader?"

"Roger, Companion Leader, but you're garbled."

"Damn again!" Curt took the standby tacomm unit out of his pocket and plugged it in. "Bravo Leader, is this better?"

"Roger! Five by! Got you located!"

"We have enemy patrol action reported. Stand by to provide some support fire."

"Roger! I can lay in the Saucy Cans firing with at high quadrant angles as mortars."

"Hold fire until I can give you target coordinates,"

Curt told her. He then turned to Adonica. "Where's the Tee-dad patrol now?"

She pointed. "About fifty meters out that way, we think."

"Kester," Curt told his master sergeant on the tacomm, "a retrograde action, please. You're probably going to come under enemy fire if you stay where you are."

"I'm well hidden," came Kester's voice in Curt's helmet. "Lemme stay and ambush them. I haven't fired or broken silence. They don't know I'm here. On the other hand, I don't have a visual on them, either."

"Mag bearing about three-three-zero, maybe thirty meters," Curt advised him.

"Wet and swampy out there. Can't see anything."

"Nick, join me" Curt told his other NCO. "Adonica, stay here. You may be shot if you try to get back."

"Not me," she replied confidently and suddenly disappeared quickly and silently into the bamboo grove to Curt's left.

He would have chewed her out the next time he saw her if she'd been one of his troops, but she was a civilian and their native guide. However, this didn't keep Curt from having an overwhelming urge to paddle her fanny for her refusal to follow orders.

Nick joined him. "What's the sit, Captain?"

"We may either initiate a frontal attack on a Tee-dad patrol, or we may catch them on their left flank if they move against Allen who's over to our left by about fifty meters," Curt explained. "Black Jack, search and identify, mag bearings two-seven-zero through three-six-zero; anticipate several humans carrying rifles proceeding either toward us or across our front from right to left."

"Searching!" Black Jack immediately began to swivel its upper turrets and look through the jungle

189

with radar, infra red laser ranging, passive infra red, visual sensors, and chemical sensors.

"Nick, keep down and ready to shoot. Kester's in defilade up to our right."

"Roger." The NCO checked his plastex grenades.

Whang! Clang! Whang!

A burst of three 5.56mm rifle rounds bounced of Black Jack's hard frontal armor. The muffled sound of the rifle they came from followed.

"Target, bearing two-eight-one, eleven meters!" Black Jack reported.

"Shoot it!" Curt told it.

When Curt saw where Black Jack's 20mm round tore through the mangrove thicket, he pointed his FA-BARMA.

A body crashed forward through the thicket with a scream, followed by the form of a second soldier carrying a rifle at the ready.

The man was still behind a lot of foliage, enough to tumble a 5.56mm round. But a single round from Nick Gerard's 7.62mm FABARMA penetrated the thick vegetation and caught the Tee-dad neatly in the chest.

"Six targets! Follow my fire!" came Henry Kester's voice over the tacomm followed by rapid rifle fire to Curt's right front.

Black Jack swivelled again. "Bearing two-eight-four, twenty-five meters," the robot reported.

"Commence firing!" Curt snapped, adjusting his sights accordingly and bringing the FABARMA into firing position against his shoulder and right cheek.

A violent fire fight began.

The survivalist war games and Grey Flag should have alerted Curt to the fact that most fire fights are extremely intense and also very short. The air was full of projectiles snapping and buzzing and whining overhead accompanied by the sound of ricochets.

About forty seconds after it started—a time period that seemed like forty hours to Curt—he noticed that the enemy fire had slacked off.

"Companions!" Curt called both in the clear and on tacomm. "Forward! Marching fire!"

Gerard didn't understand what his company commander was doing. The idea of standing up, revealing one's self, and marching toward the enemy position while firing from the hip seemed suicidal. "Captain! You'll be hit!"

"Like hell!" Curt called and fired a three-round burst in the direction of the Tee-dads. "They can't shoot if I'm making them keep their heads down!"

"We're wasting ammo!"

"Ammo's cheaper than lives! It'll take eighteen years to make your replacement; we'll get more ammo from the logistics replenishment tonight!"

Motivated by his commanding officer's example, Gerard joined Curt and Black Jack, firing as they moved forward among and around the mangrove roots and trunks.

Curt passed the two Tee-dads who'd been the first casualties of the fire fight. Curt didn't stop to check them, but they didn't move and were either dead or positively out of the fight. He did kick the SAR-80 assault rifle and Mekanika Uru submachinegun out of their potential reach and into the water.

Kester appeared on the right, soaking wet and slipping a new fifty-round clip into his FABARMA.

"Your ammo all right?" Curt asked.

Kester nodded and began firing again. "Caseless stuff is just like brass rounds. It don't get wet and fizzle if the coating hasn't been scratched."

No more firing came from in front of them in the general direction of the Tee-dad patrol.

A glint of metal on the left caused Gerard to swing.

"Hold fire! That's Alpha!" Curt shouted.

"Yo," came Jerry Allen's voice, shortly followed by his appearance around a bamboo grove accompanied by Adonica whose glinting stainless steel Mini-14 rifle barrel had caught the sunset light.

"Keep it up! Maintain contact! Let's go!" Curt exorted his troops. He stepped off through the shallow water, firing three-round bursts with the butt of his FABARMA halfway between his shoulder and hip. Allen, Adonica, Edie Sampson, and Corporals Jim Elliott and Charlie Koslowski appeared and formed a skirmish line with Curt.

"Where are your Mary Anns?" Curt called out to his lieutenant.

"Two out of action and the rest unable to follow us through this swamp," Jerry Allen replied. "I can call on them for fire support if need be . . ."

"Adonica, get the hell out of this! Get back behind the warbots!" Curt yelled at her.

She didn't reply, caught on to what Curt and the rest of the Companions were doing, and slogged forward with them through the mud and water, firing her Mini-14 from her hip.

They came upon three more dead Tee-dads. Adonica stopped firing long enough to kick their Mekanica Uru 9mm submachine guns and bandoliers of clips into deep water to one side.

"Companion Leader, this is Companion Bravo!" came the voice of Alexis Morgan on Curt's tacomm. "We detect no targets for you on this side of the river. And you're just about to the river itself . . ."

"Damn! I'd never know it!"

"Companion Leader, this is Companion Bravo. Orders: Break off the pursuit! Return to the ACP."

"Whose orders?" Curt shot back.

"Grey Head."

192

"What does she know about this?"

"She's here in my ACP. Has been since a few minutes after you left, Captain."

"Shit!" Curt muttered under his breath in frustration. He and the Companions were advancing, and he hated to give up the momentum of the advance that they'd worked hard to achieve. On the other hand, if the Lagoon River—more of a wide and swampy creek—were indeed right in front of him, he might get across but without his company warbots. Although his unit had just been blooded in personal combat, he wasn't so sure he wanted to put them in a position where they were forced to continue solo without even the limited fire support of the Alpha Mary Anns, wherever Allen had stashed them in stand-by. The 20mm on Black Jack wasn't enough powerful enough to count as heavy fire support, and the jeep might not make it across the river if it turned out to be too deep. Curt knew he'd fired off four of his clips, and others might have even less ammo than he did. Furthermore, sunset was upon them, and they'd be facing an unknown enemy on the other side of the river in growing darkness.

Hettrick was right. Time to pack it in, Curt decided. "Companion Bravo, give us a dee-eff and a line of march,"

Curt requested.

"Companion Leader, say again. You're broken."

Damn! The standby tacomm unit was crapping out on him. "Kester, give me your standby tacomm!"

Kester held up the little plastic box. Water was draining out of it. "Sorry, Captain, I couldn't keep it dry, and something obviously corroded the case."

So Curt toggled his tacomm unit again and said slowly and clearly, "Bravo, dee-eff. Dee-eff."

"Roger! Got dee-eff. Mag bearing zero-four-five, range four-oh-five meters."

"Coming home!" Curt replied, checked his compass, and set up the reciprocal. "Heading two-two-five! Move out!"

They looked like a bedraggled unit of riff-raff by the time they got back to the Bravo command post vehicle about thirty-five minutes later. But the small arms and artillery fire at the bridgehead had fallen off to an occasional brief exchange between a Tee-dad and a Hairy Fox warbot.

Both Col. Belinda Hettrick and Lt. Alexis Morgan greeted them in the ring of warm light that surrounded the ACV. Curt was about to reprimand Morgan for lighting up the place and thus providing a possibly inviting target for Tee-dad artillery or even patrol action when his platoon leader remarked, "Sentinels and outposts established, Captain. We'll have plenty of warning of any Tee-dad activity."

"And the Marauders are in position to provide supressing fire. The Warriors and Killers are replenishing," Hettrick added.

"Lieutenant Allen, that was a magnificent job you did out there finding and holding that Tee-dad patrol. And, Captain Carson, you and your Companions carried out a very valorous rescue attempt and topped it off with the destruction of that Tee-dad patrol. But, my God, you look like you've been dragged through the manure pile!"

"Kinda feel that way, too, Colonel," Curt admitted. He was suddenly very tired.

"Lieutenant Morgan, tell my aide to have logistics bring up fresh uniforms, fresh socks, fresh everything."

"And a biotech," Jerry Allen added. "Adonica's been hit."

"What? Where? Why the hell didn't you tell me?" Curt exploded. He didn't notice until right at that mo-

194

ment that Adonica was being partly supported by Allen and Edie Sampson.

"In that last advance, I got nicked by a five-millimeter riccochet in the fleshy part of my thigh when I went back to report to Jerry that I'd found you," Adonica Sweet admitted, checking a piece of synflesh that someone in Alpha Platoon had obviously applied to the wound. "It's just a scratch. I'll be all right."

"Don't believe her," Allen broke in. "That's got to hurt like hell."

Adonica nodded and sat down on the ground. "It does. But it's not a serious wound."

"A wound's a wound, sweetie," Edie Sampson told her. "This dressing's wet. Here, let me change it. Nick, get me a fresh emergency biopack out of your ACV. I'll need the aesepsis equipment, too. This place crawls with slimy things . . ."

"Especially something called gangrene if a wound's not properly cleaned," M. Sgt. Henry Kester put in, "Captain, this place crawls with slimy things like that. Speaking of slimy things, we need to strip out of these wet clothes now and check each other over for parasites. Check *everywhere!* Which is why everybody checks everybody else."

"Morgan," Curt called to his senior platoon officer, take Sampson and Adonica into the ACV where they can strip down. Check them. The rest of us, down to skin, right now. What are we looking for, Henry?"

"Leeches, especially the little ones. Snails. Anything that shouldn't be on you. Tropics are full of stuff like that. Trinidad's no different . . ."

Curt was glad to get out of his wet clothes. He found a tiny black leech about three centimeters long on his right thigh, and another one on his left calf. Kester had similar parasites, but Gerard, Allen, Elliott, and Koslowski also had little snails on their legs and lower torsos. Where it was impossible to pull them off with fingrnails, solvent and alcohol killed them and got them to turn loose of the skin.

It wasn't a pleasant episode.

The supply van showed up while they were completing this job, and everyone had donned fresh uniforms within a few minutes. To Curt, it felt good to get out of his wet boots and socks, to say nothing of the cammy uniform that he'd worn for several days. It was beginning to get a bit raunchy.

When the women came out of the ACV, Adonica was wearing a loose cammy coverall that Curt decided didn't do for her what the khaki cutoffs and white cotton halter had. But, on ther other hand, she was less of an obvious target now. She limped a bit on her leg, but otherwise seemed unaffected by her wound.

Jerry Allen was all over her like a rug, being supersolicitous, especially when the second supply van pulled up with hot meals.

It was standard field rations. But, after a day in combat, they tasted good, and Curt discovered that being shot at also stimulates hunger.

"What about the tactical meeting? It's nineteen hundred hours now," Curt pointed out to Hettrick as he sat next to her while they consumed their meals.

"Postponed two hours."

"Where, Colonel?"

"My ACV about a kilometer to the rear alongside the Southern Main Road. We'll leave here in about thirty minutes."

"Let me get my company bedded down first, Colonel. It's been a rough day."

"That it has. But that's why you've got your platoon leaders and M. Sgt. Kester. They can see to your NCOs and squad leaders."

Curt didn't try to argue or even remark further. In

battle, it was the duty of the senior officers to come to the juniors in combat, but the obligation of junior officers to come to the senior officer's commpand post for planning and operational briefings.

"And, Captain, I suggest you remind your company that this is a combat zone and Rule Ten is *definitely* in effect right now," Hettrick went on.

"I need to," Curt remarked.

"I've noticed," Hettrick said. "Please pay special attention to Lieutenant Allen."

"I will, but what's the actual status of Adonica Sweet?" Curt wanted to know.

"Civilian contractor, I think."

"Colonel, you'd better brevet her to third lieutenant," Curt advised, referring to the temporary rank assigned to West Point cadets when they joined a regular Army outfit during summer maneuvers.

"I'm not sure I can do that."

Curt sighed. "If you don't, I see trouble brewing."

"So do I. Let's put it this way, Captain: If Lieutenant Allen busts Rule Ten, I'd better not learn about it . . ."

There were times when Col. Belinda Hettrick was all female, very desireable, and very willing, but this wasn't one of them. In spite of the fact that Curt had been shot at that day and was therefore experiencing the usual post-combat horny syndrome, he realized that Hettrick probably was experiencing the same thing but was subliminating it with enormous will power. Few warbot brainies of the RI were married except to other RI personnel because of both the intensity of the post-combat syndrome in robot warfare and the power of Rule Ten. Had this been a war game instead of an honest-to-God shooting war, Hettrick herself might have been radiating a bit of coyness, even during an evening break. But Curt could see that tonight she was a colonel and all colonel with a full regiment as her responsibility. That was occupying her total existence.

Curt knew from his own experience—and it was renewed this evening—that there was a great deal of truth in the old adage about the "loneliness of command."

He really didn't want to remind Lt. Jerry Allen about Rule Ten. It applied to Curt as well.

CHAPTER TWENTY-ONE

It was all business in Col. Belinda Hettrick's Armored Command Vehicle, a bus-sized mass of armor and tracks and turrets from which sprouted various antennas, comm dishes, and light weapons. The main and largest compartment in the ACV normally used as the regimental command post during combat was filled with eight linkage couches and six bio-tech stations. The various AI computers and intellgence amplifiers, linkage transceivers, and associated electronics were tucked in racks and small compartments around the room.

It had been a very long time since a regimental commander had held a face-to-face regimental planning meeting under combat conditions. It hadn't been necessary in the past when all the Robot Infantry company commanders were in linkage under normal RI procedures during which a staff or planning meeting could be carried out without anyone leaving their respective command posts.

But being the first regiment to work the new and experimental Sierra Charlie doctrine brought with it some unorthodox operational procedures. Not everyone was used to them yet, not the least of whom was Col. Belinda Hettrick.

The commanders of the six companies of the Washington Greys—the four combat companies, the headquarters company, and the service company—were there. The commanders of the combat companies had just come out of an all-day session of linkage except Capt. Curt Carson of Carson's Companions. Manny Garcia and Samantha Walker looked and felt decidedly uneasy as all of them sat around on the linkage couches. This was new, different, and difficult to assimilate or evaluate for the regular warbot brainy officers.

Eight people made the compartment a little crowded although the environmental control system did a reasonably good job lowering the temperature and humidity to livable levels.

Curt Carson didn't say anything, but Capt. Martin Kelly did, as usual, even though the regimental commander was present. "Well, Carson," came the little man's raspy, irritable, and pugnacious remark, "why the hell couldn't your vaunted Sierra Charlies break through the Tee-dad river crossing defenses? Whatsa matter? No guts to make a frontal attack?"

When he was met with silence, he looked quickly around, seeking support from some of the other company commanders who'd been forced to break off an advance and seek roadside cover when Carson's Companions ran up against the Tee-dad defenses six hours ago.

"Captain Kelly, let me remind you," said Col. Belinda Hettrick with a slight touch of reprimand in her voice, "that the Companions were under such intense fire that they couldn't disengage and I couldn't bring one of the warbot companies forward through the fire support positions occupied by Walker's Warriors. As it was, all of you should know that the Companions attempted on their own initiative to make a swing around the right flank and were stopped by water and extremely bad footing. Frontal attacks aren't condoned by the Sierra Charlie doctrine; that's where warbots are used. But, even at that, none of you could have gotten your warbots through there. As it was, Carson's, people accompanied by their command warbots penetrated deeper than we thought possible. And they stopped a Tee-dad combat patrol in the bargain.''

''While the rest of us sat around and twiddled our warbots,'' Kelly added.

Capt. Marty Kelly was a cross Hettrick had to bear. Basically, he needed to be taught table manners and not to mess on the carpet. But he and his company were aggressive and tenacious fighters; they'd cleared out Point Fortin in far less time than Hettrick had estimated they could, taking nearly a hundred Tee-dad prisoners to boot. Kelly's Killers was a maverick outfit; no other regiment in the 17th Iron Fist wanted them because they were so difficult to control. But Hettrick had been saddled with them and had therefore been forced to work out a method of keeping Marty Kelly on somewhat of a leash. This she normally did by a method that was frowned upon in all the leadership manuals: She reprimanded and criticized Kelly in front of the other regimental officers because Kelly had not responded to private reprimands and criticism.

''Captain, shut up and listen; you might learn smoething,'' Hettrick snapped at him in a vexed tone, then went on, ''It's true that we've encountered a stalemate. Any time an engagement or fire fight at the platoon or company level doesn't resolve itself one way or the other within six hours, prolonging the effort puts too much strain on a company and leads to a waste of manpower, usually in the form of casualties even in full robot warfare where the hazard of KIA still exists. Frontal attacks never work worth a damn anyway. And when we can't hold them with fire and move around their flanks to their rear, it's time to change plans.

They've been changed for us. Captain Hampton," she remarked to her chief of staff, "will you please bring everyone up to date on the total situation as it presently stands?"

The tall, thin chief of the regimental staff with his thin black mustache and shaved head got up and taped a map of Trinidad to the bulkhead. "Sorry we don't have room for a holographic projection in here, but we're all learning new things and we have to go back to some of the old ways. I haven't got time to give you a crash course in map reading, so I presume all of you remember enough about what you were taught at West Point or OCS."

He picked up a long sliver of bamboo apparently cut from one of the groves outside. Using it as a pointer, he indicated the map as he went on, "Here's the current situation: On the southwestern front, we're stalled at the point where the Southern Main Road crosses the Oropuche-Lagoon River; two companies of the Fourth Tee-dad Regiment from San Fernando are defending. As you know, the swamps along the rivers make it difficult if not impossible to move warbots or assault vehicles around the right flank.

"The other regiments have had a straight shot thus far. The Can Do has taken Siparia and is coming up Siparia Road to our right rear.

"The Wolfhounds took Sadhoowa on schedule and are currently engaging two companies of the Fourth Regiment north of Penal where Erin Road crosses the Oropuche River just east of what's left of the Napirima Air Base; the Wolfhounds are expected to take Debe and the Air Base shortly after dawn tomorrow. That will give us a badly needed heavy air logistics base.

"The Cottonbalers have taken Basse Terre and will occupy Princes Town by dawn tomorrow.

"In the meantime, Operation Bass Boom has come

off on schedule. We were told of this only a few hours ago. The Twenty-second Double Deuces are ashore along the Gulf of Paria from Pointe-a-Pierre to Waterloo against little opposition. By noon tomorrow, they should be astride the Solomon Hochoy main highway between San Fernando and Port of Spain and engaging elements of the Third and Fourth Regiments.

"The Tee-dad tacair was destroyed on the ground at Napirima along with the coastal defense squadron. The Tee-dad transport squadron has a few aerodynes left at Piarco, and all but four or five of their Diamante interceptors remain operational. Basically, we can forget about Tee-dad air. When the Wolfhounds take Napirima tomorrow and the Air Force can begin using it as a base, we'll have absolute air superiority . . . which is not as important as it may seem in this environment, by the way, because the heavy vegetation hides things, even the roads.

"Oh, and by the way, don't worry about the Tee-dad artillery battalion. The Air Force creamed Port George on schedule this afternoon. And the Navy put the Tee-dad coastal defense forces on the bottom of the Dragon's Mouths. So this is going to be an Army show from now on," Hampton said proudly.

Now things begin to make sense! Curt thought. *The operational picture is beginning to fill in!*

"The Tee-dads have been reacting more or less as anticipated," Hampton went on. "Recon indicates that the Third Regiment moved southward out of Chaguanas shortly before noon, probably with the intention of reinforcing the Fourth Regiment around San Fernando. Latest recon indicates they've reacted to the landing of the Double Deuces on their right flank and have turned to move north and east. The Double Deuces anticipate encountering substaintial resistance from this Tee-dad regiment tomorrow morning. The

Fifth Regiment started moving westward out of Rio Claro along Mayaro Road at about fifteen hundred hours this afternoon either to reinforce the RI Fourth or to hit the right flank of the Cottonbalers moving north. However, late recon indicates they've turned right and are moving northeast up Tabaquite Road. The Second Regiment is still in Sangre Grande and the Presidential Guard remains in Port of Spain.

"As for the latest guess concerning the Tee-dad movements, it's apparent the Tee-dad high command is becoming aware of the extent of the forces being brought against them. Right now, it's two RI divisions against four of their regular infantry regiments plus their special forces battalion—which we think is still in Arima—and their engineer battalion, which probably got creamed during the Double Deuces landing at Pointe-a-Pierre. And they've still got their elite, part-warbot Presidential Guard which will undoubtedly be used to protect General Drake and the other military government personnel.

"What will the Tee-dads do? It's the best divisional sit-guess that the Tee-dads will retreat north and east to hold Port of Spain and the east-west built-up complex lying between the North Range and the Central Range of mountains. We've hit with such fury and zeal that they probably don't realize they outnumber us about two to one in combat effectives at this moment.

"Any questions?" Captain Hampton looked around.

"Yes," Samantha Walker spoke up. "Is this it? Any other forces due to come ashore?"

"We don't know," Hampton admitted. "Operation Steel Band has very tight security."

"Probably send in a company of expatriates formed on another island to capture Port of Spain and get all the glory," Marty Kelly muttered, "while we slog it out in the mud and water down here."

"Not exactly, Captain Kelly," Hettrick told him. "Thank you, Wade. Now I'm going to tell all of you what we've been told to do. Orders from division and maybe from higher than that. Listen up because we're going to get our butts out of this stalemate and shag-ass fast . . . like we're supposed to do.

CHAPTER TWENTY-TWO

Col. Belinda Hettrick turned to the map of Trinidad taped to the bulkhead and indicated what she was talking about as she spoke. "The Fifteenth Robot Infantry, the Can Do Regiment, under Colonel Walker Armistead will relieve us on this line tonight. They're a regular RI unit with the mass and firepower we haven't got because of our Sierra Charlie status. Okay, you all aren't Sierra Charlie companies yet, but we're more mobile than a standard RI regiment. About midnight, give or take thirty minutes, the Can Do warbots and vehicles will show up and dovetail into our positions. Be prepared to withdraw as Armistead's units show up. They'll move two warbot companies into the line tonight while we withdraw down Siparia Road to San Francique Road. Looks like we're not going to get very much sleep, but that's normal for combat operations. So I want you to be sure your troops are as rested as possible in spite of all this movement. Tomorrow, we sweep eastward fast, the Companions on recon, the Killers on point, the Warriors as fire support, the Marauders as rear guard and reserve.

"And, Kelly, if I get anything out of you other than compliance with orders and requests for information, I'll put you in the ass-end position," Hettrick warned her battle-eager Captain, anticipating Kelly's reaction

206

to plaing second fiddle to his competition. "So you'll follow Carson, and you'd better figure on shagging your butt to maintain contact with him; his Sierra Charlies move fast, as Sam Walker will tell you."

"Listen to the colonel," Capt. Samantha Walker agreed. "We didn't catch our breath until Curt ran up against the Tee-dads at the river."

"Rendezvous and sort out our column along San Francique Road tonight at a village called Pluck," Hettrick went on. "At dawn, we move out through Penal. We'll be moving laterally to the rear and the right flank of the Wolfhounds and the Cottonbalers, and we should meet no enemy resistance. Our first objective is Devil's Woodyard east of Princes Town by noon tomorrow. What we do and where we go tomorrow afternoon depends on the tactical situation then. We may swing north to get behind the Tee-dad Third, Fourth, and Fifth Regiments—what may be left of them by that time. Or if those regiments move into the hills above Tabaquite and Navet Dam, we may keep going east to Rio Claro and swing north to Sangre Grande." She indicated the route on the map taped to the bulkhead. "Our job is to be where they ain't and cut off any possible Tee-dad retreat into more difficult terrain and better defensive positions. If we run into Tee-dad forces, Kelly holds them in place, the Warriors act as light artillery, and the Companions maneuver around them. A lot of secondary roads can be used to flank them and cut them off. Depend on your native guides for directions. But if they don't know the roads, switch to your maps, which may not be totally accurate. Comments? Questions?"

Curt waved his hand and reported, "Colonel, our tacomm units have been going toes-up in this environment. My company has only three operable units left. We don't know when the bigger units in our vehicles might go bad, too. Supply may have to replace the tacomm units along with our ammunition and fuel ever day . . ."

"Captain Otis, can they be field-repaired?" Hettrick asked her maintenance section officer.

"Don't know, Colonel," Capt. Elwood Otis told her frankly. "We're capable only of lowest level field repair and maintenance, and this is the first I've heard about the tacomm units going bad. What's the problem?"

"Fungus," Curt explained.

Capt. Elwood Otis shook his head. "Orgasmic! Well, that's out of my league. Harriet, looks like you've got a supply problem . . ."

Lt. Harriet Dearborn of the supply section also shook her head. "Ammo, fuel, food, and the usual basic warbot maintenance parts and supplies are coming through according to logistical plan. But no replacement tacomm units are in the supply pipeline right now. Never considered we'd need them, what with the level of backups on hand. However, I'll get on it right away, Colonel. Please be advised, everyone, that it may take a day or so to get new tacomm units into the logistical pipeline."

"Do your best," Hettrick told her. "In the meantime, we'll use warbots as messengers carrying written messages, reports, and orders. Or use warbots in direct linkage mode to act as your surrogates on site. Or use the normal warbot linkage networks because those are redundant, fail-safe, and parallel function. Brush up on your recollections of Field Communications One-oh-one."

"If our tacomm units are going toes-up, are the warbots going to do any better?" Manny Garcia wanted to know. "They're full of lots more complex and sensitive electronic gear. Must be a real feast for those fungi."

"Any problems with the warbots thus far?" Hettrick asked her company commanders in general.

"Yes." It was Capt. Samantha Walker. "We've gotten glitches in some of our units. Garbled feedback, for example. Smeared sensor readouts. Failure to fully carry out commands. May be normal combat wear-and-tear because we've pushed them pretty hard today. One of my heavy weapon warbots may have taken a piece of a one-oh-six round or may have started to go bad before it was hit. Or after. I don't know which. I wasn't linked to it. Luckily, Sergeant Leslie Merritt got out of it before she had a double-lobed Lebanese systolic stroke. Some of my NCOs are acting like they're coming down with battle fatigue . . ."

"Doesn't sound like any maintenance function we can't handle," snapped Marty Kelly. "I know you guys in maintenance have to keep busy, Otis, but I've taught my people to use mallet maintenance. If something goes wrong, hit it with a hammer. Or kick the shit out of it. Usually either fixes it or gives your maintenance people something to keep them really busy. As for battle fatigue, Sammy, that's considered to be gold-bricking in my outfit. I suggest you . . ."

"Speak for your own people, Marty," Sam Walker interrupted with irritation in her voice. "Some of my warbot brainies reported having trouble today. Lot of them with headaches tonight. Came close to going into spasm mode for no apparent reason. Johanna, if you have any spare biotechs, we could use them."

Capt. Johanna Wool of the biotech section sighed and told her, "Sam, we're up to our armpits in warbot brainy symptoms that have all the earmarks of good old battle fatigue, with all due apologies to Captain Kelly. Plus the fact that we took some minor trooper casualties today, but all of them are back with their units tonight." Wool was also a medical doctor, and her biotechnical outfit was the closest thing to a medical aid station that the Washington Greys had.

"Keep me advised. Fully advised," Hettrick told her company commanders. "If our warbots start going toes-up as badly as our tacomm units have, we're in deep yogurt with a high pucker factor. We may all end up being Sierra Charlies for real in this operation, out there fighting in idiot mode with minimal robot and computer support."

"Orgasmic!" Manny Garcia muttered.

"Back to the humping infantry," Samantha Walker added.

"Possibly. If it goes that way, your troops must be at the top of their form and not suffering from fatigue. There should be no tired units, only tired commanders. So make sure your troops get as much rest as they can tonight, in spite of moving all over the map. Those not commanding or in linkage for the retrograde maneuver should grab time on the snore shelf. Anything else?" Hettrick looked around. Some officers might have wanted to say something, but they didn't. This was no war game.

The banter, the bitches, the gripes would have to wait.

So Hettrick went on, "I'm proud of you and your people, damned proud! You pulled off the first amphibious operation in the last twenty years of Army operations, and you did it without losing personnel. You came ashore out of some decidedly uncomfortable Navy boats, and you reached your initial objectives ahead of schedule. You fought like hell and took nearly a hundred Tee-dad prisoners in Point Fortin. You came up against an enemy in defensive positions you weren't equipped to handle and you tried to out-maneuver them on your own initiative. I have no doubts we could break that Oropuche River bottleneck tomorrow. But we've been told to do something we're supposed to be pretty good at. So have no pride when it comes time to get the hell out of Whiskey Creek. My guess right now is that we'll all meet in Rio Claro tomorrow night. If this fracas is over by then—and it could be if we're better soldiers than the Tee-dads—the drinks are on me in whatever Rio Claro cantina we can find. Good hunting!''

The lights in the little roadside hamlet of St. Mary's were all out, but the wan light from a the moon riding in the western sky was enough for Curt to see the road. Capt. Samantha Walker nodded her head toward her All Terrain Vehicle. ''Want a ride back up to your cee-pee?''

''It's only about a kilometer. I should walk. And so should you,'' Curt pointed out.

''We may get damned tired of walking before this is all over. Don't look a gift horse in the mouth.''

''Horses? God, I wish we had some horses, Sam. Although they wouldn't be much good in swamps . . . or against automatic weapon fire.'' Curt suddenly felt tired, whupped, beat. But a whole night of withdrawing from combat, travelling, regrouping, and moving out lay ahead of him. He decided that a quiet walk down a highway on a tropical island in the moonlight with 5.56mm things maybe buzzing around him wasn't such a good idea after all. ''Well, yeah, okay, I'll take you up on that ride, Sam. Especially after what Hettrick said about tired commanders. Guess we've got to keep from getting bushed-out, too.''

As the little vehicle whined down the road, Sam Walker asked, ''Do you really think the bots and vehicles will start to crap out, too?''

''Maybe. Probably. Be ready if it happens,'' Curt advised her. ''As usual, the Army fights with equipment designed for another war in another place. If we'd had six more months in the Vee-eye, we might have run into some of these problems and been able to start correcting them."

"We never have six months. We're lucky if we get six hours."

"Right."

The swampy rain forest alongside the road was taking on the appearance of being torn up. Trees were lopped off or up-rooted. The shoulders of the road were deeply rutted by the tracks and wheel marks of heavy warbot assault and command vehicles pulling off the asphalt into the cover of the vegetation. In the moonlight, Curt saw what remained of the little house alongside the road where he and Kester had given aid to the Trinidad family; they were nowhere to be seen, and the house had been gutted by artillery fire. Since he'd been through the hell of Munsterlagen where he'd seen a whole town ripped to shreds, it was nothing new to him. Outwardly, the wanton destruction of civilian facilities no longer affected his performance as a combat officer; such was the nature of war. Inwardly, it bothered him because those people unfortunately just happened to be in the path of war. Thus it had been throughout history . . .

Curt heard something. It began as a far-away whispering rumble and grew louder like a freight train approaching, then changed to a warbling whistle. A second similar sound came immediately with it. The night lit up with a brilliant flash that would have blinded Curt if he hadn't instinctively covered his eyes. Not five meters in front of the ATV, the road erupted in violence, noise, and heat.

Capt. Samantha Walker was momentarily blinded by the flash.

Curt grabbed the control yoke and prevented the

ATV from careening off the road. But he couldn't stop its forward motion.

"Eighty-one millimeter heat-seeker smart mortar rounds!" he yelled. "Out of this thing! Now!"

"Can't see!" Walker yelled back.

Curt grabbed her, yanked her out of the seat, and rolled out the right door of the ATV onto the pavement. Although the ATV was still moving, albeit less than ten kilometers per hour, he hit the ground and rolled. So did Walker, but the impact broke his grip on her. Fortunately, Walker had been driving on the right side of the road American fashion, so Curt only hit the edge of the asphalt before rolling into the soft dirt at the highway's edge. He came to a stop and Walker rolled into him.

The first incoming round had missed, but the second one got the ATV right in the turbine exhaust stack. The world lit up.

Curt was stunned by hitting the road and rolling into the ditch as well as from the force of the first explosion.

"Sam, you okay?" Curt asked, putting his arms around her and turning her so he could see her.

She was limp.

He suddenly realized that his hands were covered with a warm, wet, slippery goo that seemed to be pulsing from a source.

In the light of the burning ATV, Curt saw with horror that Capt. Samantha Walker had been hit by a piece of the second round's frag warhead. She was unconscious, whether from the fall out of the ATV or from whatever had hit her. Her soft body armor had stopped several pieces of shrapnel, but she hadn't been protected where something sharp and deadly had whipped past her and slashed across the left side of her throat, tearing away the scarf bearing the blue and yel-

213

low colors of the Robot Infantry. She was bleeding to death from a torn carotid artery.

Curt tried for the pressure point below her neck near the clavicle. He got it, but all the pressure he could bring to bear didn't seem to stop the blood gushing from her neck.

He grabbed for his tacomm unit and discovered it had been between his body and the road when he'd bailed out of the ATV. The heavy plastic case was completely crushed.

Hoping there might be a trooper nearby who'd hear him, he called "Biotech! Biotech! Wounded! I need help!"

Nobody came before Capt. Samantha Julia Walker, U.S. Army Robot Infantry, stopped breathing in a series of rattling gasps and her body went into a final spasm in his arms.

When the two field biotechs in their white tabards with the red cross of mercy front and back found him with Walker's body alongside the road a few minutes later, Capt. Curt Carson looked up at them and said in a husky voice, "She doesn't need you now."

"Are you all right, Captain?"

"No, I'm not. But I haven't been hit. Please guard her body. I have to find her command post and take care of a lot of things."

And it wasn't going to be easy, he told himself as he crawled to his feet, gained the edge of the road, and began to walk toward where he knew her company command post would be.

It was the first time Capt. Curt Carson had ever had anyone die in his arms in combat.

In fact, it was the first time *anyone* in the Robot Infantry had died in combat in more years than he knew.

What made it even worse was that Capt. Samantha Walker was a lovely, warm, and sensible woman, a comrade in arms, a friend. She shouldn't have been where she could have been hit by a mindless piece of metal guided to her only by the heat of the ATV exhaust. And hitting her just where she wasn't protected by body armor.

And Sam Walker hadn't even become one of the Sierra Charlies yet; she was a warbot brainy who'd been allowed into combat only because robot warfare had theoretically eliminated the chance she'd be killed in actual combat.

Curt was far too shaken and angry to either curse or pray.

CHAPTER TWENTY-THREE

"There wasn't a damned thing I could do . . ." Curt admitted.

"Oh, my God! Poor Sam! It must have hit the Warriors hard!" Lt. Alexis Morgan was pale and shaking.

"Well, we've all got to go some time, and Sam went in combat. She knew the risks. We all know the risks," Curt muttered. What could he say? It was bad enough to have a fellow officer die in his arms. It was even worse that she was a woman and, as a warbot brainy, shouldn't have been exposed to fire in the first place.

Platoon Sgt. Edwina Sampson had quietly retreated to a corner of Curt's ACV and was weeping silently.

Lt. Jerry Allen was white-lipped. He said nothing. It was his first experience of losing a fellow officer in combat. He didn't really know what to say and was almost afraid to say anything lest it be the wrong thing.

M. Sgt. Henry Kester knew about it and knew what to do. Curt's field uniform was covered with the drying blood of his fellow officer. "Captain, you've gotta get out of that uniform *now!* I think we've got a set of fresh cammies around here somewhere . . ."

Curt knew his female officers weren't skin-conscious. How could they be when they knew each other so well from warbot linkage where it was almost possible to enter another person's mind electronically? So he stripped out of his blood-soaked cammies to his seat-soaked skivvies, wondering, however, how Adonica Sweet might react.

He didn't have to worry. Even though a strong English tradition still persisted in Trinidad after years of being a Crown Colony, the English never really were prudes even on their tight little island home; it was only the cold climate of Britain and the need to maintain aloofness in their colonies that gave them the reputation of being prudish, snobbish, and always dressed properly for the occasion. Trinidad was a tropical island where clothing wasn't necessary for body warmth, only for protection against the environment. And the people of Trinidad had seen American TV and American tourists for decades, in addition to many of them being American-born like Adonica Sweet.

Adonica didn't bat an eye. Instead, she looked somber and tried to explain, "I'm sorry, it's partly my fault. I should have warned you the Brazilians had supplied heat-seeking projectiles for the eighty-one millimeter mortars . . . and that Drake's regiments have trained on maneuvers to use them along the roads at night to control any possible movement of partisan forces."

"But *how* did they know to target the road? And the ACV at that?" Curt asked savagely. They'd been a small and mobile target, and they'd been an unscheduled movement. The first round hadn't zeroed-in, but the second one fired only a few seconds behind, had demolished the ACV. No 106mm rounds from the standard Tee-dad recoilless company heavy weapon had been fired. Or, at least, Curt didn't remember any coming in after that traumatic moment in the roadside ditch. "Alexis, Jerry, did you detect *anything* in the air, like a FAC aerodyne, for example?"

"Sky was clean as a whistle," Allen reported.

"Low-orbit satellite recon?" Morgan wondered aloud.

"Trinidad doesn't have any military satellites," Curt objected.

"No, Captain, but we're fighting more than just the Tee-dads, as you call them," Adonica reminded him. "Argentina, Brazil, and Chile are supporting General Drake. Brazil has a very advanced military satellite recon system based on the old French SPOT satellites they bought years ago."

"But to detect, identify, target, and transmit the information about a single small ATV on a road in less than a few minutes? From a satellite? To some sort of general command post? And then have the coordinates and the order to fire passed down the line to a company in combat in time for them to lay two rounds in on that ATV? I don't even think an artillery regiment with full combat computer capability could do it . . ." Curt didn't believe it was technically possible.

"Many things have probably happened since you came ashore at Point Fortin this morning," Adonica told him. "You undoubtedly caught General Drake and his staff completely by surprise then. And the Brazilians do have recon satellites up at two hundred kilometers in high inclination orbits with sensors capable of resolving targets less than a half-meter. Drake has satellite ground facilities in Port of Spain as well as an excellent island telephone system which he still controls. Maybe that's what got you."

"How come you know these things, Adonica?" Curt suddenly asked.

"Because, Captain, I'm a spy. And so is my father," she replied bluntly. "And don't let appearances deceive you. My degree is in geology, and I know what earth-looking satellites can do."

Curt leaned over and picked up the handset of the

ACV's tacomm. "I want Hettrick and General Carlisle to know this. They can pass the data up the line, and maybe a couple of Brazilian satellites could be strangely blinded the next time they go over Trinidad. In the meantime, why didn't you tell us about this, Adonica?"

"Captain, there's so much data . . . I could spent tonight giving your regimental computers a data dump if you want. I'm sorry that my oversight resulted in the death of Captain Walker," Adonica apologized. "I'm truly sorry, Captain. But Captain Walker will be buried in the soil she tried to liberate."

"No, Colonel Hettrick has left orders," Curt explained tonelessly, shaking his head, "that Captain Walker is not to be buried on foreign soil. We are expected to attend the memorial service in Arlington after this is over." Capt. Samantha Walker would be buried on that solemn bank overlooking the Potomac with others who'd given their lives for their country. "She was a fine soldier and an outstanding officer. I can't understand why people like that have to die in combat . . . My God, this Sierra Charlie thing may *not* be the way to go! At least if women are involved."

"I liked and admired the Captain," Platoon Sgt. Edie Sampson put in, rejoining the conversation but wiping her eyes as she did so. "But it could have happened to anybody . . . anyone in this ACV, as a matter of fact. And it bothers me that a woman got it. But what did we expect? Sex don't mean a damned thing in the RI—except when Rule Ten isn't in force. Other than that, we're all just soldiers. Every damned one of us is equal when it comes to a bullet or a shell or when a command post full of warbot brainies takes a direct hit. Sure as hell I ain't gonna let this scare me into running tail for home!"

"In your own way, Sergeant," Lt. Alexis Morgan

said slowly. "you've echoed my thoughts. I never asked for security when I accepted my commission. Sam was my friend, too, and her loss hasn't changed my thinking a bit. I'm not going to huddle in my ACV because of it."

"Staying behind armor is a good idea, Lieutenant, and maybe you and Sampson ought to keep out of the line of fire from now on," Curt decided on the spur of the moment. "Be a good idea for you to stay in the ACVs and command your warbots from there. I don't want to see either of you mucking around in the mud and getting shot."

"Bullshit, Captain," Morgan told him bluntly in a level tone of voice and with uncharacteristic candor. "We've trained as a team, and we'll fight as a team. It's no time to get cold feet and change the rules in the middle of the game. Until the general order comes down from topside, I'll shoot it out one-on-one with the Tee-dads if I have to. Scroom!"

Curt glowered at her. "That was a direct order, Lieutenant. I expect you to carry it out."

"Seems that Sergeant Kester told me what to do if I ever got an order like that. So, following his advice . . ." She saluted smartly and snapped an emphatic, *"Yes, sir!"* Then she turned to her platoon sergeant, Nick Gerard, and said in an even voice of authority and command, "Sergeant, let's go round up the squad leaders and the warbots. We've got to be ready to pull out of here in a few hours." She slung her FABARMA rifle over her shoulder and buckled on a bandolier of clips. As she started for the sortie door of her ACV, she turned to her company commander and said, "Captain, you need to get some rest. You've been through hell. I'll get the Companions disengaged and to the rendezvous point at Pluck."

Curt realized the nature and the reason behind the

order he'd given in a moment of emotion. He knew what the problem was and knew that the Robot Infantry was no different from other aspects of life in America where it was always a matter, deep down inside, of *women and children first*. But here they were in the rain forests and swamps of Trinidad facing an enemy that would shoot to kill anyone, man or womam, not because they were necessarily defending their native soil but because they were mercenaries hired by Gen. Austin Drake to do just that.

None of Curt's people, himself included, had asked why they were here doing what they'd been ordered to do; that's what they got paid for. That was their profession, and they knew it and were proud of it. There was no easy way out of the present situation, no way to say to his female officer and NCO, *Okay, they've started to shoot at us. The war games are over. Now you girls get the hell out of here before you get hurt.*

"You have your platoon to take care of, Lieutenant," Curt reminded her, getting on an even keel again. "Please carry out your assigned responsibilities. Master Sergeant Kester and I will see to the details of the retrograde operation. Just be prepared to move when the order comes. And don't get your ass shot off. You present a bigger target there than most of the rest of us . . ."

Some of the more rabid female equality types in the Army would have put Curt on report for that blatantly sexual, chauvinistic, and derrogatory remark. But Alexis Morgan was far from being a broad-hipped woman; exercise had kept her fit and trim. So rather than take offense at Curt's remark, she almost smiled. She knew her CO was under control again when his sense of humor began to show. "Captain, I know you're basically a male chauvinist teddy bear, but if you weren't my commanding officer and we weren't in

221

a combat situation, I'd bust you in your chauvinistic chops for that remark . . . sir.'' She paused with just the hint of a smile flicking over the corners of her mouth, then asked, ''Speaking of the orders coming, are any of the tacomms still working?''

Kester shook his head. ''The Captain smashed the last one getting out of Captain Sam's ATV. The other spare went tits-up this evening. But the bigger units in the vehicles are still working. That's only because we've been running the environmental control systems and keeping everything relatively cool and dry inside . . . at least for right now.''

''Why don't we use pigeons?'' came the quiet suggestion from none other than Adonica Sweet who'd been sitting silently to one side, not fully understanding the strange cameraderie between these very unusual soldiers so unlike the mercenaries of the Trinidad Defense Force with whom she was familiar.

''*Pigeons?*'' Alexis Morgan asked incredulously.

''I seem to recall a piece of equipment bearing the military nomenclature 'UBQ-1' that worked pretty well,'' Henry Kester said wryly.

Morgan didn't seem to realize that the old master sergeant was pulling her leg, so she walked right into it. ''What the hell is it and where do we get one?''

''Well, Lieutenant, in the old alpha nomenclature, it stood for 'General utility, pigeon, special purpose, Model One.' '' Kester didn't even crack a smile. ''Carrier pigeons were widely used as message carriers as recently as World War Two.''

''Where the hell are we going to get pigeons?'' Curt asked.

''I know a family,'' Adonica Sweet put in, ''who lives in Ciperio Ste. Croix who used to race pigeons with my father. We'll go right through there tomorrow morning. I'll see if I can find Mister Tej. He's a petroleum manager in that oil field area."

"Good. Please do that, Adonica," Curt told her. "In the meantime, you're a civilian and you won't be needed as a guide during the retrograde operation. We know where the roads are. So I want you to stay here in this ACV. I've seen enough people killed today, and there may be Tee-dad patrols out there tonight guided by those Brazilian recon satellites you warned us about."

Adonica shook her blonde head. "Captain, the space snoops can see you on the roads, but not in the forest. No one in his right mind would go out in those swamps at night. The place literally crawls with things you want to see before they get too close to you. I guarantee no Tee-dad patrols will come through that swamp tonight. So I'd like to go back to the Alpha Platoon cee-pee."

Curt knew something indeed was brewing between Lt. Jerry Allen and Adonica Sweet. It hadn't come to a boil yet, however. He made a mental note to himself to ask Sgt. Edwina Sampson to keep an eye on things for him. He didn't want the additional worry about young Allen's gonads taking control of his brain. Maybe he should mention to Colonel Hettrick the possibility of a brevet commission for Adonica.

When the ACV had cleared out except for Henry Kester standing watch up in the turret, Curt rang up Hettrick on the tacomm. He was surprised to discover that she wasn't in linkage but answered the audio call personally once her aide had given it to her. "You all right, Captain?" she asked formally.

"Best I can be, under the circumstances," Curt told her.

"Captain Walker has been picked up by divisional Graves Registration," the Colonel informed him, anticipating his question. "She's the only fatality thus far in the regiment. The Wolfhounds lost a platoon sergeant, and Colonel Calhoun's aide is the only Cottonbaler casualty. By the way, Curt, since you were present, I presume you'll attest to her posthumous citation for the Bronze Star . . ."

Curt shook his head although Hettrick couldn't see that. "No, Colonel, only for the Silver Star. She died in combat."

"Technically, we're not in an official state of armed conflict, Captain. Bronze Star is the best that Division staff believed they could justify."

"Goddamit, Colonel, we have been shot at today, and a damned fine officer has been killed in the process! If that isn't armed conflict, what the hell is?" Curt exploded. "Find the sonofabitch who doesn't believe that and put him with my company for a day! I won't stand still for anything less than the Silver Star for Sam Walker! All day the day of her death, she exhibited valorous conduct in the face of an enemy who was shooting at us and trying to kill us! Without her fire support, my company would have been dead meat!"

"Nothing's been submitted yet, Captain," Hettrick told him levelly, "so cool your circuits, sir. What did you want to talk to me about? Problems you can't solve?"

"No problems here I can't solve . . . yet." He was thinking of Jerry Allen and Adonica Sweet. They could become his major headache if nothing worse happened. "But I got some Gee-two out of my native guide about Brazilian low-level recon satellites . . ."

"Thank you. We know of them."

"Then why were Sam and I hit on that road?"

"Satellites didn't spot you," Belinda Hettrick told him. "The target coordinates were called in on the island's telephone network by someone on our side of the line. We heard it, and we couldn't get to you in time because your portable tacomm wasn't working.''

"A spy behind our lines?''

"Captain, we did our best to cut overhead telephone cables leading north, but we couldn't have gotten them all. And we didn't cut any underground cables because we don't know where all of them are,'' Hettrick explained. "Don't worry about ABC satellite recon; the Navy's got them blinded and jammed. But ten thousand or more Trinidad civilians are now in our rear area; not all of them like the idea that we're here. They know how to use a rather good and extensive telephone system on this island. The Trinidad government was proud as hell when they got the island wired up to modern direct-dial telephone service back in the 1980s . . . and the system's been pretty well maintained and updated. The spies use it. So what are we supposed to do? Round up ten or fifty thousand people on this end of the island and put them in a pen somewhere? Not according to our rules of engagement!''

"So are we combat officers free to assume that all natives are hostile?''

"Negative! Remember the rules of engagement which, by the way, are still in effect in spite of what happened to Captain Walker. So just cover minus-x all the time. We're likely to run into partisans working for either side . . . or for themselves. That will be especially true tomorrow when we're moving fast through back country.''

"Orgasmic!'' was all that Curt could think of to sputter.

"And, by the way, Curt, Lieutenant Joan Ward has assumed command of Captain Walker's company. I've just been informed that they will continue to call themselves the Warriors . . . except now it's Ward's Warriors.''

"That's nice to know. Sam would have liked that," Curt remarked quietly. "I'll give Joan a call. Do you want me to write or telex Sam's family?"

"I've already undertaken that grim and unwanted task . . . but she was unmarried and survived only by her father, retired out of the Fifty-Eighth Regiment, the Patriots, who by the way just this last hour took the Solomon Hochoy Highway at Freeport. Looks like we've got three and maybe four of the Tee-dad regiments boxed in between Port of Spain and San Fernando . . ."

"And now we've got move fast enough around to the east to keep them from heading into the hills," Curt added. "Thank you, Colonel. I still haven't gotten over Sam, but I feel a little better. The Companions will be ready to move out when relieved."

"I know you will. And, by the way, I want to pass along to you something that General Carlisle requests," Hettrick added almost as an afterthought. "The scribblers and alarmers from the Fourth Estate have picked up on Sam Walker's story that Jimmy Hodge filed when the news hit Carlisle's cee-pee. Hodge is a good media man—fair, impartial, understands the need for military units even in today's world . . ."

"I think I talked to him after Zahedan," Curt recalled, remembering that the little man was one of the few newspeople who'd treated him like a human being rather than as a war robot. "But I thought Operation Steel Band was running under a general news media blackout . . ."

"It was. Only a couple of pool people—Hodge among them—came ashore with us," Hettrick explained. "But it isn't a blackout now; it's become a greyout. We've got practically every major news organization in the world on Trinidad now."

226

"So I noticed. We creamed one of their camera planes making an unauthorized pass over our column."

"That was just the beginning. They're likely to be all over you like a rug tomorrow. Let me know if they bother you to the point that our operation is endangered."

"I'd just as soon not talk to them at all until this is all over," Curt growled. "Colonel, please keep them away from the Companions. We're on recon point, and we can't be bothered with them."

"I'll try. But there are a lot of them."

"How are they getting in here? Where are they coming from?"

"Anywhere they can get airlift . . . and in some cases anywhere they can hire a boat. The fixed-wing Caravan you creamed was registered in Tobago. They're getting aerodynes, Vee-stol airplanes, even old helicopters from Guyana, Tobago, Barbardos, anywhere they can find them . . . and ignoring warnings from both the Tee-dads and ourselves that they'll be fired upon if they stumble into a combat area . . . which they're doing."

"Well, Colonel, if those bastriches happen to get in the line of fire, I can't help it if they have an 'accident.' "

"I know it. Happily, nobody has asked about the Caravan you shot down earlier today; they may not even know it's missing. I'm sure as hell not going to tell them about it; that's not my job. We'll let someone up in General Brooke's staff worry about that one." Hettrick paused. "But the reason I brought it up is this: The only casualty taken by the Washington Greys thus far has been one of our women officers. And we're the new Sierra Charlie experimental outfit figuring out how to mix warbots and human soldiers in a new army

227

tactical doctrine. Samantha Walker is going to be lead-story news tomorrow morning, and the Army is likely to be accused of unnecessarily exposing women to the hazards of being killed in combat. The Army's been hassled about this since World War Two. Now it's going to intensify."

"Do you have something specific in mind that you want me to do, Colonel?"

"Not really. I think you can handle any of the hand-wringing scribblers without a problem. Just wanted to warn you that they're probably going to descend upon you and make your life miserable by trying to get you to criticize long-standing Army policy."

"Thank you, Colonel, I know you'll try to keep them off my back. But even if they get by you, they've got to find me. And it looks like Carson's Companions are going to be moving rather fast pretty quick."

CHAPTER TWENTY-FOUR

Pulling one unit out of the line while another moved it to take over never was an easy tactical job—especially at night with no lights allowed and with verbal commands and hails kept to an absolute minimum.

But it was made a lot easier with the help of night-vision goggles and personnel wearing brassards that emitted only specific infra red wavelengths easily spotted by other Army night goggles and warbot sensors. This sort of identification technology was relatively new to the Army, and G-2 was absolutely certain that the Tee-dads and their supporting ABC Allianza organizations didn't have it yet because it involved some very special temperature-sensitive processing of fabric dies containing some rather rare, esoteric earth minerals not generally mined and refined anywhere but in North America. Curt flew a small i-r identification pennon from the whip of one of his comm antennas to qualify his vehicle as a non-target, and a small 25-centimeter square i-d cloth hung from the rear of the ACV to complete its identification.

Curt also put his General Purpose command robots on duty as outposts twenty-five meters from his ACV. They, too, were suitably marked. The Can Do might shoot any unmarked and improperly identified object, even a warbot, even though everyone knew the only Tee-dad warbots were still with the Presidential Guard around Gen. Austin Drake somewhere in the vicinity of Port of Spain.

Curt quietly brought both Alpha and Bravo platoons within visual range, even in the jungle. To make the front a little less deep for the change-over, Ward's Warriors had moved up the road from their fire base position to cover the hole left when Curt moved Morgan's Bravo Platoon to the right.

About midnight, Curt remarked to his master sergeant, "Henry, tell me if you hear the same thing I do. It's dead-ass silent outside. No incoming Tee-dad one-oh-six or even high-angle eighty-one mortar rounds. Quiet as hell. Shouldn't be that way. The Tee-dads are either retreating or their conserving ammo for daylight."

The old sergeant didn't answer right away. Finally, he opined, "They may not know what's going on, Captain."

"Hell, if they've got any recon at all, they must know the Can Dos are moving up toward our positions."

"Maybe they haven't got any recon capability left," Kester guessed. "Don't forget, Captain, the Tee-dads are a garrison army, not a field force. Three hots and a cot every day, and maybe shoot a few peasants for kicks in between. They've been fighting on this line since noon. Maybe they're tired. Maybe they're low on ammo. Maybe their losses are more than S-2 guessed. Or maybe they're fighting the clouds of mosquitoes and other irritable flying beasties in this tropical paradise called the Oropuche River swamps."

"Or maybe they've withdrawn under cover of darkness," Curt added. "They've got to know the Double Deuces landed in their rear at sunset."

"Possible. Possible. The 'Save Our Ass' maneuver is pretty damned compelling if there's nobody guarding minus-x," Kester observed quietly.

"My God, with all this silence, maybe we ought to try to force the river crossing tonight," Curt voiced a sudden thought.

"Captain, a frontal attack through dense forest is dangerous enough in the daylight. At night, it's disastrous. We don't know where we're going, and we don't know where the enemy is until he shoots. So we'd have to advance in column on the roads while the woods give the enemy cover. Anyway, we've been ordered to stand fast and be relieved. Let the Can Dos bust their butts forcing the river crossing tomorrow; they've got the warbots and firepower to do it. We tried all afternoon and couldn't."

Curt shook his head sadly. "If the Tee-dads are retreating, we shouldn't lose contact with them."

"Yeah, Captain, but if they run, we can catch 'em, and when we catch 'em, we'll make 'em run again. Standard offensive tactics. When you get right down to the lickin' log, war is a pretty simple thing . . ."

"You're right, Henry. Here I've got the jitters after only one day in combat."

"Captain, fatigue can make cowards of us all. Get some sack time. I'll let you know when the Can Dos show up."

Curt checked the time. "They're due now."

"Then they'll be here on the tick," Kester pointed out. "The 15th Regiment has a pretty strong tradition about that."

As if on cue, the tacomm loudspeaker announced, "Companion Leader, this is Jeep One. Friendly command vehicle approaching from minus-x. Identity verified by infra red signatures."

Curt reached out and toggled the pre-arranged frequency and skip-code. "This is Companion Leader calling the command vehicle approaching from my rear. Acknowledge and identify yourself verbally!"

"Companion Leader, this is Copperhead Leader. We have a visual and an infra red check on you. My unit is prepared to relieve your unit, sir."

Curt initiated the standard procedure of verification. "Copperhead Leader, please transmit the given name of your commanding officer."

"This must be Kay-det Curt Carson, the cock of the Corps! George Crook of Crook's Copperheads, in case you've forgotten!"

No one but a classmate at West Point would have known of Curt's legendary monicker gained one memorable night when Curt, driven rather hard by the lust of six months' of barrack's life, went Absent Post between bed checks, didn't get caught, and only his roommate George Crook knew. It had turned out to be a dry run insofar as Curt was concerned because the summer camp counsellor from nearby Bear Mountain State Park stood him up. Only George Crook knew that, too. But Rumor Control ran away with the yarn as usual, adding embellishments to it with every transmittal to the point where Curt was the prime target of every tactical officer's nighttime scrutiny of the barracks for months to come.

"I haven't forgotten, and thanks for hiding the rope ladder." Curt's reply would serve as positive identification of himself. Only Crook knew about that quiet purchase in a Newburg sporting goods store.

He toggled over to his company tac frequency. "Companions all, this is Companion Leader. The Copperheads of Can Do are moving into position in your minus-x. Give way and complete the handoff. Report on tacomm once you've reached our reassembly point and are ready to move to the rendezvous and move-out point. Execute!"

"Call in the jeeps, Henry," Curt said to his master sergeant. "Dog down the sortie door once they're aboard, and let's quietly make our little retrograde maneuver . . ."

"You mean retreat."

"No, Sergeant, and you know better. We never retreat. At the very worst, we make a tactical withdrawal to a previously prepared position. And we've got a lot of kilometers to cover after that . . ."

"You really going to go for the pigeons, Captain?"

"Damned right! Better than nothing out here in the jungle, particularly if the rest of the tacomms get eaten by fungus. What are we going to do? Stand up and wave semaphore flags? And I'll bet even *you* don't remember semaphore code; hasn't been used for about a hundred years. We've got to have some way to communicate while we're balling along through this jungle." He flipped on the ACV's command circuits to talk to his vehicle. "Companion One, this is Companion Leader. Verification code Pluck. Start up, back out of position slowly, allow the ACV in your minus-x to move in, then retrace that ACV's path back to Siparia Road. Execute and report!"

"Your order is received and verified. Starting up. Backing out."

"Henry, put your helmet on, stick your head out of the turret, and make sure this goddamned beast

233

doesn't back into Crook or a tree. I don't trust electronic circuits any more. And I'm not going to bust this vehicle; I don't want to walk all the way to Rio Claro . . ."

CHAPTER TWENTY-FIVE

The nature of a battle, a campaign, or a war—euphemistically called an "armed conflict" because the nations of the world outlawed "war" in the United Nations' Charter in 1945—depends on viewpoint, which in turn depends upon the information in hand.

Gen. Austin Drake sat in the heavily-guarded War Room hastily established in the basement of the Red House in Port of Spain. His aides and staff had just up-dated the maps. He studied them with his clean-shaven chin in his massive hands. His expression was impassive. Inwardly, he was depressed.

In the first twenty-four hours of the invasion, his Trinidad Defense Forces had been caught by surprise.

The American landings of what appeared to be four robot infantry regiments—a full division—had been made on the south and southwest coasts with no initial resistance.

A bombing attack on Fort George had knocked out his heavy artillery battalion. All of his Brazilian X2A106 self-propelled 106mm guns were smoking hulks lined up side by side in the Fort George motor pool. More than two-hundred of his Brazilian and Argentine mercenary soldiers and officers in the 1st Regiment's artillery batallion were dead or wounded. He attached the survivors immediately to the roboticized

First Battalion of the First Regiment, the Presidential Guard still based in Port of Spain.

Napirima Air Base had been attacked by American strike fighters. His own tactical strike squadron of 24 Embraer Piranhas had been destroyed on the ground before it could even get into the air to make a good accounting of itself. The attack had even destroyed the eyes of his naval forces, twelve IA-88 Delfin maritime patrol aircraft.

Without air surveillance, his two naval flotillas had been lured out of Port of Spain and San Fernando on the previous morning by a heavy concentration of enemy naval vessels approaching the Dragon's Mouths. His corvettes and hydrofoil gunboats were now on the bottom.

What was left of his air capability, a few fighter interceptors and some transport aerodynes, was protected under heavy guard in revetted hangars on the marge of Piarco International Airport. He didn't tell his staff that he was holding those aircraft as his last resort; he could get out of Trinidad as long as he had those transport aerodynes and enough fighter cover to protect them until he got to the coast of Guyana, now controlled by the ABC Allianza.

This was typical of the careful and discreet behavior of Austin Drake. He was a student of military and political history. If he was ever deposed as President of Trinidad—which he always held as a definite and probable possibility—he did not intend to end up like Ferdinand Marcos or General Federico Luis Pinedo with his assets traceable and seizable. If he were forced to leave Trinidad, he had to worry only about himself. The mistresses and his military aides would just have to fend for themselves. All treasures of a negotiable nature had been quietly dispatched overseas in the weeks and months preceeding the invasion.

So all he had to worry about that morning was defending himself against a massive American invasion.

Gen. Austin Drake was fuming inwardly at his allies for not providing him with intelligence that might have kept him from being surprised. He didn't know that the Brazilians and Argentines had been fed false data by the United States intelligence and that the Chileans, who had picked up some solid intelligence through their own networks, had been pooh-poohed by the other two Allianza members. The United States invade Trinidad? Impossible, *señor!*

Everyone on the ABC Allianza general staffs knew that the United States had only four divisions of robot infantry and three light armor divisions because of the historic American trait of maintaining only the bare minimum of military forces. There were, of course, numerous half-staffed reserve divisions and the National Guard militia, which the ABC Allianza really couldn't understand, although Drake had continued to warn them of the possibility the Americans could activate them as temporary replacements for regular Army units.

The ABC Allianza didn't believe Drake about the National Guard because they were constantly amazed at American congressional penury for maintaining adequate force levels contrasted with profligate American military spending for weapons technology, primarily warbots.

Furthermore, unlike many other militaristic nations of the world, the American government hadn't used its military units as internal police forces since the Indian Wars of the 19th century, and this was alien to the ABC Allianza, too.

And the United States was widely believed to be reluctant to use its meager military forces for anything more that "showing the flag" in parts of the world where American business interests might be threatened by either terrorism or political potential of nationalization. American Army units were stationed in Europe, the Mid-East, northern Africa, and northweastern Asia as a show of force. But except for several local campaigns, the American Army hadn't fought a major war in more than a decade. Other professional military leaders of the world thus considered the Americans to be amateurs. Even the simple hostage rescue mission to Zahedan in eastern Iran had nearly failed; Brazilian analysis of that operation had concluded that only the application of magic-like high technology against poorly-educated religious fanatics had saved the American troops and image.

Gen. Austin Drake, President of Trinidad and Commander-in-Chief of the Trinidad Defense Forces, now knew that the ABC Allianza had been trapped by their own wishful thinking and distorted analysis of American military capabilities. The last twenty-four hours had proved that beyond a shadow of a doubt.

But Austin Drake was a graduate of West Point. He'd risen through the U.S. Army ranks to Lieutenant Colonel, enjoying a spectacular career in the then-new Robot Infantry. He was a "twenty-year wonder," making light colonel well before he would otherwise be eligible by time on the promotion list. Drake was not an outstanding soldier; he was a political officer, one who knew where bodies were buried and therefore who and how to curry for favors. He might have made it all the way to the general officer ranks if he hadn't voluntarily resigned before he was caught doing the commonplace in some Army circles: dealing quietly with certain defense contractors for rewards that were numbered bank accounts in Singapore and assurances of well-paid consulting contracts after retirement. Austin Drake managed to get the hell out with his "honor" and Singapore accounts intact but his promised consultancies shot out from under him.

However, he'd always had the reputation for landing on his feet; the world needed experienced military men, and governments were anxious to hire those with a knowledge of American military technology. The ABC Allianza had supported him as the late Clarke Chamberlin's Minister of Defense.

In spite of the fact that Austin Drake now ruled one of the most economically powerful countries in the Caribbean—albeit with the backing of the ABC Allianza who had plans for the island—he was in trouble and he knew it.

But he didn't dare reveal the full depth of his fears.

He'd taken personal command at noon the day before. With his knowledge of American doctrine and tactics, he'd deployed his forces against the invasion, using the mobility of his regular infantry forces plus terrain features to slow or halt the more ponderous robot infantry. The Brazilian and Argentine mercenaries in his regiments were experts at fighting in the environment of Trinidad.

He was proud of the fact that his non-robot 4th Regiment in San Fernando had held the American warbot forces at the Oropuche River near St, Mary's and between Penal and Debe.

But he sat back and listened as his chief of staff, Col. Sebastiao José de Carvahlo, briefed him on the current situation.

"At your direction, the Third Regiment has deployed southward out of Chaguanas to reinforce the Fourth. According to your orders, the Fifth Regiment left Rio Claro at fifteen hundred hours yesterday to attack the right flank of the invading Americans," Carvahlo indicated the map with a long wooden pointer. "But, General, we did not anticipate the landing of a second American robot infantry division on our heavily industrialized west coast, especially at sundown when our gunners had to look directly into the sun.

"A robot infantry *division?* Where did the Americans get a second RI division? Are you certain of that information, Colonel?"

"Yes, sir, I'm certain. Reports that came in from the Third Regiment last night reported full RI division strength."

"Troop commanders have a strong tendency to grossly overestimate the forces opposing them, if for no other reason than to justify their retreat. And especially at night," Drake muttered darkly.

But if it was true, Drake knew he was now outnumbered. He'd have to win by maneuvering. He knew his TDF infantry regiments, could move faster than the American Robot Infantry. He'd have to pull back, conserve his forces, and watch for the soft spot. There was always a soft spot, a place where a sudden thrust could split the enemy and permit smaller units to chop them up piecemeal.

"Where's the Fifth Regiment I moved out of Rio Claro?"

"They're attacking east of Point Lisas at this time."

"Who changed the route of march? They were supposed to engage the American regiment coming up from Basse Terre."

"The Americans entered Princes Town against no opposition at twenty hundred hours last night, General." Carvahlo said this with a great deal of trepidation; the news had come only after the General had retired for the night, and Carvahlo had agonized for hours over whether or not he should awaken the commander-in-chief with the information.

"So where the hell is the Fifth Regiment?"

"We should be very proud of the Fifth, General.

240

They moved over hilly back roads at night and engaged an American regiment east of Point Lisas at dawn.''

"Who ordered this change in plan?" Drake's anger was rising.

"Sir, you had retired with direct orders not to be disturbed, telling me that the commander above all other people needed rest for a clear mind." Carvahlo swallowed and went on, "General, since you were not available, I took the responsibility for issuing the change of orders. It seemed to me that the Fifth would be cut off by the Americans otherwise, and that concentrating our forces was in accordance with the best principles of combat—"

"Goddamn it to hell, Carvahlo, you should have informed me!"

"I tried, sir. You were . . . uh, in the company of a lady. You told me to get the hell out, if I may use your exact words."

Drake now remembered the intrusion into a moment of passion. But he mentioned nothing more about it. Instead, he went on the offensive. "Well, for chrissake! Now I'm going to have to pull the Fourth Regiment out of San Fernando to the northeast to save their asses! Which means we can't hold the Oropuche River line! Colonel, you really fucked up the situation around San Fernando! I won't have my subordinates going over my head giving orders that screw up a carefully-made plan! You're relieved of your duties!" He called toward the closed basement door, "Captain of the Guard!"

A gaudily-uniformed officer of the Presidential Guard stepped in, accompanied by two large war robots. He saluted snappily. "Sir!"

"Colonel Carvahlo has been relieved and is under arrest. Confine him to quarters!"

Sebastiao José Carvahlo looked surprised. "General! There is more that I must report on the tactical situation!"

"I'll get that from my observers' network! Take him away, Captain! Dammit, am I going to have to do *all* the fucking staff work around here to make sure it's right?"

Only after the Guard officer and the two warbots had left with Carvahlo did Drake simmer down enough to realize he as going to have to replace his chief of staff. But with whom? Now he was beginning to distrust his own staff men. Who could he count on?

Well, he could certainly handle incoming field reports from his civilian observer organization throughout the island. The Americans hadn't disabled Trinidad's excellent telephone network yet. So he could find out where the Americans were, even without aerial recon. But he needed more than that.

Even from a cursory study of the map, he sould see that something very unusual was happening in the vicinity of Monkey Town and Ciperio Ste. Croix. Movement. A lot of movement. Fast movement. But he knew from his own experience that the American Army didn't and couldn't move like that. Their warbot tactical doctrine was strictly oriented to small unit actions, usually at the battalion level and rarely above the regimental level.

Because of the limited range of several kilometers— actual numbers classified—over which humans could control warbots through nonintrusive electronic links to their nervous systems thence through computers thence through various communications links to the warbots out in the field where the action was, warbot tactics had to be small unit tactics. Warbot companies were trained to pin down the enemy with dense fire and move mobile warbots in platoon or company strength to seek soft spots in the line where deep penetration could be made far behind enemy lines where the enemy unit could be outflanked and brought under murderous cross fire from warbots. Warbots were murderous in their firepower, of course, because they could be designed to handle the weight and recoil of weapons far larger than a human soldier could use. Furthermore, most of their internal volume could be used for ammunition supply.

On the march, the American warbot doctrine was the leap-frog maneuver, putting one warbot unit in front, letting another warbot unit advance through it, then moving the first unit forward again. It was slow and ponderous, but it was murderous. However, the American forces east of San Fernando weren't behaving that way. What was going on?

Drake knew he had to have better intelligence data. With it, he could beat the Americans with maneuver. He also needed heavier weapons; 5.56mm SAR-80 assault rifles and CETME light machine guns using identical ammo were ineffectual against warbot armor unless a round caught a warbot in the sensors. As for the Mekanika Uru 9mm submachineguns that were so useful in keeping the Trinidad people in line, they might as well have been peashooters against warbots.

The Brazilian military advisor came in with several members of his staff. Gen. Joao Bonifacio Deodoro was a wiry but balding little man who wore the badges of parachutist, pilot, and astronaut. "Good morning, General!" he snapped. "How are your forces holding the Americans?"

"Surprisingly well!" Drake said as brightly as he could. "Look here: My special forces battalion moved from Arima overnight and has stopped the Americans at Chaguanas. The Third Regiment performed a valiant reversal of movement and is holding east of Couva.

The Fifth Regiment conducted a difficult repositioning at night over bad back roads and is holding the line at Gasparillo east of Point Lisas.''

Deodoro knew that a numerically inferior force could successfully defend against a stronger force. In spite of all the taechnological changes in warfare, the principles set forth by Sun Tzu and Carl von Clausewitz centuries before were still valid. ''But how long can you hold them?''

''I'm concentrating on pinning them between the Caroni Swamp to the north, the Solomon Hochoy Highway to the east, and the hills south east of San Fernando,'' Drake explained, indicating the map. ''We've lost Napirima Air Base, but you can still bring in reinforcementss because we're in control of Piaroco International Airport.''

Deodoro was silent for a moment. ''We did not anticipate this invasion. It will take time to marshal reinforcements for you—assuming, of course, that the officials in Brasilia decide to become more deeply involved.''

''What do you mean, General?'' Drake suddenly asked. ''Trinidad has a joint defense treaty with the ABC Allianza.''

''*Com caerteza*. But the ABC Allianza ministers are now meeting to discuss the American invasion of Trinidad. It is a serious matter to become involved in an armed conflict with the United States and its allies.''

''But we *knew* the possibility existed!''

''Bue we did not expect it this soon, General.''

Austin Drake gritted his teeth. ''Very well, I'll hold them. It'll help if I can regain some air capability. I still have pilots left. If you'll send some new Piranha strike aircraft to Piarco Airport, I'll hit the Americans from the air with impunity. I've got an advantage.''

"An advantage? What would that be?" the Brazilian asked.

"It appears the Americans aren't being allowed to attack any of the industrial or petroleum facilities," Drake pointed out to his allied advisor. "They've gone to extreme lengths to prevent damaging the steel plants, the chemical factories, and the petroleum refineries along the Prime Industrial Belt between San Fernando and Waterloo. These still belong to American and Saudi companies, even though we've already nationalized some of them. From the American actions thus far, I don't believe they'll do anything to harm those expensive industrial plants."

General Deodoro smiled. "That may indeed change the picture. How many American units do you estimate are currently involved?"

"Two robot infantry divisions."

"Which ones?"

"I don't know yet" Drake admitted, but went on quickly, "But they've had to put those two divisions together out of regimental units from other locations around the world. Which tells me they don't anticipate reinforcing them because they don't have any reserve units available. They're looking for a quick victory without the need for reinforcement. And, General, the world news media are already trying to swarm into Trinidad. The longer I can engage the Americans, the more casualties I can create. With media coverage, I can turn world opinion against the Americans for invading and turn Americans against their own government because of the casualties. We can win this one!"

"Tell me, General Drake, what do you need in addition to Piranha strike aircraft?" the Brazilian asked quietly.

"Mobile artillery. With that and strike aircraft, I can pin those robot infantry units into their present positions and create those casualties which will be splashed all over the TV screens of the world . . ."

"But I understand that American Robot Infantry regiments have some rather effective anti-aircraft measures."

"Self-guided tube rockets like the old Strellas and some quad-mount fifty-millimeter chassis. Americans depend on their Air Force gaining air superiority over their battlefields," Drake pointed out.

"But we've seen no air-ground combined arms co-operation from the Americans in this operation," Deodoro objected. "They struck the air fields and Fort George. But they have put no strike aerodynes over their troops for deep interdiction."

"Because of their rules of engagement, General," Austin Drake said. "It's damned difficult not to clobber civilians or to keep from damaging industrial facilities with tacair. The Americans have done this before. In fact, this seems to be a very straightforward replay of the old Bahrain occupation I took part in eleven years ago," Drake paused, then added, "It's a well known fact that Americans always fight a current conflict with the plans and tactics that were successful for them in their last similar operation . . ."

"You seem to have the American plans and intentions well analyzed, General."

"I do," Drake lied. "But I need some help to win this thing. My staff is showing itself to be inexperienced, and I've lost some excellent field officers."

"I'm sure we can bring in the Piranhas. Would some additional military advisors be useful as well?"

"Very much so!"

General Deodoro turned to his aide and spoke in rapid Portugese. The aide, a Brazilian colonel, jotted some notes on a pad of paper, then in turn handed it to an aide who was only a captain and who quickly disappeared out the door of the War Room.

Drake arose and extended his hand to the Brazilian. "General, we're going to beat these American bastards after all!"

"*Com certeza!* We know very well the sort of man we have supported here on Trinidad! After I contact Brasilia to make my full report and justify this request, I will be in touch with you in a few hours. Please come over and have lunch with me at the Brazilian Embassy . . ." So saying, General Deodoro swept out of the War Room with his retinue.

Austin Drake didn't know how he was going to get away from the War Room for the necessary three-hour Brazilian luncheon, but he knew he'd have to do it. He'd have to find a replacement for Carvahlo this morning. That wouldn't be easy.

And that on top of the current situation. He slipped into a chair and stared at the map. It was going to be tough, and it was going to be close. But, with the support of the ABC Allianza as promised in the treaty— or even with some minimal reinforcements—he knew his five regiments of battle-tested mercenaries could hold their own against the eight regiments of American robot infantry. The Americans had never fought their warbots in the tropics before; they didn't know how to do it right, and Austin Drake was going to make this lesson in warfare an expensive one for them to learn . . . and beat them in the process. Eight to six weren't bad odds. He'd accept those.

Capt. Julio Roca, Drake's Argentinian aide, slowly entered the War Room. His face was white, and his hand trembled as it held the message. "General Drake," Roca said with hesitation, "the situation has drastically changed, but I did not wish to interrupt you and General Deodoro . . ."

Austin Drake turned to face his staff man. "Well? What is it?"

Roca gave him the handwritten message, anticipating the usual response of the messenger who brings the bad news to the dictatorial leader. "We just received a telephone call from two of our observers on the north coast. "An estimated multi-national force of fifteen hundred infantry have succesfully landed at La Vanche Bay and Blanchisseuse. Troops from Venezuela, Panama, Colombia, and two other nations have been observed. They are moving rapidly over the North Range toward Port of Spain and Arima. We have no units available to meet this third invasion except your roboticized Presidential Guard here in Port of Spain . . ."

CHAPTER TWENTY-SIX

If Gen. Austin Drake was having his political, organizational, and strategic problems at the very top of his own hierarchy, the problems down at the fighting level of his enemy were no less compelling although they might have been of a different degree.

From the viewpoint of Capt. Curt Carson, Operation Steel Band was one of bone-weary travel over kilometers of road, always on the alert for snipers, enemy units, or even the partisans that he'd been warned about.

Fortunately, there was no dust. The roads were well paved with asphalt as Adonica Sweet had pointed out.

But the heat and humidity made up for the lack of dust. The ACV's environmental control system just couldn't keep up with it because it was impossible to dog down the hatches and depend solely upon the ACV's sensors. Curt or Kester had to stay alert, helmeted head out of the top turret hatch, binoculars and infra red goggles in use, scanning the surroundings as they moved past.

God knows the scenery was something right out of a tourist' handbook—lush tropical ran forest lining both sides of the road, the brilliant colors of flowers, and the incredible sounds of uncountable birds. Adonica Sweet had mentioned to Jerry Allen that many of the gaudy blooms were wild orchids. Back in the States, the domesticated versions of these lovely flowers would have each been worth a small fortune. Curt had raised hell with Allen for debouching from his moving platoon ACV unarmed to pick a bouquet of these wild orchids; Allen was properly contrite and submissive to Curt's verbal discipline, but it was obvious that the platoon leader's thoughts were elsewhere. A few minutes later, Curt noticed both Allen and Adonica in the turret hatch of their leading ACV; Adonica had plaited those wild orchids into her straw blonde hair.

Combat and a love affair didn't exactly go together in Curt's mind. But they were depending on Adonica Sweet, and she had to ride the lead vehicle because the Companions were not only the recon outfit of the Greys but also the pathfinders in the quick sweep around the right flank. He couldn't get along without her because the maps weren't that good.

Almost without warning, Kester called down from the turret, "ATV approaching from minus-x up the column!"

"Who is it?" Curt asked.

"Looks like the Colonel."

Curt undogged the view hatch in the aft sortie door in time to see the ATV sweep to the left side.

"We're being hailed down," Kester reported.

"Companion One, pull to the right side of the road and halt," Curt gave the verval order to his Armored Command Vehicle.

"Do you want the rest of the column to stop?" Kester called down.

"Negative."

"We'll be out of column order, Captain," the master sergeant reminded him, "and on these narrow roads we can overtake with this monster only at wide spots."

250

"Worry about that later," Curt advised him. When the Colonel came forward to visit, she took priority.

"Lower the sortie ramp," Curt told his ACV.

The blast of hot, wet air invaded the interior of the bus-sized vehicle as the rear ramp came down. Almost immediately, Col. Belinda Hettrick debouched from her ATV, dashed across the intervening space, and came up the ramp. She was fully dressed for personal combat, wearing cammies, helmet, and cammy cream. She was carrying her Hornet submachinegun. Quickly returning Curt's salute, she told him, "Get that ramp up! Damn, it's humid in this place! And get moving again! My ATV will follow you."

It would take a few minutes for the enviromental system of Curt's ACV to wring all the humidity out of the air that had invaded the interior of the vehicle. "Companion One, this is Companion Leader. Join the column at the first opportunity." He turned and asked his commanding officer, "What's going on, Colonel?"

Hettrick unslung her Hornet and pulled off her helmet to reveal her shaved head covered with beads of sweat like her face and arms. "I would have sent an aide up to learn the answer to that question, Captain, except we're moving so fast I figured I'd better come up myself. Your tacomm must be out. Have you heard any of my calls in the last hour or so?"

Curt shook his head. "Not a sound. I haven't even been talking to my own company, so I don't know whether or not any of the comm gear is working."

"Call my command vehicle," Hettrick told him.

Keying in the tacomm code, Curt spoke into his headset boom mike, "Grey Head, this is Companion Leader. How do you read?"

Silence.

"Getting out?" Hettrick wondered.

Curt indicated the equipment. "Indicates it is."

"Call your point vehicle."

"Companion Alpha, this is Companion Leader. How do you read?"

The audio reply came back with strange noises that sounded like Sgt. Edie Sampson was gargling. "Companion Leader, this is Companion Alpha. I read you with difficulty."

"My God, Alpha is less than fifty meters ahead!" Curt breathed.

"Sounds like the digitizer circuits are dropping in and out at random," Henry Kester said from his perch up in the turret.

"Electronic equipment is dying slowly and in random fashion throughout the regiment," Hettrick told him. "How's your computer?"

"Companion One seems to be working all right thus far. No reports of trouble from my other units."

"Pull that tacomm unit, the one that's garbling incoming and failing to send outgoing," Hettrick directed him.

Twisting four fasteners, Curt pulled the thin plastic package out of its slot. One look at the multiple-pin connector in the back was all it took. "Goddamn thing is green with gunk!"

"Corrosion," Hettrick said.

"On gold contacts?"

"Or fungus," the Colonel added.

"What the inside of this thing look like?" Curt wondered.

"Have you got a spare?"

"Yes."

"Plug it in, then pop the seals on this one."

After Curt had inserted the standby tacomm transceiver in the slot, he took the inoperative unit, stood it on its edge on a shelf, pulled his survival knife from its sheath at his belt, inserted the edge of the blade in one of the minute cracks, and pried the plastic casing open.

"What the hell?" Curt saw the tiny plastic boards and other miniature electronic chips and components inside were supporting various coatings and lumps of yellow, green, and blue; some were smooth, and some were furry.

"I was right. Fungus," Hettrick muttered. "Throw it away. It can't be fixed. It's being eaten."

"Panama," M. Sgt. Kester put in cryptically.

"You ought to know," Hettrick told him. "You were there. What do we do, Sergeant?"

"Couple of things," the old soldier remarked. "First, keep the warbots—all kinds of warbots—inside where they're cool until they're absolutely needed. That'll keep the residual fungus in them from growing faster than the internal inhibitors can kill it . . . which is what happened to that tacomm. Second, keep our vehicles closed and cool; they'll prevent the other Hyper High Speed circuitry from getting eaten. Third, be prepared at all times to override any and all computers and go into idiot mode with our head-mounted computers. Last, we get our hands on some UBQ-1 communications units like Adonica Sweet said she could find in this area . . ."

"UBQ-1 units? Never heard of them. What are they?" Hettrick asked.

"Carrier pigeons, Colonel."

CHAPTER TWENTY-SEVEN

"Carrier pigeons? Dammit, Henry Kester, this is no time for jokes!" Col. Belinda Hettrick exploded.

"Colonel, I'm not kidding. We also oughta be ready to go back to the old hand signals for visual-range column work. Or whistle signals. Do we have any whistles available?" Kester asked.

"Whistles?"

"Every old drill sergeant used to carry one. Best auditory signalling system the Army ever had. Caught your attention for sure, it did. Better than bugles or drums."

"No whistles," Hettrick admitted. "But I remember what you're talking about. And we have no buglers left, either; they were replaced long ago with audio recordings." She paused for a moment, evaluating the deteriorating electronics communication systems they had come to depend on. She knew they'd have to come up with a subsitute—and possibly very soon—until Supply could bring up new tacomms. "Sergeant Kester, you woldn't happen to know the old hand signal system, would you?"

"Matter of fact, I do, now that you mention it, Colonel."

"While the tacomm system is still working, pass a

verbal description of some very simple systems up to regimental cee-pee for distribution."

"Yes, Colonel. Do you want me to run a quick briefing when we stop for the chow wagons to catch up with us at noon?"

"Please do." Hettrick looked grim. "Dammit, the history books are going to laugh like hell at us . . ."

"Better than being caught with no communications whatsoever, Colonel," Curt pointed out. "I'll bet the Department of the Army is likely to look rather favorably on us for having enough military knowledge to be able to fall back on those old systems when the new ones fail." He suddenly had a thought. "When we stop in Ciperio Ste. Croix in a few minutes to pick up our pigeons, let's see if our native guide can find us some native drummers, too . . ."

That was almost too much for Colonel Hettrick. "Drummers haven't been used on the battlefield since the Civil War! And where the hell are we going to find drums and drummers on an island like Trinidad?"

"Colonel," Curt Carson told her slowly, "Trinidad is the birthplace of the steel band. There's hardly a town or village on this island that doesn't have its steel band and people who can make drums out of old fifty-five gallon oil containers! How much time do you think it would take them to work out a signalling code?"

Hettrick was quiet for a moment. She felt rather naked and vulnerable because she was out of instantaneous telecommunication with her regiment, a factor that wouldn't have concerned any commander in pre-radio days. Like most people, she'd grown accustomed to rapid communication when she wanted it. It was obvious to her that something had to be done to solve the growing communications problem. She'd taken the necessary first steps, and was unafraid of the consequences. Unlike many commanders, she didn't fear

255

criticism or even censure for using such primitive methods on the modern battlefield. But she was afraid these might not work quite as well on the modern roboticized battlefield as they had in prior times. Combat success was her goal, not conformity to doctrine.

She was also worried about the very real possibility that the warbots and the associated computer intelligence amplifiers, nervous system linkage circuitry, and up-down-link communications between warbot brainy and warbot might deteriorate. This would mean that her troops, most of whom were still regular RI, would have to "go personal" or "into idiot mode using the head-mounted computer." In short, they'd have to go into personal combat as Carson's Companions had done, but without even the minimal amount of training and experience that the Sierra Charlies had gotten in war gaming and survivalist training. This would also put them at a severe manpower disadvantage because the Washington Greys had a TO of only 92 people versus an estimated 2,000 troops in each Tee-dad regiment.

She *had* to keep her three warbot companies operational! If they began to succumb to the tropical environment like the communications systems had, she didn't have the capability at regimental level to repair them, and her maintenance section would be heavily overworked doing nothing more than replacing "blackboards," as the modular encapsulated electronics and computer components were nick-named. First priority for Lt. Harriet Dearborn in supply would be to turn on the faucet for every type of blackboard used in the regiment so that Capt. Ellwood Otis would have something for his maintenance platoon to replace. She might even have to authorize field replacement of some blackboards if Otis' people got overworked.

Once she got back to her regimental CP, she'd get

her staff on the job and talk with General Carlisle at divisional headquarters. If the whole division—nay, the entire warbot contingent of Operation Steel Band—was facing this problem, G-4 *had* to know about it and be ready for it, even though they were only a little more than one day into a planned five-day campaign. It could last a lot longer if the warbots and high-tech were clobbered by an enemy the Army had once known how to fight but had forgotten about in the long years since Panama . . . or even the South Pacific back in World War II.

First priority, however, was to get the communication systems properly backed-up. She turned to Curt asked, "No drums. Too noisy. Might attract enemy fire. But pigeons are another matter. How do you intend to run this carrier pigeon system?"

"I don't know," Curt told her frankly. "It was Adonica Sweet's idea."

"Your native guide? Then get her back here. I want to talk with her," Hettrick snapped. She didn't want to return to her own regimental ACV until she'd seen the pigeon and hand signal systems in operation. Most of all, she couldn't afford in this stage of the rapid flanking maneuver to be out of touch with her recon company, and she would be if she left then.

Curt got through to Jerry Allen's ACV on the tacomm well enough to pass the order to send Adonica back. He watched the forward visual monitor with Hettrick and saw Adonica jump off the lead vehicle and run back down the road toward them with her steel Mini-14 glinting in the sunlight.

"Rather young to be doing this, isn't she?" Hettrick commented.

"She knows what she's doing," was Curt's response. "The Tee-dads imprisoned her father on espionage charges, so she's pretty well motivated against

257

the Tee-dads. She also wants to find her father if she can. And he's retired, disabled, a Captain in the Washington Greys back in the Panama fracas."

"Really! But aren't you worried about her riding the lead ACV with young Allen?"

"Yes, but Sgt. Edwina Sampson's up there, too."

"That may not keep young Allen from becoming distracted by her. Very distracted, I might add, judging by her looks."

"Colonel, her father is on Trindad as a manager for Texarco. She's an American citizen," Curt pointed out.

Hettrick smiled. "She is? Good! Then I can brevet her to third lieutenant so Rule Ten will apply . . ."

"I was hoping you would," Curt admitted. It would take some stretching of the Army regulations, but Colonel Hettrick had the authority. Ever since the War of 1812, regimental commanders in the field had the authority to brevet Indian scouts and other locals as "third lieutenants" in a campaign; it was still done with cadets and midshipmen from the academies when they were temporarily assigned to an operational unit or ship during their annual six-week, in-service tour of duty prior to their senior year. The "third lieutenant" brevet hadn't been used in a campaign for a very long time, but the authority to give such temporary "commissions" was in the Army regs, albeit hard to find but there nonetheless.

Adonica came in through the turret hatch rather than the rear sortie ramp whose lowering would have dumped more hot, wet air into the ACV. She seemed quite delighted to meet Hettrick. When the Colonel offered to brevet her to third lieutenant, Adonica accepted eagerly and without hesitation.

"Good! Now, how is this carrier pigeon system of yours going to work?"

"I don't know. Zeenab Tej will be able to explain it. She and her father used to race pigeons with my father, but I was only a bystander. I never got actively involved. We should be passing through Ciperio in a few minutes. I'll find her. Shouldn't take very long to get things organized."

When the column entered the the village of Ciperio Ste. Croix on the northern edge of one of Trinidad's oil fields, it looked just like any other village on a Caribbean island. Because the Fifth TDF Regiment had detoured to the north last night and thus not engaged the Cottonbalers of the 17th Iron Fist, there was no indication of battle anywhere. In fact, there was little if anything to indicate that an invading army in the form of the Cottonbalers had passed through. The Cottonbalers were a proud old regiment with a tradition to uphold; their officers and NCOs both felt a strong obligation to maintain the image of the American Army as one that did not loot, rape, and pillage in the field.

As a result, the refinery and oil field workers and their families lined the road through the little village, cheering and waving whatever scrap of fabric they could find.

Curt, Hettrick, and Adonica Sweet rode the glacis plate while Kester manned the turret hatch. The mid-morning sun was already hot, and the humidity was so high that it felt like a wet cloth pulled over Curt's face. These people didn't seem to mind the island's climate, but they were used to it.

"A surprising mixed bag of people, aren't they?" Hettrick remarked.

"I've been amazed," Curt replied. "I didn't realize Trinidad was such a melting pot . . ."

"Oh, the people of Trinidad have come from almost everywhere," Adonica Sweet told them brightly. "Americans like myself, Britishers, Dutch, Latvians, former African slaves, Hindus, Pakistani, Saudi, Malays, Chinese . . . It's a long list. And we get along quite well with one another. Until General Drake took over, there was always plenty for everyone . . ."

"We'll see if we can't let you bring back the plenty," Hettrick told her, "without someone at the top looting it all."

"Yes, of course! We know that's why you're here." Adonica suddenly jumped off the glacis plate and ran to the side of the road. "Zee! Zeenab Tej!" she called.

It sounded like a man's name, which was why Curt was surprised when Adonica threw her arms around another young woman slightly older than herself but with an exotic, fascinating beauty greatly different from Adonica's fresh, all-American girl look.

Zeenab Tej had not traded all of her heritage for the easy-going tropical garb of Trinidad. There was a hint of the Punjab, of Bombay, of the ancient civilization of the Indus in the silk and color and drape of her garb and the complexity of the golden jewelry that she wore on her wrists and ankles. Yet she didn't have the full face of most Hindu women, but could have posed for any of the classical Greek statues of goddesses.

Adonica brought her over to the ACV. "Colonel Hettrick, Captain Carson, this is one of my oldest friends, Zeenab Tej!"

The woman spoke in the lilting English dialect of Trinidad but with an overlay of formal Oxonian English. "It is indeed a pleasure to meet you and to thank you for your efforts to help Trinidad! Adonica tells me you would like my help."

"We understand your father has pigeons we might use for messages," Hettrick began bluntly.

Zeenab Tej shook her head sadly. Her long, black hair was tightly wrapped in a complex bun behind her head and a filmy orange silk scarf hung from it, swinging back and forth as she moved. "My father was called to a supervisor's meeting in Couva two days ago. I'm afraid he may have been caught in the invasion."

Hettrick tossed up her hands. "Well, there goes our carrier pigeon system! I'm just as glad. Pigeons are filthy birds. Had too many of them in Philly where I grew up . . ."

"Oh, do you want to use our pigeons for message duty?" Zeenab asked with a smile. "Of course! You don't need my father for that! I'll set up the system and keep the birds for you. Just tell me how you want to communicate with one another, and I'll establish the cages in the proper locations!"

"Actually, Miss Tej, we need to communicate between moving vehicles," Curt explained.

"No problem! How many vehicles? Can you help me bring the birds and cages here? I'll likely need a bit of help if we're to do it quickly . . ." When she saw hesitation in Hettrick and remembered the colonel's previous comment, she turned and added, "Colonel, our birds are not the street pigeons you knew in America. My father has spent decades cross-breeding the Inca doves and white fronted doves of tropical America with the green fruit pigeons my grandfather brought from India. They will always fly to their mate because they are strongly monogamous. And we keep them clean, healthy, and well fed; one does not mistreat an athlete, especially an animal that can fly for more than a thousand kilometers if necessary. I think you may be surprised by their beauty . . ."

Curt was as amazed by the unexpected appearance or the birds as he was by the unanticipated beauty of Zeenab Tej.

He, too, had known only the street pigeon as a grey, dirty-looking bird, often with white or tan spots and markings, that still inhabited North American cities by the billions as scavengers. Zeenab's birds in their clean and coloful cages sported glistening, almost fluorescent green, white, and blue plumage. They emitted the same "coo-coo-coo" sounds as the street pigeons he'd known, and they strutted and nodded like all pigeons.

"The females will always return to their specific cages," Zeenab explained. "The males will always fly to their selected lifetime female mate. Therefore, we take the females in strange cages and leave the males in familiar cages. The males or the females will therefore always return no matter who releases them in what sequence."

"Doesn't take very long for the system to stabilize itself with females back in their own cages and the males with them," Hettrick observed.

Zeenab nodded. "True, so there must be physical redistribution of the system quite often."

"Damned nuisance," Hettrick muttered.

"But better than human messengers trying to find their destinations," Curt pointed out.

"We'll probably end up using human messengers, too, even as short-handed as we are . . ."

"Oh, but I can find local messengers for you," Adonica put in. "Lots of youngsters know these roads very well, and they'll be happy to act as message carriers for a dollar or so . . ."

"Pretty damned expensive," Hettrick said. She wasn't really sure she liked all of this non-reg procedure that was being forced upon her by the failure of the Ordnance and Signal Corps to consider fighting in the tropics. Deep down inside, she was concerned with the effect these local women were going to have on her crack Sierra Charlie company, the one she was counting on.

"A Trinidad dollar is about twenty-five cents American," Adonica explained.

"Well," Hettrick replied with a shrug, "we'll use runners if we have to." She looked at her watch. She should report to Carlisle soon. And she didn't feel comfortable being away from her command post for this length of time. "Give me what I'll need to pigeonate back and forth with my four companies on the march," she told Zeenab, creating a new Army term in the process. "Captain, better get moving again. We've got to cover another fifteen kilometers before noon."

CHAPTER TWENTY-EIGHT

Six pigeon cages were strapped to the mizzendeck of Curt's ACV, but only after Curt and Kester rigged a tarp shade at Zeenab's insistence to keep the pigeons out of the direct sun.

Then it was a matter of move out, move fast, move forward.

Curt still had marginal and garbled communications with his point vehicle over the ACV's last reserve tacomm unit. He ordered Kester down out of the turret cupola and told him to dog it down. "We've got to keep things cool enough in here that our remaining tacomm doesn't quit," Curt explained.

"We can do it," Kester agreed, "as long as the command computer keeps on working and we have x and minus-x video monitors."

"How's you manual control skill?" Curt wanted to know.

"Hell, I can drive this thing," Kester replied with easy confidence. "It's easier to let the automatics do it, but I can wheel this bus if I have to. We used to have to, you know . . ."

"Damned good thing the Cottonbalers cleared this road on their forward sweep," Curt said outloud. "We'd be in a hell of a mess if we had to fight for every meter.

Kester didn't take his eyes off the video monitors or the computer readout that assured him that Companion One was still running the ACV properly. "Captain, I've been thinking," he remarked. "If we've had trouble with our tactical communications and are starting to see some glitches in our other computer electronics, what's happening in the other units? Hell, they're even more vulnerable than we are. Their warbot brainies are hooked right into the computers. How can they keep on fighting if their gear is going tits-up?"

Curt didn't answer for a moment, He was savoring Zeenab Tej's quiet, exotic beauty, something he hadn't expected to encounter in this campaign. Certainly, the probabilities of encountering a fresh young woman such as Adonica were themselves astronomical, but running into the exotic Zeenab Tej as well was totally improbable and unaccountable. She distracted him, and he knew it. He forced himself to think about Kester's question.

"First of all, Sergeant, I don't know how much fighting they're doing. We haven't been told the big picture, probably on purpose. But it looks like the other units haven't done much. Maybe the Can Do did when they took over from us. But when the Cottonbalers came through here last night; they didn't fight, they just had to advance and keep on advancing. But there's something else I think we've forgotten, and we shouldn't have because we're old warbot brainies ourselves . . . The RI companies and regiments not only have the latest state-of-the-art technology, but they're right inside it. You know what it's like to run warbots . . ."

"Sure do." A warbot brainy used a warbot as a complete extension of himself—sight, sound, movement, the works—as the warbot sensors and feeback systems reported directly to the human's nervous system and the human gave direct commands from his nervous system to the warbot.

"And what's it got that we haven't got much of?" Curt went on.

"Redundancy. Lots of back-up. Can't afford to have the system go bad when there's a human being involved."

"More than that, I think. Ever had a warbot go bad on you?"

"Hell, yes, Captain! We all have!"

"You know it when it starts to happen, just like you know when your arm goes to sleep or you stubbed your toe or you have a cold and your sense of smell is shot to hell," Curt went on. "So you'd switch to backups immediately or withdraw from the warbot and yell for maintenance to step in. Right?"

"Right."

"And as Sierra Charlies we have taken ourselves partly out of that loop. We know when a gadget is going bad only when it fails to work right. We have little if any advance notice."

"Yeah, that's one of the problems of the Sierra Charlie concept . . ."

"And one we didn't get worked out before going where we could get shot at. Tacomm is our big problem at the moment, right? Don't answer that; it was a rhetorical question, Henry; it wasn't asked to find out whether or not you're stupid. Where is tacomm used in this Army?"

"Well, sure as hell not in the RI! We didn't need it! We had direct communications back and forth everywhere through normal warbot linkage channels!"

"Yup! Tacomm has been used only in the rear echelon, out of combat range, in protected environments so that people up at divisional level could actually talk to one another just like the paper pushers have done for centuries. We're not only using rear echelon equipment right up at the front where it takes far more beating, but we're also working with stuff that should still be labelled experimental back at Aberdeen Proving Ground. Does that answer your question?

Henry Kester thought about it for a moment. "Yeah, but it doesn't make me feel any better knowing that we're an unproven, untested, highly exprimental unit forced into combat long before we were ready. Hettrick and the Greys are counting on us. We're up at the head of the pack. We could get ambushed at any moment. And the minute we do, are you ready to bet that Kelly—whose right in our minus-x—wouldn't trample all over us to close with the enemy, particularly when he tries to communicate with us on tacomm and doesn't get an answer?"

"I don't know what you're doing in a Sierra Charlie infantry company, Sergeant," Curt told him without rancor. "You've got enough imagination today to warrant shipping you back where you could dream away with the divisional or even the Army staff stooges . . ."

"Captain, you can't insult me. First place, a hell of a lot of officers, good and bad, have chewed my ass or pulled my leg, so I'm sorta used to it. But don't be surprised if Captain Kelly climbs up our ass if we get into a fracas . . . and don't be surprised if one of the Saucy Cans or a Hairy Fox accidentally gets its azimuth coordinates one-eighty out and shoots his lips off—"

"Excuse me," Zeenab Tej put in quietly, "but who are you fighting?"

"Soldier talk, Miss Tej," Curt explained. "You'll probably hear a lot you don't understand. The Sergeant and I go way back together. Don't worry about what you hear. Just concentrate on making the pigeon system work when we need it."

267

"I can also help as a guide," Zeenab volunteered. She was radiating something that Curt thought must be part of her heritage, a projection of desire, a message of willingness, the quintessential exotic projection of promises of joys and pleasure beyond a man's wildest imaginings, something that must have become part of her genetic background from forebears who'd lived on a subcontent where it was a young woman's duty to be attractive to men. "Adonica must get some rest occasionally. And I know the southern part of Trinidad very well. Unlike Adonica, I was born here. I grew up here."

"Thanks. I may take you up on that," Curt told her. He was unusually blunt and sharp. Part of it was his own reaction to what she had just told him and partly because of the subliminal way Zeenab Tej was acting.

And Curt had been concerned about Jerry Allen becoming infatuated with Adonica Sweet and thus losing his combat edge! Well, he'd solved that. Third Lieutenant Adonica Sweet was as thoroughly bound by Rule Ten as Jerry Allen himself.

Now Curt was finding himself becoming fascinated with Zeenab Tej. Strong feelings surged through him, ones that he shouldn't have to worry about as a company commander in combat, ones that he'd trained himself to sublimate because of Army Regulation 601-10.

By God, you're going to have to discipline yourself, Carson! he told himself viciously. This is no time to get involved with a woman . . . any woman!

Although Gen. Austin Drake was certainly having his problems at one end of the campaign spectrum and Capt. Curt Carson was having ones that were different only in kind, not degree, over on the other side on the firing line, Col. Belinda Hettrick herself was engrossed in a multitude of her own difficulties stemming, in a like fashion, from both personal and professional sources. Back in her regimental command post and into computer linkage for the maximum effectiveness and data transfer, she was reporting to Maj. Gen. Jacob O. Carlisle of the 17th Iron Fist in his divisional headquarters near Penal.

"We're on schedule, General," Hettrick told him, "but we may have some field communications problems down on the company level."

"What's the problem, Colonel?"

"Failure of the rear echelon tacomm units, both vehicular and portable, that were all we had available for Carson Companions, our Sierra Charlie outfit. They weren't designed for the sort of rough abuse they're encountering in tropical combat conditions. We've arranged for some back-up systems, some of which I consider to be rather primitive . . ."

"What are they?"

Hettrick was afraid Carlisle might ask that question. "On the local tactical level, Carson is going back to hand signals. For command tactical between regiment and company, he'll be using carrier pigeons . . ."

Carlisle didn't seem surprised. "Well, they've worked before, Colonel."

That was a response she hadn't anticipated. It made her feel better. "Carson's people are being very innovative, General. They've even considered the use of the Trinidad steel bands to provide drum signals . . ."

Carlisle chuckled. "Well, Carson's people are intelligent; he leads them well. That's why he was selected to debug the Sierra Charlie concept, if it's valid at all . . . But you seem unusually worried, Belinda. Is it this wide right sweep I've asked you to do? With your Sierra Charlies, you're the best outfit to do it."

"Yes, sir, I am a bit worried. We've got our neck a
269

hell of a long way out. We're going to be a long column with exposed flanks. The Tee-dads could exploit that when they find out."

"Colonel, if you keep on moving according to schedule, the Tee-dads won't come anywhere near you," Carlisle told her. "Here, let me show you the situation."

A holographic map swam into reality in front of her; actually, it was projected into the visual cortex of her brain by the actions of the intelligence amplifiers at both divisional and regimental headquarters.

"The Can Do and the Wolfhounds both have broken the Oropuche River line and taken Napirima. The Fourth Tee-dad Regiment is in retreat, pulling out of San Fernando to the northeast. The Cottonbalers will hit them on the flank near Bonne Aventure. That's well to the north of you by almost ten kilometers. The Double Deuces have pushed inland beyond the highway and both the Third and Fifth Tee-dad regiments are withdrawing. Looks like everyone is heading for Piarco International Airport because the Carib forces made their successful landing this morning and are already on the northern outskirts of Port of Spain. The Presidential Guard seems to be moving eastward toward Piarco. I think they're going to make a stand at Piarco where the ABC Allianza might be able to airsupply them."

"Looks like the Greys are moving away from the action, General," Hettrick observed. She didn't like that. Even with her communications problems, she didn't want to be shuffled off to some quiet corner of the island to hold down a flank position while the final fight took place elsewhere.

"Maybe so at the moment, but we don't know exactly what the Tee-dads have in mind at this point," Carlisle explained. "They're withdrawing and conserving their forces. At this time, we want Rio Claro in our hands to secure the eastern side of the island. Otherwise, our rear may be totally unprotected if an ABC Alliance force puts ashore along the east coast.

"In the meantime, don't worry about your flanks. We have no reports of Tee-dad partisans in the Central Range. Or have you run into any?"

"No, sir, the locals seem quite happy to see us."

"Same report coming in from everywhere on that. So proceed to Rio Claro and occupy it by eighteen hundred hours tonight."

"Uh, General Carlisle, that's better than fifteen kilometers to traverse in only about six hours."

"You should meet no resistance, Colonel. And don't worry about your flanks; there are no Tee-dad forces that could threaten them because we've got them all engaged at the moment. Get to Rio Claro. I'll have further orders for you then when the overall enemy disposition and possible ABC Allianza involvement become more clear. Be prepared to move in *any* direction out of Rio Claro. The Washington Greys are my maneuvering unit; I'm going to put you behind the enemy so you can hassle the hell out of him. Don't worry; you'll get your fight . . ."

saving their forces. At this time, air was in Clare
in our hands to secure we chosen store of the Islands
Otherwise with less may be totally overrun well as
the Aubron force pass under these weapon once C
to his hand-picked close fighters. You must finally
to have an edge and he and release of the General
General. Or have you had this ....

CHAPTER TWENTY-NINE

On the approach to Rio Claro, Curt kept his ACV
within visual distance of Lt. Jerry Allen's Alpha Platoon vehicles consisting of Alpha's command ACV
with its little All Terrain Vehicle in tow followed by
Alpha's Robot Transport Vehicle and Light Artillery
Maneuvering Vehicle with its Saucy Cans.

But he instructed Lt. Alexis Morgan to keep her
Bravo Platoon vehicles 500 meters behind him.

Curt had some tacomm contact with Alexis, but he
had to use hand signals between his vehicle and those
of Alpha Platoon. Alexis' equipment apparently
hadn't yet succumbed to the fungus rot that had
somehow infested the innards of their electronic gear.
He warned Allen in a written order which Sergeant
Edie Sampson dashed back to pick up:

*Exercise caution entering R. Claro. Proceed to 5th Reg ca-
sern. Housekeeping troops may be there. Return fire if fired
upon. If engaged, go straight. Bravo will flank right. Killers
will support.*

The order had been as succint as he could write it.
It had been a very long time indeed since he'd actually written a field order.

A similar message went back by tacomm to Alexis,
whose equipment was in shape to relay it rearward
down the column to Kelly's Killers, Ward's Warriors,

Hettrick's CP, and Manny's Marauders in that order.

Curt didn't know if any of the other company commanders were having trouble with their equipment because of the heat and humidity. He had his own problems to worry about.

And the Priority Number One problem right now was entering a town that had been garrisoned less than twenty-four hours before by several thousand troops of the Tee-dad 5th Regiment.

Army units everywhere weren't very different; they always had some sort of rear echelon types who often did nothing more than cover the unit's actions with the necessary paperwork—now done almost totally in megacomputers by the U.S. Army, of course, which didn't necessarily mean that less actual paper was generated. Curt knew that computers hadn't eliminated hard copies; they proliferated them. Even when the Washington Greys moved out of garrison, a platoon of Headquarters Company troops was usually left in place for housekeeping purposes, gathering up all the loose ends before following the regiment to its new garrison or campaign.

Their route from the Devil's Woodyard eastward had been along the southern foothills of the Central Range, a low spine of hills about 1,000 meters high that cut diagonally across Trinidad from the southwest to the northeast. The going had been easier than coming up the Southern Main Highway along the west coast, but they had to move more slowly toward Rio Claro because the two-lane road wound and twisted over ridges and rivers. The area, once sugar cane fields, had been reforested late in the last century by the government to provide a supply of softwood for the economy. As a result, the countryside wasn't the dank rain forest they'd encountered south of San Fernando, but relatively open forest with a great deal of secondary growth. However, where the new growth was concentrated, it was dense indeed. As Trinidad's economy had progressed, the need for softwoods had declined, and some of the areas along the road hadn't been harvested in decades.

Curt was fatigued. The initial tension of waiting under water in the dank confines of the *Tally Puss* had been followed by the shock of battle at the Oropuche River and then by a day of rapid and seemingly endless travel along roads where they could have been ambushed at any moment.

Fortunately, Gen. Austin Drake's regime hadn't garnered the sort of popular support needed for the formation of effective partisan groups to repel invaders. On the other hand, the American troops had found an underground anti-Drake network already in place and in communication with someone beyond the island who'd managed to coordinate their efforts. Curt didn't worry about such things. The ins and outs of the spooks were more than he cared to play with. That wasn't his game. Early in his Army career, he'd opted to serve in the RI rather than Intelligence or other support branches. He figured that if he survived as a warbot brainy and if the vagaries of an Army career allowed him to climb what was vulgarly known as "the greasy pole of promotion," he knew he'd eventualy find himself in staff positions and higher commands eventually. No need to rush it.

About a kilometer out of Rio Claro, Curt ordered the Companions to combat-sit level. They'd spent most of the afternoon inside the vehicles anyway because the regular afternoon thundershower had soaked the countryside for thirty minutes shortly after 1400 hours. Now the clouds had broken. They were driving eastward into a beautiful double rainbow generated by another rainshower out in the Atlantic off the coast.

"My birds will be all right, won't they?" Zeenab had asked anxiously.

Curt looked around to the bird cages riding on the rear deck, then ducked his head inside and told her with a smile, "Well, they look all right. A little wet, maybe. They won't melt, will they?" He didn't tell her that they could be raked by rifle fire coming from the sides of the road if they were ambushed. He'd used a carrier pigeon about an hour ago to communicate the situation and his intentions back to Hettrick. He was fascinated by the gentle and almost loving way Zeenab treated those beautiful birds. It was obvious that the woman had a great deal of love in her. Curt was having difficulty keeping his mind on the combat situation. He forced himself in an almost Prussian fashion to concentrate on his job because the lives of eleven people in Carson's Companions depended on him and those eleven had given him trust and obedience far beyond that required by Army regulations and manuals.

"Hardly, Captain," Zeenab replied. "But I don't want them to get too hot."

"They won't," Curt promised her and managed to tear his eyes away from her and return to "riding shotgun" for his ACV with his helemeted head extending through the turret hatch only to the extent that he could see over the rim. He preferred to do it that way. He'd learned during the exercises and war games in the Virgin Islands that video sensors and displays lacked depth and discrimination when compared to his eyes, especially in this short-range, semi-jungle environment.

The town of Rio Claro was absolutely quiet as the Companions' column entered it. The shops were shut.

No one was in the streets. There was no grand welcoming throng as there had been when they'd passed through Ciperio Ste. Croix or even Princes Town.

"Captain, there's gotta be some of the Tee-dad Fifth Regiment left here," Henry Kester's voice came to Curt's ears from the ACV's main compartment below.

"Yeah. No civilian welcome. Everybody's hiding. But I don't see any evidence of Tee-dads, Where the hell could they be?"

"Probably holed up in the casern with ammo and communications."

"Sounds reasonable. Got any good guess where the casern is located?"

"Last high-resolution satellite image indicates maybe on the southeast quadrant of the town square where the main roads cross." Kester replied. "They probably don't expect us."

This last comment surprised Curt. "Eh? Why?"

"If I was them, and if I was expecting us, I'd cover the road with one-oh-sixes and bring the column under fire before it entered the town," Kester told him. "We didn't take any incoming. So they're not expecting us. So they'll react after we're in the town. So it's street fighting. Like Munsterlagen. Or Zahedan."

"I'll sign off on that," Curt muttered, slightly changing his planned tactics in his mind. He'd grown to respect and trust his master sergeant's combat-honed hunches as well as his expertise. "We go to team combat dismounted mode with command warbots." He snaked his right arm up through the hatch alongside him and waved it back and forth.

Jerry Allen in his ACV turret hatch ahead of him saw it and responded in kind.

Curt moved his arm from the vertical down forward to the horizontal, signalling, "Forward!"

Allen responded by repeating the arm signal back.

Then Curt pumped his clenched fist downward several times, then swung his arm horizontally left and right: "Line of foragers, dismounted."

Jerry Allen repeated this.

Arm signalling seemed crude, slow, and ineffective, but Curt realized that he'd become wedded to the electronic umbilical of tacomm. Up until the twentieth century, radio hadn't been available to control troops in combat. But the old methods still worked for those who knew them, which is why West Point still taught them . . . much to the disgust of cadets spoiled by instant high-tech communication all of their lives.

He saw the sortie hatch of the Alpha Robot Transport Vehicle drop. Six Mary Anns swarmed out. Then came Platoon Sgt. Edwina Sampson followed immediately by Cpls. Jim Elliott and Charlie Koslowski followed in turn by six more Mary Anns. The platoon split. Six command warbots moved down each side of the street toward the town square.

Curt turned in his cupola but gave no hand signal to Alexis following behind him. Instead, he keyed the tacomm and hoped it was sill working. "Companion Bravo, this is Companion Leader. Do you read?"

"Garbled, but readable, Companion Leader."

"Dismount squads. As foragers on each side of the street. At the town square, column right. Repeat; at town square, column right. Casern is probably on southeast quadrant of square. Inform column."

"Roger, I read that as dismount squads, as foragers, each side of street. At square, column right. Casern on southeast quadrant. Passing it back."

Curt watched with careful eyes as they proceeded along the middle of the street. The townspeople hadn't evacuated; he caught the slight movement of a window curtain and the motionless shadow of a person

277

behind a partly closed door. The lack of an open reception seemed to confirm Kester's suspicion that a housekeeping contingent of the Tee-dad Fifth was still in town and that the townspeople were staying under cover because they expected bullets and shells to be snapping down the streets.

Nothing happened until Allen's ACV entered the town square.

The beautiful old flowing fountain in the middle of the square suddenly disappeared in a mushrooming cloud of dust and smoke. The concussion wave smacked Curt's helmet.

The next explosion demolished the wall of a shop behind Allen's ACV.

The Saucy Cans on the following LAMV swiveled in its turret, took aim, and got off two rounds.

Surprisingly, Lt. Jerry Allen suddenly erupted from the hatch of his ACV's turret, rolled down the back side of the vehicle, and hit the ground on his feet but crouched. The rear sortie hatch flopped down in emergency extension and Adonica Sweet ran out, helmet clutched in one hand and her silvery Mini-14 in the other.

"Why the hell are they abandoning the vehicle?" Kester yelled up to Curt.

Curt didn't get the chance to answer his Master Sergeant. A fraction of a second later, the ACV took what was apparently a 106mm HEAT round in the right forward armor plate. Even at an angle, the round punched right through the layered armor and caused the innards of the vehicle to erupt in gouts of flaming shards from the pyrophoric effect of the projectile's spent-uranium core.

"The vehicle's computer told 'em someone had pinned the targeting laser of that one-oh-six launcher on them," Kester guessed.

Curt didn't see what had happened to Allen, Adonica, or the Alpha Platoon. The square was suddenly full of dust and smoke and fire.

But he heard the sudden, sharp, unmistakeable *bam-bam-bam* rapid-fire report of the 75mm Saucy Cans on Alpha's LAMV.

And the rapid and ripping tearing-box sound of the high-rate fire of 20mm cannons on the Mary Anns.

He brought his ACV to a stop well short of the square.

A small form in cammies dashed and dodged out from the smoke, stopping occasionally to fire a silvery rifle from the hip in the general direction of the incoming fire. It was obviously Adonica Sweet. She ran up to Curt's ACV and ducked into the lee of it for protection. "Platoon or less!" she shouted between gasps of breath. "In the casern! Southwest corner of the square! Submachineguns and a single one-oh-six, we think. Alpha is proceeding down the street straight ahead to try to get behind it!"

Curt expected that response. Standard urban street fighting tactics modified for Sierra Charlies. Allen was following orders and knew what he was doing.

Ducking down inside the ACV, Curt yelled at Kester, "Move this humper to the side of the street. Dismount with the warbots! We're gonna find an alley and move south to the right flank. Only about twenty Tee-dads in the casern. A one-oh-six and burp guns."

"If that's all they got, they're housekeeping troops like you guessed," the master sergeant replied, moving quickly to power up warbots waiting in standby mode. "What we going to do about Zeenab?"

In her bright clothing, Zeenab Tej would be easily visible on the street. "Can you shoot?" he asked her.

She looked at him without the slightest trace of fear

279

in her expression and calmly replied, "I don't know. I've never tried. Give me a gun. I'll try."

"Damn!" This was no time to teach her to shoot. But he didn't want her to be unable to defend herself. The FABARMA assault rifle would be too much for her. He jerked open a small arms cabinet. Although the Companions had opted for the larger and heavier FABARMA assault rifle, the standard-issue M26A3 Hornet submachine carbines hadn't been removed from the ACV; there hadn't been time. He grabbed one, shoved two clips into it, cocked and armed it, and handed it to Zeenab. "Keep your finger off the trigger. That's this guarded button here. If someone comes at you, point this at him and push the trigger. Got it?"

"Yes." Her icy coolness was strange. She showed absolutely no wonderment, fear of the weapon, or reluctance to take it.

"Okay, stay with me."

"What about my birds?"

"They're protected behind the turret. Nine millimeter parabellum rounds can't penetrate the turret." He didn't tell her that if the ACV took a 106-millimeter flat trajectory high-velocity HEAT round as Allen's vehicle had, the pigeons would become fried squabs.

Kester had ordered the ACV to the side of the street tucked up against a flower shop with its bright and colorful blooms. He put it in automatic defense mode as the rear sortie hatch came down to ramp position.

"Ready, Captain," Kester said curtly.

"Follow me," Curt told the two of them and dashed down the ramp.

It was hot and damp in the street. Sporadic bursts of small arms fire continued, punctuated by the louder sounds from the Mary Anns. Curt heard the heavier reports from the 50mm on the Hairy Foxes; Alexis must have gotten some of her warbots into position. The rapid rippling fire of the Tee-dad submachine-guns was almost lost in the noise of the robotic fire-power of the Companions.

Looking back down the street, he could see Alexis' Bravo Platoon vehicles moving to the sides of the streets, ducking into alleyways, and otherwise moving to the south in the flanking maneuver.

Curt had to move fast. He and Kester couldn't stay in the street. Right behind the ACV was an alleyway leading south off the main street. Curt dropped to the hot concrete of the sidewalk and peered around the corner of a building to look down the alley. It was close quarters, barely three meters in width. Plenty of places for snipers to hide. Plenty of places to hide an ambush party. But there was no movement that he could see.

Some sixth sense told him the alley was clean, un-defended.

"Cover me," he snapped to Kester, "and follow me."

"Right with you," Kester fired back.

Curt jogged down the alley, moving quickly from one side to another at random. About fifty meters along, he began to curse the weight of the personal combat gear he was carrying. Hell of a lot easier to use a warbot, he told himself.

He came upon a passage space between buildings leading to the left. About ten meters down, there was a wooden fence about a meter high across the passage.

Someone was behind that fence.

"You behind the fence! Stand up slowly, hands in sight! Do it *now!* If you don't, I'll shoot!" Curt prob-

281

ably didn't mean it, and he knew that. If the huddled form turned out to be a civilian, the rules of engagement prohibited him from shooting.

The form didn't move.

CHAPTER THIRTY

Curt put a three round burst of fire from his FA-BARMA into the fence above the form. The impact of the bullets shattered the wood and threw splinters.

Two open hands appeared and a young boy slowly stood up. "Do not shoot! Do not shoot!" he suddenly screamed.

Curt didn't shoot. The boy was obviously too young. He was a noncombatant.

Moving quickly, Curt went up and vaulted the fence. The youngster was unarmed. "What the hell you doing here?" Curt wanted to know.

"I live here! I want to watch the fighting!" The boy was now terrified.

Curt reached out with his left hand and clapped the boy on the shoulder. "Get inside. You damned-near got killed. Go on!"

The boy disappeared into a door which slammed shut behind him.

The passageway opened onto the north-south street just below the casern.

Kester was alongside him as Curt cased the situation. "Nobody on this side of the casern . . . I think. They must be shorthanded and putting up their major fight down there in the square."

"Damned stupid. Shouldn't fight. They're 'way

283

outnumbered. They ought to surrender," Curt muttered.

Kester shook his head. "Not until they put up a token fight. Don't forget, Captain: The Tee-dads are Brazilians or Argentines. They think it ain't *macho* to give up without a fight."

"The hell you say. These guys aren't the same as the Panamaniacs you fought."

"The intelligence reports said Drake's Tee-dad troops were mostly Brazilian and Argentine mercenaries. They're *macho* all right." Kester observed with finality. "They'll fight, then surrender with their personal honor intact because they showed they weren't afraid to fight."

"Yeah, after they took out one of our ACVs in the process," Curt recalled glumly. "Okay, so we get them to surrender. How to we get into that casern from here?"

"Simple," Kester said. "Sally port door over there. Blow off the latch with an M20 grenade." When Curt started to say something, the master sergeant went on, "The casern ain't no civilian facility, Captain. ROEs don't apply."

"Okay, do it," Curt said and turned around. "Zeenab, you stay here . . . Where the hell did she go?"

Zeenab Tej was not to be seen. She hadn't followed them at some point in their trek from the ACV down the alley and passage.

"Shit! I haven't got time to go look for her," Curt exploded. But he knew she was armed. She could protect herself if necessary. But Curt didn't think it would be necessary. The town seemed benign except for the small contingent of Tee-dad troops defending the casern. "Okay, let's winkle the bastards out of there and get them to surrender."

The massive wooden double doors of the casern yielded all too easily to the detonation of the M20 plasticex grenade. Curt and Kester were inside immediately through the smoke and dust, taking advantage of the shock and surprise of the explosion.

But then all hell broke loose outside the casern toward the town square.

The big building shook on its foundations.

Out in the central courtyard visible from the demolished sally port, the casern was slowly being demolished by heavy weapons fire.

Curt wanted his tacomm in the worst way. He desperately needed to talk to Hettrick or *someone* to pass the word to ease up the heavy stuff because he and Kester were already inside the casern.

Shouts and yells drew Curt's attention. The corridor from the left was suddenly full of men runnning at full tilt toward them. They were dressed in the gaudy grey and orange garrison uniforms of the Tee-dad forces. Curt saw a submachinegun in the hands of one of them.

Curt swung his FABARMA and his finger tightened on the trigger.

"Captain! Don't!" was M. Sgt. Henry Kester's quick shout.

The man carrying the submachinegun saw Curt and Kester, dropped the weapon to the floor, came to a sudden halt, and raised his hands. Two men behind him ran into him, staggered, and raised their hands as well. "Surrender! We surrender!" one of them cried out. He was soon joined by a chorus of voices.

"Make them stop!" another yelled. "They are destroying the casern!"

"We tried to surrender to them! But the robots kept shooting!" came another cry.

"Let us out before they blow up the building!"

285

"Who else is in the building? Any other soliders?" Curt asked quickly.

"No, no!" one of them said. "Uh, there are some women, *señor*. They are not armed. We were just awakening after *siesta* . . ."

"Yeah, I've heard it's better on a warm aftrnoon. But now you're prisoners of the combined Caribbean forces." Curt waved his FABARMA toward the grenade-destroyed doorway to the street. "Out onto the street!" he ordered.

"No! No! The robots, they will shoot us!"

"I'll take care of this, Captain," Kester said and moved out of the destroyed sally port into the street.

And immediately ducked back into the shelter of the doorway. He yelled down the street in his parade ground command voice, "God damn it, you stupid sons of bitches! Crank up the discrimination on your warbot visual sensors! Stop shooting into your own troops! Cease fire, damn it!"

Two light assault warbots rolled up alongside him, their 25mm weapons focused on the master sergeant. A third warbot, a Mark 40 with audio output, joined them. "Sorry, Sergeant, didn't recognize you. Didn't mean to shoot at you. Was trying to kill Tee-dad bastards."

The warbot spoke in the voice of Capt. Marty Kelly who was commanding the machine from the remote company command post.

"Damned lucky you can't shoot straight," Kester replied to the company commander without using his rank or title. It was obvious to Curt that Kester was pissed.

"Kelly, this is Curt Carson! I'm bringing out prisoners!" Curt called loudly. "Stop shooting or I'll bring you up on a Hague violation."

"Okay, okay! I've passed the order to cease fire! But

how the hell did you get into the fucking casern? What you doing there?''

"Getting troops to surrender." It was obvious to Curt what had happened. Kelly's Killers had been following the Companions. When the shooting started in the square, Kelly had ordered his Killers forward as the support company and assumed the attack, rolling right over Morgan's Bravo Platoon as it tried to deploy. Kelly had obviously acted before Hettrick could get out an order to the contrary. And, in the assault, Kelly had followed his usual operational code: *Kill 'em all and let God sort 'em out.* Kelly's heavy weapons warbots had gone into action with typical Kelly overkill, intent on destroying the casern rather than getting only twenty or so housekeeping troops inside to surrender.

"Put a couple of your warbots to guarding and escorting these Tee-dads. Get 'em out of here and back to the rear echelon," Curt snapped. "Division Ineligence will want to interrogate them."

"Hey, Carson, you're not in charge here! I was the one who creamed the casern and forced the Tee-dads into your arms," Kelly's voice objected.

"The hell I'm not in charge. Ranking officer among equal ranks is the one on site. Haven't got time to argue with you." Curt was pissed off that his arch rival was trying to grab the command as well as the glory for the capture of the Rio Claro casern. "I've got to find my people!"

Three Killer warbots moved in to escort the nineteen Tee-dads who'd surrendered.

Back in the town square, things were a mess. Allen's ACV was burning with flames licking out of every opening and a dense black cloud of acrid smoke billowing up into the cloud flecked sky. Arrayed in streets and alleyways around the square were the heavy fire and assault warbots of Kelly's Killers. Curt's own ACV appeared to be unharmed where Kester had parked it alongside the street. He couldn't see Morgan's equipment.

He and Kester were quickly joined by Allen, Adonica, Edie Sampson, and the two Alpha Platoon squad leaders.

"Shit, what a mess!" Curt growled as he looked around. Several of the buildings opposite the casern were holed. The casern itself was heavily damaged. The pretty little fountain in the center of the square was in rubble; water squirted randomly into the air, splashed to the street, and ran off in rivulets. He shook his head; this shouldn't have happened, but it had been the Teedad housekeeping platoon in the casern that had started it. Kelly's Killers had helped turn it into a heavy fire fight when small arms would have carried the day just was well since the Greys were up against only a small contingent with light weaponry. The 106mm recoilless would have been limited in its usefulness once Curt's troops and command warbots had dismounted and maneuvered using urban tactics.

But, no, Kelly had to thrust in and do his usual hero routine.

"Head count," Curt said, looking over his people. "Alpha Platoon! Lieutenant, looks like you've got everyone."

"Uh, yeah, including Adonica," Jerry replied. Adonica Sweet's face was dirty and smudged, and her borrowed cammies two sizes too large hung on her, wet with sweat. Her silvery Mini-14 was cradled in her arm. But she stood next to Jerry Allen and looked at him with obvious adoration. "We lost one Mary Ann to a one-oh-six round. Last one they fired. Took Mary Ann Three dead-on. We can probably salvage the ammo and some of the robot modules."

"Leave it for regimental maintenance. I'll request a

288

backup unit be brought up tonight," Curt replied. "Kester, what the hell happened to Zeenab Tej?"

Kester shook his head. "We got to that passageway where the kid was hiding, and I plumb forgot she was supposed to follow us. Sorry, Captain."

"Don't apologize. I should have told her to duck into a doorway and make herself invisible until this was over." Curt reflected that it would be damned difficult for Zeenab to make herself inconspicuous, not only because of her bright clothing but also because she unconsiously projected her beauty which was far more bright than her attire. "We've got to find her. But first, where's Bravo?"

"Moved off to the south," Kester recalled. "The Lieutenant's savvy. She's heard the firing quit. She'll regroup the platoon and head back here."

Copl. Jim Elliott waved his hand. "Captain, let me take two of my warbots and I'll go looking for her in case she didn't get the word."

"Okay, go! Allen, you and Sampson and Koslowski come with Kester and me. We've got to find our pigeon tender and our other platoon," Curt said.

"Don't bother," Adonica Sweet put in. "Here they come."

The street south of the square was filled with people whose cheering and shouting grew in volume and intensity as more joined the throng. Leading it was the proud figure of Lt. Alexis Morgan. Her whole platoon of soldiers and warbots stretched across the street ahead of a throng of Rio Claroans that grew behind them.

And accompanying Alexis Morgan was the brightly clothed Zeenab Tej.

When they were about ten meters from Curt and the rest, Zeenab suddenly broke away and dashed up to Curt. Impulsively and with none of the calm couth she'd exhibited earlier, she threw her arms around

289

Curt's neck and buried her head on his chest. She started to cry.

This sudden show of emotion on the part of Zeenab in front of Curt's company was slightly embarassing to him. Put he put his arm around her and held her. "Hey, hey, hey! What happened, Zee? Did you get lost?"

"No, no . . . When you blew up the door to the casern, I got frightened . . . and I tried to go back where the youngster went inside . . . Then the explosions in the casern began . . . and I started to run away . . ."

Alexis Morgan simply looked at Curt and added, "I saw her run out of an alleyway carrying that Hornet, and I damned near shot her before I recognized her." It was obvious from her tone that she didn't like Zeenab Tej and furthermore didn't like the whole idea of two civilian women accompanying the Companions, regardless of whether or not they were good guides.

But the growing crowd of Rio Claro citizens was all around them now, and others were streaming into their ruined civic square. Musical instruments seemed to appear, and Curt heard the unmistakeable tinny clattering of a Trinidad steel band beginning to play as it marched up one of the streets.

The local fire brigade had somehow showed up and got busily to work checking the ruined buildings for potential fires. Edie Sampson was trying to convince the fire chief that trying to put out the raging fire in the ruined Alpha ACV was a hopeless task.

Other contingents of the Washington Greys were beginning to clog the street leading into town.

Curt hoped to hell that the Tee-dad tacair units had truly been put out of business. This sort of concentration of troops was a perfect target for a strike, and it could be even more disasterous because of all the civilians joining what appeared to be evolving into a celebration.

But he suddenly discovered that he had other worries than a potential enemy tacair strike or the beautiful Zeenab Tej with her arms tightly around him or his Companions looking on with various expressions on their faces. Or even with Capt. Marty Kelly whose own ACV was trying to make its way down the road into the square.

A man stepped up to Curt and said formally, "I am the mayor of Rio Claro. Although we are happy to welcome you and rejoice that you have rid us of the oppressive presence of General Drake's soldiers, I am afraid that I am forced to ask the question: When will you pay for all the destruction you caused? To whom must I present the bill for this damage?"

CHAPTER THIRTY-ONE

Col. Belinda Hettrick stood up. "I told you I'd buy the drinks in Rio Claro! Well, I think we can afford to relax for a moment in the middle of a campaign," she announced to Curt and her other company commanders as they finished dinner in a cafe off the main square. "We took this town with only one Tee-dad casualty. We have orders to remain overnight here to regroup and replenish. Our warbot sentries are out on picket and there are no Tee-dad units nearby. And General Carlisle just told me that the large infantry contingent from five Caribbean nations landed on the north coast this morning and took Port of Spain this afternoon. We didn't know much about this ahead of time because of security, of course, so Operation Steel Band may have just turned into a mopping-up operation. And that's a damned good thing. This is a pretty island with a lot of nice people. It shouldn't be torn up by a war. So here's to the United States and Trinidad!" She raised her glass filled with a rum concoction and gave the traditional Army toast, "How!"

A chorus of "How!" echoed throughout the little cafe.

"And we have he sad duty of recognizing our collegaue, Capt. Samantha Walker, whom we shall remember in the regimental records for her valor as well as her comradeship. May I have a moment of silence, please?''

This dinner might have seemed incongruous after the battle for the Rio Claro casern that afternoon. But the people of the town had recovered with amazing speed and resilience. Except for the three shops on the square that had been damaged by the Tee-dad 106mm recoilless and the casern which had taken heavy fire from Kelly's warbots, the rest of the town had been untouched and was again open for business. It had been several days since the Greys had eaten anything other than Army rations, so Hettrick had reserved this cafe for a meeting of her officers over a meal and had told her chief of staff, Captain Wade Hampton, to arrange parties for the NCOs in other cafes nearby. There didn't seem to be a shortage of places to eat. Obviously, the Fifth Regiment's former presence had stimulated the local entrepreneurs to provide adequate places to enjoy one's self. Then, too, Rio Claro was more than the roadside villages through which the Greys had passed in the last two days. It was the largest town they'd seen on Trinidad.

Hettrick raised her chin and went on, ''Sam, farewell. But I welcome to the Washington Greys the company that shall henceforth be known as Ward's Warriors, and I offer a toast to its new commanding officer whose field promotion has just been confirmed by the 17th Iron Fist, Captain Joan Ward. How!''

''How!''

''Now we must finish this campaign and find Gen. Austin Drake,'' Hettrick went on.

''Hasn't General Drake surrendered yet?'' Zeenab asked in surprise from where she sat next to Curt. The various Trinidad guides were also at the dinner meeting, and Adonica sat next to Jerry. Alexis made certain she got the seat on the other side of Curt.

293

"Unfortunately, no. Not only that, but we don't know where he is," the Colonel added.

"I think I know, Colonel," Adonica spoke up. She was somewhat out of order, but that was tolerated from a field-brevetted third lieutenant who wasn't aware of Army rank protocol. "Have we taken Piarco International Airport yet?"

Hettrick shook her head. "No. It's being heavily defended by the Tee-dad Third Regiment and the Presidential Guard."

"Then that's where General Drake is," Adonica maintained.

"I've got to agree with Adonica," Jerry piped up. He, too was busting protocol. Curt reminded himself to have a few words with Allen; his obvious infatuation with Adonica was visibly apparent. It was also apparent to Curt that Jerry's brain was getting switched off by his gonads. But, then again, Curt was worried about that happening to himself because of Zeenab. The encounte in the town square after the casern battle was hard for him to erase from his mind. In his arms, Zeenab had felt soft and small and vulnerable.

"The Tee-dads will circle the wagons there," Allen went on boldly. "They can be re-supplied by Allianza airlift . . ."

"Not a chance, Lieutenant. The Air Force holds air superiority over the island," Major Ed Canby put in.

"Major, you're probably right, but where the hell *is* the Air Force?" Capt. Marty Kelly asked brashly.

"Yeah. We didn't see an aircraft of any kind all day," Curt added. "Damned good thing we made that dash without contacting the Tee-dads. If we'd been ambushed and gotten into a fur ball, we sure as hell could have used some air support."

"We were damned lucky," Capt. Manny Garcia pointed out. "We were strung out along that road so

294

loosely that we were sucking for an ambush or even an air strike . . .''

"Hang in there, Captains," Hettrick put in gently. She knew her officers had been in combat only hours before and were on the hot edge. And she knew that Curt had been in personal combat where he could be shot at, even though his body armor would stop most small arms fire. "The Air Force and SeaBees are repairing Napirima Air Base right now. According to estimates, it'll be operational tomorrow morning. Then the Air-Force will move in some short-range tactical aircraft for air cover. Right now, they have to fly so damned far that every little tac strike becomes a strategic mission requiring air-to-air refuelling."

"So here we sit on our asses in the rear of the enemy," Marty Kelly complained, "out here in the boonies away from the big fight. When do we get a piece of the real action? What the hell is Division staff doing?"

"Colonel, I recall that our orders said we be told where to move after we got to Rio Claro," Curt deliberately interrupted. "Where do we go from here?"

"Without a map, I can't describe it to you because I don't know the terrain that well by memory," Hettrick admitted. This wasn't unusual in the RI. Officers tended to concentrate on other tactical matters, leaving to the computers the problems of sorting out and filing and finding the little details like maps.

"I do," Adonica piped up. "In Rio Claro, we've got the Nariva Swamp to the northeast, savannahs and Trinity Peak to the south, and the Central Range to the north and west."

"Thank you, Third Lieutenant Sweet," Hettrick said, stressing the girl's temporary rank. "I appreciate your input. As you point out, we can move out in any direction from here. And you're right, Captain Carson; we were told we'd be issued orders when we got to Rio Claro. We've received those orders. Listen up:

"At oh-five-hundred tomorrow morning, the Companions will move out, followed by the Killers, the regimental cee-pee, and the Marauders. This main force will drive northeast along Cunapo Southern Road to Sangre Grande. The objective is to get around behind the Tee-dads and prevent them from retreating into the Sangre Grande area to turn it into a redoubt."

"Colonel, you didn't mention the Warriors," said Captain Joan Ward.

"I've been told to split my command." It was obvious from the tone of Hettrick's voice and the way she said it that she didn't approve of the idea. Curt wasn't sure he did, either. Economy of force and mass were two timeless verities of combat. He felt that the planners and staff had already screwed up plenty by neglecting these and other verities. Crossing the rear of the Can Do, Wolfhounds, and Cottonbalers regiments of the 17th Iron Fist had been hassle enough at the road junctions. If the communications had been as bad earlier in the day as they were now, the Greys might never have pulled it off. But he listened as Hettrick went on, "The Warriors will move out eastward to Pierreville, then up the east coast to join up with the regiment in Sangre Grande. Joan, the task of the Warriors is to forestall the possibility that the ABC Allianza might attempt to reinforce the Tee-dads by landing along the east coast."

Captain Joan Ward nodded. "Yes, Colonel. The Warriors can probably detect and offer some resistance to such a landing. But how do I communicate with you?"

"You having trouble, too?"

"Yes. Tacomm units are dying. And our warbot brainies are reporting difficulties in the remote up-links and down-links with their warbots," the new Captain reported. "Drop-outs mostly. They're suffering momentary loss of contact with warbots in a random sequence and at random times. The only thing that's kept them from something like being KIA is that the drop-outs are short and they're running several warbots in parallel."

"I had the same problem this afternoon," Marty Kelly added. "Things got wild during my assault on the casern because some of my warbots went . . . Well, *berserk* is the best word I can think of to describe what happened. They were reporting back great on the down-links, but my warbot brainies couldn't maintain continuity or control on the up-links. The warbots sort of went automatic or something . . . and totally at random."

Pretty damned flimsy excuse! Curt thought. There were ways to overcome such linkage problems—for example, working through other warbots that did have good up- and down-links. Curt knew that in the heat of battle Kelly and his warbot brainies had simply let the rogue warbots run berserk with unbridled and undirected force while they worked with those they had control over, all because of Kelly's basic combat policy of utilizing force to the maximum rather than surprise and cafeful tactical work.

"Colonel," Curt put in, "with all due respect to my fellow company commander, I'd greatly appreciate it if he would instruct his officers and NCOs to push the panic switch and disable those warbots if they start going spasmodic from now on . . . especially since he's going to be following us up the road to Sangre Grande. Our Bravo Platoon under Lieutenant Morgan would have suffered some equipment losses today if she hadn't had the smarts to move out of the way to the right flank when the Killers rolled through her. We'd just as soon

297

not have unreliable warbots nipping at our heels for fifty kilometers . . ."

"My warbots aren't unreliable!" Kelly objected.

"You just reported they were," Curt replied quickly.

Hettrick moved to head off the usual confrontation in her command: Carson versus Kelly. "Captain Kelly, you will muster your company tonight to inspect and operationally check *all* equipment. Major Benteen, please see to it that Captain Otis and his maintenance people are available to Captain Kelly. Manny, your Marauders are next in line for second-level maintenance service because you won't move out until a few hours after the Companions depart. Captain Ward, be prepared to move as instructed, but also be ready to change plans and move up the Cunapo Road to Sangre Grande with the rest of the Regiment. I'm going to contact General Carlisle and see if he'll agree to keep the Greys together because of our growing communication problem. In the meantime, enjoy this food—the *callaloo* is delicious!—and get some rest. And I wish to remind you that this is combat and Rule Ten is in effect."

CHAPTER THIRTY-TWO

The food was good, and the pause in Rio Claro gave Curt and his company a chance to take baths as well, the first in several days. He spent the rest of the evening resisting the temptation to check out the festivities in the town. The sounds of steel band, calypso, and carousing were plainly evident. If the American troops weren't taking part—and some were—the people of Rio Claro didn't really give a damn. The occupation of the town by the Washington Greys was a good excuse for a party. Under the increasingly oppressive regime of General Drake, there had been few opportunities for carnival. So the people of Rio Claro had plenty of pent-up steam to release.

Instead, Curt checked his two platoons bivouacked in a park-like field on the north edge of town, made certain that their equipment was in shape to move out at 0500 in the morning, and saw to it that they'd been resupplied with rations, fuel, fresh clothing, and ammo.

Alpha Platoon took over the spare ACV from Ward's Warriors. It was Capt. Samantha Walker's former company command vehicle. Curt felt a great deal of sadness when it joined his unit; it still had something of Sam's aura in it. But with only two officers, one of whom was both company commander and platoon leader, the Warriors weren't using one of their ACVs.

Curt knew that an empty ACV is not only as useful as tits on a turret but provided a bus-sized, robot-controlled target that might as well be manned and defendable. So his Alpha Platoon got their necessary replacement vehicle.

Curt checked M. Sgt. Kenry Kester. He wanted to make sure the older man was really in good condition after the personal combat today. Kester insisted he was all right, although he had an ugly blue bruise on his left side. "Captain, I caught a nine-millimeter getting out of the ACV. Didn't seem worth making a fuss over. I'm a little sore, but I can function," he pointed out. "Matter of fact, sir, I could probably go one-on-one with you right now and plow your field because you're dragging your ass more than just a little bit."

Curt grinned. "Want to check that out, Henry?"

"No, sir. My ass is dragging, too. I said I *probably* could do it, not that I particularly *wanted* to. I'd rather check out the party in town then get some sack time. But—" He looked up at the pigeon cages lashed to the rear deck of the ACV. "I ought to report to you that I think at least one of Zeenab Tej's pigeons is missing."

Curt looked up at the cages, too. "So? I told her to dispatch one to Colonel Hettrick early this afternoon."

"Yes sir. I know that. She's still short one pigeon."

Curt gave a snort of laughter. "Henry, we don't have to account to quartermaster for one each pigeon model UBQ-one, serial number whatever. I'm not signed out for it. Neither is Zee. And you're not on the line as the company clerk. So don't worry. She probably used it to send a letter home saying she's all right. Go do a little partying and get some sack time."

"Yes, sir. You should do the same, sir," the old master sergeant remarked.

"I'll sack out. I haven't got the poop to party," Curt

admitted. "Sleep in the ACV with the air conditioning on. Dry and cool."

"I'd planned to. Good night, Captain."

"Good night, Sergeant."

Kester patted the side of the ACV and sauntered down the street toward the carnival in Rio Claro.

Curt made the rounds of the other platoon ACVs just to check. Platoon Sgt. Nick Gerard was leaning against the side of the Bravo vehicle, eating some fruit. " 'Evening, Captain. Want some melon? Some guy gave me one big enough for the whole damned company to eat."

"Thanks, Nick. Don't you want to get inside and stay dry and cool?"

Gerard shook his head. "No, sir. Ever spend a summer at Fort Leonard Wood?"

"Yeah. They've got square days there—ninety degrees temperature and ninety percent humidity."

"That was easy to take. I was raised in St. Louis. I got used to this sort of weather when I was a kid."

"Good. Maybe you've got some suggestions on how we can handle the green and purple stuff that's growing all through our electronic gear," Curt said.

Nick shook his head. " 'Fraid not. Just gotta learn to think rust, that's all."

"Thought I heard conversation." Lt. Alexis Morgan's head appeared through the turret hatch. Curt had grown used to her as a warbot brainy with her head shaved to make the helmet contacts more positive. However, in the past six months as a Sierra Charlie, she and the other members of the company had let their hair grow. It was sort of a badge of difference. Curt hadn't seen her without her helmet for several days and noticed that six months plus the high humidity of Trinidad had given Alexis an abundant head of rather sexy-looking, curly auburn hair.

"You look rather ravishing in the tropical moonlight, Lieutenant," Curt bantered easily.

She cocked her head and looked at him provocatively. "I believe the line is, 'Come up and see me some time.'"

"In front of the help?" Curt joked back. "And in spite of Rule Ten?"

Alexis sighed. "Ah, yes, Rule Ten! Oh, if the United States Army really understood what we do or don't do for it . . ."

"The hired help will find a native companion and a nearby bush if you want me out of the way," Gerard put in.

"As long as you don't bust Rule Ten," Curt told him. "No army has ever been able to control fraternization with the natives . . ."

"Is that what they call it? I always thought it was called—"

"That's enough, Sergeant!" Alexis interrupted him. She was on edge. Curt knew why. Because of the combat today, his libido was high. In short, he was horny. He knew Alexis was, too. But this wasn't a war game that was over at sundown, allowing them to enjoy the evening together after drinks and dinner at the Club. Rule Ten was designed quite frankly to keep combat troops from going into total and complete rut instead of doing their job as combat soldiers. In some outfits, it was honored in the breach. But enough court martials and dishonorable discharges as a result of either being caught or being snitched on by a disgruntled partner served to deter serious career officers of both sexes. Curt didn't know whether Rule Ten was a good rule or not. But it was there, and it had to be obeyed. He had accepted his commission knowing it was there.

"Yes, m'am." Gerard tossed the remainder of the fruit away and began to walk toward Rio Claro.

"Think I'll take a little walk before a sack out. Sure hope we can get this whole thing over and done with in the next couple of days . . ."

Alexis looked down at Curt again and formally told him, "Good night, Captain. Please get a good night's sleep yourself."

"Good night, Lieutenant. You do the same," he told her, firmly intending to do what she asked.

At the new Alpha Platoon ACV, Curt found Lt. Jerry Allen stretched out on the aft deck in the open air. The young man wasn't asleep. He turned on his side upon Curt's approach. "Evening, sir."

" 'Evening. It's more comfortable inside," Curt pointed out.

"Yes, sir. But Third Lieutenant Sweet is there."

"So?"

Jerry shook his head violently. "I . . . I . . . I just couldn't stay inside with Adonica tonight, Captain. I . . . I'm not sure I wouldn't bust Rule Ten. Fact is, I'd bust it for sure. When I explained it to her, Adonica said she'd end up busting it herself. So I'm trying to sleep out here. I guess I really need a cold shower. Goddamned discipline! Sorry, sir . . ."

Curt shrugged. "Rule Ten isn't just discipline for the sake of discipline, Jerry. Or tradition. Or prudishness. Didn't you understand it when they explained it at the Point?"

Jerry picked nervously at his fingers and muttered, "Yes, sir. Some cadets figured it was one of the usual stupid regs and they'd be okay if they didn't get caught or snitched on, in spite of the Honor Code. Then a couple of cadets got their buttons and epaulets ripped because of it." He gave an explosive sigh and sat up. Running his fingers through the stubble of hair on his head, he went on, "Yeah, I know it's intended to keep the Army from becoming one big orgy at taxpayers' expense. But, dammit, sir, why *tonight?* We've got war-bot pickets out. We won't get ambushed. And we don't move out for another six hours or more. What's wrong with it *tonight?* Adonica or I could get killed tomorrow . . ."

"That's always the first excuse in a combat situation," Curt tried to explain. "Somebody put a lot of thought and study into Rule Ten before it was put in the book. We've got to accept the fact they knew what they were doing. Otherwise, in the crunch we'd toss other rules in the latrine when we didn't like them. This affects personal discipline. Jerry, the most difficult kind. The kind that keeps intelligent, trained, bright people from turning tail and running like hell to save their ass when the shooting starts. Keeps you and me from letting other animal instincts take over under the gun. Makes us do what we're getting paid for. Even the warbot brainies who don't get shot at . . ."

Jerry Allen scratched the stubble on his chin. "They ought to modify Rule Ten for the Sierra Charlies."

"Not tonight." The fatherly chat was getting nowhere. Curt went Patton on his young officer. "Lieutenant, tomorrow morning at oh-five-hundred, I want to see that stubble shaved off your face. Clean! I want to see Alpha Platoon bright and sharp as a tack. We've got a long haul tomorrow, and this fracas isn't over yet. Not until Drake is out of the picture and the Tee-dads holler quits. Sharp! Understand?"

"Uh, yes, sir."

"Good night, Lieutenant."

"Good night, Captain."

Curt walked back to his own ACV, aware of his own problem.

And unable to come to any calm, rational solution for other reasons.

Maybe Zeenab would already be asleep inside the

ACV so he could doss down outside on the ground with centimeters of armor plate between the two of them.

But he wasn't that fortunate. He was forced to confront the situation.

Zeenab was atop the rear deck of the ACV tending to her pigeons. She straightened up with a start when Curt stepped up to the vehicle. "Oh! Sorry! You surprised me, Captain."

"Putting the birds to bed?" Curt asked.

"Yes. And making sure they know they haven't been abandoned on the back of this big armored car. And that I still care about them." She straightened up and cooed to the birds, saying soft things in a soft voice to them. Then she descended down the steel ladder from the deck to the ground and walked over to Curt.

"I was just doing the same thing with my troops," Curt managed to say, folding his arms across his chest and leaning back against the warm side of the ACV.

"Yes, people need the same reassurances, don't they?" She moved close to him. She took no overt action, but she was projecting desire and sensuality. Curt knew that some women could do that. Zeenab was doing it very well.

Curt gritted his teeth and managed to reply, "Yeah . . . and it's the commanding officer's job to provide it. Goes with the glory of leadership."

"And who provides it for the commanding officer? Other higher-ranked commanding officers?"

Curt shook his head with his arms still folded. "Not in the Army. Not on duty. Not in a combat situation like this."

Zeenab tilted her head and a querulous look came into her large eyes. "Adonica told me something about it this evening. Some rule you have about men and women not sharing one another. She couldn't understand it."

"I don't have to understand it. I only have to obey it."

"Rules are only guidelines for proper behavior."

"Not this one."

"What is it? What does it *really* say?"

"I can quote it verbatim from the regulations. Every officer can." Curt looked up at the starry sky overhead and recited by rote, " 'Army Regulation Six-oh-one-dash-ten: No physical contact of any sort whatsoever, except that required for the conduct of official Army business, shall occur between male and female armed forces personnel of any rank or relative rank while on duty or in a combat situation as defined by the officer in command. Violation of this regulation is a Class One violation of Army regulations punishable under the Uniform Code of Military Justice as ammended.' "

Zeenab was silent for a minute, then said, "Oh. Good. It doesn't apply."

"Huh? What do you mean?"

"It doesn't apply to you and me."

Goddammit, she's right, and I knew it all the time myself! Curt thought furiously. "Yeah, but it doesn't mean that you and I can make love tonight."

"Oh? Why not? I want to make love to you. Do you want to make love to me?"

"Goddam right I do, and you know I do!" Curt said savagely, still looking at the stars above, trying valiantly to stem the raging river of sex that coursed through his loins.

"Then why not? Do it. Make love to me," Zeenab demanded in a soft voice. She reached up into the tightly bound hair on her head and did something to it. It suddenly fell in a shimmering cascade behind her to her waist. "Take me over under the trees and make love to me. Now. Do it."

If Curt had ever wanted a woman in his life, he wanted this one. And he wanted her now. This moment. "My troopers can't. My officers can't. I've got to set an example. I'm their commanding officer. They're Carson's Companions."

"So that's why Adonica was made an officer? To keep her from sleeping with Jerry?"

Curt nodded.

"Very stupid of her. I told her she should never have accepted the brevet. She could have done her job just as well without it."

"Yeah, but Allen couldn't have done his job unless it was done. And you should have been brevetted, too!"

"Really? I would have refused. So now both Jerry and Adonica are totally frustrated. Does that improve Jerry's performance as a soldier?"

Curt had a twinge of doubt race through his mind. Maybe this exotic woman was right. "The regulation's there. I can't change it."

"Do you think a simple regulation, mere words, can keep two people apart?"

"Probably not."

"Certainly not. And would you enforce the regulation if you knew they were violating it?"

"Goddammit, Zee! You're tossing some damned difficult questions at me!" he complained. "Okay, let me put it this way: If Jerry and Adonica bust Rule Ten and I happen to stumble on them, I'd have to do something. I couldn't ignore it. But if they're discreet about it, I really don't want to know about it."

"Adonica told me she wouldn't let a simple regulation keep her from the ultimate joy two people can experience with one another."

307

"Well, I don't intend to beat the bushes looking for them. Or for any or my troops if they decide to slip into town . . ."

"So you recognize that 'Rule Ten' as you call it doesn't keep them from bedding any man or woman in Rio Claro? Curt, plenty of men and women in town tonight would enjoy going to bed with one of your soldiers," Zeenab pointed out, still talking in her soft voice but doing something to the colorful sash wound around her narrow waist. "Captain, not everyone stayed here after you made your rounds. Even Master Sergeant Henry Kester took 'a little walk before turning in.' "

Kester. And Gerard. Some of the squad leaders, no doubt. Maybe even Sgt. Edie Sampson. Curt thought. But he said nothing. Zeenab had pushed him beyond the point where he wanted to think about it. Fatigue was beginning to draw a thin haze over his mind between reality and fantasy. But fatigue didn't reduce the feelings he had within him for this woman standing quietly beside him, unwilling to move away from him, unwilling to give up, unwilling to accept his rationalizations, and slowly removing her clothing in a provocative manner.

His silence caused Zeenab to ask him softly, "Curt, my dearest, do your beloved troopers know and understand Rule Ten?"

"Of course they do!"

"And do you?"

"Certainly!"

"And you must know them well enough to know what they're doing."

"I know them damned well."

"And are they 'busting Rule Ten'?"

"Two of them, maybe. The others aren't."

"So? And you? Curt, my darling, you're a good and brave soldier. Show me that you're also a human being. Let us make love . . . without breaking Rule Ten

308

at all . . ." This time when she reached up and put her arms around his neck, she didn't just bury her head on his chest.

It was a warm, moonlit tropical night. Robots stood guard. And human beings were human beings.

CHAPTER THIRTY-THREE

It didn't look bad. But, on the other hand, it didn't look good either. Gen. Austin Drake sat behind a command-and-control console deep in the communications bunker at Piarco International Airport and glowered at the maps and charts. He was very much a loner and always had been, preferring to make decisions on his own after his staff had briefed him. Like many other despots in history, he did it his own way, often ignoring the advice and suggestions of his expert advisors. The Argentines liked him for that and had convinced the Brazilians to support him because he was viewed a a "one-man junta." The Brazilians, far more accustomed to working in teams, had gone along only because the Chileans, also accustomed to juntas and strong men, had supported Argentina.

So Drake sat alone and tried to figure out what was going on and what he could do about it until the ABC Allianza could bring in the promised reinforcements. He'd already initiated one master movement, but he was being threatened from several directions now.

The roboticized Presidential Guard and units of the Third Regiment were fighting hard to hold Piarco International Airport. Drake had deduced from battle reports that the invaders were laboring under a rule of engagement prohibiting them from attacking or damaging non-military facilities. So he'd ordered the Presidential Guard to turn the civilian commercial air terminal and the air cargo areas of Piarco into strong points which they could defend with their heavily-armed and armored Brazilian and Argentinian warbots. Hundreds of millions of dollars of commercial aircraft had already been destroyed and the new international terminal building, once the pride of Trinidad as its "Gateway to Paradise" was under attack, its south wing already engulfed in flames.

The invaders shouldn't be doing attacking those civilian facilities! Drake shook his head in amazement. In the U.S. Army, rules of engagement were sacred, broken in the field only under conditions of dire emergency. It was part of the Navy's *Stark* legacy that had extended over into the Army. Perhaps their rules of engagement on Trinidad permitted them to attack civilian facilities when his forces had commandeered and fortified them. If so, that was going to hamper his operations.

As he watched the video monitors from the sensors up at ground level, he began to wonder how much longer he could hold Piarco against the overwhelming forces that now occupied the island of Trinidad.

But he took some solace in the fact that the world news media were gladly taking video feeds from his sensors. He'd encouraged this and, as a result, the media were giving prime coverage up the destructive holocaust of this invasion, milking it for all its horror and killing as a "nasty little war" over the Caribbean's weathliest island. He'd managed to convince most of the media people—he considered most of them airheads who'd believe almost anything that happened to match their classical media liberalism—that the energy and industrial interests in the United States had put pressure on Washington to come in and save their interests from being turned over to the people of Trinidad by his government. So he'd managed to get the news reports slanted to implicate that this was a war instigated by the greedy Wall Street and Houston bankers against the happy people of Trinidad who enjoyed the highest standard of living in the Caribbean basin.

Actually, very little killing was going on. Warbots were occasionally destroyed, but his mercenary Trinidad Defense Forces troops from Argentina, Brazil, and Chile were surrendering rather than fighting to the death as he'd ordered them. For all of the action and movement in the past two days, only fourteen Americans had been killed, according to his battle reports. But he'd lost several thousand men in the air strikes on Fort George, Piarco Airport, Napirima Air Base and during the sinking of his naval forces in the Dragon's Mouths. He didn't tell that to the news media people.

His line regiments had suffered about 22 percent casualties, enough to worry him but not enough to cause him to tap replacements from his Second Regiment being held in reserve in Sangre Grande. Fortunately, his units weren't burdened with wounded; he'd ordered his regiments to abandon their wounded to the enemy, thus saddling his opponents with the problems of transporting and caring for them.

But far too many of his Trinidad Defense Forces troops were surrendering. He was disgusted with the battle performance of some of his mercenary troops. Only the Fifth Regiment had put up a fight south of San Fernando, but too many of the Fifth Regiment had then surrendered to the Americans in the San Fernando area; only a few units had managed to retreat out of the trap as the robotic pincers of the 17th Iron Fist and 22nd Double Deuces divisions had closed on the city. Then yesterday the Venezuelans and Panamanians accompanied by token forces from Curaçao and Jamaica had entered and taken Port of Spain without a fight and without losses, his own Presidential Guard retreating before them, covering his own minus-x as he relocated his headquarters at Piarco.

Gen. Austin Drake knew he was on the defensive. This bothered him because the actual count of his troops showed that he outnumbered the invaders by more than 4 to 1. However, when the effectiveness factor of warbots was taken into account—and Drake had only about 200 warbots in his Presidential Guard against an estimated 4,000 warbots in two full U.S. Army RI divisions—the two sides about even. He was heavy on human soldiers while the invaders were strong in warbots.

He'd started to use this critical difference to his advantage.

Warbots had firepower, protection, and durability. He knew his units enjoyed mobility, speed, and versatility.

It had been a hard job, but he'd worked out the tactics for the counteroffensive. His staff had been carrying out his orders all night. He planned to cut the Americans off where they were thin, then he'd open up and hold the east coast of the island for the arrival of ABC Allianza reinforcements.

His new chief of staff, Col. Affonsio Fernandos Lima, formerly commandant of the southern military district which had covered the area from San Fernando to Rio Claro and Pierreville—now in enemy hands—knocked at the door to the bunker room. Drake turned in his chair and straightened his uniform. "Come in, Affonsio! What's the word from General Deodoro?" he asked.

313

Lima saluted stiffly. "Sir, General Deodoro and his aide, Captain de Sousa, request to see you."

"Sure! But why the formality? Deodoro doesn't need all the formal protocol to come talk with me," Drake said easily.

"Captain de Sousa specifically requested it, General."

"Shit, he must have gotten some bad news from Brasilia!" Drake muttered. He braced himself mentally for the worst and told his chief of staff, "Ask them to come in, Affonsio.

Lima saluted again and left. Shortly, General Deodoro and his aide came in. Deodoro took off his gloves and set them on the table along with his riding crop. Captain de Sousa dutifully picked them up.

"Good morning, General!" Drake greeted him ebulently. "When can we expect the airlift from Anapa and Manaus?"

"You can't expect it at all," Deodoro told him sourly.

"Oh? What's the problem?"

"The government of Guyana has refused to grant us overflight privileges in spite of considerable diplomatic pressure," the Brazilian military advisor reported.

"Refused? Why doesn't Brasilia exert some diplomatic pressure?" Drake wanted to know. "Guyana is supposed to be in the ABC Allianza camp . . ."

Deodoro sat heavily on the edge of the table and twisted one end of his thick moustache absently. "They say they do not wish to become involved in a possible conflict with Venezuela . . . much less the United States. They have threatened to intercept any ABC Allianza aircraft penetrating their airspace en route to Trinidad . . . We know what we've supplied to Guyana in the way of air defenses, and the authorities in

314

Brasilia don't wish to test the effectiveness of that system. Naturally, the government of Guyana will pay dearly for this."

"Well, goddammit, so will I! Are you bringing that airlift in over Venezuela?

Deodoro shook his head firmly. "Of course not! The Venezuelans in company with the Panamanians are in possession of Port of Spain at this moment! The Security Council in Brasilia is not yet ready for war with Venezuela, Columbia, and Panama, all of whom have contingents in the invasion force . . ."

"So I'm not going to be reinforced by air? Orgasmic!" Drake fulminated, unconsciously slipping into the slang of his former U.S. Army service. "How about ground forces? When will they reach Trinidad?"

General Deodoro looked at the map on the wall. Unlike the American Army with all its computers and displays, the Trinidad Defense Forces were organized like a twentieth century army. High-tech was expensive. And a high-tech warbot army wasn't the best for internal constabulary and police purposes as the TDF was. He took his riding crop out of the hand of his aide and used it as a pointer while he addressed the map. "The Allianza Security Council in Brasilia has agreed to assist you and place troops under your command to repel this invasion. Our Second Division, the Pernambuco Grenadiers, will depart Belem by sea tomorrow; twenty-four hours later, they will land at Manzanilla on the east coast. The Argentine Third Division is being transported today to Sao Luis and will depart by sea later tomorrow, but they will require more than thirty hours to reach Manzanilla."

Two divisions! That would swing the balance, Drake told himself. His confidence began to return. Now all he had to do was to hold on for another two days, allowing for some delays in bringing in the Brazilian

315

and Argentine divisions. But everything had to work and work just right. There was no room for him to make a mistake.

"Excellent! Orgasmic! General, this means that I can withdraw from Piarco if the pressure gets too great, retreat to Sangre Grande, and hold until your troops land to reinforce me. This should tip the balance because the Americans have no other troops available to reinforce those already on Trinidad!" He refrained from clapping General Deodoro on the shoulder; one didn't do that with Brazilian general officers.

"You're considering giving up Piarco Airport?" Deodoro was querilous.

"I may have to in order to conserve my forces for the defense of Sangre Grande," Drake explained. "Don't worry: I'll leave Piarco in such a mess that it'll take the Americans months to put it back together . . . Just like I did with Napirima."

The bunker suddenly rocked with a distant explosion. Plaster dust fell from the ceiling.

Drake checked his video monitors. They were blank. Colonel Rocas suddenly stuck his head through the door. *"Perdoe-me,* General," the man said, trying to control his agitation but lapsing into his native Portuguese in the excitement. "Piarco Airport is under tactical air strike by American Air Force A-Twenty aircraft and A-A-Ten attack aerodynes!"

"What the hell? Those are short-range tac strikers!" Drake exploded. "Where did they come from?"

"Napirima," Rocas reported.

"So the Americans have rebuilt it already," General Deodoro observed quietly. "Now they have quick response tactical air support as well as air supremacy . . ."

Drake recovered enough to boast, "General, when my Fourth Regiment combined with my Special Forces

Battalion breaks through at Rio Claro today, I'll sweep around the left flank and take Napirima back! And we'll have the whole east coast free for your landings!"

"Be that as it may, General Drake, in the meantime I think it wise to evacuate Piarco," Deodoro advised him. "You cannot hold Piarco if the Americans have quick-response tactical air. I, for one, do not wish to be captured by the Americans. I strongly stuggest you withdraw at once to Sangre Grande."

Drake sighed. "I was planning to, General. But, before the day is out, we'll hold the entire eastern half of the island."

"If you break through in the south."

"I will," Drake promised.

CHAPTER THIRTY-FOUR

But in the south, it was still very quiet. The road north out of Rio Claro twisted through the foothills of the Central Range of hills to the west. It was only a two-lane highway, but it was paved, making it easy going for Carson's Companions in the recon slot ahead of Kelly's Killers on point. A few kilometers out of Rio Claro as they crossed the Killdeer River, the vegetation got lush with the western fringes of the Nariva Swamp occasionally visible off to the right. So Curt rode high in the turret of his ACV in spite of the growing heat and humidity that caused sweat to run down into the corners of his eyes, making them smart.

"Zee, please hand me a towel," he called down to Zeenab who was riding in the coolness of the ACV.

She quickly came up into the turret hatch with him. The hatch wasn't very big, which brought the two of them into intimate touch . . . which Curt didn't mind at all after last night and which Zeenab appeared to relish herself. "Here, my captain, let me wipe your face," she told him softly.

"I sweat too much in this climate," he admitted.

"I enjoyed your sweat last night. It made you taste good. It made you feel good to me. You are a man, dear Curt. Very much a man. And good men perspire. Like the oil field workers after a hard day on a rig . . .''

Zeenab had a strange and stilted way of speaking the English language with a Caribbean accent and lilt. Curt liked it. He liked this woman a great deal. "You're all woman yourself, you know," he told her.

"Do you feel guilty now?" she asked.

He shook his head and grinned. "You were right. I didn't bust Rule Ten."

"Of course you didn't."

"But I feel sorry for Jerry and Adonica."

"Don't," Zeenab told him. "And don't ask questions."

"I won't. Just as long as Allen does his job."

"Colonel Hettrick has a great deal of power, doesn't she?" Zeenab asked rhetorically. She wiped her own neck, now exposed because her long, black hair was again bound into a complex bun of braids on the back of her small head. "With a simple decree called a brevet commission, she can separate two people."

"Hettrick has never acted from spite or jealousy, Zee."

"Perhaps not. But I sense that the women of the Washington Greys are certainly capable of jealousy when it comes to outsiders and their men."

And I hope to God Alexis didn't sense anything this morning! Curt thought savagely. "Zee, that's why we have Rule Ten. Now I have to get my mind on the business of combat survival. All day, as a matter of fact. Much as I'd like us to enjoy one another again right now, that's a hell of a difficult situation to be in if the shooting happens to start—"

"What can start?" Zeenab asked, looking around. "All of the fighting is going on elsewhere."

"Anything can start. Especially when you don't expect it," Curt warned her. "Now get below. I've got work to do."

A few minutes later, Master Sergeant Henry Kester touched Curt's leg. Curt ducked his head into the turret. "What's up, Henry?"

"Tacomm's completely out. Can't even maintain contact with Lieutenant Morgan now."

"Okay, I'll switch to hand signals."

"Let me take the message back, Captain. I think the Lieutenant should close the interval so she can maintain a visual. This road is pretty damned crooked."

"Go do it, but don't tire yourself. You look a little bagged."

"Combat, sir."

"Enjoy the party in town last night?"

"Yes, sir. You should have come with me. Good time. Needed the relaxation."

"Well, I sort of relaxed by staying home," Curt admitted.

"Yes, sir." Kester was being unusually quiet and respectful this morning. "She's quite a woman. Makes me want to be about thirty years younger."

Curt forced himself to laugh. It was somewhat of a forced laugh because Kester had just signalled him with discretion that the old master sergeant had figured out what had gone on in Rio Claro. "Kester, you old banty rooster, you'd still bed every wench you could get your hands on! And do a good job of it, too!"

"I'd try, sir," Kester admitted. The subtle communication had taken place, and Kester had signalled that whatever his captain did was his captain's business as long as it didn't affect the performance or survival of Carson's Companions. "Would you let me out, Captain? I don't want to drop the ramp and dump the interior air. Our tacomm may be out, but I don't want to expose the warbots and other gear any more than I have to.''

Curt dropped into the ACV and let Kester out the turret hatch, then resumed his position. It seemed to him that it was going to be another long day of travel. Hours and hours of boredom, always on the alert for a flanking ambush although Adonica Sweet had advised that it would be extremely difficult for any sizeable Tee-dad force to cross the roadless Central Range and take them from the left as they moved along.

Nonetheless, Curt required that his Companions maintain vigilance. Far too many cavalry thrusts in military history had been hit by abmush or flanking attack. The Washington Greys were going to be strung out along the road with their flanks exposed, a prime target for that sort of thing. And Curt wouldn't put it past the tropical-trained Tee-dad soldiers to exhibit the ability to cross the Central Range, even without roads. Warbots couldn't do it, but human soldiers could do it and had done similar things in the past. Curt didn't want to take chances. Sierra Charlie warfare was new to him, but it did have its roots in the past. Curt certainly didn't want to be guilty of forgetting the lessons of history and reinventing the square wheel. His Sierra Charlies had already done enough of that to suit him.

Thus Curt was seated in the turret hatch and sweeping the surrounding underbrush and forest visually as they crossed the trickling Navet River with an abandoned gas station and small store on the left when all hell broke loose somewhere at the rear end of the column.

Morgan's ACV suddenly closed the gap between the vehicles, and he could see Alexis high in the turret. She was yelling at him, but her voice was drowned

321

in the sound of the vehicles and the rapidly increasing noise of battle coming from the rear. But he caught her hand signals.

Enemy to the left.

He passed the hand signal up to Allen. Then signalled both his platoon leaders, "Dismount. Fight on foot."

"Companion One!" he yelled at his ACV as he dropped into the vehicle. "Enemy to the left. Sensors out! Drop the ramp and dismount warbots! Execute!"

"Companion one, executing!" The rear ramp dropped. Curt saw the turret swivel to the left.

"Zeenab, stay inside! Don't come out! It's going to be deadly out there!" he yelled at the beautiful woman seated in the forward end of the ACV bay.

"But my birds . . ." she started to complain.

"They'll be all right," he lied to her. "Warbots! Power up! Enemy is to the left of the vehicle. Deploy as skirmishers on the west edge of the road. Do not enter the jungle. Fire at any and all targets out there."

His two General Purpose Mark 33 warbots had been in pre-combat standby. Now they replied verbally in sequence that they were ready. And then they trundled out the hatch and down the ramp.

The 75mm Saucy Cans on the LAMVs suddenly opened up on targets with their distinctive *blam-blam-blam* in three-round bursts, seeking range and targets.

But Curt didn't get the chance to dismount the ramp. 5.56mm small-arms fire was in the air over the road, and he heard the rounds whanging the armor of the ACV. Slugs bounced off his two Mark 33s as they deployed to the side of the road. So he yelled, "Companion One, raise the ramp!" And he clambered back up to the turret whose 20mm cannon was now registered and firing bursts into the underbrush

322

at targets only its infra red and chem sensors could detect.

Curt poked his helmeted head over the lip of the turret hatch and saw that the whole column was under fire from the left. Allen had his Alpha warbots deployed and his vehicles were firing.

Swinging his gaze to the rear, Curt just managed to glimpse Alexis Morgan taking a hit on her helmet. She disappeared into her ACV.

Goddamm it, Alexis has been hit! he thought savagely and wanted more information. How badly had she been hurt? Was she still conscious? But the tacomm was out.

He had to satisfied with the knowledge that, while the standard M6 composite plastic helmet couldn't be penetrated by a 5.56mm caseless round at even a hundred meters, the impact was enough to stun and even knock a person unconscious. Better that than the round penetrating skull and brain. But taking a round in the helmet wasn't something relished by any warbot brainy. Better not to be shot at, but that was part of being one of the new Sierra Charlies.

Curt suddenly got a visual on one of the attackers. Human. Bright electric blue beret above cammy coveralls. That meant only one thing. The Tee-dad Special Forces batallion!

He saw Allen's equipment suddenly deploy abreast the road and begin firing forward, Alpha's Mary Anns sweeping the road ahead in an apparent attempt to keep the Tee-dads from crossing it.

But his recon picket company wasn't taking the brunt of the attack. It was concentrated on his ACVs. The main fight seemed to be taking place to the rear.

A wiry form in cammies darted along the right ditch of the road under cover. It was Kester, returning from Morgan's ACV. Once in the fire shadow of Curt's

ACV, Kester scrambled up the right side of the vehicle. Curt moved aside to let the master sergeant drop through the hatch.

It took a moment for Kester to regain is breath, then the old fighter reported between gasps, "The Lieutenant's okay. Conscious. Headache. Bruise. Like getting clobbered in the head with a beer bottle . . . Looks like the whole column has been hit from the left flank . . . This is only a flanking force . . . Couple of squads of Tee-dad Special Forces . . . Main attack seems to be concentrated on the rest of the Greys to the rear . . ."

Curt glanced at the map display. "Some Tee-dad units must have come down the Tabaquite Road during the night. Looks like these flanking parties worked their way down the Killdeer and Navet Rivers . . . Zee, I'm going to get a bird. Which one? I have to send a message back to the Colonel!"

"Curt! You'll be killed out there!" Zeenab objected.

"Maybe . . . Which bird? Describe it?" Curt asked as he clambered into the turret again. But when he poked his head gingerly over the lip of the hatch, he saw that he wouldn't be able to use Zeenab's pigeons. The cages had taken bursts of 5.56mm fire; there was nothing left but some framework, screening wire, and feathers.

Nothing to do but fight it out here and hope the other Greys units were doing the same.

He checked his warbots. They were deployed alongside the road and firing sporadically into the jungle. The warbots and heavy weapons of both Alpha and Bravo were in action. While the 20mm and 50mm cannons of the Mary Anns and Hairy Foxes were doing their jobs, the 75mm Saucy Cans of the LAMVs were literally up-rooting trees.

324

Lots of heavy firing was coming from the rear. That's where the main battle was still raging.

Then the firing of the Companions' warbots and vehicles stopped. Curt checked his displays below the lip of the hatch, and the reason became clear: they'd run out of targets.

Their attackers had been about two squads of Tee-dad Special Forces. The yells and cries of the wounded came from the forest. But no more firing.

Curt dropped down into the ACV again. "We're not sending a message," he said simply without explanation. Zeenab would discover soon enough that her birds were gone. It was time to do something other than sit on that road like ducks in a shooting gallery. "Henry, go forward with Alpha and help hold the road against any Tee-dads trying to get around us there. Companion One and our command warbots will hold this position. I'm going back with Bravo, and we'll sweep west of the road and try to flank the main force attacking the rest of the Greys."

"Captain, the warbots are going to slow us down out there in the puckerbrush," Kester pointed out diplomatically as only a master sergeant with twenty-plus years can. "This terrain calls for the speed and mobility of Sierra Charlies with fire support from our warbots on the road. Why not get the troopers from Alpha, join up with those from Bravo, and we'll sweep in idiot mode, fast and surgical?"

It sounded better to Curt than his own plan. "Okay, you called it and I buy it," he told Kester. He'd learned to pay attention to his master sergeant when it came to non-warbot operations with the new Sierra Charlie company. Kester had fought in this same sort of environment a long time ago, and he hadn't forgotten how to do it. "We'll be against other human troops out there. So we'll let our warbots and auto equipment form the fire base and we'll hit them the same way they hit us . . . and they're probably not expecting us! Give the warbots your i-d code and scoot. Get Alpha and meet me at Bravo ACV. Go!"

Kester went.

Curt looked at Zeenab as he strapped on his field harness with ammo and grenades. "Zee, stay here; you're behind armor and protected. Still got that Hornet?"

"Yes, but—"

He identified his IFF transmitter code to the warbots and told her, "Use it if you have to, but you probably won't have to. No time for explanations." Curt grabbed his FABARMA, went out the top hatch, and rolled down the right side of the ACV behind Kester.

He still took the protective option of scurrying down the eastern drainage ditch of the road in defilade, even with his warbots providing fire cover for him and no fire coming from the enemy. Kester went forward to get Allen and his people.

When Curt got to the Bravo ACV, Sgt. Nick Gerard stuck his head out of the turret. "Dismount!" Curt called. "Everyone. We're going flank skirmishers in idiot mode."

"The Lieutenant's in no shape to do that," Gerard replied.

"Can she dismount for a con?"

"Wait one, sir." Nick disappeared. Then Corporals Tracy Dillon and Tom Cole rolled out, followed by Gerard and Lt. Alexis Morgan.

Alexis didn't look very good. "Never took a round in the helmet before," she told Curt when she got to the ground. "I'm shook up a bit. Headache mostly."

"Okay, I don't want you crawling around out there in your condition. I want you to stay with the vehicles. Zeenab's back in my ACV," Curt told her "Listen up to what we're going to do, and give us fire support."

"I'm sure as hell not going to stay here just to protect *her!*" Alexis snapped with irritation. Her head hurt, and she had a very good idea of what must have happened last night between her favorite company commander and a woman she was growing to dislike for many reasons.

"No, Lieutenant," Curt replied sternly. "Not just to protect Zee. That's not the order I gave. You're hurting, and someone who knows how to do it has got to tell these vehicles what to do. The twenties won't reach very far, but the Saucy Cans will cover us out to several kilometers . . . if the computers don't screw up. That's why you're staying. You've got to ride herd on the fire control computers just in case they freak out with fungus."

"Yes, sir," Alexis replied somewhat more meekly. She was hurting, but at least she was alive.

Within a minute, they were joined by Jerry Allen, Adonica, Kester, Sgt. Edwina Sampson, and squad leaders Elliott and Koslowski.

Curt knelt down in the dirt of the ditch and used the oldest visual aid known to the military: a map scratched in the dirt. "Okay, here's what we're going to do. We've put down that Tee-dad platoon that hit us. There are wounded out there, but they aren't shooting. So we'll walk over them and swing out west of the road, go to line of skirmishers, and move south to flank whatever Tee-dad troops are giving the Greys a hard time to our rear. Twenty meters between us. Use marching fire. Your rifles have superior range and penetration, so keep firing. We'll catch the Tee-dads on the left flank and roll 'em up. Lieutenant Morgan, put a Saucy Can rolling barrage over our heads. Adonica, you stay here with Lieutenant Morgan."

"Captain, you're short one officer, and you'll need a pro-tem Bravo Platoon cee-oh," Adonica pointed out.

"Can't let you. You're—"

"I'm a third lieutenant, Captain. You made it quite clear last night that I was no longer a civilian. And I played in these forests when I was a kid," Adonica Sweet snapped with just the right amount of sass and respect in her voice.

Dammit, she's right, and she's good, Curt told himself. *Alexis isn't going to like it, but that's just tough shit. I'm in command of this outfit.* "Okay, Lieutenant Sweet is in *temporary* command of Bravo Platoon until we complete this maneuver. Adonica, if you're smart, you'll pay attention to Sergeant Gerard. Nick, you know what to do."

Gerard nodded. If his commanding officer wanted to put this pretty little recent civilian in temporary charge, he'd go along with the protocol because he would in fact be running the platoon.

"I'm going to be right next to you, Sergeant," Adonica told the NCO.

"Smear some mud on that shiny rifle of yours, Lieutenant," Nick told her. "It glints in the sun. Could give you away or make you a target."

"I'll use cammy grease," Adonica told him, patting the Mini-14. "Forgot about the stainless steel shine. but better stainless steel than rust. Old Betsy here belonged to my grandfather . . ."

Curt checked his watch. It was 0635. The fighting had been underway for only about fiteen minutes. It seemed like hours. He looked around. "Any questions? Okay, let's move out. Its only about two kilometers back to the Killdeer River, and that's where

328

we're likely to find another Tee-dad unit attacking. We'll hit 'em hard on the flank and keep going. We'll pick up other fire support from the Killers and the Marauders when they see our IFF beacons. But be careful. Everybody. They might shoot at us thinking we're Tee-dads. Henry, take the left side of the skirmish line next to the road and pass the word to the other Greys as we contact them. We're going to show them what Sierra Charlies are really all about . . . Follow me!''

CHAPTER THIRTY-FIVE

It had been more than a quarter of a century since any U.S. Army soldier had advanced through tropical foliage in the assault against an actual enemy. Warbots had been used instead, these mechanical and electronic extensions to human bodies taking the physical punishment while the soldiers remained safe in a warbot linkage command post. That was easier and far safer.

Curt discovered that personal combat was not only hot, sweaty, and dirty as he'd learned in survivalist and war games over the past several months but also full of fear and foreboding. He'd been taught that all people going into combat are frightened and the more intelligent they are, the more they're frightened. But discipline, pride, self-respect, and self-confidence can make people courageous even when they're afraid. He'd made Carson's Companions into a taut, disciplined unit. With his own brand of gentle but fair and firm discipline, he'd overcome the innate resistance to obedience that's in each new member of a combat unit. He'd forged a team of people who actually liked one another and got along together. They took pride in their company and the discipline they had. Now, he knew his Companions would react subconsciously in a split-second to signals and crises in personal combat. And they knew what the other members of the team would do. Even the squad leaders, newest of the Companions, had become team players even though they'd yet to learn how to take part in the talk and chatter that went on among the Companions.

Adonica Sweet worried him, however. She was smart, savvy, and as brave as a kitten. But how would she react under fire?

He couldn't worry too much about her. He had to stay alert and aware himself.

He took the center of the line of skirmishers a hundred meters off the road. The line was two hundred meters long. Lt. Jerry Allen held down the right flank out in the tropical forest while M. Sgt. Henry Kester was twenty meters from the road itself, holding down the left flank and ready to pass the word along to Kelly's Killers and Manny's Marauders when they got back to them.

He couldn't see the road and Kester, and he couldn't see Allen. The foliage wasn't thick, but it was heavy enough so that he could see only Cpl. Jim Elliott on his left and Cpl. Tracy Dillon on his right.

In spite of the racket of battle ahead of them, the Companions could communicate reasonably well between each other by voice. They hadn't deployed more than a few minutes when they found dead and wounded Tee-dad special forces troopers less than fifty meters from the road.

"Wounded Tee-dad here! What do I do him?" Koslowski called.

"Kick his gun out of reach. Disarm him and leave him," Sgt. Edie Sampson's voice replied.

"He's pretty badly wounded. He'll die."

"You've got no time to help him, Elliott. The biotechs will pick him up in less than an hour. Keep moving!'' Sampson's own personal combat experience with Curt in Zahedan was making itself evident.

Sampson wasn't heartless in telling her corporals to leave the wounded; she just had no milk of human kindness for an enemy who'd been shooting at her a few minutes before and no desire to jeopardize herself or the skirmish line by dropping back to help a wounded enemy. In the first place, none of the Companions were equipped with anything more than simple emergency medical kits which wouldn't do very much in any case.

Curt made a mental note and filed it. Biotechs were going to have to move right along with the Sierra Charlies in order to handle Sierra Charlie casualties. A damaged warbot could be left standing in the field until maintenance came along to haul it back and fix it, but a wounded human soldier often needed biotech help quickly. *So many little things we used to know and took for granted . . . and we've forgotten them because of the warbots!* Curt thought, then turned his attention back to the battle.

''Captain, they're carrying only nine-millimeter submachineguns and a few CETME light machine guns! No body armor either!'' came Sgt. Nick Gerard's call.

''Of course!'' Adonica added. ''Blue berets. Special Forces platoon. Used mostly for supressing insurgents. We've seen a lot of this outfit lately around Point Fortin.''

Alexis started the barrage. The 75mm shells going overhead made a sound that was a ripping, roaring, tearing noise of incredible loudness, the sound slipping up the scale as the shell came up overhead and then down the scale as it went forward and away. Doppler, Curt thought. A constant bedlam of Saucy Cans shells going overhead assaulted his ears along

332

with the muffled booms of their warhead explosions on landing.

Tracy Dillon yelled at Curt, "Kester reports Kelly's Killers want to send their warbots into the jungle behind us to provide covering fire! They're not under attack on their sector of the road. It's all to the south of them!"

That stupid sonofabitch Kelly's going to get his warbots tangled up in here and lose them! Curt thought. Maybe Kelly's big Mark 88s could get through by their sheer weight; the ground didn't seem to be too soft. But the lighter Mark 50s would have trouble moving between the trees and didn't have enough mass to knock some of them over. The little P-40s would do all right, but a standard RI company only had about a dozen of tose, and their 20mm cannons were too light for a rolling artillery barrage and too heavy and slow-firing for close-in jungle anti-personnel fighting, which was what this was. And when it came to crossing the Killdeer River, all warbots might get into trouble if they didn't have floation gear installed . . . which they didn't.

"For crissake, no!" Curt yelled back. "Tell Kelly to send his warbots back down the road to provide Garcia with some fire support from the flank! His warbots can't move fast enough out here and they're not equipped for this environment!"

Then Curt didn't have the luxury of time to worry about Kelly.

"Tee-dad platoon!" came the cry from his left followed by the sudden ripping report of a FABARMA rifle on full auto. Others joined in. The right flank was quiet. Then he saw the bright electric blue beret of a Tee-dad Special Forces soldier and he opened fire, shooting in three-round bursts with his FABARMA's butt snug against his right hip as he walked.

333

The blue beret disappeared; he didn't know whether or not he'd hit the man or just caused him to stop shooting and seek cover. He didn't really want to know; he just wanted the Tee-dad not to shoot at him.

"Hit the dirt!" someone on his right yelled. The sound of a 106mm self-propelled projectile aimed high and going over quickly followed.

"Negative! Negative! Forward! Marching fire!" Curt hollered back. Hitting the dirt made matters worse. What he wanted was a continuous stream of withering fire to make the enemy hit the dirt instead. With his head down, the enemy couldn't return fire . . . or couldn't return as much of it, even with 106s.

He did, however, crouch instinctively when a 9mm round hit the tree next to him.

But, strangely, the small amount of 9mm stuff that was being returned by the Tee-dads was going high. Curt remembered that a man with a submachinegun tends to shoot high when surprised and forced to the defensive.

Special Forces didn't carry the sort of heavy weaponry needed to put down a warbot outfit. Mekanika Uru 9-millimeter submachineguns and CETME 5.56mm LMGs were peashooters, useful only for urban fighting against people, not jungle combat against armored warbots. *Why did they send boys to do men's jobs?* Curt wondered.

Alexis's rolling barrage of Saucy Cans fire had partially devastated the forest of young mahogany and palm trees. And it was still rolling out ahead of them, the shells ripping through the skies overhead.

The Tee-dad Special Forces platoon wasn't expecting either the rolling Saucy Cans barrage or the assault on their unprotected left flank by rapid-firing American foot soldiers. They'd been told the American forces were roboticized. The possibility of encountering other troops on foot hadn't been in their battle plans, and they were totally unprepared for the assault by the Companions with marching fire.

Faced with a flanking attack by unsuspected, dismounted infantry, the Tee-dads started to give up, dropping their weapons and standing up with their hands in the air. *"Paré!* Stop! I surrender!" the cries began to come.

"Dillon!" Curt yelled. "Tell Kester to have Kelly send in warbots to take and escort prisoners!" That was something warbots could indeed do very well in these circumstances. Curt didn't have the manpower to spare; he had to use everyone to keep the skirmish line moving forward, and no one could afford to stay back to guard prisoners.

"They're already coming in!" Tracy Dillon reported back.

"Companions! Turn any prisoners over to Kelly's warbots! Let me know when you're ready to move forward again," Curt passed the word right and left along the line.

Alexis's Saucy Can barrage was lobbing its shells higher now, arcing them partly over the winding road.

The Companion's skirmish line crossed the Killdeer River shortly thereafter, putting the Tee-Dad Special Forces platoon out of action with about 50 percent killed and the rest taken prisoner by Kelly's warbots. Gerard and Elliott had taken hits from 9mm submachinegun fire on their body armor, but neither's armor had been broached.

Within a hundred meters after crossing in running water up to their waists, the Companions discovered and assaulted the flank of a larger Tee-dad unit of company size engrossed in a fire fight with Ward's Warriors on the road. This Tee-dad outfit wasn't a lightly-armed Special Forces unit but a heavy weapons company from one of the standard Tee-dad regiments. They were pounding the Greys on the road with 81mm mortars and 106mm recoilless launchers. About half of the men carried the light SAR-80 5.56mm assault rifles.

It was another brief fire fight with Curt and his company advancing as they shot their FABARMA rifles from the hip.

Warbots from the Killers and Marauders were now moving south along the edge of the road abreast of the Companions, helping to roll up the enemy left flank with the sort of massive heavy-caliber fire that warbots can provide because they were designed and built to handle much larger weapons than a human could possibly withstand when it came to both weight and recoil.

Curt caught a 5.56mm round on the left side of his soft body armor at the waist. It glanced off and thunked into a nearby tree. Even though the round couldn't penetrate even at normal incidence, the blow was enough to temporarily knock the wind out of Curt, and he fell to his knees. The punch in the ribs hurt like hell, but he decided he hadn't been penetrated. One of Kelly's P-40 warbots rolled past him, firing as it went.

The fight got fiercer. Saucer-shaped gunship aerodynes with Air Force markings were suddenly in the skies.

Then there were no more Tee-tad soldiers to shoot at, only beaten men who'd dropped their weapons and surrendered, plus the devastation and death wrought by the heavy warbot gunnery and the aerodyne gunships. The firing stopped. The Saucy Cans shells quit ripping overhead. The warbots ceased their insistent shooting. Save for a few bursts of automatic weapon

336

fire here and there as a Tee-dad decided to give it one last try and a warbot returned the fire, the battlefield on the northern outskirts of Rio Claro fell silent.

Curt's watch said it was 0852.

CHAPTER THIRTY SIX

The Battle of Rio Claro had lasted less than three hours. It seemed much longer than that to Curt. But modern battles don't last very long because of their extreme intensity. In this one, Curt discovered he'd used up more than 450 rounds of ammo. He had only about 50 rounds left, and they were already in the clip in his FABARMA.

Putting his fingers between his lips, Curt gave a loud whistle and then yelled, "Companions, assemble on me!" And he fired a three-round burst into the air from his FARARMA.

It didn't take them long to come in from the skirmish line.

They were all there—wet with river water, beads of sweat running down their faces over the cammy grease, cammy coveralls torn and ripped, and with a look in their eyes that was at the same time exhuberant with victory and filled with the stress and tension of personal combat. Nick Gerard limped, and the left sleeve of Jim Elliott's cammies was torn off. Jerry Allen's right hand was cut and bleeding, but Adonica had wrapped it in a synflesh dressing from his medikit and was hovering over him like a mother hen.

Somewhere in the heat of battle, Adonica had stripped out of her oversized cammy coveralls and now

338

wore only her shorts and halter. She was still soaking wet from the river crossing and had a bruise on her right leg.

Damn, I'm proud of these people! Curt thought exhuberantly. So he told them so. "You just took on two platoons of Tee-dad Special forces and a company of Tee-dad regulars," he announced. "And you whupped the hell out of them and probably saved the regiment in the process! Good work! Damned good work! Well done!"

"I'll echo that." Col. Belinda Hettrick appeared from the direction of the road with her aide and four warbots from the headquarters company as an escort. "Nice work, Companions. You did some things I didn't expect, but you turned the enemy flank."

"Maneuverability and speed. That's what Sierra Charlies are all about, Colonel," Curt reminded her. "And you saw what we can really do when it isn't a war game with staff stooges for umpires. And stupid rules written by warbot types that tried to tell us what and what not to do . . ."

Hettrick looked at him reproachfully. "Agreed. But don't go bragging about how much smarter you were than the umpires. Your actions spoke for themselves, so let it rest at that."

As the Companions gathered around Hettrick, Curt asked the regimental commander, "We only saw our small part of this. What the hell were the Tee-dads trying to do?"

Hettrick ran her hand over her face to wipe away the sweat. "They thought they could move in behind us and retake Rio Claro. That's the best the spooks can dope out. The Tee-dads figured the Division was heading either for Pierreville or Sangre Grande and they could flank us and chew us up from behind. Didn't work. Their timing was off in spite of the fact that some of the prisoners said they'd spent the night moving down the road from Tabaquite. They thought we'd also move right through the night and keep on going past Rio Claro. But we took a break instead. So they ran right into the whole damned 17th Iron Fist even before the support batallion started to move out of Poole. The Can Do got around behind them to the west at Poole and cut them off. Then the Cottonbalers and Wolfhounds held Rio Claro, protected our rear, and are mopping up what's left."

"How many of them, Colonel?" Henry Kester wanted to know.

"From what we can tell, they threw their whole Fourth Regiment at us plus their Special Forces company that you clobbered."

"The Fourth Tee-dad regiment? Wasn't that the outfit that stopped us at Oropuche River, Colonel?" Jerry Allen asked.

"It was. They got out of San Fernando and combined with some units of the Fifth Regiment that didn't manage to get chewed to pieces by the Can Do, the Wolfhounds, and the Golden Dragons of the Double Deuces in the Battle of San Fernando. They say Drake sent them down here with the Special Forces to break the back of the American invasion. But you Sierra Charlies stopped them because they weren't expecting you. So don't worry about the Fourth Tee-dad Regiment stopping you at Oropuche River day before yesterday, Lieutenant. The Companions vindicated themselves at Rio Claro! There's only one unit more elite than the Tee-dad Special Forces, and that's the Presidential Guard." She looked them over. "Support companies are on their way up from Poole. I'll get fresh uniforms and ammo up to you. Anybody need a biotech?"

"No, m'am. Just a bruise from a nine-millimeter on the thigh armor," Nick Gerard said.

"Elliott?"

"Sore arm Colonel. I'll live."

"Catpain, you look like you took one in the torso."

"I did, Colonel," Curt admitted. "That's why I insisted that Sierra Charlies wear body armor. Hot and sweaty, but it saved three of us."

"That hand cut badly?" Hettrick asked Jerry Allen.

Adonica Sweet answered for him. "He got cut by a flying wood splinter, Colonel. I've got the bleeding stopped now."

"You might have the biotechs bring us some analgesics," Curt suggested. "I think we're hurting from bruises more than just plain hurt. Lieutenant Morgan took a five-point-five in the helmet when this thing started. Last I saw of her, she had a splitting headache."

"Done! You'll get a biotech. Head back for the road and report to Capt. Manny Garcia. He'll have his vehicles take you back to yours. We've also just gotten a shipment of new tacomm units, so we can get under way for Sangre Grande and be in communication with one another."

"Sierra Hotel!" Sgt. Edie Sampson said happily. "Arm signals work, but tacomms are a hell of a lot easier!"

"Your company in shape to continue moving, Captain?" Hettrick asked.

"Yes, m'am, unless something happened while we were out in the puckerbrush, as our master sergeant would put it."

"Damned good thing you took the near flank of that skirmish line, Sergeant Kester," Hettrick pointed out. "Every one in the Greys can recognize you."

"Yes, m'am. That was the whole idea," Kester admitted.

Hettrick started to walk back to the road, but then turned to face them. "And, by the way, in case I forgot to tell you, damned good work, all of you! Good show! Well done!"

By 0930, the Companions were dropped off at the company ACV. Alexis was on the ground alongside it, ready to welcome them. She saluted smartly as Curt debouched from the Marauder ACV. "Was the barrage suitable, Captain?"

Curt returned her salute. "Damned right! Good job, Alexis."

Why is she so damned cold and formal? Curt wondered.

"I'm glad I performed to your satisfaction, Captain."

"What do you mean?"

"The fire control computers went down. I controlled that rolling barrage manually by watching your beacon returns on radar and computing barrage impact points by map coordinates."

"Damn, Alexis, that was good!" Jerry complimented her. "I haven't done that since I left West Point, and I'm not even sure I still could."

"When you have to do it, you do it," Alexis observed. "I also had to handle a slightly hysterical civilian you left with me, Captain . . ."

"What? Zee went into spasm mode?" Curt asked.

"Zeenab Tej lost her cool when she discovered her birds had been blown away," Alexis explained.

"Oh, for crissake!" Curt began. That explained part of the aloof coolness exhibited by Alexis Morgan.

"She also got real worried about you, Captain, and unloaded a data dump on me about you. I'll tell you about it later if you want," Alexis remarked offhandedly.

So that was it! Curt thought. Maybe he should have applied Rule Ten to himself anyway. Or maybe, as Zeenab herself had pointed out, Rule Ten needed to be modified. But it was too late now. What had been done was done. Time to see if he couldn't patch things up a bit with Alexis. "Can it wait?"

"Yes, sir."

"Okay, later." Curt looked around at the Companions. "You all look like you could use a shit, shine, shower, shave, and shampoo," he remarked with a slight smile, using the warbot brainy slang for a general clean-up following combat.

"Yes, sir, I'd sure as hell like a bath right now. Maybe I'll go jump in the river—" Sgt. Edie Sampson began.

She was interrupted by Zeenab who came out of the turret hatch, dropped quickly to the ground, and threw her arms around Curt while she sobbed, "Oh, Curt, Curt, my darling, you're all right! My birds have all been killed! I couldn't stand the thought of losing you, too . . ."

Edie Sampson viewed this display with a noncommittal expression, then added, "Yeah, I guess Sherman was right. War is hell . . ."

Curt was more than merely embarassed by the behavior of Zeenab. He disengaged her arms from around his neck. "Lieutenant," he said to Alexis, "let's get a tranqulizer into this woman. She's still hysterical."

"Yes, sir. She's got two tranks in her now," Alexis pointed out.

Curt had inwardly suspected that Zeenab was going to be trouble, but he hadn't expected this. She was a beautiful woman, and her pigeons had helped out in a tight spot, but she'd caused big problems for him in his company . . . and he didn't need that. Best to get rid of the problem right now before it got worse. With-

343

out the need for her pigeons—and without her pigeons, in fact—because of new tacomm units, he didn't technically need her any longer. He should send her back to Rio Claro. But when he looked around, the ACVs from Manny's Marauders had left. So he turned to his master sergeant. "Henry, get on the hooter to regimental cee-pee. Tell them we've got a civilian here who's effectively gone into spasm mode. Battle fatigue. Tell them to send someone up to get her."

"Yes, sir!" Kester snapped and mounted the ACV to drop through the hatch.

"In the meantime," Curt went on, "Lieutenant Morgan will resume command of Bravo Platoon . . . if you're up to it, Lieutenant. How's the head?"

"Much better, Captain. I can resume my command, sir."

"Good. Lieutenant Sweet, Zeenab here is your friend. You're reassigned to my ACV; you can navigate us just as well from here, and there's only one road to Sangre Grande. And I need you to comfort your friend if she doesn't get sent back to the rear."

Adonica looked properly forelorn and chagrined at the same time. "Yes, sir, but I should ride up with Lieutenant Allen—"

"Lieutenant, that's an order."

"Yes, Captain," the young woman replied, then remarked after a brief pause, "But if you don't think you need my services, I'd be happier resigning that brevet commission and going back to Rio Claro with Zeenab . . ."

"What do you mean?" Curt asked.

"I think, Captain, and with all due respect," Sgt. Nick Gerard put in carefully, trying to let Curt know that his personal assessment of the behavior of his company commander toward Zeenab Tej and Alexis Morgan—which was perfectly transparent to the

344

Companions— to say nothing of Curt's failure to recognize Adonica's part in the flanking assault was basically overreaction on Curt's part, "that she's politely told you she wants to get the hell out of this chicken outfit . . ."

"You think so, huh?" Curt snapped back, but with the edge gone off his voice this time. "Well, Sergeant, she's in it for the duration like the rest of us unless I hear from the high brass. In the meantime, I gave an order. Until I get a contrary order from a superior officer, I'll expect you all to hop to and carry it out." He checked his watch. Somehow, it had gotten sweat or condensation inside of it, and he could barely read the digital numbers through the film of water inside the crystal. "And I've got my orders, too. We move out at ten-hundred hours. Which means we've got about five minutes before the rest of the Washington Greys start running up our ass. We're expected to get moving. So mount up. Do it. Now. On to Sangre Grande."

The way he said it caused the Companions to move, scattering to their respective vehicles. He turned to Adonica and Zeenab, indicated his ACV, and said politely, "Ladies, if you please?"

"I wonder if we ought to. I busted my buns for this outfit. So did Zee. Discipline notwithstanding, and even though the morale of your outfit may be pretty good, it doesn't seem to extend to us," Adonica said with disgust in her voice.

"It's a long walk back to Rio Claro in this heat and humidity," Curt reminded her.

"Captain," Adonica said with a touch of acid in her voice, "it'll be a hell of a lot easier to walk back to Rio Claro than it was walking through that jungle with you, shooting at people and being shot at . . ."

In spite of the fact that Curt had had some reservations about how Adonica might perform under fire, he

345

had to admit to himself now that she was a damned good soldier. She'd stood up and been shot at with the rest of the Companions. By rights, he shouldn't treat her like an ordinary native guide. Zeenab had come unraveled under stress, but Adonica had shown guts. Not many women would have willingly done what she'd done.

"My apologies, Lieutenant Sweet," Curt told her, using the formal address of rank to help smooth up what might otherwise become a very rough situation. He knew he'd been badly rattled by Zeenab's embrace in front of his troops. "I didn't intend to demean you, and I apologize if I offended you. Chalk it up to the aftermath of combat, and I'll try not to let it happen again. You did an outstanding job during that flanking assault, and I intend to see that you're properly recognized for it in public. I also know you're hoping to find your father. So please stick around. I'd appreciate it if you'd help Zeenab through a difficult time for her. As soon as I can, I'll transfer you back to Lieutenant Allen's ACV. Or would you prefer that I had Zeenab ride back with Lieutenant Morgan and let you go back to Alpha Platoon now?"

Adonica slung her grease-covered Mini-14 over her shoulder by its carrying strap. She suddenly grinned. It was a fresh, young smile that cut through the sweat and cammy grease on her lovely young face. "Captain Carson, flattery will get you anything, so keep talking. This is also a hell of a lot more fun than sitting around the oil patch watching the grass grow. Come on, Zee, let's climb aboard. On to Sangre Grande!"

346

CHAPTER THIRTY-SEVEN

It had been a long day. A damned long day. Curt was bone tired. M. Sgt. Henry Kester briefed him in the turret of the ACV as the kilometers rolled past. They had proceeded in a generally northward direction along the Cunapo Southern Road paralleling the Central Range of 300-meter hills. Their green slopes looked steep and difficult.

"Not many troops can operate over that sort of terrain," Kester pointed out. "Maybe some insurgents or guerrillas, but not regulars. Takes time for troops to cover that sort of ground, and we've been moving too fast for them to react."

The old soldier was right, of course. But this didn't prevent Curt from maintaining an intensive surveillance of the left side of the road as they proceeded north. The maps showed only a few short primitive roads leading off into the hills, and they didn't go more than a kilometer or so before the charts showed them dead-ending.

"No problem, Captain Carson. Sergeant Kester is right," Adonica confirmed. "If any wilderness is left on Trinidad, it's in the Central Range up there around Mount Tamana. Some of the most beautiful hummingbirds the the world up there—"

347

"Bird watching is about the last thing on my mind right now," Curt admitted.

"Pity. The original Amerindian inhabitants called this island *Iere,* the land of the hummingbirds," Adonica remarked as they sat together in the main compartment of the ACV.

"How's Zeenab doing?" Curt asked the young girl, indicating the older woman sleeping on a padded bench toward the rear.

"Okay, I guess. She's pretty upset about losing her birds."

"I gathered that. She getting over it?"

Adonica looked puzzled. "It's hard to tell. She's acting strangely. Certainly not like the Zeenab Tej I used to know."

"What do you mean?"

She shrugged. "I can't put my finger on it. More quiet than I remember her. Subdued may be the word. Fearful, too. Lost, perhaps. And, well, just maybe a little guilty, but I don't know why she'd want to feel guilty. One thing for sure, Captain: seems she sure fell for you. Hard."

"Maybe," was all that Curt thought of to say. He recalled last night in Rio Claro. Zeenab hadn't exhibited caring love as much as she'd projected outright sensuality. It was almost as if she'd deliberately tried to seduce him. The thought had crossed his mind last night, but he'd dismissed it then just as he did now. At the time, it had seemed something they both wanted badly. Now, the stress of the morning's battle, the likely endless trek up the Cunapo Southern Road toward Sangre Grande, and possibly a new battle had all apparently been more than she could take.

Curt had asked Hettrick whether or not he should send Zeenab back since her pigeons were no longer available for message duty and workable tacomms were in hand. But Hettrick replied that the Washington Greys didn't have the personnel available to shepherd a civilian to the rear. It would have immensely complicated the movement of the regiment along the road. The convoy of vehicles stretched back for almost ten kilometers, and there were few places where a vehicle bound southward for Rio Claro could have passed the huge ACVs and other warbot vehicles on the winding road that was often only one lane wide.

"What about you, Captain?" Adonica asked.

"What about me?"

"Yesterday you couldn't take your eyes off Zeenab, Captain. That was obvious. Do you love her?"

Curt sighed. "I don't know, Adonica. I'm a soldier—and a field soldier at that. Right now, I'm a company commander in combat, and what love I have must be directed toward my outfit. Maybe Zeenab just happened to come along at a time when I needed her. Being shot at does things to a person."

"Yes, so I found out," the young woman replied somberly. "Which is why I've got to tell you, Captain Carson, that I'm still upset at you for not letting me ride up in the Alpha Platoon ACV."

"I know that. And Jerry's pissed off at me, too. But I couldn't afford to have you up there today distracting him."

"Distracting him!"

"That's what I said. If you thought I had the hots for Zeenab, it's been blantly obvious that you and Lieutenant Jerry Allen had 'em for each other in an even worse way . . ."

Adonica tossed her blonde hair out of her face. "That's a private matter between me and Jerry and none of your goddam business . . . Captain."

"It is my business, Lieutenant," Curt replied, deliberately stressing her rank. "This is combat and any
349

of us could get killed. Everything my people do has got to be my business. If you're nervous in the service, there's not a whole hell of a lot that either of us can do about it until we take Sangre Grande and get this fracas over with." Curt sighed. Technically, the discipline of Carson's Companions was his responsibility. But so was its leadership. Balancing the two had often been a delicate process. And since Adonica Sweet had never taken an oath for her commission, he probably didn't have a damned bit of real authority over her. On the other hand, she'd taken on the role of guide willingly and had accepted a brevet third lieutenant's commission willingly, too. So, whether he was legally or technically correct or not, Curt *had* to assume authority.

"That's part of what discipline is all about," he went on in a gentler tone. "Without it, even warbot brainies safe on their linkage couches would throw in the towel when the going got tough. An outfit has to have even better discipline to hang together in personal combat. You're in it up to your pretty neck, Adonica, and you can't get out of it right now. You may not like it, but I think you've got the guts to stick it out. You're still a lot of help . . . and it's more than maintaining Jerry's morale. You're a damned good soldier. When and if Morris Priest starts to put things together again on this island, he damned well ought to ask for your help . . . and I'm going to suggest just that to Colonel Hettrick."

"A woman would never be allowed to serve in the Trinidad Defense Forces," Adonica maintained. "Besides, playing soldier with the boys was fun when I was a kid because I was always a tomboy . . . and the boys got more interesting as the years went by. But I'm not sure I'd like to play soldier for real. I just want to find what Drake did to my father . . . and see to it that Jerry gets through this alive."

"He'll do all right, Adonica. Just don't distract him. As for General Drake, I'll give you first shot at interrogating him if we're lucky enought to catch him . . ."

The ACV's tacomm unit signalled. It was the Washington Greys command post calling. "Attention, all Grey units, this is Grey Head. Orders follow. Stand by to copy.

"Companions, turn right on Plum Road and proceed to Upper Manzanilla. Secure the Eastern Main Road out of Sangre Grande against possible Tee-dad offensive. Bivouac tonight near Upper Manzanilla.

"All other Grey units, proceed to Warren Road, deploy to the right along Warren Road and the ridge. Stand by to provide possible heavy fire support to the left flank. Bivouac on Warren Road tonight.

"Logistics aerodynes will be over you between nineteen-hundred and twenty-one-hundred hours. Be ready to reprovision with food, ammo, and any other materiel which you inform Ess-Four you need before seventeen-hundred hours today.

"Company commanders will meet at Grey cee-pee at nineteen-hundred hours. Tac aerodyne transport will airlift a few minutes before that time, so be ready to go.

"Hard copy will come up on the net in two minutes.

"Signal receipt and ready to comply."

Since the Companions were first in line and also first mentioned in the orders, Curt keyed the tacomm and replied, "Companion Leader, roger, orders received. Wilco."

One by one, the other companies of the Washington Greys were heard to report in.

Curt looked at the map. Adonica indicated where they were supposed to turn onto Plum Road. "Right after we reach the ridge line and start down. We have to go back up the ridge and over it again to get to Upper Manzanilla.''

Curt shook his head in puzzlement. ''Why is Hettrick splitting her command? And why send us down the back road there?''

''She might want some more troops on that road,'' Adonica guessed. ''Look, that's the only way out of Sangre Grande if Drake's units are being forced back from the west. It leads to the coast. Drake might try to break out of Sangre Grande along that road . . .''

Curt continued to shake his head. ''Doesn't make sense. The Wolfhounds are coming up the coast road.'' He shrugged. ''Well, maybe I'll find out at the company commander's meeting tonight. Adonica, I would like you take over Bravo Platoon during my absence while Lieutenant Morgan stands in for me here.''

''Sure! No problem, Captain! Sergeant Gerard pretty much runs Bravo Platoon anyway when Lieutenant Morgan isn't around.'' She suddenly looked at him. ''Uh, Captain, judging from Lieutenant Morgan's behavior, there wouldn't be something between the two of you that Zeenab is disturbing, would there?''

''What makes you think that?'' Curt asked suddenly.

''Well, just say it's a woman's intuition.''

Curt cracked a small smile and replied, ''As you told me, it's a private matter, and R-H-I-P.''

''What's that mean?''

''Rank Hath Its Privileges, Lieutenant.''

''Oh.'' Adonica was silent for a moment, then added softly, ''I thought so. Poor Zeenab . . .''

Curt relayed the information to Allen, and shortly after crossing the ridge, the Companions turned right, went back over the ridge line and down across the L'Ebranche River, then followed along its right bank until they reached the Eastern Main Road and the little village of Upper Manzanilla at 1725. Curt could see Manzanilla Bay and the ocean through the trees.

"We'll circle the wagons here for the night," he passed the word on the company tacomm when they got to the intersection of Plum Road and Eastern Main Road where the latter crossed the L'Ebranche River. "Dog down and stay inside unless you put on insect repellent. Kester reports that the mosquitoes outside are many and large enough to take on an A-Twenty in a dogfight!"

"Matter of fact," the old soldier remarked as he closed the turret hatch, "tell everyone to disable the anti-air sensors. Those damned things are big enough for the radar to get a range gate lock-on and trigger the triple-A defenses!"

"Companion Alpha Leader and Companion Bravo Leader, please come to Companion Leader for a conference. Bring your rations; we'll chow down in here," Curt added. He wanted to talk with his platoon commanders before heading off to the regimental pow-wow.

Both Morgan and Allen dropped through the turret hatch. Morgan was slapping at something. "Damned bugs! Repellent didn't do a bit of good!" Alexis complained.

"You must taste pretty good," Allen remarked.

"She usually does," Curt put in lightly.

"I haven't noticed," Allen came back with a raised eyebrow.

"Damned good thing," Adonica said.

"All right!" Curt snapped. "Sorry I got the witty repartee started. It's been a long, hard day. Sit down, all of you, and let's chow-down. You too, Zee. Adonica, move over and let her sit next to you. Sergeant, is the galley hot to trot?"

Everyone was a tad testy and on edge. Food, even in field ration form, helped immensely. So did the relaxation because, as Curt pointed out on the map, the Companions that night weren't immdiately threatened. They were serving as a second line of defense behind Kelly's Killers further up the Eastern Main Road with the Wolfhounds coming up from the south behind them all. It was almost as if Hettrick had sensed their fatigue and slipped them into a safe slot for the night.

"I've got to go to a meeting at regimental," Curt explained to them as they finished eating and stuffed their used utensils in trash bags. "I'll probably want to talk to you after I get back so I can give you the latest scoop with the group. Or at least bring you up to the same level of ignorance and confusion that I'll be enjoying at that time. Alexis, I want you to take temporary command of the company while I'm gone, as usual. Adonica will assume temporary command of Bravo Platoon. While I'm at the meeting, I'd like you to check your troops and equipment; Adonica, Alexis and Nick Gerard will help you with Bravo."

"And what am I supposed to do?" Zeenab asked petulantly.

"Help Alexis and Sergeant Kester here in my ACV," Curt told her.

"I repeat: What am I supposed to do? I know nothing about your equipment."

"You can make yourself useful by helping out. Henry will tell you what needs to be done. For example, drain excess condensate water from the dehumidifiers. Help load and store tomorrow's rations when the logistical aerodyne lowers them in. And help tidy up in here; this place is a mess after a day on the road, and we may be fighting again tomorrow. So we've got a lot of work to do tonight before taps."

"Orgasmic! More work! I'd could use about a week's sleep right now," Alexis put in. "Know something? I miss the biotechs."

"Come to think of it, so do I," Curt added, thinking fondly of the petite Tech Sgt. Helen Devlin who'd helped him getting into linkage with warbots and out again, a tricky biological, physiological, electronic, and psychological feat.

"One of the disadvantages of being a Sierra Charlie, I guess," Jerry said philosopically, then added, "But we need at least one physical trauma biotech NCO in every platoon of Sierra Charlies. My left hand is still sore where I cut it this morning."

"I think all of us are hurting a little bit here and there," Alexis remarked.

"How's your head?" Curt asked her.

"How's your side, Captain?" she asked back.

"It hurts, but I'll live, Lieutenant."

"Same here, Captain."

"We're hurting mostly because we went into combat before we were ready," Kester remarked.

"No outfit is ever ready, Sergeant," Curt observed. "We needed a lot more training. Hell, we didn't even have most of our procedures worked out before we had to go and get shot at. By the way, if I didn't tell you before, all of you did a damned fine job back at Rio Claro. Do you realize we took on two Tee-dad Special Forces platoons and a regular infantry company, all used to fighting in this tropical paradise? And we did it off the top of our heads without any prior experience in a skirmish line?"

"That's not what I meant, Captain," Kester said. "We're bruised from hits on our body armor and from the general wear and tear of field combat. Our muscles are sore because we haven't used some of them in a long time. We're beat to the socks tonight because we're badly out of shape. You gotta be in top physical condition for personal combat. It tears the hell out of you and uses up a lot of energy in a damned quick

355

hurry. We didn't have near enough physical condition-ing before we hit the beach. Army's going to have to relearn that, too."

"Amen, Sergeant!" Alexis breathed.

"Yeah, I was surprised how quickly I'd gotten out of shape after West Point," Jerry added.

"We all are and were and did, Mr. Allen," Curt told him and then added in a lighthearted mood, "So I'm going to start ordering in raw meat for you, Allen. Maybe that will help turn the lead in your ass into tiger milk."

"No problem with that here, Captain," Allen shot back.

"I'll attest to that," was Adonica's remark, then she suddenly shut up in embarassment. Curt didn't even glance in her direction.

"A bath would feel damned good right now," Alexis voiced her thoughts.

"Yeah, if it wasn't almost three klicks to the beach, I'd wander down there after the work is done and go for a swim," Allen replied.

"Too far. But go swish your feet in the river outside; they could use it," Alexis told him.

"Hell, we'd get eaten alive by mosquitoes before we could get there and back," Kester put in.

"Oh, you were thinking of skinny dipping in the river, Sarge?" Alexis wanted to know. "After all this time, I didn't know you were that kind of party animal . . ."

"There may be frost on the roof, but there's still a fire in the boiler, Lieutenant," Kester replied quietly with a twinkle in his eyes.

Curt sat back, tired but relaxed. This was the sort of loose banter that characterized Carson's Compan-ions when they started to relax and let off steam. He was glad that Alexis appeared to have snapped out of

356

her snit. He watched Adonica and Zeenab; they were a little mystified by this frank chatter between men and women. That sort of thing probably wasn't a part of their world on Trinidad. But this was a close-knit outfit and always had been. They were intelligent and courageous and young . . . except Henry Kester who was young in heart.

CHAPTER THIRTY-EIGHT

At 1830, Curt peeled out of his body armor; no need to wear it to a regimental meeting. But the logistics aerodyne hadn't arrived yet, so he had to crawl back into his sweat-soaked cammies. As a precaution, he sprayed on some insect repellent. Then he strapped on his supply harness just in case; better to have it than run into a tough situation and discover he'd left it back in the ACV. Grabbing his FABARMA, he left the group in the ACV, slipped up through the turret hatch, and witnessed the most beautiful tropical sunset he'd ever seen.

The bug juice apparently worked for him. And his contemplation of the sunset was interrupted by the rumbling, swishing, muted roar of a tac aerodyne that slipped down the road and came to hover above the ACV. A pick-up harness loop flipped out of a hatch in its bottom, Curt slipped it under his arms, and the aerodyne lifted him aboard.

At 1900 hours, he found himself in Hettrick's big regimental ACV, seated on a bench down one side of the main bay between Manny Garcia and Joan Ward. And the regimental commander got the show on the road right on time.

"You all did a hell of a job today. Whupped the ass off the Tee-dads at Rio Claro after they ambushed us, then moved thirty klicks over the crookedest road I ever saw. I'm proud of you! You're Washington Greys! You're goddamned good! Now, today might have been rough, but tomorrow's likely to be a real bitch." Hettrick was loved by the Washington Greys because she didn't mince words when the fighting got going. On the other hand, she could be as gracious and diplomatic as a queen when social conditions required it. "As the old cliche goes: This is it! This is what we've trained for!"

In spite of the fact that her regimental CP had all the latest electronic display screens, a map of Trinidad was taped up on the wall behind her. Superimposed on it were the presently known locations of all military units. Blazoned across its top were the words, "CLASSIFIED TACTICAL SENSITIVE."

"We've got Drake and what's left of his forces cornered in Sangre Grande. He can't get out. Tomorrow, he gets a surrender ultimatim at oh-five-hundred under a white flag. The Deputy Supreme Commander, Land, of Operation Steel Band, Lt. Gen. Louise Montcalm, will carry it into Sangre Grande under a white flag of truce in a logistics aerodyne. With discreet fighter cover, I might add. Gen. Austin Drake will have two hours to throw in the towel. But we'll be in position by oh-seven-hundred to push off the final assault on Sangre Grande because General Carlisle knew Drake personally when the man was still in the Army, and he believes Drake will try to fight his way out; if he can't, he'll try to get his troops to fight to the last man. Which they won't do because they're mostly mercenaries from Brazil and Argentina."

She reached into a campaign bag and pulled out a folded paper. After unfolding it awkwardly—she wasn't used to doing it, she taped it up on the wall over the Trinidad map. This new map was a 1:50,000-scale map of the Sangre Grande region. The location of the various units were marked.

"To the north and west of the city, the Carib forces under General Sturdevandt have already made contact with the warbots of the Tee-dad Presidential Guard southeast and east of Valencia. The Caribs—Venezuelans, Panamanians, and Columbians; the companies from Jamaica and Curacao were constabulary outfits and are taking care of Port of Spain and San Fernando—they may have some trouble making headway against an elite warbot unit. We'll just have to see how much heavy fire those Brazilian and Argentine warbots can put out and how good their armor is.

"The Tee-dad Third Regiment—what's left of it plus units from the Fifth Regiment—will be confronted by the Twenty-Second Double Deuces moving in from the west. The Tee-dads have a pretty good line of defense along the Cunapo River, but they're badly outnumbered and the Iron Fist will probably be the outfit which turns their southern flank later in the day if our push succeeds.

"The Iron Fist has been given the southern jaw of the Sangre Grande nutcracker. The Wolfhounds will pass through Upper Manzanilla shortly after oh-one-hundred tomorrow morning to form the eastern end of the Iron Fist line. Carson's Companions are currently bivouacked in Upper Manzanilla and Kelly's Killers are stationed at the intersection of Eastern Main Road and Warren Road. Curt and Marty, you'll have to let the Wolfhounds move through you and past you tonight. Tomorrow at oh-seven-hundred, the Cottonbalers and the Can Do will move toward Sangre Grande along the Cunapo South Road, deploying as shown.

"The Greys have been ordered to stay put on Warren Road and provide heavy fire cover. I'm forming and taking command of the First Temporary Tactical

Battalion made up of the Marauders and the Warriors. The First Batt will act as a mobile reserve, ready to move where the action warrants."

Sensing a rustle among her company commanders that signalled their disciplined dissatisfaction with the fact that the Greys were essentially being left out of the fight, Hettrick quickly added, "I don't like it either, but the Washington Greys have taken the brunt of the action south of the Central Range thus far. General Carlisle knows that both our warbot and Sierra Charlie contingents are flexible and have learned to be very mobile. He wants to use that to the best advantage. Manny and Joan, don't fret; your outfits will get the chance to shine."

She turned and looked in turn at Curt and Marty Kelly. "And if you two can keep from spitting at each other for another day I've got a job for you. Curt, I want you to give me another one of your end runs tomorrow. Marty, I want you to go with him in support."

"Give you anything you want, Colonel. Name it," Curt told her.

"Colonel," Marty Kelly broke in, "I'll follow your orders, but I'm damned tired of having to eat Carson's dust. All I've done is follow him for two days—"

"And you've done a damned fine job of it because you've not only pushed him but you've responded quickly to threats and assaults, Marty," Hettrick told him, deliberately giving him a little ego grease. She knew very well the rivalry between the two company commanders, and she wanted to harness that in a way that meant trouble for the enemy rather than for her. Curt was the easiest for her to handle; Marty often gave her the most trouble.

And he continued to do so. "I haven't trained-up

my outfit for this sort of cavalry-style operation. We're an assault outfit, not a strike unit."

"Captain!" Hettrick's voice now had an edge on it. To her company commanders, it meant that her patience had run out. She rarely chewed-out a subordinate publicly, but right then she saw no alternative. "You were transferred to the Greys because the Killers are a problem outfit . . . but I thought your aggressiveness would be useful if I could get it under control. I haven't always succeeded because you're like mercury fulminate, Kelly. You fulminate! And you screw up. You screwed up in Zahedan. You screwed up two days ago. Now you've got the chance to turn the enemy's flank and chew him up from the rear along with a Sierra Charlie outfit that's proved it can combine its shock and maneuverability with your concentration of force and fire power. You two have a combat team going, whether you know it or not. And whether you like it or not. So shut up and listen to what I want you to do. . . .

There was silence for a moment. Curt didn't need to speak up. But Kelly finally said, "Yes, Colonel."

"The Venezuelan Second Battalion under Colonel Miranda is going to move east on Valencia Road and sweep down on Sangre Grande from the north along Toco Main Road," she went on, pointing to it on the map. She took a deep breath, knowing the potential consequences of what she was about to say. "Curt, I want you to take over the Companions and the Killers as my Second Temporary Tactical Battalion. Cut right along Caigual Road to Lower Fishing Pond, then sweep into Sangre Grande from the east on Sangre Grande Road. You'll link up with the Venezuelans about a kilometer east of the city. Go in and get Drake's command headquarters. If we cut off the head of this

Tee-dad monster, it will drop dead in our hands. And then we can all go home."

"How far do we have to move?" Curt asked. To hell with Kelly. Curt would put the rivalry behind him whether Kelly would or not. They were being given orders, and they were supposed to be professionals and carry them out, not snipe at one another.

"About twelve to fifteen kilometers; maps aren't that accurate and surveillance satellites can't see the roads in some locations because of the vegetation."

"When do you want us to be where?"

"Plan to link up with Miranda and his Venezuelans about noon."

"What if he isn't there then?"

"Go in without him. Don't give up your advantage of shock and surprise."

"If Drake runs," Kelly observed, "the only way out of Sangre Grande is Toco Main Road up to Toco Bay. What are the chances of him doing that, Colonel, and will we be able to get the hot poop if he tries it?"

"I'll do my best to keep you up to date on the latest reconaissance data," Hettrick promised. "But be prepared to either tangle with Drake and part of his Presidential Guard trying to get out of Sangre Grande . . . or to get in behind him if he leaves before you get there and engages the Venezuelans." She paused and went on, "Now, listen to me, you two. I'm sticking my neck the hell out on the block and taking a risk by putting Sierra Charlies and an aggressive warbot company together in a tac batt. Nobody's worked out the tactical procedures for that, but I think you two can hack it. Frankly, I'm doing it because we don't know exactly what Drake will try to do. If you two will work together as I know you can, you can handle anything that comes your way in this maneuver. Bury the goddamned

363

hatchet—and not in each other's skull—and go do the job."

Curt looked over at the other captain and merely asked, "Kelly?"

"Okay, Carson. You confuse 'em, I'll clobber 'em."

CHAPTER THIRTY-NINE

The tactical transport aerodyne dropped Curt on the pick-up harness alongside his ACV. He slipped out of the padded loop of rope and gave it three sharp tugs. It began snaking back upward into the aerodyne as the saucer-shaped aircraft increased its slot flow and blasted away to the southwest, returning toward regimental headquarters to pick up another company commander.

Save for the ever-present mosquitoes, nothing appeared to be moving around the cluster of ACVs, ARTVs, and LAMVs. Then, in the tropical moonlight, Curt saw Lt. Alexis Morgan and 3rd Lt. Adonica Sweet sitting together on the ground alongside the vehicle. They got silently to their feet and began walking over to him.

He knew something was wrong. Very wrong.

"The meeting go well, Captain?" Alexis asked.

"Educational. We've got another end run to make tomorrow with the Killers on our ass."

"Orgasmic!" was Alexis' acidic comment.

"Call Jerry and have him come over; I need to go over the details with everyone." He paused, then asked, "Al, I thought the mosquitoes chewed you up even when you used repellent."

"They do. But we need to talk to you, and we

365

wanted to snag you the instant you got back." Alexis slapped at her arm. "Missed."

"Can we do it inside the ACV?"

"I'm in favor, but not inside the your ACV. We need to speak privately," Alexis was acting strangely. Curt couldn't put his finger on it. He could usually read the woman very well; tonight, he couldn't. Yes, he decided, something was indeed wrong if she wanted to talk with him privately and yet in the company of Adonica Sweet.

"Oh? Okay, then let's go over to your ARTV and get inside," Curt suggested. "The warbots are powered down. They won't eavesdrop."

"Uncomfortable, but private. And privacy we need. Comfort can come later," Alexis observed.

Once inside Bravo's Armored Robot Transport Vehicle with the sortie hatch closed, Curt voice-commanded the lights to turn on. The interior was designed to transport the thirteen warbots of Bravo Platoon, not human beings. But there was an area in the aft end where technicians could perform warbot maintenance. The three of them found a place to sit on the traction plastic floor covering, surrounded by the silent warbots.

"Okay, now spill it. What's going on?" Curt wanted to know.

"We've got trouble," Alexis told him.

"Big trouble," Adonica added.

"While you were gone, Adonica and I got Zeenab to open up," Alexis went on.

"I thought that might happen. That's why I left the three of you together," Curt admitted. "So, what transpired?"

Adonica began slowly and almost apologetically, "I've known Zee for years. We grew up together near San Fernando. She's a little older than I am, so she always played big sister for me and I was her tomboy kid sister. I was the one who'd rather play war and cricket and football with the boys instead of holding doll tea parties and such. Zee used to tease me for playing with the boys, but later on she developed her own fascination for men—"

"Your life story have something to do with the reason the two of you are upset?" Curt pressed. He always tried to cut through to the meat of the matter, but he thought that perhaps tonight he should let Adonica tell it her way because she was somehow distressed . . . and he was worried about Alexis' behavior.

"I think it does. You have to understand a little of the background to understand Zee. Her father was a refinery shift supervisor near San Fernando. She always complained that he didn't get the big promotions because he was Hindu. A lot of Hindus came to Trinidad in the last couple of centuries, and most of them sort of merged their culture into that of Trinidad. Zee tried to be less Hindu and more Trinidad; I never saw her dress in traditional saris and stuff. But yesterday she surprised me in Ciperio; she was wearing all those bright colors and bracelets. She didn't look at all like the Zeenab I used to know. I haven't seen her in the past two years, and people change, but she seemed almost like a stranger when we met again," Adonica went on. "We got to talking about old times tonight, and I got her to talk about herself. Captain, she's scared half out of her mind."

When Adonica paused that this point, Curt put in, "I've got news for you: We've *all* been scared in the last couple of days, This operation's had a very high pucker factor. So go on."

"Zeenab's been hiding something from all of us. But she couldn't hold it in any longer, especially from an

367

old friend," Adonica explained. "She was devastated by the loss of her prized birds and scared of what her father would do to her when he learned she'd taken them without his permission."

"And she was pretty damned well shaken up about you," Alexis interrupted.

"Me? What the hell did she tell you, Alexis?" Curt wanted to know.

Adonica answered instead, "The Lieutenant told Zee quite gently and politely that she'd have more than a little competition. Zee couldn't accept that. Captain, it seems you're the embodiment of her girlish fantasies about strong, powerful, athletic military men."

"Orgasmic! I don't quite know how to take being considered the embodiment of a fantasy," Curt admitted bitterly. "So what was she hiding from all of us? And why did she reveal it to you two?"

"She sees herself on the losing side," Adonica explained, "and told us she'd better confess in the hope we'd go easy on her. Zee's a secret police agent. And she used one of her pigeons to report on us to her father who's apparently with Drake."

"What!" Curt exploded in disbelief. "How the hell could that possibly be? We didn't plan for our tacomms to crap out. We didn't plan to pick her up with her birds in Ciperio. Bringing her along was strictly an accident!"

"It was indeed," Alexis tried to clarify the situation. "She hadn't planned to do it, either. But she seized the opportunity."

"But a secret police agent? I find that hard to swallow," Curt said, shaking his head.

Alexis went on, "Kester discovered one of her pigeons missing; she tried to cover up that she'd dispatched it with a message to her father revealing our location. He's apparently on Drake's spook staff. She claims that's why the Tee-dads swung south and hit us at Rio Claro. She thinks she's responsible for Drake's troops getting slaughtered, and she can't deal with that."

"Drake's secret police had undercover agents everywhere on the island," Adonica went on to explain. "They apparently recruited her father because of his dissatisfaction with the multinational petroleum companies. They had a policy of bringing in outside managers—like my father—and wouldn't promote the local experts like her father who in turn recruited her. Zee claims she got involved initially for his sake. Eventually, she began to believe Drake's propaganda and started to enjoy the little perks that came with being involved with the secret police . . . except the men who were too distrustful and violent for her . . ."

Curt shook his head sadly. "I know the type. Closet paranoids or sadists who covet power over people by controlling information or physically coercing them. But all you've told me thus far doesn't tell me why she'd suddenly lay this data dump on you."

"What Zee knew of soldiers she learned from the secret police and the Brazilian and Argentine mercenaries of the Fourth Regiment in San Fernando," Adonica explained. "She believed what they said about American soldiers."

"The usual anti-American line?"

Alexis replied with disgust, "Yeah, we're just warbot drivers. Mean, vicious, and uncaring automatons. War mongering butchers, the hired gangsters of the greedy capitalist pigs . . . We've heard it for a long time—"

"She was scared to death of all of you at first," Adonica pointed out.

"It didn't show," Curt said. "She managed to hide it because she was a deep spook for Drake."

"Not totally, Captain," Adonica cautioned. "She didn't understand why I was working for you. She thought we could work together and protect one another because I was also a Drake spook, but it became obvious I wasn't during the Battle of Rio Claro, and that confused her. Tonight she told me she'd learned how wrong she'd been about Drake *and* about American soldiers because of the past two days with Carson's Companions."

Alexis allowed just the hint of a smile to show as she added, "She's amazed that we were the same as the Americans in the Trinidad oil industry."

"Captain, you had a great deal to do with that because she told me it was the first time she'd really been treated respectfully as a woman," Adonica explained and then added wistfully, "I know what she means. When I was a kid, I was supposed to do girl things although I was just as good at playing soldier as any of the boys. In Trinidad, men have never treated me as an equal; the island's stuck in the past from that social standpoint. But in Carson's Companions—and in the United States Army, for that matter—you work together as people then play together as men and women. I don't know how you've done it, but you've got a military organization with both men and women in it . . . and everyone knows and respects the differences . . . and no one pays much attention to those differences when it comes to doing the jobs you're supposed to do."

"Believe me, Adonica, it isn't easy," Curt admitted.

"Damned right it isn't," was Alexis' comment.

"Takes a lot of respect for one another and forgiving and working around personal shortcomings," Curt went on looking at Alexis. Zeenab was sensual, alluring, and exotic, but Curt preferred the quiet strength, intelligence, and compassion of the first lieutenant. "Everyone thinks of the Army as being on the technological cutting edge; they don't know we're also on the social cutting edge because we can get killed doing our jobs."

"And she liked *you*, Captain. She told us."

"What did she tell you?" Curt asked anxiously.

"Woman talk," Alexis told him in a tone that indicated she knew about last night. She went on, apparently choosing her words carefully and trying to hide her own feelings in the matter, "She claims it started as an attempt to suborn you and get you to reveal any secret plans so she could get the information to her father. Then her beloved birds got destroyed in the ambush, and you—we—continued to treat her as one of us in spite of the fact her apparent usefullness was at an end."

"She's very confused," Adonica explained.

"Zee took an enormous risk in revealing all this to you," Curt reminded them. "Did she understand the consequences of it?"

"I'm not sure any of us understand the consequences," Alexis put in. "It's pretty convoluted, Curt. We recruited her as a carrier pigeon tender at the suggestion of Adonica who didn't know her connection with the secret police."

It *was* a complicated matter! Curt nodded and observed, "Yeah, I don't think any of us will take her out and shoot her as a spy."

"I'd sure as hell flatly refuse to carry out that order, insubordination or not!" Alexis said emphatically then added thoughfully, "I actually got to like Zee a little bit in spite of the circumstances leading up to this. Deep inside that woman is a desire to be considered worthy and useful."

Curt thought that was an interesting observation,

coming from Alexis as it did. Alexis had somehow managed to get her personal feelings under control again, and he guessed it was probably because she realized she had little reason to be jealous.

"Do you have to report this to Colonel Hettrick?" Adonica asked anxiously.

"Eventually. But it isn't critical that I do it at once. The colonel hasn't got time for it right now. She's responible for a very complex operation."

"So what do we do with her?" Alexis wanted to know.

"Keep her with us for now. She can't harm anyone here," Curt observed then quickly added, "I don't say that because of what happened between Zee and me. I'm thinking about tomorrow. We may tangle with Drake and his Presidential Guard. Chances are, the secret police may be part of the Presidential Guard. Or at least accompany Drake if he runs. Zee might have some insight that could be critical. She knows things about the secret police that we don't. So I'm reluctant to scrub a potential information source, especially since she's blown her cover and can be kept under control . . ."

"I'll watch Zee, Captain," Adonica volunteered. "I know we're closing in on Sangre Grande, which means this war will probably be over pretty soon. Drake has nowhere to go. You won't be needing my services as a guide because this is pretty much a set-piece battle from now on."

"I hope it's a set piece, and set up for our side. However, Adonica, you've just outlined your assignment," Curt told her and got to his feet resuming his command personality. "I don't want to bother Colonel Hettrick with this problem; it doesn't materially affect the wrap-up of Operation Steel Band. She'll get a full report once the shooting stops. Lieutenant Morgan, I

want you and Lieutenant Sweet to sleep in my ACV
with Zee tonight; give her a trank if she needs it and
get her under control if she's still verging on the hysterical. She needs you two women, not a man to help
her forget her problems. The master sergeant and I will
sack out with Nick Gerard in the Bravo ACV. Tomorrow, the platoon ACVs are likely to be busy places, so
Adonica and Zeenab will ride with me. Now let's have
a quick head-to-head with everyone. Adonica's right;
we've got Drake trapped, and tomorrow is likely to be
a bitch . . .''

CHAPTER FORTY

Gen. Austin Drake was rapidly coming to that same conclusion himself.

Col. Affonso Fernandos Lima, Drake's chief of staff, finished outlining the current situation. "The Presidential Guard has presently stalled three Caribbean battalions near Valencia. The heavy warbot firepower of the Guard can keep them there tonight, possibly through noon tomorrow."

"They are to hold at all costs!" Drake snapped. "They're not to give a millimeter of ground! No one is to surrender! No one!"

"Yes, General," Lima replied dutifully. The Brazilian knew very well that a warbot battalion might—*might*—hold out for a day or so against regular infantry, but there was a matter of the dwindling ammunition supply that Lima didn't mention right then. He went on, "The Third Regiment combined with units from the Fifth is staging a successful retrograde operation to a tactical defense position along the line from Cumuto to Mamon with a fallback line from Guaico to Nestor. We've lost contact with some of the enemy units from their Twenty-Second Division in that area, but the regiment is prepared to defend against them. The Second Regiment has moved out of Sangre Grande to hold the line from Nestor around a loop to Warren Road. We know that the American Seventeenth Division is now holding the ridge line on Warren Road and has its regiments scattered back down Cunapo Southern Road. A report from an agent in Pierreville says that a regiment of the Seventeenth Division—he thinks it's the Wolfhounds—has moved north along the coast toward Manzanilla.''

Drake looked at the map darkly. ''We'll hold them. We've got to hold them. And we'll break their assaults tomorrow. That will give us the necessary time for the ABC Allianza relief force to land at Manzanilla Bay the day after tomorrow as planned—''

''I am afraid that will not be possible now,'' said Gen. Joao Bonifacio Deodoro, the Brazilian military advisor.

''Not possible? What do you mean?'' Fear gripped Drake's belly.

''Brasilia reported to me about thirty minutes ago that the seaborne relief expedition has been aborted. Cancelled.''

''Cancelled? Why?''

''The Americans have taken control of the sea and the air. In the opinion of our military planners, the Allianza reinforcement operation would not be able to get through,'' Deodoro explained. ''In addition, the American Wolfhound regiment now holds the landing grounds at Manzanilla Bay and can offer heavy warbot fire in opposition to our landing there.''

''All right! I'll pull every unit out of Sangre Grande and launch them on an offensive down the Eastern Main Road to Manzanilla!'' Drake suddenly decided. ''It's far more important that we secure a beachhead at Manzanilla Bay for the Allianza landings! If I time it properly, I can catch the American Seventeenth Division with our full forces just as your landing hits

375

them from the rear. Together we can crunch them up. We can do it!''

''We cannot. The landing has been cancelled,'' Deodoro repeated flatly and went on to explain, ''General Drake, Brasilia does not wish to risk its forces at this time. It would certainly result in a sure and certain war with the United States and other nations having interests in Trinidad. I am advised to tell you that the ABC Allianza joint high command now believes Trinidad is lost and relief forces should not be squandered here. The Americans moved much faster than anyone anticipated.''

''Then I'll fight to the death!'' Drake announced. ''They won't take me alive . . .''

''Perhaps that will be you, but it will not be me,'' Deodoro told him firmly. ''I must withdraw the Brazilian military advisory group. I request that you provide me with transportation at once to Salibea where a submarine will pick us up in Saline Bay.''

Drake hesitated and didn't immediately answer. He faced a difficult, if not impossible, situation in trying to hold Sangre Grande for reinforcements that would never show up. The game was over. He had to get out of Trinidad. He ran over the elements of it in his mind.

Outside waited a Brazilian-made ACV manned by a warbot squad of the Presidential Guard. It could carry only him and his bodyguard.

To get the additional vehicles necessary to carry the Brazilian military advisory team, Drake would have to call in at least one company of the Presidential Guard currently defending the eastern approaches to Sangre Grande.

If he did that, he knew that the one remaining Presidential Guard company couldn't hold off three battalions of Caribbean infantry. It would be wiped out in a matter of hours. Therefore, the Guard would have to stage a slow, meter-by-meter retreat toward Sangre Grande, fighting as they withdrew. His Second Regiment would *have* to hold the American 17th Division coming up from the south.

How what about the timing? Could the Presidential Guard move fast enough in retreat to get the additional vehicles into Sangre Grande before the defenses collapsed under the assault of two disivions of American warbots?

It would be very close.

One thing was certain: If he let Deodoro have the transportation and escort now available in the street outside, Drake would end up being trapped in Sangre Grande. Drake wasn't about to sacrifice his hide, the "fight to the death" statement notwithstanding. That had been bluff. But his bluff hadn't worked; General Deodoro hadn't tumbled for it.

For an instant, Drake considered ordering his bodyguard to shoot the Brazilians.

But Deodoro and his advisors were armed; the General carried two Astra pistols and his staff had Mekanika Uru 9mm submachineguns slung from their shoulders. It would be a shoot-out, and Drake didn't like the odds. He might not survive it.

He had to compromise his way out of this one.

"General, I haven't got transportation available at the moment," Drake told the advisor.

"Then I shall be forced to commandeer the Presidential Guard vehicle outside."

"General, I think you might find my Presidential Guard more than a little reluctant to hand it over to you, much less take you where you want to go, unless I gave them a direct and personal order to do so. Otherwise, they'd resist. That's an armed warbot squad out there, not just soldiers. Are you and your advisors prepared to shoot it out with warbots? You supplied those warbots, General; you should know their capabilities. And I do not intend to place myself in jeopardy just so you can save your ass, General. A lack of planning on your part does not constitute an emergency on mine.''

Gen. Deodoro knew he'd hit an impasse. But there was a way out despite the fact that the ABC Allianza was prepared to abandon General Austin Drake on Trinidad.

The ABC Allianza had knowingly gambled on Drake's ability to turn the island nation into a northern outpost of the Allianza. They'd been willing to invest a limited amount of money, manpower, and war materiel on a high risk basis to establish a strategic presence at a critical South American choke point. Nothing ventured, nothing gained. And the price had been considered to be relatively small in any event, win or lose. The gains to be made and the advantages to be achieved were enormous if everything succeeded. The Allianza had decided to shoot crap on Trinidad.

But General Austin Drake had turned out to be a poor bet. The American soldier of fortune had been enormously successful in staging the coup that overthrew the democratic government of Morris Priest, and he'd been very successful in eliminating the leftwing radical, Chamberlin. But his military government had been lackluster and incompletely organized. And when it came to something Drake should have been able to handle without question—military affairs—the man had chosen to use military force to intimidate and terrorize people in order to consolidate his power rather than to defend the island. Drake hadn't counted on outside military invervention; he'd claimed history didn't justify it.

General Deodoro and the ABC Allianza high command might not have been so reluctant to provide continued support if it had been simply a matter of Drake's forces being overwhelmed by superior numbers. Enough additional military force could have been pumped into the island to handle that . . . if Drake had shown himself capable of military leadership.

Instead, Drake had proved he was a loser. He'd been caught flatfooted by the Americans. He'd allowed his air force be destroyed on the ground. His naval forces had been suckered into a direct confrontation with superior U.S. Navy forces in the Dragon's Mouths, sending the whole lot to the bottom and eliminating any possibility of maintaining sea control around the island. He'd moved too little and too late with inadequate intelligence data. He'd deployed and maneuvered his units badly. He'd failed to exploit enemy weaknesses when and where they presented themselves. His troops had been so poorly motivated, and led, that they'd deserted or surrendered, often without a fight. His island-wide network of secret police agents had either defected or proved to be ineffectual. The last straw came when Drake finally wasted more than a whole regiment on a flawed and undermanned offensive at Rio Claro organized with wishful thinking on the basis of a single piece of unconfirmed intelligence data.

Deodoro also knew he'd delayed too long with Drake, but he'd done it knowlingly out of self—interest because the Brazilian general officer had a stake in the success of the Trinidad experiment. However, he, too, had been guilty of wishful thinking, counting on the ABC Allianza reinforcements to turn the tide. But the Americans and their Caribbean allies had moved far faster than anyone had anticipated. The Americans must be using some new types of very fast warbots, especially in the southern portion of the island. The American 17th Division had covered ground almost twice as fast as normal warbot forces could move. They obviously had some new technology.

As a result, the Brazilian was caught. He had to get himself and his advisors out of Trinidad. To be captured in Drake's Sangre Grande headquarters by the Americans or the Caribbeans would not only create a difficult diplomatic situation for the Allianza, but would mean the end of his own military career. On the other hand, if he got out safely, he could tell a story of hanging on until the last moment to save the situation but being forced to withdraw as Gen. Douglas MacArthur had left the Phillipines in World War II. He'd even play with the statement, ''I shall return!''

''I will strike a bargain with you, General Drake,'' Deodoro announced. ''Get me and my people out of Sangre Grande . . . and you may come with me. I will see to it that you will be welcomed aboard that Brazilian submarine with me. In that way, we can withdraw from this untenable situation and be in a position to return in the near future. The Americans will not occupy Trinidad; they've given back their military conquests ever since their war with Mexico. Within a year, Trinidad will be under a new government and ripe for plucking again . . . with the lessons of the past learned well and with greater military strength behind us.''

Actually, Deodoro had no intention of making any sort of recommendation that would put Drake back into Trinidad. But the mercenary could be taken to Brazil where he'd be given military make-work and kept under control so he didn't dash off somewhere and make some other military mistake. The price was cheap.

To Gen. Austin Drake, Deodoro's offer was a fortuitous answer to Drake's biggest problem at the moment: his personal survival, the Trinidad Defense Forces notwithstanding. The TDF was a hollow shell of beaten mercenaries. His government in Port of Spain had collapsed with the capture of the city yesterday by an embarassingly few troops from Curacao and Jamaica, two Caribbean nations known for their miniscule armies that were more constabularies than fighting forces. He had no tight strings attaching him to Trinidad now. He, too, had shot crap on the future of the island once he'd gotten control and become a puppet of the Allianza, a deal that had sounded good and promised well but had fallen through. He shrugged mentally. Some deals were just that way. *You can't win 'em all,* was his philosophy. *You can't hit a home run every time you come to bat.* It looked like this one was down the drain. Time to get out of there and look for the next opportunity. By accepting Deodoro's offer, he could get to Brazil and wait for something to turn up. He'd have to give up Trinidad, but he was beginning to doubt that he could save the situation on the island in any event. In Brazil, he'd continue to be beholden to the ABC Allianza, but he'd get out of this with his hide. The price was cheap.

"You've got a deal, General. But I can't do it immediately. I'll have to disengage a Guard company and pull them out of the line at Valencia," Drake explained. "I'll expedite it by ordering them to abandon their warbots so they can move faster, but we probably won't be able to get out of Sangre Grande until morning in any event. Not to worry. The defenses to the south and west will hold. And we'll make that noon rendezvous with the sub at Saline Bay without trouble. By the way, I'm sure you won't mind if I take along my personal bodyguard . . . Just in case. After all, it will provide protection for everyone in the party . . .''

CHAPTER FORTY-ONE

The rain began about midnight as a violent thunderstorm accompanied by lightning and high winds which whipped the palms and ferns. Water ran off the road in thick sheets, accumulating in muddy pools in the ditches. But, unlike the other short-lived thundershowers experienced thus far on Trinidad, this time the storm didn't stop. It continued to rain.

"The end of the Petite Careme," Zeenab Tej explained to Curt.

"Your monsoon season?" Curt asked the beautiful woman who seemed to have come out of her depression.

"Not really. Possibly a hurricane, although we get very few of them."

Curt checked in with regimental headquarters. The tacomm was still working. The Colonel had gone to bed, but S-3 confirmed Zee's observation. Hurricane Pauline, a late season storm, was passing westbound about 150 kilometers north of Trinidad. The forecast was for rain, heavy at times, during the next twenty-four hours as the storm went past.

"We're going to have mud, lots of mud," Zee advised.

"The bane of a campaign," Henry Kester remarked. "Hasn't been an army in history that hasn't had to fight the mud too. Looks like we've joined the club on this operation."

"Sergeant, the Wolfhounds will be coming through in less than an hour," Curt pointed out, checking the surroundings with the night vision sensors of the ACV; they were also having trouble discriminating through the rainfall. "Are we going to get bogged down in the unpaved areas alongside the road here?"

"I'll check," the old master sergeant replied.

"Take a slicker."

"Just slow me down. I've been wet before. Actually, since we didn't get the chance to go skinny dippin' in the river like I wanted, a rain bath will feel pretty damned good . . ."

Curt didn't get too much sleep that night. Neither did most of the Companions who stayed up checking their special voice-commanded, artificially-intelligent warbots to make sure the vital electronics circuits wouldn't get soaked by leaks in the warbot hulls. And making certain that the rounds of caseless ammo hadn't had their sealing coats scratched in a way that would allow the propellant to get wet.

The Wolfhounds came barrelling through about 0100, slipping and slithering on the wet road, spraying water and mud everywhere. It took them nearly three hours to pass. The Companions' vehicles no longer were coated with the grime of travel but covered with mud that hid most of their camouflage paint patterns.

But in spite of the delay in letting the Wolfhounds through and the inevitable problems of getting the company started to move in the mud and rain, Curt was able to stay on schedule. By 0500, the Companions were on the roll, beginning their third day of fast, long-distance maneuvering.

The side roads were paved, but the heavy rain was eating away at their shoulders. The passage of the

Companions' vehicles created a series of worsening chuck holes full of water and mud. The streams they crossed had become murky, muddy, rapidly-flowing torrents. Ragged clouds hung over the hills and often down to the tops of the trees. Occasionally, the rain fell so hard that visibility dropped to nearly zero.

It was tough going, and Curt resigned himself to being wet for most of the rest of the day.

The weather rarely cooperates when the big fracas comes around, he told himself. Chancellorsville, Gettysburg, Chattanooga, the foggy victory at New Orleans— these and other American battles came back to Curt's mind from his studies of military history. *Now it's going to affect the Battle of Sangre Grande . . . but we don't know how.*

The Companions' part of the Battle of Sangre Grande began innocently enough about 1400 hours, almost as a sideline to the real battle that Curt could hear plainly through the rain and mist off to his left as his 2nd Tactical Ballation (Temporary) of the 3rd RI, the Washington Greys, drove cautiously eastward on Sangre Grande Road toward the city ahead. The wide sweep to the right around the east of Sangre Grande had been made without incident except for sliding around in the mud near Lower Fishing Pond where they'd had to make their own road through the jungle for about a hundred meters. No contact had been made with the enemy. The rain was coming in bursts now, and the clouds scuttling eastward had occasional breaks through which the sun and the blue sky above appeared. When this happened, Curt could see Air Force- and Army-manned and robot recon aircraft wheeling in the sky over the battle. *Good! Maybe we'll get some idea of the situation when we need it,* Curt thought, although he knew his vehicles weren't equipped to receive the real-time visuals from the recon ships; there was only so much data that a commander could process down at

385

the company level. Regimental would get the data and forward applicable bits of it to him.

Jerry Allen's Alpha Platoon at the head of the column was within approximately two kilometers of Sangre Grande when the sound of small arms fire came suddenly from the right.

"Grey Head, this is Companion Leader," Curt spoke into the tacomm. "Suspected engagement to our right or north."

Static. Nothing. Beeps and clicks and chuckles from another frequency-hopping tactical communications unit that had given up the ghost.

"Shit!" Curt exploded and yelled, "Henry, do we have a standby tacomm unit for Grey Head's net?"

"Negative. Lucky to get the single replacement," came the voice of his master sergeant.

"Goddamn thing's gone tits-up, too. Hand me the headset for the company tacomm net," Curt snapped, referring to the vehicle-mounted unit which had been maintained in the cooler, drier environment of the ACV. "Maybe someone can relay for me."

Slipping on the headset that Kester handed up, Curt keyed it and called, "Companions and Killers all, this is Companion Leader. Kelly, how do you read?"

"Loud and clear, Carson. Shooting's started over on the right."

"I hear it. Is your tacomm to regimental cee-pee working?"

"Affirmative!"

"Call Grey Head. Report the sound of a fire fight. Get me a recon report or anything that will tell us what's going on there. It isn't very far away."

"Rog. How about the Killers going over to have a look?"

"Negative, Marty. Don't get your water hot. There's a river between us and Toco Road, if that's

386

where the fire fight's taking place. And that river's full of water right now . . ."

"Carson, if some one starts shooting at me, I'm gonna start shooting back!"

"Roger that! Now get me that information if you can, Kelly. Companion Alpha, you read?"

"Loud and clear," came Jerry's voice.

"Companion Bravo?"

"We're with you."

"Continue forward until we pass Crocobar Road. Watch for suitable paths through the foliage to the right. Bring weapons to bear to the right and get them up to fire-ready condition. Command warbots to power-up and dismount on order. Sierra Charlies, prepare to dismount. Standard procedure and equipment, including body armor."

"What do you think, Captain?" Alexis asked.

"I get the feeling our Venezuelan colleagues have engaged a Tee-dad unit making a run for it up Toco Road, as we suspected they might," Curt gave them his own gesstimate of the situation.

"Carson, you're right," Marty Kelly's voice came in. "Grey Head recon reports a column of vehicles, unit unidentified but company strength, heading up Toco Road and the Venezuelans heading south on that road. Engagement appears to have started where the road crosses the Oropuche River—"

"Another Oropuche River?" Allen broke in.

"Check your map, Mister Dumb John! Two of them on this island," came the gravelly voice of Lt. Russ Frazier of the Killers.

"Kelly, pass the word to your people to knock off the sarcastic remarks," Curt snapped to his counterpart. "We'll damned well act as a team, or those who don't choose to do so will be reported afterward. The tapes will be ample evidence . . ."

"Killers, this is Killer King. Knock it off! We've got the chance to shine here, so don't screw it up! Pay attention to the real fight . . ."

Curt ducked down into the ACV, slapped the hatch shut against an oncoming rain squall, and told his master sergeant, "Henry, take the conn." He slipped over to where he could see the simple tactical display. Checking the coordinates, he told the computer to calculate firing points, then he keyed the tacomm headset, "Companion Alpha, six hundred meters past the intersection of Crocobar Road, pull off to the right and halt. Don't worry about getting the vehicles into the mud; looks like this may be the big encounter today. I'll be with you. Prepare to dismount with the Mary Anns. Companion Bravo, at the same point, pull off and stand by to dismount the Hairy Foxes if the ground looks anywhere near like they won't sink clear through to China. I'm passing firing coordinates to you on the uplink *now!*" Curt keyed the terminal, and the necessary information for Alexis to feed into her Mark X60 Heavy Fire warbots and both platoons to use in laying their Saucy Cans went out in a string of digital pulses that sounded like a Bronx cheer on the audio portion of the system.

Curt went on snapping orders, "Killer King, this is Companion Leader. I want you to pass through the Companions on the Sangre Grande Road and go eight hundred meters past the intersection of Crocobar Road. Then go flankers right. The ground is likely to be soft and muddy, but you've got only about four hundred meters of mixed open field and jungle to traverse before coming to Toco Road. Work to the left and get behind the Tee-dad unit on Toco Road. Remember that the Venezuelans are engaging them on the right, so do not—repeat, do not—fire on the Tee-dad unit in

388

such a way tht the rounds go into the Venezuelans. Understood?''

"Understood, Companion One. Killers, go get 'em!''

"EEE-YAA-HOO! Killers on the loose!'' came the bloodcurdling cry from both Killer company commanders. "Killer King, this is Companion Leader. Caution: Companion Sierra Charlies will be advancing dismounted in skirmish line on your right flank. Keep your sensors tuned to our beacons . . .'' Curt gave an additional warning to the impetuous Kelly and his company.

"You mean you're going to go out there in the frigging mud and put your pink bods in the line of fire again?'' Kelly asked. "Hell, Carson, let us warbot brainies do the job! Let the warbots take the incoming!''

"I don't want to take the chance that your warbots are going to get bogged down in the mud out there. Even if you can't get to the road, use your firepower to sweep it clean and keep the Tee-dads from retreating back into Sangre Grande! My Sierra Charlies will hit 'em from the flank. This Tee-tad outfit is probably their Presidential Guard warbot unit; they won't know how to handle an American Sierra Charlie outfit on their flank.''

"The Venezuelans are regular infantry,'' Kelly pointed out.

"Yeah, and there's a whole battalion of them to keep the Tee-dad warbots occupied out front,'' Curt pointed out. "The Venezuelans won't be able to do much against the concentrated firepower of a warbot unit except keep the Tee-dad attention on them. We've got both infantry and warbots, so you hit 'em with warbots from the rear if you can, and I'll bring my Sierra Charlies in on their right flank—''

"I've got a visual! I've got a visual!" Jerry called. "Tee-Dads! I can see four vehicles. They don't look like warbot command vehicles. No heavy armored stuff. And no warbots in sight."

"I'll betcha we caught Drake trying to run!" Curt said to Kester.

"I don't bet on sure things," Kester replied quickly.

"Zeenab," Curt called over to the woman riding in the rear of the ACV, "I need your help."

"How can I help soldiers in battle?" Zee asked darkly. "I'm just a prisoner now . . ."

"Like hell you are! Listen, I could damned well have turned you over to Hettrick and her S-4 intelligence people last night. I decided not to do it in the heat of combat. Why? Because you came clean with us and there isn't anything more you can do for Drake even if you wanted do . . . and I don't think you want to now . . ."

"You're right, Curt—"

"I hope so! I'd better be! But if I catch you trying to help Drake or giving me false data, I'll have no heartburn about shooting you dead on the spot. But I don't think I'll have to. Show me I'm right. Would you please shag over here and give me a hand? You could help keep us from getting hit with something we might not be able to handle. And you can probably tell me something about the Tee-dad Presidential Guard . . ."

Even though she looked defeated, Zeenab Tej was still a stunningly beautiful woman as she flowed to her feet and walked over with that peculiar swaying motion of her body. Her dour expression, so out of place on her beautiful face, didn't change. "What do you need to know about the Presidential Guard?"

"What about their warbots? How do they operate them? What sort of weapons do the warbots carry? Do

390

the Guard soldiers themselves carry weapons, and if so what kind?''

''Their robots come from Argentina and Brazil. They have cannons. I think each platoon has its own command unit, but the chain of command upwards keeps tight control on everything that goes on. The warbot operators are under strict control in their command tank.''

''Sounds like they don't trust their troops.''

''The commanders don't. They don't want the warbot operators to be able to act on their own initiative. Drake has always been afraid that someone in the Presidential Guard would stage a warbot coup. So the secret police also ride along, one in each platoon command car.''

He gently laid his hand on her shoulder. ''Thank you, Zee. That was very important. We've come up against that sort of positive warbot control before. It's typical of highly centralized regimes run by dictators and juntas.''

Surprisingly, she laid her own hand on top of his. It was a soft touch. A slight smile flicked across the corners of her mouth. ''The Presidential Guard and its warbots really aren't a combat force,'' she added, seemingly starting to open up a little bit. ''Drake organized them strictly as a show and parade unit to impress people with the high-tech power of his armed forces. But I've never seen them out of Port of Spain. I don't think they go on maneuvers with the other regiments at all. They're just what their name implies: a presidential guard unit.''

''Okay, we can handle them,'' Curt told her. He looked at her carefully. Gone was the radiance she projected so easily in Rio Claro. She was still a beautiful woman, but now she looked beaten and defeated. It was apparent to Curt that she's seen more war than she wanted and that combat was far bloodier and terrifying than she'd ever imagined when she'd spooked for Drake.

She hadn't really known what she was doing and hadn't realized the consequences. Now it was telling on her. *My God, she's really got a bad case of battle fatigue!* Curt said to himself.

But he keyed the battalion tacomm network mike and spoke using slang as code, "Companions and Killers all, I've got the scoop from the spook. Bypass the Tee-dad warbots. Take out the cee-pees and warbot brainy control units. The Tee-dads use linear decision-downward control procedures. Strictly Sov in nature." Everyone on that tactical communications net understood exactly what Curt meant.

He felt the ACV pull off the road to the right and stop. This was it. Time to get out and face combat again. Curt hoped it would be the last skirmish in this war.

CHAPTER FORTY-TWO

And Curt now had to make a tough decision. His other Companions would dismount with the voice-command warbots of the Sierra Charlie forces, and they'd cross the few hundred meters between the roads to assault the Tee-dads. If Curt left the ACV, he'd be out of communication with the tactical battalion. On the other hand, he was a member of the Sierra Charlie team and should dismount with the rest of his company. It was really no decision, but it bothered him a little bit to key the headset and call, "Killer King, this is Companion Leader. I'm dismounting with the Sierra Charlies. Put a warbot on me to pick up voice and hand signals. In you lose me, assume command of the battalion."

"Carson, you're out of your goddamned mind, but I'm with you," Kelly's voice came back. "We're in position and moving, but it's muddy. Move it fast or get stuck."

"Henry, power up the bots and let's go. Zee, you stay here, understand?"

"No. I'm coming," Zeenab said suddenly.

"Like hell you are! In those brightly colored clothes, you're a prime target! Besides, you're not a soldier . . ."

"Neither is Adonica, but she's going with you."

"No, goddamn it! Stay here!"

"I don't have to follow your orders, Curt. Besides, I can identify Guard warbots and soliders and maybe even some people."

"I won't have you going out there and getting shot! Now that's all there is to it! And I don't have time to argue with you! Henry, let's move!"

"You're afraid I'll get hurt?" Zeenab asked quickly.

"Yes. Or killed," Curt had to admit.

"I didn't think you cared about me any longer."

"Damned nonsense! You're a civilian. I'm under rules of engagement not to endanger civilians. Henry, dump the ramp!" He grabbed his FABARMA and went down the ramp into the rainshower behind the two General Purpose warbots and followed by M. Sgt. Henry Kester.

"Companion One and Companion Two," Curt ordered his warbots, "Check the ground ahead of you as you go. Try to keep up with Sergeant Kester and me. If your data indicates you'd get stuck keeping up, do the best you can anyway. But do not get stuck in the mud? Understood?"

"Understood!" came the synthesized voice from the two warbots who were essentially serving as fire cover for Henry and him.

The rainy air was full of the sound of battle. Most of it was dead ahead of Curt. Through breaks in the vegetation on his left, he waw the Killer warbots moving slowly forward, cautiously checking terrain footing as they went. His company was out and ready to move, already formed in a skirmish line with their Mary Anns and Hairy Foxes moving ahead and behind the line respectively. The Mary Anns would draw any initial enemy fire, thus pinpointing enemy targets while the Hairy Foxes would provide cover with their heavy 50mm overhead fire.

394

Curt passed a house tucked in amongst the trees. A scared young woman peered out the door. "Get back in there," Curt told her gently. "Keep your family inside and out of sight. We don't want to hurt you, and this will all be over in a few minutes."

A hundred meters from the road, they came to a rain-swollen creek. Two substantial foot bridges crossed it. Without orders, the Companions went into the river and through water up to their chests, holding their FABARMA rifles over their heads. On the other side, they waited while Curt and Henry filed the warbots over the bridges to the other side. They had still taken no incoming fire, and they couldn't yet see Toco Road a few hundred meters ahead of them.

A small form in baggy, ill-fitting camouflage coveralls and a helmet that was far too large came dashing from behind and up to Curt. She was barefoot and carrying a Hornet submachine carbine.

"Goddamn it, Zeenab, I told you to stay in the ACV!" Curt yelled.

"So shoot me," she snapped.

"Shit! I haven't got time to coddle you! Stay behind me!"

"Yes, Captain."

One of Kelly's warbots trundled across the bridge and up to Curt. In a synthesized version of Kelly's voice, it reported, "About fifty percent of my force has made it to the road behind the Tee-dads, Carson. You were right; the going was pretty damned muddy in there for my heavy warbots. I'm short on firepower although I can have some of the stuck bots lob heavy stuff into the Tee-dad column. Want to co-ordinate the assault?"

It was unusual to get that sort of cooperation out of Kelly, but Curt knew that the Killers' commander didn't want to admit that he might fail alone on a rear assault and would rather share the glory that resulted from a victory brought about because of a combined attack. "Okay, how far does your computer show our beacons from Toco Road?"

"About two-ninety meters."

"Okay, we'll go up to the edge of cover and signal you through this warbot. Pour it into them from the rear while we give it to them with small arms fire from the flank."

"Gotcha!"

Curt didn't advance with his Companions in skirmish line more than another twenty meters before the forest thinned out and they had a clear shot at the road before them. At a range of 270 meters, his people couldn't miss with their powerful FABARMAs. The Presidential Guard—recognizable because of their somewhat gaudy uniforms with braid and aiguillettes and other "chicken guts" hanging from fringed epaulets—was apparently so confident that they hadn't put on combat clothes, or maybe they didn't have them. They were fighting from the vehicles and from the mud of the roadside ditches. Their fire was directed forward at the as-yet-invisible Venezuelans.

Curt saw that they had no warbot-type vehicles, only the regular EE-9 Cascavel reconaissance vehicles and EE-11B Urutu armored personnel carriers of the regular Tee-dad forces.

And there wasn't a warbot to be seen!

"They've left their goddamned warbots behind!" Henry Kester remarked in disbelief.

"Must have been in a hell of a hurry to get out of Sangre Grande," was Sgt. Edie Sampson's remark from her position beyond Kester.

Curt turned to look over his shoulder at Kelly's relay warbot. "Kelly, open fire on the vehicles. Companion Leader One, if you read me on the tacomm battalion net, order Companion vehicles to open fire on coordinates from the data bank!''

"Killers read you! Companion vehicles read you!'' said Kelly's warbot.

A maelstrom of hell opened up before their eyes on Toco Road. Heavy fire from Kelly's warbots came in from the left and caught the rear vehicle. Curt heard the sound of shells from Mademoiselle Saucy Cans on his own LAMVs rush overhead and erupt in flashes on the road, catching another of the vehicles. For this encounter, the Saucy Cans amounted to heavy artillery.

Tee-dad soldiers in gaudy uniforms erupted from the hit vehicles and from other vehicles on the road.

"Companions, open fire! Fire at will!'' Curt yelled over the bedlam.

At a range of 1000 meters, a FABARMA round will penetrate 5 millimeters of steel armor plate and show a shot group of 36 centimeters' radius. Now the Companions were firing their FABARMA assault rifles at a range of about 270 meters, and the accuracy and penetration of these small arms was extremely deadly indeed. The FABARMAs simply out-shot the SAR-80 5.56mm assault rifles carried by the Tee-dad Guardsmen. Curt had put his reputation and career on the line by insisting on those Mexican FABARMAs for his Sierra Charlies because he'd known all along that they'd need a powerful personal weapon that shot straight and could penetrate. Now he was being vindicated. Some of the Companions' shots riccocheted off the Tee-dad vehicles when they hit an an angle, but others penetrated dead on. None of the FABARMA rounds were deflected by hitting the vegetation alongside the road; the rounds went right on through it. The Tee-dads lucky enough not to be hit in this fusilade managed to get around. behind the vehicles and out of the murderous fire.

But this didn't protect them against the deadly heavy fire coming in from Curt's Saucy Cans. The real value of those 75mm weapons had been taken for granted by Curt up to now. But he gained a totally new appreciation for them from the perspective of watching what happened on the delivery end as their shells hit the road and the vehicles. *Thank God the Army was smart enough to license that weapon from the French!* Curt thought. At least somebody high up in Army Ordnance had been thinking and planning. The results showed.

It was a different sort of a fight than the Battle of Rio Claro where the Tee-dads had tried to ambush a superior force with inferior tactics. Here the Tee-dad Presidential Guard had been stopped by a Venezuelan battalion in front, cut off by an American warbot company with its heavy firepower being brought to bear from behind, and assaulted on the flank by the new American Sierra Charlies with their equally-heavy vehicle support artillery and very powerful assault rifles.

The return fire from the Tee-dad Presidential Guard was extremely ineffective because they were armed with Mekanika Uru 9mm submachineguns and Astra Model A-80 9mm automatic pistols. None of these had the range or hitting power to match that of the Americans and Venezuelans. There was a single CETME 5.56mm light machinegun mounted on each of the Urutu APVs, but most of these weren't manned.

Some of the Tee-dads tried to escape into the jungle on the other side of the road, but the Companions could shoot well with their FABARMAs and dropped most of the fleeing men.

Others members of the Presidential Guard started to give up, dropping their weapons and trying to surrender with their hands in the air.

Then out of the grey, overcast, rainy skies came a pair of A-20 tactical strike aircraft moving at high speed

398

about ten meters above the road toward Sangre Grande. The pilots apparently saw that the American and Venezuelan ground forces had the fight well in hand because they didn't open fire but merely went into afterburner as they passed over the Tee-dad vehicles. The psychological effect alone was enough to bring the fight to an end.

The Tee-dads were now convinced that further resistance was useless in the face of overwhelming ground fire plus the demonstrated American capability to bring them under tactical air attack. They came from around vehicles and out of vehicles with their hands in the air in mass surrender. White flags appeared and waved from the turrets of two of the vehicles.

But a man stood up in the turret of a lead APV, brandished an Astra pistol, and yelled loudly enough that he could be heard even over the bedlam of small arms and light artillery fire, "No, you bastards! Pick up those guns! Get in those vehicles! Goddamn it, we can fight our way through! Don't you dare desert me now after all I've done for you!" It was General Austin Drake.

Surprisingly, Drake wasn't shot at. Curt brought his own FABARMA to bear on the man, but witheld fire. He wanted to capture Drake alive.

Across the intervening open space on Curt's right ran four figures in cammies carrying FABARMAs and one carrying a Hornet. Platoon Sgt. Nick Gerard led the charge, running toward Drake. "Get out of there, General!" Gerard yelled as he ran. "Drop that pistol! Hands up!"

Austin Drake took aim with his 9mm Astra and fired off a shot at Gerard. The General was a marksman because he caught Nick in the chest with the first shot, spinning him around but failing to knock him to the ground. Again, Nick's body armor saved his life.

Zeenab Tej, running alongside Gerard, stopped, brought the Hornet submachine carbine to her shoulder, and fired a three-round burst. It missed Drake.

Drake's second shot hit Zeenab. The Hornet flew into the air and she fell backwards into the wet grass.

Seeing that, Curt aimed and fired.

What had been General Austin Drake's head suddenly erupted in a crimson explosion as the 7.62mm high-velocity FABARMA round caught him directly between the eyes.

Captain Curt Carson was a marksman, too.

It was all over.

Then all the Companions were at the road and being joined by the warbots from Kelly's Killers.

Tee-dad Presidential Guard soldiers stood alongside their vehicles, hands in the air. But a strange group of six men in unidentified uniforms also stood there in the rain, but they didn't hold their hands up in surrender. Instead, one of them with complex insignia, lots of gold on his shoulder boards, and an array of ribbons on his chest stepped forward toward Curt. He also had two pearl-handled Astra pistols holstered at his waist.

"Hold it right there!" Curt snapped at him. "Drop those pistols!"

"We are not Trinidad troops," the man replied in a strange accent. "We were forced to come along with General Drake. I am General Joao Bonifacio Deodoro, the military attachè from the Brazilian embassy in Port of Spain, and these gentlemen are members of my staff. Although I have been separated from my papers, I believe you can obtain my bona fides through your own channels."

"General," Curt replied in a respectful tone without taking his FABARMA off the man. "What the hell are you doing here?"

"Many of us sought refuge and safety with General

400

Drake when he moved the seat of government to San-gre Grande,'' Deodoro replied smoothly. "We were forced to come along with General Drake when he left Sangre Grande.''

"Sure you were,'' Curt told him, but the sarcasm in his voice also told the man that Curt didn't believe a word of it. "Drop those pistols. You're in uniform and without identification. I have to assume that you and your staff are prisoners of war, and you'll be treated as such until a higher command decides oth-erwise . . .''

"I am the Brazilian military attachè, and I demand diplomatic—'' Deodoro began haughtily.

"You're probably also Drake's Allianza military ad-visor,'' Curt told him bluntly, then added, "Drop those pistols!''

Slowly, Deodoro removed his beloved pearl-handled pistols, the ones personally presented to him by the President of Brazil, and handed them butt-first toward Curt.

"Henry, take them,'' Curt told his master sergeant. "General, have your staff do the same. Then over against the vehicles! Move it!''

Thus did Gen. Joao Bonifacio Deodoro move out of the history books, a prisoner of war later to be repatri-ated to Brazil and never heard from again.

"Captain!'' Jerry called out, "more troops coming along the road from the west!''

Another group of strange infantrymen in cammys cautiously approached. Curt knew who they must be. They were wet and muddy and had the exhausted but enthusiastic look of victorious troops.

The Venezuelans.

A tall man with a neatly trimmed moustache but the stubble of a beard on his chin stepped up to Curt. He'd obviously seen a lot of action recently. "Captain Carson? *Coronel* José Antonio Miranda," he introduced himself, proffering his hand. "*Muchas gracias* for the assistance."

"You've come a long way, too, Colonel," Curt replied, remembering to salute the superior officer out of courtesy before he took the man's hand. "I think it was inevitable that we'd meet like this!"

"And it seems you have solved the problem of what would be done with General Drake. Nice shooting!"

Sgt. Nick Gerard was up at the turret of Drake's machine. "You got him dead on, Captain," he reported. "But I'll let Graves Registration take care of him. Too damned much blood for me . . ."

"You all right, Nick? Did you get an Astra round in your armor?" Curt asked anxiously.

"Yup. Easier to take than a high-velocity five millimeter round."

"Why did you try to assault an armed general in the open, Sergeant?" Curt admonished him lightly.

Gerard dropped to the ground with a splash of mud. "Captain, the sonofabitch wasn't going to surrender unless I threatened him and got him out of that vehicle. He was shooting up our outfit—"

"Ohmigawd, where's Zee?" Curt suddenly remembered and turned around.

Adonica, Alexis, and Edie Sampson were huddled over someone in the grass. Curt trotted over, expecting the worst. He didn't notice Colonel Miranda and Henry Kester trotting next to him.

Adonica looked up as he approached. Zeenab Tej, her face drained of color, was in her arms. "Zee's been hit. Didn't have body armor. Took Drake's bullet in her abdomen."

"She needs a biotech," Alexis put in. "Soon. Looks like internal bleeding."

"Kelly!" Curt yelled. "Call regimental! Get one of

our biotech units over here!'' Then he said to the three of them hovering over Zeenab, ''Dammit, a Sierra Charlie unit's got to have its own field biotechs for just this sort of emergency like the old real infantry . . .''

''Captain, if you will please allow me to assist a valorous young lady,'' said Colonel Miranda. ''My medics will be here immediately. We can stabilize her until she can be transported.'' He flipped his tacomm unit from his belt, raised it to his mouth, and rattled off a stream of Spanish into it.

''As I said, just like the real infantry has,'' Curt remarked, relief in his voice as he saw two Venezuelan soldiers running across the field toward them. They wore white helmets and tabards bearing the red cross of medical specialists.

''With no criticism intended, Captain, because your troops certainly fought valiantly and courageously under fire,'' Colonel Miranda remarked, slipping his tacomm back on his belt, ''it has always amazed me that you Americans would permit women to serve in combat units . . .''

''Colonel,'' Curt said proudly, straightening up and speaking clearly so that the three women could hear him, ''our women fight as well if not better than our men, and we're damned proud of them. Having them around even on the battlefield keeps us men reminded of what all of us are really fighting for . . .''

AFTERMATH

Any time is Carnival time when there's something to celebrate. It was Carnival time.

The tropical night in Port of Spain was warm, and the light breezes off the water were like silk across the faces of Carson's Companions as they tried to battle their way through crowds of people who were trying to give them things to eat and things to drink and other things to make them feel good. They were off duty—definitely off duty—having exchanged their camouflaged battle clothing for the lighter, airy, more comfortable cottons they'd tried to purchase in Sangre Grande and Port of Spain; but no one would let them pay for anything.

The sounds around them resembled a very badly maintained old ACV trying to fight its way through a junk yard while creaky warbots threw scrap at it. Steel bands were everywhere, making strange and beautiful music from old 55-gallon oil drums whose ends had been carefully stressed and tuned.

"Let's get the hell out of here and find a place where we can get a quiet drink or two or three . . ." Curt Carson yelled to his troops.

"And a good meal or two or three . . ." M. Sgt. Henry Kester added.

"Before they ship us back to the Vee-Eye," Alexis Morgan finished.

The older man with his arm around Adonica Sweet raised his other arm and yelled over the noise, "Carson's Companions, follow me!" Roger Sweet, erstwhile Captain in the Washington Greys, had been found in Port of Spain by the Companions who were able to locate him because of the efficient job done by the Jamaicans identifying and cataloging Drake's political prisoners. The man looked none the worse for a week of imprisonment. But a day of freedom can do wonderful things for a one's psychological condition which in turn does much for one's physical condition.

Loose ends remained to be tied up and work remained to be done helping repair the damage caused by the four-day conflict. So all the American and Caribbean troops had yet to be shipped out. In addition, getting troops off an invaded island is often a lot harder than getting them onto the island in the first place.

Things were a bit confused after the Battle of Sangre Grande brought the whole "Affair Drake" to a rapid close. Colonel Belinda Hettrick found herself so completely occupied with the administrative details of wrapping up an invasion that she'd almost automatically given Curt and Carson's Companions what amounted to a open-ended pass with a admonition and a lecture spiced with gripes that went about as follows:

"Yes, yes, *all right!* Go ahead, get out from under foot here! Check into some hotel in Port of Spain and let Major Canby know where you are so he can ship all of you out to Charlotte Amalie when we've got the transportation arranged!" she'd told him hastily while her staff tried not to pester her but *had* to see her for her approvals or directions or orders. "I've got no

405

place to billet you around Sangre Grande anyway, so you might as well go to Port of Spain and let me get this mess straightened out. It could take a week or more. So here, take an Army charge card with you . . . but be damned careful not to run up any bills I can't justify to Finance, or I'll have them garnisheed from your pay! And if anybody tells you that the work is all done once a war is won, send 'em around! See you in Carlotte Amalie! By the way, Curt, the Companions did a hell of a fine job! When we all get back to the Vee-Eye, I want to talk to you about it . . ."

So the Companions found themselves high and dry in Port of Spain with a bottomless supply of plastic money and an open pass with no report-back time. "Don't call us; we'll call you!" That was the best sort of pass to get!

It had taken very little time to locate Roger Sweet because the Jamaican constabulary had captured all the records of political prisoners before Drake's Presidential Guard had had the time to wipe the computer memories and destroy the data banks. It was almost Old Home Week because, as Adonica had mentioned, her father had served in the Washington Greys during the Panama Relief Expedition, and one Private First Class Henry Kester, then nearly a raw recruit, had been in his company, Sweet's Stilettos.

"Henry, you old trooper, you haven't aged a day!" Sweet told him.

"Damned right I have! And so have you, Captain. But you've done a little too much keypad punching, it looks like to me!"

"The only place I can fight these days is from behind a desk," Sweet admitted. "But since Adonica found you and then you found me, the least I can do is show you Trinidad . . ."

406

"Captain Sweet, we've just seen a hell of a lot of Trinidad, sir," Henry remarked.

"Yeah, but you haven't seen Port of Spain during Carnival . . . and even if it's now too rich for your blood, Henry, these youngsters you're mothering will sure as hell enjoy it!"

"Not very many things have gotten too rich for my blood, Captain," Henry said in his usual low-key manner.

Carson's Companions agreed. And they could hardly refuse to go along for the ride, so to speak. Adonica Sweet had, in effect become one of them. And her father always had been, or so it seemed.

But the Carnival in Port of Spain was almost too much for them. The Companions were bone tired as people only can be after several days of getting shot at and giving their all. Curt and the rest of the company gladly followed Roger Sweet who led them through the crowds along Independence Square down to Wrightston Road. There, Adonica's father simply stepped in front of a jitney, secure in the knowledge that the driver would stop and thus not run him down. After a minute of quiet haggling with the driver, Sweet motioned to them and called out, "All aboard!"

"Where we going?" Alexis wanted to know.

"You Washington Greys have started to ask too many questions. Don't ask questions. Just have fun," Roger Sweet advised her.

Adonica grinned. "I know where we're going! I know! You'll love it, Alexis!"

"I'd love going just damned near anywhere after being in hell for the last few days!" Jerry remarked.

Henry Kester grinned, the first time many of the Companions had seen him do it. Henry was feeling good and releasing a lot of tension. "You'll never go to hell, Lieutenant, in spite of what some people will

407

try to tell you. None of us ever will. Remember the song?''

And he launched into an improptu ditty, obviously modified from another old Army beer call song which he blasted out in an off-key voice:

> *And when he gets to Heaven,*
> *To Saint Peter he will tell,*
> *'I'm a Sierra Charlie reporting, sir!*
> *I've served my time in Hell!'*

''What's a Sierra Charlie?'' Roger Sweet wanted to know. So Henry spent the rest of the ride telling him all about it.

They drove for an indeterminate length of time and distance with the Carnival sounds of Port of Spain fading behind them. When the jitney stopped and Adonica's father got off, motioning them to follow, they were somewhere down by the water and a beach. The sound of a steel band rattled in the distance. A rough wooden sign announced ''The Bucket of Blood'' and pointed toward the beach.

It was an old beach club, and it was in full operation. A mixture of about fifty people was there. Under a rusting corrugated tin shed of ancient vintage with sides open to the tropical breeze of evening, people sat around tables lit by candles, eating food that looked strange and drinking concoctions of unknown contents. Or they danced to the loudest steel band Curt thought he'd ever heard. The tin shed did wonders for the acoustics of the 16-man assembly with its big bass booms, baritone pans, tenor pans, pie plates, garbage pan lids, old skillets, maracas, wood blocks, and guords. The music—it really was music—filled the old tin shed of the beach club with sound and rhythm that would bring out the ballroom savage in anyone.

Again, Roger Sweet seemed to know who was who

and what to say and how do to things because the entire group of Carson's Companions found themselves seated at a huge round table covered with a gleaming white cloth and lit by many candles.

The older man explained to all of them, "The Bucket of Blood has been here as long as I can remember. Been in the family for generations. Best beach club I know. Best food I know. Drinks will knock you on your ass if you let them. See the people? Oil patch types, mostly. But you'll find anyone and everyone here at some time ot other. And tonight we're here, and it's on me because Adonica told me all about what you did and how you finally trapped and killed that bastard Drake. No, no, shut the hell up, Carson, because your goddamned Army plastic card won't pay for anything here because I told them so! Waiter! Hi, John! You know what I like! Bring one for everyone, and keep them coming!"

Curt relaxed and let him run the show. Sweet knew what he was doing, and Curt was too exhausted to care. He'd done all the fighting he cared to do for a while. So he found himself seated next to Jerry Allen who was, of course, next to Adonica who was, naturally, next to her father. Alexis made very certain that she was on the other side of Curt.

"Okay, soldiers," Roger Sweet told them, "you just let me take care of ordering and such. You tourists don't know what's really good. And, since you saved this island, you ought to learn something about it. You'd damned well better like rum because we've got lots and lots of it . . ."

Things got a little hazy after several tall ones. The food was excellent—*sans coche* and *callaloo;* an East Indian affair called a roti whose sharp curry flavor Kester claimed had "character and personality;" delicious bean-sized oysters and *chip-chip,* little shellfish that

409

tasted like clams; and some sort of meat stew called "quenk" that Sweet didn't bother to describe but which tasted like pork.

"You couldn't buy ambience like this anywhere else for any price," Alexis remarked to Curt. "I'm stuffed. For the first time in days, I feel I've had a real, honest-to-God meal of real, Honest-to-God food . . ."

"Yeah, aren't you glad we saved this island?" Curt replied.

"Was worth it for this alone," Alexis said. "Too bad Zee couldn't enjoy it with us."

"Funny you should mention her, Al," Curt said.

"Why? Because she caught you when I happened to be restricted under Rule Ten?" Alexis shrugged. Bathed and fresh and with her hair washed and wearing a frilly white cotton dress that had frills and ruffles and other feminine touches in all the right places for a woman, she seemed to be anything but a hardened combat soldier in the candlelight. She smiled. "No, Zee came through when the chips were down and it counted. Sure, I was jealous, but Zee is one of us."

Nick Gerard, sitting on the other side of Alexis, turned his head and said, "I checked with Colonel Miranda's field hospital after we hit Port of Spain. Their MASH surgeons got the bullet out of her and patched her up. Lost some blood, but that's all. No permanent damage. She'll be transferred to the hospital here in Port of Spain tomorrow . . . And you're right, Lieutenant. I'll drink to her health with the Companions any time! And with you, too, Adonica!"

"I'll damned well second that!" Alexis said firmly. "Adonica, I talked to the Colonel. Our Colonel. She's sort of busy finishing up the paperwork for a war. But she agrees. You're a fighter who's just as mean and nasty as Edie or me . . . and you'll get a shot at OCS where they'll make you even meaner and nastier. And commission if you want it. No problem; you're an American citizen.''

''But—'' Adonica began.

''Shut up and don't complain, dammit!'' Alexis interrupted her sharply. ''You don't have to make a decision for a while. But you are indeed a damned good fighter and leader . . . and this isn't a bad life if you overlook some of the crap and enjoy the fun parts. You're pretty, hon, so one thing you're sure to like is the chance to meet men who are by-God *men!*'' She dropped her voice and spoke to Curt, ''Present company included, by the way . . .''

''I know all about by-God real men,'' Adonica Sweet said simply, looking at Jerry.

''Adonica—'' Roger Sweet started to say.

''Daddy, look at me! Don't be parental-protective! I'm a big girl now! I've also fought a war!''

''That you are and that you have. I was about to commend you for inheriting your mother's outstanding ability to choose excellent men.''

''Well, I think it's time we girls all let our men know that we're damned glad they're around when everything goes to slime,'' Edie Sampson spoke up and raised her glass. ''Here's to our men, our Companions! We fight with 'em but don't like to fight without 'em! How!''

''How!'' came the chorus of feminine voices around the table.

M. Sgt. Henry Kester was known as a man who held his liquor pretty well. But something had come unglued that night. He got to his feet, swayed, and said, ''I've had it. But I don't know when I've had so much fun having it. This is the way to live. And the way to fight if you've gotta fight. Sure, it's tough duty. But let me tell you something . . . You fight even better as Sierra Charlies than you did as warbot

411

brainies! Our Sierra Charlie women are the roughest, toughest troopers I ever served with!'' The old soldier raised his glass in the air. "Here's to our fighting women! How!'' And he downed he rum punch in one gulp. The Companions cheered.

"If I'm going to be a soldier,'' Adonica remarked, "I want to serve in the Companions. So I don't know whether I'll take that OCS offer or not. Your TO seems to be full . . .''

"Won't always be,'' Kester observed.

"You don't have to serve in the Companions,'' Jerry observed. He'd had a lot of rum to drink and he was still young and somewhat undiplomatic, which was reflected in his remark as he continued, "You could resign your commission, come back to Trinidad, and take over the government. You'd do a damned sight better job than Drake did! Uh, oops! Did I just say something wrong? Put my foot in my mouth or something?''

"Yeah, you did, and I'll make you pay for it later,'' Adonica promised. "No, Trinidad doesn't need to be ruled. It needs to be nurtured.''

"This is the first time,'' her father pointed out, "that a war or even a battle has been fought on this island. I hope to God it's the last. Which is why I don't exactly like to see the American military pull out again . . .''

"Well, I agree with you, Captain Sweet,'' Nick Gerard said. "I grew up in the cities of the American Rust Belt, and I think we oughta do what we can to protect the real beautiful places of the world like this . . . and the real people that live in them. Help them out when they want it. Keep the sonsofbitches of the world from looting them. Honest. It ain't just the rum talking for me, either . . .'' Nick had had a lot of

412

rum, and the tensions of the past few days were beginning to release themselves.

"No, but the rum is helping, Nick!" Edie observed and got to her feet. "Come on, soldier. How about dance with this gal?"

The steel band was making beautiful music with a mambo beat. Roger Sweet stood up and yelled to them, "Mambo Number Five!"

"I can't do these crazy dances!" Nick complained.

"Neither can I! But who gives a damn?" Edie yelled joyfully and hauled Nick to the dance floor.

It was contagious music. "Where the hell do they learn to play music like that?" Curt asked Sweet.

Sweet shrugged. "Natural. Not a one of them can read a single note of music . . ."

"Started about a hundred years ago when African tribal drums were banned by the British," Adonica explained. "The Americans came down here during World War Two and left lots of oil drums . . . and some forgotten genius named Lord Humbugger figured out how to tune the end of an oil drum with a cold chisel . . . This outfit calls itself the Brute Force Steel Band." Curt noticed that Adonica left the final "d" off the word "band" in accordance with the local dialect.

The Brute Force swung into a calypso:

> Hol' 'em, Joe; Hol' 'em, Joe;
> Hol' 'em, Joe; I know, let 'im go!
> My donkey love rum,
> My donkey love bum . . .

. . . and on and on with a seemingly endless series of verses.

It got to be too much for Alexis. She didn't ask Curt to dance with her. She simply got to her feet and pulled Curt up with her.

413

Surprisingly, Curt discovered he wasn't exhausted. And he could dance to the music. Maybe it was the rum. Maybe it was the steel band. Maybe it was Alexis.

"This should never end . . ." Alexis remarked when the band wound down from one number and began to tune up for the next with a clatter of banging and rattling and chatter.

"Yeah, I think we've got to come back here," Curt agreed.

"Nick's right. Places like this *must* be nurtured."

"Again and again and again," Curt remarked as the band clattered into a calypso he later learned was called "Brown Skinned Gal" and dated back to another time when Americans had been here:

> *Don' feel bad,*
> *You're on my mind, baybee!*
> *Don' feel bad,*
> *You're on my mind, baybee!*
> *Goin' away in my sailing boat*
> *And if I don't come back,*
> *You're on my mind, baybee . . .*

"I'm going away in a sailing boat. Want to come along?" Curt asked Alexis.

"Sure. You're on *my* mind, baybee!"

"And I don't feel bad about it, either," he told her.

He looked over her shoulder and noticed that Jerry and Adonica were gone. But Roger Sweet didn't seem to care. He knew his children were only loaned to him and he had to give them back some day. His daughter was now a big girl and he'd given her back. He was talking old times and drinking with Henry.

"I don't want to dance any more," Alexis said.

"Neither do I," Curt agreed.

"Rule Ten isn't in effect."

"How'd you know?"

"Let's go for a walk on the beach in the moonlight."

"Best way to end a war . . ."

GLOSSARY OF ROBOT INFANTRY
TERMS AND SLANG

ACV: The Armored Command Vehicle, a standard warbot command vehicle highly modified for use as an artificially-intelligent, computer-directed command vehicle in the Special Combat units.

Aerodyne: A saucer- or frisbee-shaped flying machine that obtains its lift from the exhaust of one or more turbine, fanjet engines blowing outwards over the curved upper surface of the craft from an annular slot near the center of the upper surface. The annular slot is segmented and the sectorized slots can therefore be controlled to provide more flow and, hence, more lift over one part of the saucer-shaped surface than another, thus tipping the aerodyne and allowing it to move forward, backward, and sideways. The aerodyne was invented by Dr. Henri M. Coanda following World War II but was not developed until decades later because of the previous development of the rotary-winged helicopter.

Artificial Intelligence or *AI:* A very large-memory, very fast computer which can duplicate or simulate certain functions of human intelligence such as bringing together or correlating many apparently disconnected pieces of information or data, making simple evaluations of importance or priority of data and responses, and making decisions concerning what to do, how to do it, when to do it, and what to report to the human being in control.

ARTV: Armored Robot Transportation Vehicle, a highly modified artificially-intelligent, computer-controlled adaptation of a warbot carrier which is used by the Special Combat units to transport their voice-commanded, artificially-intelligent Mary Anns and Hairy Foxes (see below).

Biotech: A biological technologist, normally a non-commissioned officer in the Robot Infantry but can often be a specialized non-combat officer.

Bot: Generalized generic slang term for "robot" which takes many forms as *warbot, reconbot,* etc.

Bot flush: Since robots have no natural excrement, this term is a reference to what comes out of a highly mechanical warbot when its lubricants are changed during routine maintenance. Used by soldiers as a slang term referring to anything of a destestable nature.

Cee-pee or *CP:* Slang for "Command Post."

"Check minus-x": Look behind you. In terms of coordinates, *plus x* is ahead, *minus x* is behind, *plus y* is to the right, *minus y* is left, *plus z* is up, and *minus z* is down.

Dee-eff or *DF:* Direction finding using transmissions from electromagnetic sources such as radios, lasers, infra red transmitters, etc.

Double-lobed Lebanese systolic stroke: Warbot brainy slang for being killed in action, suddenly losing all contact with one's war robots.

Down link: The remote command link or channel from the robot to the soldier.

FABARMA: The 7.62-mm M3A4 "Novia" caseless ammunition assault rifle designed by Fabrica de

Armes Nacionales of Mexico and used by the Special Combat units.

Fur ball: A complex and confused fight, battle, or operation.

Go physical: To lapse into idiot mode (see below) to operate in a combat or recon environment without robots; what the Special Combat units do all the time.

Golden BB: A lucky hit from a small caliber bullet that creates large problems.

Greased: Beaten, conquered, overwhelmed, creamed.

Hairy Fox: The Mark X60 Heavy Fire warbot, an experimental voice-commanded artificially-intelligent war robot mounting a 50-mm weapon and designed to provide heavy fire support for the Special Combat units.

Humper: Any device whose proper name a soldier can't recall at the moment.

Idiot mode: Operating in the combat environment without robot support; especially, operating without the benefit of computers and artificial intelligence to relieve battle load. What the warbot brainies think the Sierra Charlies do all the time.

Intelligence Amplifier or *IA:* A very fast computer with a very large memory which when linked to a human nervous system, serves as a very fast extension of the human brain allowing the brain to function faster, recall more data, store more data, and thus "amplify" a human being's "intelligence."

Jeep: Word coined from the initials "GP" standing for "General Purpose." Once applied to an Army quarter-ton vehicle but subsequently used to refer to the new Mark X33 General Purpose voice-commanded, artificially-intelligent robot which accompanies Special Combat unit commanders in the field at the company level and above.

KIA or *"killed in action"*: A situation where all of a soldier's data and sensory inputs from one or more robots is suddenly cut off, leaving the human being in a state of mental limbo. A very debilitating and mentally disturbing situation.

LAMV: Light Artillery Maneuvering Vehicle, a computer-controlled, robotic vehicle used for light artillery support of Sierra Charlie units; mounts a 75-mm "Saucy Cans" weapon originally designed in France.

Linkage: The remote connection or link between a human being and one or more war robots. This link or channel may be by means of wires, radio, laser or optical means, or other remote control systems. The robot/computer sends its data directly to the human soldier's nervous system through small electrodes positioned on the soldier's skin; this data is coded in such a way that the soldier perceives the signals as sight, sound, feeling, smell, or the position of a robot's parts. The robot/computer also picks up commands from the soldier's nervous system that are merely "thought" by the solider, translates these into commands the robot can understand, and monitors the accomlishment of the commanded action.

Mary Ann: Slang for the Mark X44 Maneuverable Assault warbot, an experimental voice-commanded, artificially-intelligent warbot developed for use by the new mixed-operation Special Combat forces to accompany soldiers in the field and provide light fire support from its 25-mm weapon.

"Orgasmic!": A slang term that grew out of the observation, "Outstanding!" It means the same thing.

Pigeonate: A concocted word relating to operations with carrier pigeons.

Pucker factor: The detrimental effect on the human

420

body that results from being in an extremely hazarous situation such as being shot at.

Robot: From the Czech word *robota* meaning work, especially drudgery. A device with humanlike actions directed either by a computer or by a human being through a computer and a remote two-way, command-sensory circuit. Early war robots appeared in World War II as radio-controlled, drone aircraft carrying explosives or used as targets, the first of these being the German Henschel Hs 238 glide bomb launched from an aircraft against surface targets and guided by means of radio control by a human being in the aircraft watching the image transmitted from a television camera in the nose of the bomb.

Robot Infantry or *RI:* A combat branch of the United States Army which grew from the regular Infantry with the introduction of robots and linkage to warfare. Active RI divisions are the 17th ("Iron Fist"), the 22nd ("Double Deuces"), the 26th ("R.U.R."), and the 50th ("Big L").

Rule Ten: Slang reference to Army Regulation 601-10 which prohibits physical contact between male and female officers and/or soldiers while on duty other than that required for official business.

Rules of Engagement or *ROE:* Official restrictions on the freedom of action of a commander or soldier in his confrontation with an opponent that act to increase the probability that said commander or soldier will lose the combat, all other things being equal.

Saucy Cans: An American Army corruption of the French designation for the 75-mm *"soixante-quinze"* weapon mounted on a LAMV.

Sierra Charlie: Phonetic alphabet derivative of the initials "SC" meaning "Special Combat," the experimental Army soldiers trained to engage in personal field combat supported and accompanied by voice-commanded, artificially-intelligent warbots.

Sierra Hotel: Shit hot. What a warbot brainies say when they can't say, "Hot shit."

Simulator or *sim:* A device which can simulate the sensations perceived by a human being and the results of the human's responses. A simple toy computer with an aircraft flight simulator program or a video game simulating a human controlled activity is an example of a simulator. One of the earliest simulators was the Link Trainer of World War II that provided a human pilot with the sensations of instrument or "blind" flying without leaving the ground.

Sit-guess: Slang for "estimate of the situation," an educated guess about the situation.

Sit-rep: Short for "situation report."

Snake Pit: Slang for the highly-computerized briefing center located in most caserns and other Army posts.

Spasm mode: Slang for killed in action (KIA).

Spook: Slang term for either a spy or a military intelligence specialist.

Staff stooge: Derrogatory term referring to a regimental or divisional staff officer.

Tacomm: A portable computer-controlled, frequency-hopping, tactical communications radio transceiver used primarily by rear echelon troops.

Tiger error: What happens when an eager soldier tries too hard to press an attack.

UBQ-1: Humorous alpha-numeric model designator of the carrier pigeon.

Up link: The remote command link or channel from the soldier to the war robot.

Warbot: Abbreviation for "war robot," a mechanical device that is operated remotely by a soldier, thereby taking the human being out of the hazardous activity of actual combat.

Warbot brainy: The human soldier who operates war robots, derived from the fact that the soldier is basically the brains of the war robot.

ORDER OF BATTLE
OPERATION STEEL BAND

Supreme Allied Commander—Gen. Otis R. Brooke
  Deputy Supreme Commander, Land—Lt. Gen. Louise J. Montcalm
  Deputy Supreme Commander, Sea—VADM Arthur D. Hamlen
  Deputy Supreme Commander, Air—Lt. Gen. Phyllis C. Cochran

17th "Iron Fist" Division (Robot Infantry)
  Maj. Gen. Jacob O. Carlisle

3rd RI "Washington Greys"—Col. Belinda J. Hettrick

    1st Company, "Carson's Companions"
        Captain Curt C. Carson
        1st Lt. Alexis M. Morgan
        2nd Lt. Jerry P. Allen
        M. Sgt. Henry G. Kester
        Platoon Sgt. Nicholas P. Gerard
        Platoon Sgt. Edwina A. Sampson
        Corp. James P. Elliott

Corp. Charles S. Koslowski
Corp. Tracy C. Dillon
Corp. Thomas C. Dole

2nd Company, "Walker's Warriors"
Capt. Samantha J. Walker
1st Lt. Joan G. Ward
2nd Lt. David F. Coney

3rd Company, "Manny's Marauders"
Capt. Manuel X. Garcia
1st Lt. Joshua M. Rosenberg
2nd Lt. Eleanor S. Aarts

4th Company, "Kelly's Killers"
Capt. Martin C. Kelly
1st Lt. Russell B. Frazier
2nd Lt. Phillip B. Messenger

Headquarters Company—Maj. Edward R. Canby
Chief of staff—Capt. Wade W. Hampton
Aide—1st Lt. Hensley Atkinson

Service Company—Maj. Frederick W. Benteen
Capt. Johanna W. Wool—Chief of Biotechnology
Capt. Elwood S. Otis—Chief of Maintenance
1st. Lt. Harriett F. Dearborn—Chief of Logistics

7th RI Cottonbalers—Col. Emmett J. Calhoun
15th RI Can Do—Col. Walker A. Armistead

27th RI Wolfhounds—Col. Charlotte B. Gatewood

22nd Double Deuces Division (RI)—Maj. Gen. Daniel O. Miles

        14th RI Golden Dragons—Col. Willa J. Fetterman

        28th RI Lions of Cantigny—Col. Leslie Anne Merritt

        58th RI The Patriots—Col. Nelson A. Miles

        187th RI Raddasans—Col. Josephine W. Wheeler

Caribbean National Forces—Gen. Col. Hans Van S. Sturdevandt

        2nd Battalion, 1st Regiment, Army of Venezuela—Col. Jose Antonio Miranda

        1st Battalion, 1st Regiment, Army of Colombia—Col. Rafael de Paulo Herrera

        5th Battalion, Special Forces, Army of Panama—Col. Ricardo Francisco Amador

        Company A, Curacao Guard—Maj. Johannes van Dusen

        3rd Company, Jamaican constabulary—Capt. Sydney A. W. Baker. Jr.

49th Tactical Strike Wing, USAF—Col. Leo R. Vance

55th Tactical Fighter Wing, USAF—Col. Jack W. Pucker, Jr.

94th Tactical Strike Wing, USAF—Col. John D. Sturgis

89th Military Airlift Wing, USAF—Col. Anna M. Ryan

313rd Air Refuelling Squadron, USAF—Lt. Col. Rhea O. Stone

Task Force 58, USN—RADM, Francis A. Ericksen

      Task Group 50.10, USN—Capt. Willard A. Lee

      Task Group 50.20, USN—Capt. Robert E. Davidson

      Task Group 50.30, USN—Capt. Merill B. Gardiner

Task Force 38, USN—VADM Warren E. Sample

HIGH-VOLTAGE EXCITEMENT AT ITS ELECTRIFYING BEST FROM PINNACLE BOOKS!
Warren Murphy and Richard Sapir's
THE DESTROYER!

#1: CREATED, THE DESTROYER (036-7, $3.50)
Framed and then fried for the murder of a slimy dope dealer, ex-New Jersey cop Remo Williams is resurrected as the most efficient human killing machine the world has ever known!

#2: DEATH CHECK (037-5, $3.50)
Remo Williams sets out to derail a sinister top-secret brain trust's mad dream of world domination!

#3: CHINESE PUZZLE (038-3, $3.50)
Remo Williams and his Korean mentor Chiun must smash an insidious oriental conspiracy before the U.S. and China come to nuclear blows!

#4: MAFIA FIX (039-1, $3.50)
Remo Williams sets out to destroy a shipment of fifty tons of heroin — and any Cosa Nostra chump who gets in his way — before the powdered death hits the streets!

#5: DR. QUAKE (140-5, $3.50)
A madman threatens to make California disappear with his deadly earthquake machine, and only Remo Williams can prevent the terrifying West Coast crackup!

#6: DEATH THERAPY (141-3, $3.50)
Remo races to put a sexy seductress and her army of mind-slaves out of business before they can sell America's top military secrets to the highest bidder!

Available wherever paperbacks are sold, or order direct from the Publisher. Send cover price plus 50¢ per copy for mailing and handling to Pinnacle Books, Dept. 061, 475 Park Avenue South, New York, N.Y. 10016. Residents of New York, New Jersey and Pennsylvania must include sales tax. DO NOT SEND CASH.

HIGH-TECH WARRIORS IN A
DEVASTATED FUTURE!
C.A.D.S.
BY JOHN SIEVERT

#1: C.A.D.S. (1641, $3.50)

Wearing seven-foot high Computerized Attack/Defense System suits equipped with machine guns, armor-piercing shells and flame throwers, Colonel Dean Sturgis and the men of C.A.D.S. are America's last line of defense after the East Coast of the U.S. is shattered by a deadly Soviet nuclear first strike!

#3: TECH COMMANDO (1893, $2.95)

The fate of America hangs in the balance as the men of C.A.D.S. battle to prevent the Russians from expanding their toehold in the U.S. For Colonel Dean Sturgis it means destroying the key link in the main Sov military route—the heavily defended Chesapeake Bay Bridge-Tunnel!

#4: TECH STRIKE FORCE (1993, $2.95)

An American turncoat is about to betray the C.A.D.S. ultra-sensitive techno-secrets to the Reds. The arch traitor and his laser-equipped army of renegades must be found and smashed, and the men of C.A.D.S. will accomplish the brutal task—or die trying!

#5: TECH SATAN (2313, $2.95)

The new U.S. government at White Sands, New Mexico suddenly goes off the air and the expeditionary C.A.D.S. force must find out why. But the soldiers of tomorrow find their weapons useless against a killer plague that threatens to lay bare to the Soviet invaders the last remaining bastion of American freedom!

Available wherever paperbacks are sold, or order direct from the Publisher. Send cover price plus 50¢ per copy for mailing and handling to Zebra Books, Dept. 061, 475 Park Avenue South, New York, N.Y. 10016. Residents of New York, New Jersey and Pennsylvania must include sales tax. DO NOT SEND CASH.